By JENN MOFFATT

Bad, Dad, and Dangerous Anthology
Christmas Ghosts

Published by DREAMSPINNER PRESS
www.dreamspinnerpress.com

By Bru Baker

All in a Day's Work
Bad, Dad, and Dangerous Anthology
Branded
The Buyout
Campfire Confessions
Diving In
Downward Facing Dreamboat
Holidays Are Where Your Heart Is
Homemade from the Heart
King of the Kitchen
Late Bloomer
The Magic of Weihnachten
More Than Okay
With Lex Chase: Some Assembly Required
Talk Turkey
Traditions from the Heart

DREAMSPUN BEYOND
CAMP H.O.W.L.
Camp H.O.W.L.
Under a Blue Moon
Hiding In Plain Sight
CONNOLL PACK
Stealing His Heart

DREAMSPUN DESIRES
Tall, Dark, and Deported

DROPPING ANCHOR
Island House
Finding Home
Playing House

Published by DREAMSPINNER PRESS
www.dreamspinnerpress.com

By TA Moore

Bad, Dad, and Dangerous Anthology
Every Other Weekend
Ghostwriter of Christmas Past
Liar, Liar
Take the Edge Off

BLOOD AND BONE
Dead Man Stalking

DIGGING UP BONES
Bone to Pick
Skin and Bone

ISLAND CLASSIFIEDS
Wanted – Bad Boyfriend

LOST AND FOUND
Prodigal

PLENTY, CALIFORNIA
Swipe
Bone to Pick
Skin and Bone

WOLF WINTER
Dog Days
Stone the Crows
Wolf at the Door

Published by DSP Publications
Collared

Published by DREAMSPINNER PRESS
www.dreamspinnerpress.com

By Rhys Ford

Bad, Dad, and Dangerous
Anthology

RAMEN ASSASSIN
Ramen Assassin

415 INK
Rebel
Savior
Hellion

MURDER AND MAYHEM
Murder and Mayhem
Tramps and Thieves
Cops and Comix

SINNERS SERIES
Sinner's Gin
Whiskey and Wry
The Devil's Brew
Tequila Mockingbird
Sloe Ride
Absinthe of Malice
Sin and Tonic
'Nother Sip of Gin

COLE MCGINNIS
MYSTERIES
Dirty Kiss
Dirty Secret
Dirty Laundry
Dirty Deeds
Down and Dirty
Dirty Heart
Dirty Bites

MCGINNIS
INVESTIGATIONS
Back in Black

HALF MOON BAY
Fish Stick Fridays
Hanging the Stars
Tutus and Tinsel

HELLSINGER
Fish and Ghosts
Duck Duck Ghost

WAYWARD WOLVES
Once Upon a Wolf

There's This Guy
Dim Sum Asylum
Clockwork Tangerine

Published by DSP Publications
Wonderland City Anthology

INK AND SHADOWS
Ink and Shadows

KAI GRACEN
Black Dog Blues
Mad Lizard Mambo
Jacked Cat Jive
Silk Dragon Salsa

Published by DREAMSPINNER PRESS
www.dreamspinnerpress.com

A PARANORMAL ROMANCE ANTHOLOGY BY
**BRU BAKER, JENN MOFFATT,
TA MOORE & RHYS FORD**

BAD,
DAD, AND
DANGEROUS

REAMSPINNER
PRESS

Published by
DREAMSPINNER PRESS

5032 Capital Circle SW, Suite 2, PMB# 279, Tallahassee, FL 32305-7886 USA
www.dreamspinnerpress.com

Trade Paperback ISBN: 978-1-64405-713-1
Digital ISBN: 978-1-64405-712-4
Library of Congress Control Number: 2020943089
Trade Paperback Published October 2020
First Edition
v. 1.0

Printed in the United States of America
(∞)
This paper meets the requirements of
ANSI/NISO Z39.48-1992 (Permanence of Paper).

To Holly and Mike… for everything.

Contents

Monster Hall Pass
by Bru Baker

Thanks to my own Gaga ball enthusiast, who was definitely the inspiration for Ruby and all the antics she gets up to at summer camp. This also wouldn't have been possible without Rhys, Tamm, and Jenn, who took this crazy idea for a short story and turned it into an amazing anthology. Much love to all of you.

CHAPTER ONE

SOMEONE KNOCKED softly on Hugh's glass office door, breaking his concentration. He needed his A game on this call, so he did something he hated—he held up a finger, telling the knocker to wait. He couldn't do much over the phone, but if he focused hard enough, he could use his powers of persuasion on the person outside the door.

He recognized the shock of bright blond hair, and his mouth watered involuntarily. Dammit. This phone call was all that separated him from his vacation, and he needed to make sure his brain was here and not leaping ahead to, ah, other appetites.

"That sounds frustrating. I'm sorry your experience has been so stressful," he said, wincing when he heard his voice. It had lost the soothing, honeyed tone of persuasion, which meant he would be back at square one with the caller.

The woman on the line plowed ahead with her litany of complaints, as he'd known she would. Mrs. Simmons was a frequent caller, and he knew better than to interrupt her before she hit full steam. It would start the excruciatingly in-depth explanation of her problems all over again, and he didn't have time for that now.

Hugh muted his headset and waved Cassandra into his office.

"Hey, Cass," he said warmly, standing up to take her hands in his. Not everyone on the staff embraced his literal hands-on approach to management, and he was careful to respect each employee's boundaries. But Cassandra always sought it out, so Hugh didn't feel bad about the pulse of power he sent her way. She shivered slightly, her eyes glazing over for the fraction of a second it took for him to drain off the worst of her anxiety. A nice snack for him, and a heady punch of relaxation for her.

He checked to make sure his headset was muted before motioning her toward the cozy chair he kept for employees. Call-center work was hard enough without having to deal with an uncomfortable work environment. He'd paid for the cushy chair himself—officially because it made his office welcoming, unofficially because some people went a bit weak after he fed on their auras, and it helped to have a soft place for them to land if their knees went out from under them.

"I'm so sorry," Cassandra said as soon as she sat down. "I know you're trying to get out of here early to get Ruby, but I just couldn't get her to calm down."

The bitter-hot smell of her frustration tinged the air, and if his stomach could growl, it would have. He needed a decent feed before he left or he'd never be able to handle summer camp drop-off with Ruby. So much anxiety and excitement and fear—it was like a smorgasbord of emotions, and going in starving could be a disaster.

"Hey, hey. It's fine." He let a little of his power slip into his voice, and her shoulders dropped noticeably as she reacted. "You've only been here a month, Cass. You're doing a wonderful job. Mrs. Simmons is a tough one. There likely wasn't anything you could have done. She always escalates to a manager. That's not a reflection on your abilities. It's just how she is."

Hell, the fact that Cass was still working there after a month meant she was better than most of the new hires. Not everyone was cut out for working in a health-insurance call center. Most people couldn't handle the stress and anger, not to mention the desperation and fear. It was hard to talk to angry people day in and day out.

It even took a toll on Hugh, and he thrived on intense emotions.

No one called their insurance company because they were happy with their service. Literally every call was a complaint. If they were lucky it was something they could actually help with, but most of the time it wasn't. Hugh wished he could shape the company's policies and reverse claims denials, but he couldn't. He and his employees were working from a limited scope, and that put them on the front lines with very little power to actually do anything.

"I know, but I just wanted to come tell you I'm sorry," she said, her head hanging.

Crap. If he didn't handle this right, she wouldn't last much longer. He needed employees like Cass. She really was good at her job, but she was also empathetic. Hugh had come to rely on her as one of his main feeding sources because she felt so bad for all of the customers.

Mrs. Simmons paused long enough in her diatribe for him to get a word in edgewise, so he put a hand out to motion to Cass to be quiet and unmuted his headset.

"I can't imagine the stress," he said, agreeing with what she'd said. "And I am so sorry that you feel Unity Health isn't serving you well. I am putting a note in your file that we've spoken and asking our billing department to take another look at that claim."

Mrs. Simmons went off again, and he listened for half a beat to make sure it wasn't anything new before muting her again.

"Cass, you absolutely did the right thing escalating her to me. I'll finish up with Mrs. Simmons, and by then Doug will be in to take over for the evening shift. Why don't you take a ten-minute break to go unwind in the employee lounge?"

She nodded and got up, her scent already lighter from his affirmation.

He was a good manager. And when you took his special abilities into account, he was a great manager. Vampires often worked in high-stress environments because it gave them so many emotions to feed from, but few used their abilities to help people feel better. Darker emotions like hate, anger, and lust were the best feeds, but they were hard to find unless you went hunting for them—literally. And he hated treating humans like prey.

The day-to-day emotions that swirled around a white-collar office were much more mundane. The desperation, fear, depression, and anxiety he siphoned off when he fed made a measurable difference in his coworkers' lives. He was a Good Samaritan. Kind of. Feeding on them wasn't great for keeping him sated, but it contributed a lot to office morale.

"Mrs. Simmons," he said, cutting her off when she finally took a breath, "you're absolutely right that we haven't been able to help you here in the call center. So I will refer this to our case-management team. You have a complicated claim, and a case manager will be able to give you the time and attention you deserve."

Anyone who called more than seven times in a calendar year was eligible for the case management program, and she definitely qualified.

He'd selfishly been letting her go into the main call-center pool because it was good for his feeding schedule, but that had been going on long enough.

"The system will assign you a case manager tomorrow, and they'll be in touch. I'll follow up with you myself on Monday to make sure they have contacted you."

That took the wind out of the old hag's sails, and he could end the call with minimal threats and sputterings from her. He put a note in his calendar to remember to call her from the road on Monday.

He filed a report on the call and did the escalation paperwork that would hopefully ensure Mrs. Simmons wouldn't drive Cass into a nervous breakdown before his return. Once he'd cleared his inbox, he could shut everything down and officially be on vacation for the next three weeks.

Hugh tried not to think about his monster hall pass, as he liked to call it, much during the year. He put a lot of effort into suppressing his vampire side when he was playing at being human, and that meant those three precious weeks were his only time to give in to his more demonic nature. Vampires weren't meant to subsist on the kind of diet he allowed himself, at least not long-term. He got weaker and weaker throughout the year, though it didn't matter much since even at half power he still had to work to conceal his abilities in order to fit in with humans.

Hugh just had to hang on until he could get Ruby to camp, and then his break could begin.

Hugh shivered and his mouth watered as memories of past trips flitted through his mind. He'd settled down when Ruby came into his life and tried to go cold turkey from feeding frenzies and general debauchery. That lasted until she'd been old enough to go to sleepaway camp. He wasn't sure how he'd survived those first six years, only giving himself a few hours away from his humanity a month while Ruby was with a sitter. Even that hadn't been nearly enough, since he was careful never to break his rule about draining people within a hundred-mile radius of his home. He'd survived on the residual energy from sketchy Tinder hookups and craigslist orgies.

But once she was old enough to spend time away at Oak River, that had changed. At first she'd gone for a week, then two. Now she was ten, and he'd finally been comfortable signing her up for a full month this summer. It was a huge financial drain, but so worth it. The last few years of summer hall passes had helped him feel more grounded and happier. Between his call-center job and his monster hall pass, he'd really been able to get into a groove. Sure, he had to fit all his orgies, feeding frenzies, and hunting into his brief respite from the responsibilities of parenthood every summer, but it was enough. It had to be.

Ruby needed him to be human, and humans did things like attend PTA meetings instead of attacking rapists in crack dens and draining them of their life force.

Hugh closed his eyes and took a deep breath. He needed to focus. His vacation hadn't officially started yet, and it wouldn't begin until he finished up here. He'd already made all the arrangements for his stay in Detroit, so the best thing to do was put it out of his mind until he'd done everything on his list.

Then he'd get Ruby packed up for camp, and they could get on the road. There was a sleazy truck stop on the way to Michigan—maybe he'd reward himself by stopping there to hunt after drop-off.

CHAPTER TWO

HUGH RIFLED through the pile of duffel bags at the bottom of the stairs, sighing heavily when his hand closed over a box of granola bars. He pulled it out and kept digging, coming up with a dozen chocolate bars, a box of cookies, and, inexplicably for his vegetarian daughter, a handful of beef jerky sticks.

He confiscated the contraband and rezipped the bag, moving on to the next one. It yielded even more candy. Ruby had a sweet tooth, but this was ridiculous. Did she really think he wouldn't check her bags? He wasn't sure if he was angrier that she was trying to sneak food to camp or that her effort was so weak. All she'd done was pile clothes on top of the boxes. Amateur.

Hugh sensed Ruby coming around the corner, her curious absence of scent preceding her. His daughter was the only person he'd met who was immune to his powers. He couldn't even scent her aura, which was how he'd found her.

He'd been stalking a man with an aura of violence so strong Hugh could practically see it when he'd come across a curious blank spot behind the dumpster of a Ruby Tuesday. He could tell there was something there, but he couldn't read it. The surprise was enough to distract him from his hunt, and three months later he'd gone before a judge and adopted her.

It had only taken a little of his persuasion to grease the wheels. On paper he was a great choice as an adoptive parent. He'd been a nomad before finding Ruby, but in the weeks after he'd held her for the first time, shivering and swaddled in a too-thin blanket, all alone in the world, he'd changed his entire life. He'd gotten the job at the insurance call center and used the modest amount of money he'd had in the bank to buy a house.

It was the stuff that wasn't on paper that would have caused problems.

Like the fact he was a vampire.

His daughter had no idea, which was part of the reason she was heading to summer camp for a month. He'd be able to hunt to his heart's content and not worry about staying out past the sitter's curfew or running into the PTA president with his fangs out.

Ruby stopped short when she saw her open bags, her eyes comically wide.

"I can explain."

He might not be able to read her emotions, but luckily she was predictable. He didn't need the upper hand provided by his powers when it came to his daughter.

Hugh spread the food out on the floor and quirked an eyebrow at her, letting the silence build until she burst.

"It's not for me!"

He cocked his head to the side a bit, waiting her out.

"Last year Emma got a care package from home with snacks, and everybody wanted some," she blurted.

"Ah. And you thought having contraband snacks would be the way to make friends?"

She'd been going to the same camp for years and had a group of girls she always bunked with. They were pen pals during the year, and they'd even visited a few of the girls who only lived a few hours away. Why did she need to make new friends?

Ruby hesitated and then shook her head. "No. She didn't have enough to share with everyone, so kids started offering her money."

Hugh bit back a laugh. He needed to be stern, no matter how amused he was by her scheme. "And you thought you could make money selling snacks?"

It was admirable, really. And if his health didn't hang in the balance, maybe he'd let her do it. But he really couldn't afford for her to be kicked out of camp. The small meals he could get during the year weren't enough. He needed to drain a few victims to keep himself going, and that couldn't happen here in Cincinnati. He needed the anonymity of a bigger city, one where a few unexplained deaths wouldn't spark an investigation.

"Sorry, kiddo. You know the rules. No food from home."

Ruby sighed and gathered up the pile. He followed her as she trudged into the kitchen.

"There are good reasons for the rules, Rube. Ashlynn's diabetic, isn't she? And Cadence is allergic to nuts."

Sometimes the ridiculousness of his life snuck up on him, and this was one of them. He was a vampire. He killed people to stay alive. Yet here he was in his suburban kitchen, listing off his daughter's friends with food allergies.

"And there are bears," Ruby said knowingly.

"I don't think there are bears, Ruby."

"Gina saw one last year!"

He shook his head and let it go. There were no bears in Ohio. Or very few, at least. And certainly no bears at the camp Ruby attended. He'd spent months picking it out, reading tons of reviews and even touring the camp itself before enrolling her. He was a total helicopter dad, and he knew it.

"No contraband. Take a final pass through your room and make sure you haven't forgotten anything," he said like he wouldn't do a double check himself before they left. His baby girl would be gone for a full month this time—there was no way he would leave anything to chance. What if she forgot the lavender-infused eye mask she needed to fall asleep every night? Or the natural silk pillowcase and sheets that were the only bedding her sensitive skin could tolerate without breaking out into rashes?

"Fine," she said, flouncing up the stairs. "But see if I make you a bracelet to match your necklace now! I was going to, but that was when you were nice."

He stifled a laugh as she stomped her way upstairs, his fingers automatically seeking the pendant he never took off. She'd made it in a rock tumbler last year at camp, and she'd been so proud of it. She'd found the piece of celestite in a riverbed when they'd been rock hunting and told him she'd known the moment she saw it in the mud that he needed to have it. He'd thought she was being dramatic, but she insisted he wear it at all times. He only took it off to shower, and if he forgot to put it back on, she'd pitch a fit.

He'd worn it dutifully ever since. After a few weeks, wearing it had become such a routine that he felt naked without it. He used it almost like a worry stone whenever he was troubled over something involving her. Like this latest blowup.

But the parenting blogs all said he needed to let her assert her independence and start taking more responsibility for things, so that's what he'd do. Within reason. And only when it wasn't actually important.

He huffed out a laugh at himself. He'd be in the running for dad of the year in no time. Except for his pesky habit of killing humans. That might give the awards committee pause.

Hugh puttered around while he waited for Ruby to finish up. He'd already packed, but he busied himself with small tasks like making sure the garden hose was off outside and that he hadn't left the oven on or something like that. He'd be leaving for his vacation from camp, so no one would be here for the next few weeks.

He'd already emptied the refrigerator and taken the trash out. Mundane chores like that grounded him and helped keep his mind off the gnawing hunger that had been building in his gut as his anticipation of his holiday grew.

By the time they were in the car headed toward camp, he was a bundle of nerves. Leaving Ruby was necessary. It was good, even. They lived in each other's pockets eleven months out of the year, so this break was healthy. He glanced in the rearview mirror at Ruby, who had her headphones on and was staring out the window at the endless expanse of farmland.

He wasn't a neglectful father for needing time away. Plenty of parents did.

Only most of them didn't murder people while they were gone.

CHAPTER THREE

GOD, HE was hungry.

He'd dropped Ruby off at camp a few hours ago, and it had taken a toll on him. He was attuned to emotions since he relied on chi to survive, and boy did summer camp drop-off have a lot of them.

He'd watched dozens of families have tearful goodbyes. Many had seemed outwardly happy, but every aura there had been tinged with sadness, even amid all the excitement and nervousness.

Meanwhile his kid—the only one whose aura he couldn't read— had barely been able to stand still through registration before she'd given him a single wave and then darted off into the crowd to find her friends.

He had been so tempted to feed a bit while swimming in that miasma of emotion. Not from the kids—he'd never do that. But there were plenty of parents who were distraught at leaving their precious babies.

It would have been easy to put a comforting hand on the shoulder of the mom who was openly sobbing. Hell, it would have helped her, drawing out a bit of that sadness. But he'd always been careful never to mix Ruby's life with his vampire needs. Even that time at the PTA meeting when a fistfight broke out over whether the annual bake sale could include items with tree nuts.

Ruby deserved a life free from supernatural shenanigans. He wasn't sure he'd ever tell her about his true nature.

Not that he thought she'd take it badly. She'd probably be thrilled.

Her self-sufficiency was almost scary. It was good she felt so comfortable at camp, but it stung a bit to know she didn't need him. She hadn't even batted an eye when he'd told her he was traveling while she was at camp and wouldn't be home to get her letters. Usually he took a few weekends away but stayed close in case she needed him.

She never had, of course. Ruby was a fierce little thing. Opinionated and wicked smart, cunning and manipulative, but always honest when it counted. She could take care of herself, and she'd proven that over the last few summers.

So here he was, living the dream, a free man for nearly a month.

What he needed was a good feed to clear his head. His mouth watered at the thought of feasting on a trucker hell-bent on taking advantage of a lot lizard. Truck stops were like fast food for a vamp. Open twenty-four seven and always serving something, even though the quality wasn't great and you'd probably be hungry again in an hour.

Hugh scolded himself for his paranoia and got out of the car, taking time to stretch his limbs. His Corolla was a good family car, but it wasn't exactly the most comfortable thing to drive. Sometimes he felt like he was peeling his six-foot-three frame out of a clown car when he got out.

Two big rigs were parked in the truck lot, and three sedans were scattered through the lot he was in. Probably meant a clerk and maybe a customer or two inside. Not ideal, but if there wasn't anyone to feed on, he could at least get himself a stale sandwich and a drink.

He hung out near the car for a few minutes, pretending to check the air in his tires and inspect the vehicle. Nothing that would draw suspicion in a place like this. It only took two passes around the Corolla before he scented someone whose aura was dark enough to make his skin prickle with anticipation. He spent a lot of the year feeding on people with gray intent. People who could go either way, who he could siphon the dark energy off of and let them go on their way, harmless. A small snack for Hugh; a big benefit for humanity.

This guy was not one of those, and Hugh had never been so happy to see a rapist. He straightened out of his crouch as the man came into view. He was wearing a tattered baseball cap pulled low over his face. His T-shirt had a trucking-company logo on it, probably the one he drove for. A big rig that hadn't been there when Hugh arrived was now parked in the truck lot.

The trucker's aura was saturated with malice. This was clearly not the first time he'd done whatever he was about to do. Hugh wondered how someone this stupid had never been caught. Not that Hugh was going to wait and catch the guy in the act. The acrid tang of murder was in his aura, so Hugh wasn't going to feel bad about draining every last drop of his chi out of him.

Unlike the trucker, Hugh had already scoped out the parking lot and confirmed the only camera was one directly aimed at the door to record people coming in and out of the truck stop. He could grab the guy and haul him off into a darkened part of the lot without attracting any attention.

He sprang into action as soon as the guy was in reach. Chronically underfed as he was, Hugh was still much faster than a human. Even if there had been a camera, it wouldn't have registered much more than a blur tackling the trucker and dragging him to the ground. It would be easy to bundle him into the back of his sedan and kill him there, but Hugh had a rule about keeping his feeds as distanced from his daughter as he could, and that included not bringing them into his car or home.

Hugh eyed the camera, confirming it was pointed solidly at the sickly yellow pool of light that illuminated the front door, one of the few security lights in the parking lot. He could feed on the guy here in the shadow of his car, but then he'd have to drag the body away later. That would be hard to pass off as a buddy helping his friend get somewhere to sleep it off if anyone discovered them, which was his go-to ruse when he was dealing with scumbags like this. He'd done it for years and never had anyone question it.

It wasn't as safe as feeding in clubs and areas where the bouncers and police knew who he was and what he was doing. Hugh had a decent network of people who helped point him toward criminals to drain during his hall-pass trips, which made things a lot safer and easier for him. But he wasn't going to pass up a golden opportunity to feed to his heart's content and get a dangerous predator off the streets for good.

Hugh headbutted the struggling man to knock him out, then wrapped him in a bear hug and stood up. He could walk with the added weight easily, but he staggered around in case anyone was watching. There were dumpsters around the side of the building, and he headed in that direction, restraining himself from siphoning off any of the trucker's aura as they walked.

He'd made it into the patchy brightness of the lights near the dumpster area when someone grabbed him from behind.

The shock of being snuck up on was a harder blow than the scrape of his face against the dirty cinder-block truck-stop wall. He'd had no inkling they weren't alone in the parking lot. How was that possible? His attacker had no aura. No scent.

He lost his grip on the trucker, who fell to the pavement with a thump. Hugh saw him crawl away out of the corner of his eye, but he let him go, his attention focused on the man who was attacking him.

Hugh fought back, moderating his strength so he didn't hurt the person. He could toss a human twenty feet if he wanted, but attracting that kind of attention was never good. Instead he pushed back, surprised when he found that even if he tried, he couldn't free himself from the iron-like hold.

"Demon! How dare you feed so brazenly?"

Hugh struggled, unleashing his full strength in a panic. Even trying his hardest, he barely moved his attacker an inch. This wasn't good.

The man leaned in and took a deep sniff. Despite himself, Hugh's pulse jumped at the intimacy. His power pulsed, taking on a life of its own as it probed his attacker. He couldn't stop it, and it was good, letting his humanity take a back seat to his vampire instincts. Like being alive for the first time in a long time. He hadn't lost control like this in decades.

Tendrils of his aura encased the man behind him, caressing skin that was so curiously free of any scent. Hugh reared back when he realized that even with his extra senses at full blast, he still couldn't smell his attacker.

Just like Ruby.

That put the brakes on his bloodlust like a bucket of ice-cold water. He'd never met anyone else that he couldn't sense. It explained how the man had snuck up on him, but it also opened up more questions. What was he? And why did he lack a smell like Ruby did?

He struggled in the man's viselike grip around his chest, his lungs screaming from lack of air as his breath came in tiny gasps.

"Do not try your tricks on me, you disgusting bottom-feeder," the man muttered.

So he'd been able to feel Hugh's aura? But it hadn't weakened him like it should have. Usually when fully deployed, his powers were almost like a numbing agent. They prevented his victim from struggling and allowed him to feed without drawing attention.

Hugh stopped moving. "What are you?"

The man flipped him around like he weighed less than a rag doll. Hugh's head bounced against the cinder block with a thud. He managed a few deep breaths before the man dug a forearm into his windpipe, choking him.

Hugh grasped at his attacker's shoulders to dislodge him, but fighting only cut off his airway further. His lips tingled, and spots crowded his vision.

The man didn't look like he should have enough strength to hold down a vampire, but he hadn't even broken a sweat. He must be supernatural, but Hugh had never heard of a creature that didn't have a scent. He'd suspect a spell or talisman that was hiding it if he hadn't experienced the same thing with Ruby.

Did that mean she was supernatural? She'd never shown signs of superstrength or any other latent abilities, aside from her lack of scent. God. Ruby. He had to get out of this for her sake.

Hugh struggled harder against the man. He needed to get the upper hand so he could find out what kind of supernatural he was. What kind of supernatural Ruby was.

Fear for his daughter flooded his limbs with a well of new strength, and Hugh landed a punch to his attacker's solar plexus. The man gasped and faltered for a split second, but it was enough time for Hugh to duck out of his grasp and pull the man's arms behind his back. The move would have wrenched both shoulders out of their sockets if the man had been human.

Hugh swung him around and pinned him to the dumpster.

"Who are you?" he rasped out, his throat sore and raw.

"Someone duty bound to avenge the lives of the innocent humans your kind murders!"

"I have never killed an innocent," Hugh said evenly. "Tell me what you are."

The man renewed his struggle but remained silent.

The irony of this being very similar to the place he'd found Ruby gave him a renewed sense of purpose.

A terrified scream from inside the building made them both stop. He held the man's gaze, both of them barely breathing as they listened.

Hugh was tempted to loosen his hold on the man, but he'd been on the receiving end of his brutality too recently to underestimate him. He kept the pressure on the man's arms steady even though he hated the thought of how much pain the man must be in. His own injuries were throbbing in time with his heart, which was beating much slower than it should be. He needed to feed… and soon.

The man he'd been about to drain must be inside the truck stop now. Hugh was torn between the desire to go help the woman who had screamed and pressing his advantage with the man he had up against the dumpster so he could find out what he was.

Another scream rent the air, followed by a gunshot. Hugh gritted his teeth and made a decision.

"The man you 'rescued' from me is a criminal," Hugh said, his voice low. "And he's inside right now attacking a human that he intends to kill. When I grabbed him he had murder in his aura. Nothing but ill intent. I don't kill innocents. I feed off men like him to save innocents from situations like this one."

His attacker seemed to be weakening the longer they spoke. His tanned skin was turning sallow, and his breaths were becoming more labored.

"If I release you, will you try to kill me again?"

The man closed his eyes. "My name is Rykoff of Harlow. You have my word as a servant of the fae summer court that I will not harm you."

Hugh sent up a prayer that he wasn't being a soft-hearted idiot and let go of the man. He stepped back, ready to defend himself, but the man slumped forward into a heap on the dirty ground.

"Will you heal?"

The man looked up, and the color of his eyes struck Hugh. They were gray like Ruby's, and in this light they almost looked amber. Like hers did when she got upset.

"Aye, but not in time to help. I need to get away from this iron before I can regain my strength. Go."

Hugh hoped he wasn't signing his own death warrant as he turned his back on the man, but unless he was a terrific actor, the guy wasn't in any shape to attack. Hugh tried the back door, but it was locked from the inside. Cursing, he ran around the perimeter of the building and wrenched open the front door.

An electronic chirp sounded when he stepped inside, but neither of the occupants acknowledged him at all. The truck stop smelled like burned coffee and stale hotdogs, all overlaid with the overwhelming stink of lust and hatred.

He hadn't been lying when he'd told the man he never drained innocent people. It was one thing to siphon off a little greed or sadness—or even excitement and attraction—to get by, but he didn't believe in killing innocents so he could live.

Hell, he rarely even drained people who weren't innocent. His powers didn't work that way. He fed off a person's chi, and he was very good at directing what part of the aura he consumed. If he was at an orgy, he'd sample a little lust from everyone. If he was just with one person, he'd feed at the moment of their orgasm, siphoning off the burst of pleasure but leaving them with the endorphin high.

When he fed off criminals, it was different. He'd dig down deep, pulling out all their darkest emotions and motivations. Unlike when he fed off innocents, he didn't worry about going too far. He'd search out every bit of lust, anger, or hatred that the person harbored and yank it out. Besides giving him the nourishment he needed to stay strong, it also had the basic effect of chemically castrating the offender. The only time it killed them was if there was no redeemable part of their aura left. He didn't feel bad about those.

This guy, though.

This guy he was definitely gonna kill.

The clerk must have been restocking energy drinks when he'd come up on her, and the man had her forced up against a pallet of them, one hand holding a gun on her while the other pawed at her clothes. The gunshot they'd heard must have been a warning, since Hugh didn't smell any blood. The woman was unharmed. Physically, at least.

Hugh didn't bother masking his speed as he rushed the man, hitting him with his full body weight and sending the gun skittering across the floor. The woman jumped up and ran to the front of the store, and Hugh figured he had a few minutes before the police arrived. Not ideal, but he could work with it.

Since vampires drained psychic energy and not blood, contrary to pop culture's portrayal of them, there wouldn't be any sign of Hugh's feeding when the medical examiner autopsied the body. Vampire kills were recorded as strokes or heart attacks. The abrupt severance of the chi from the body could cause both.

Hugh flattened himself over the man's body, and from the clerk's view it would look like he was just holding him down until the police could arrive. That would be the statement he gave the officers too.

Hugh nestled his head against the man's throat, using the man's heartbeat to help ground himself. He gathered his energy and cast it out like a net around the man's body. His own muscles went stiff as he drained him, the influx of power both exhilarating and painful. He normally liked to take his time to avoid this, but he had to finish before the police interrupted them. There was nothing to salvage in the man's aura. If Hugh didn't kill him, he'd do the same thing again.

CHAPTER FOUR

"AND YOU two don't know each other? You don't know how he came to be all banged up?"

Hugh looked over the cop's shoulder to watch the paramedics tending the man who'd jumped him. Rykoff, he'd said his name was. Hugh doubted they'd be able to do anything to help him, since he was supernatural, but they probably couldn't do anything to hurt him either.

He sent up a silent prayer that the fae had excellent hearing, like vamps. He needed Rykoff to give the same statement he did so they could get out of here without raising any alarms with the police.

"He was on the pavement when I got here. He told me some lunatic had jumped him and then gone inside, and I ran in when I heard the woman scream and a gunshot."

He saw Rykoff incline his head a fraction, and Hugh almost sighed in relief. So yes on supernatural hearing.

The cop had Hugh hold out his hands so he could inspect them. Ten minutes ago they'd been scraped and bruised from his fight with Rykoff, but feeding off the guy inside had healed him. There wasn't a scratch on him, which supported Hugh's story that he'd tackled the man and then done nothing but hold him down until the police came. He'd added a bit about the man going stiff and gasping for breath, which the clerk could confirm if she'd been watching. The autopsy would show a heart attack, most likely.

"What was your business here? You just happened to stop?"

The best lies were ones sprinkled with truth, Hugh had learned. "I'm heading up to Detroit for vacation, and I got hungry and pulled in to grab something to eat."

The officer nodded and tucked his pen back into his pocket. "Thank you, Mr. Whitby. The paramedics are going to check you over just in case, and then we'll see if we need any further statement from you. Please don't leave the scene."

Hugh wandered over to the ambulance, keeping his distance from the hysterical clerk who was being treated inside. He hoped they could give her something to calm her down. He'd do it himself, but he didn't think she'd let him anywhere near her. Not that he blamed her. She'd had a hell of an evening.

The same officer who'd questioned him had Rykoff off to the side now, so Hugh took the spot he'd been in earlier, leaning on the bumper of the ambulance. He waved the paramedic away when she tried to poke him.

"I'm fine," he said, remembering he should be shaken up a beat too late. "I mean, physically I'm okay. I didn't hurt myself when I grabbed him."

The paramedic ignored him and slapped a blood pressure cuff around his arm. Hugh swallowed a curse. His blood pressure and heart rate ran low, especially after a good feed. The last thing he needed was a trip to the hospital because the EMT thought he was in shock.

He bit down hard on the inside of his cheek, hoping the sudden pain would raise his heart rate. He stood like he was craning to see what was happening, which drew an annoyed noise out of the EMT, who frowned at him.

"Please sit still while I get your vitals," she said. "You may feel fine, but you could still have an injury."

She put her stethoscope against the crook of his arm and started pumping the cuff. His gaze darted to Rykoff again, who was running a hand through his messy hair as the police officer took his statement. He was telling him the same thing Hugh had, adding more details about how the man had jumped him. Good.

"Have you ever been told your blood pressure is very low?" the EMT asked. "What is normal for you?"

Fuck.

"Uh, I don't know," he mumbled. What was a normal blood pressure? He didn't want to spit out numbers that would be unreasonable. "I'm, ah, healthy? I don't really go to the doctor."

The paramedic made a low noise. "I'm not happy with your vitals. Sit tight, and we'll check them again in a few minutes, okay?"

She patted his knee and climbed into the ambulance to check on the clerk. Hugh knew he could refuse treatment, but that would create a paper trail, and he didn't want that. Supernaturals were supposed to keep a low profile. Being found at the scene of a crime, especially one where the criminal died, was bad enough. He didn't need to add to the situation by causing a scene about refusing medical care.

They'd let Rykoff be taken for questioning, which had to mean he'd convinced them he was okay. Did that mean fae vitals were closer to humans than vampires were? Or maybe he could glamour or do some other mind control?

Hugh's limited powers of persuasion hadn't affected Rykoff at all. He wouldn't be able to finesse his way out of the paramedic's concern either. His abilities hinged on manipulating emotions, and the EMT was very professional. She had no emotional involvement for Hugh to pluck at. As for Rykoff—Hugh didn't know if fae were immune to vampire powers or not. It could be that or a strong set of mental barriers. Very little was known about the fae because they rarely left their secluded realm.

Hugh could barely sit still. Power thrummed through him, roiling under his skin from his feeding. It had been months since he'd been this well fed. He hadn't drained anyone since winter break, when Ruby had spent the weekend at a friend's house and he'd dipped down to Chicago to hunt.

He had so much energy. He wanted to run. To fuck.

Too bad Rykoff had made it clear he hated vampires. Hugh would love to see what he was like in bed. If he was a quarter as fierce as he'd been while they were fighting, he'd be well worth the effort.

Would Rykoff be rough in bed? He was stronger than Hugh, which meant Hugh wouldn't have to hold himself back. Excitement rippled up Hugh's spine, his breath quickening as he thought about what it would be like to have Rykoff underneath him.

He shifted his gaze from Rykoff to the paramedic when she joined him a moment later.

"Okay, let's get that blood pressure one more time."

Hugh watched her carefully as she took his vitals again, relaxing when she seemed satisfied.

"That's better." She took the cuff off him. "No chest pain? Dizziness?" She shined a light in his eyes.

"No, I'm fine."

Horny as hell, but it had brought his blood pressure up, so mission accomplished.

"You could still go into shock later," she said, packing things up. "Give your doctor a call or go to the ER if you experience shortness of breath, light-headedness, or anything out of the ordinary tonight, okay?"

He nodded. "I will."

The officer was still talking to Rykoff, so Hugh walked over to his car and sat on the trunk. This was shaping up to be a terrible vacation, even if he had just drained someone.

Rykoff was fae, and unless he was mistaken, so was Ruby. Hugh had to learn whatever he could about them from Rykoff, and that would probably be a difficult task, given that the guy had tried to smash his head in an hour ago. Fae were a mystery in the supernatural community. They were one of the few groups that didn't take part in the governing councils tasked with protecting the supernatural secret. It had never been an issue before, since they stuck to their own realm. Until now, apparently.

Hugh wasn't used to not having any inkling what other people were thinking. He could read everyone but Ruby, and luckily the kid wore her emotions on her sleeve.

As far as he could tell, Rykoff had none of Ruby's tells. He was stone-faced, his emotions held firmly in check. Hugh was flying blind.

At least he wasn't actively trying to kill Hugh anymore. That was a plus. Though who knew if the truce was temporary or not. They hadn't exactly had time to negotiate terms when Hugh had dashed off to kill the bad guy.

He dangled his feet off the trunk and rested his head in his hands, listening to the surrounding conversations. Two officers were talking about a baseball game. The techs were chattering about inane things as they processed the scene inside. Rykoff was feeding the cop who was interviewing him a load of crap about why he didn't have his driver's license on him.

Shit.

He needed to get Rykoff out of there before the cop ran him through the system and came up empty.

One of the perks of being registered with the Greater North American Supernatural Council was having help in situations like these. He'd worked for the council before adopting Ruby, when he'd taken a big step back from everything related to the supernatural world in an effort to keep her safe.

Hugh didn't know what kind of safeguards, if any, the fae had to protect them from discovery. He sure as hell wasn't going to wait around and hope Rykoff had enough sense to pull himself out of this.

He hopped off the trunk and jogged across the lot. His muscles screamed for a real run, but he forced himself to keep a very human pace. Rykoff looked about two questions from an explosion when he got to him.

Luckily the cop was frustrated too, which Hugh used to his advantage. He pretended to stumble and put his hand out to brace himself, grabbing the officer by the shoulder. He drained off the frustration and focused on replacing it with euphoria.

"This is an open-and-shut case. Isn't it nice for a change to have things all wrapped up so neatly? I bet when you run the attacker's prints, you'll find a lot of unsolved cases too. This will be great for your career. It was lucky for you that Rykoff and I were here and were able to take the attacker down."

The cop's eyes glazed over briefly, and he grabbed a hold of Hugh.

"Careful there, Mr. Whitby. You wouldn't want to come through a violent crime unscathed and then fall in the parking lot afterward."

Hugh grinned and sent another burst of goodwill through their link before he let go. "Thanks for catching me. I was coming over to see if you had everything you needed from us."

The cop looked a bit dazed but nodded. "The clerk was lucky you were both here. I don't think this was the first time that perp did this, and we can all rest easier knowing he's not going to hurt anyone else."

Hugh nodded. "Definitely. You have my contact information if you need anything else. We've had a long night, and we're going to leave now."

"Yes. I'll be in touch if we need more details. Both of you should go get some rest."

Rykoff looked angry but followed Hugh when he walked away. He waited until they were out of earshot before laying into him.

"What did you do to him? I told you I won't abide you harming humans."

"I didn't hurt him," Hugh snapped. "You're the one traipsing around without a human cover story. He would have tried to run your information, and then what?"

Rykoff scowled. "I move through the mortal realm as I please."

"In a car you don't have a license for, you mean."

"I do not require a vehicle to travel."

Wait, what?

"This truck stop is in the middle of nowhere. The only way to get here is off the interstate. How did you get here without a car?"

A small smile curved Rykoff's lips. "Magic."

Hugh doubted that. Magic had a very noticeable scent—like burned ozone. And there wasn't a trace of it here.

The ambulance had left, but the parking lot was still teeming with police. Unless Rykoff's method of travel was inconspicuous, he wasn't getting out of here anytime soon. From the look on his face, he seemed to realize that around the same time Hugh did.

"I opened a portal. I can move through the mortal and fae realms through them," he said with a sigh.

Hugh grinned. This was his chance to find out more about the fae.

"Well, then, it seems you might need a ride. How fortunate that I have a car."

CHAPTER FIVE

"YOU MAY drop me at the next exit," Rykoff said as Hugh merged onto the interstate.

He still didn't look good. His skin was sallow, and his wounds hadn't healed. He appeared weak—if Hugh didn't know better, he'd say Rykoff was human. Hugh wondered if summoning a portal took a lot of energy, because that wasn't something Rykoff had much of at the moment.

"The exits out here are pretty far apart. We're in the middle of nowhere, if you hadn't noticed."

"My task preoccupied me, and then I came upon you attacking a human. I am not here to sightsee."

"If you were, you sure landed in the wrong place for it. We're about two hours from Detroit, which is the biggest city around here but also not really a place on many tourists' to-do lists. And really, we've established that the human in question was far from an innocent. I'd think even the fae would agree he needed to be dealt with."

"The fae rarely meddle in the affairs of humans. When we do, it is to protect the innocent from supernatural threats such as yourself."

Hugh ignored the obvious taunt. "Why were you at the truck stop?"

"I was on the trail of a rogue. A fae who left the realm without permission and needs to be brought back to face judgment."

"So there aren't fae who live here? In, what did you call it? The mortal realm?"

Rykoff wrinkled his nose. "Precious few. The mortal realm doesn't have much to offer the fae. Humans view nature as something to tame. The fae rely on it for survival. We have a symbiotic relationship with it—it's not something that can easily be sustained here."

Fucking hell. What did that mean for Ruby? She was a healthy kid by human standards, but if she wasn't human, was she okay? What did the fae need to survive?

"You said back at the truck stop that you couldn't heal there. What did you mean by that?"

"Fae draw our life force from nature. I need to be surrounded by it to heal."

"But it was like flipping a switch. You had me bested, but when I got you up against the dumpster it was like all your strings had been cut."

Rykoff looked at him, like he was gauging his trustworthiness. Luckily, he seemed to pass, because Rykoff continued.

"The iron," he explained. "It weakens us. That much of it, with skin-on-skin contact? I didn't stand a chance. I thought you had used it strategically."

Jesus. Ruby was allergic to iron. She'd had several bad skin reactions and once landed in the ER after eating a portobello mushroom he'd cooked in a cast iron pan.

"And what kind of nature do you need to heal?"

"Ideally, I need the forests of the fae realm. But here any large stand of trees and grass will do. For minor wounds, at least."

That wasn't good news for Ruby and their postage stamp yard.

Rykoff shifted in his seat and pulled a polka-dotted sock out from underneath himself. Hugh's apology was barely formed when Rykoff cut him off with a feral shout. Hugh had to stop him from lunging across the console. He held him at arm's length, fighting to steer the car as Rykoff went ballistic.

"How dare you defile a fae youngling! Did you think I wouldn't be able to catch the scent? Where are you keeping the youngling? What have you done to the child?"

Goddammit. Rykoff was holding one of Ruby's socks. She must have left it in the car, and he'd probably tossed it onto the passenger seat without thinking. It was next to impossible to keep shoes on that child. She stripped them off, along with her socks, at the first opportunity.

"I haven't done anything!"

"I should have killed you. You talk of not feeding from innocents, yet you have clothing belonging to a fae youngling. How many children have you killed?"

He didn't feed off children. He wasn't a monster, no matter what the world thought of vampires. Most of them weren't. They were predatory

29

by nature, but there was a moral code among them. Adults were fair game, but not children. Never children.

Hugh bit back his response and focused on navigating the car to the side of the road. They'd barely passed a dozen cars since they'd left the truck stop, but he didn't want to drive while Rykoff was actively trying to claw his way over the center console to attack him. In Rykoff's weakened state, there was no real risk of him injuring Hugh, but Hugh didn't want to hit another car because he was distracted.

"The fae child. Where have you hidden it?"

Could he trust Rykoff with the knowledge of Ruby's existence? All signs seemed to point to no.

"I don't know what you're talking about." Hugh forced the words out, fear making his throat dry.

"How did you capture the youngling?"

He wasn't going to give this asshole any information about Ruby—not their familial connection and certainly not her name.

"I can smell the child all over this vehicle now that I have the scent. You must have bathed in their essence, you soulless bastard."

Wait. Rykoff was saying he could smell Ruby. That must mean she did have a scent, and that it was just masked from Hugh. Fascinating.

"You can smell her on me?"

"Her? So the youngling is a female? Where have you hidden her?"

Shit. So much for not giving away any details about her.

Hugh fisted his hand in the fabric of Rykoff's shirt and pushed him back against the window. "Why can you smell her when I can't? Why don't you have a scent either?"

Rykoff sneered at him. "The girl smells like all fae do. Of wildflowers and sunshine. The same scent I carry."

"What makes you think the child is fae?"

Rykoff snarled wordlessly, his eyes glowing in the dim light. The hatred in them was unmistakable, even if it wasn't accompanied by the hot-sour tang Hugh could usually taste in a person's aura.

"The child is unimaginably precious. Fae younglings are rare. You will die for what you've done."

Ruby was unimaginably precious, but it wasn't because she was fae. She was his daughter. It was his job to keep her safe, and right now that meant figuring out what the hell she was so he could do whatever was necessary to protect her.

Rykoff had to know he was outmatched. He hadn't healed from their last fight, and Hugh was stronger than ever thanks to feeding. Yet Rykoff was willing to put his own life in danger to avenge a child he'd never even met. The way his voice shook when he talked about her told Hugh more about him than anything else could.

Hugh made a split-second decision.

"She's not dead."

Rykoff snorted. "Even if you left her alive, she's as good as dead. Her scent is thick on you."

"Her scent is on me because we live together. I assure you she's safe."

That made the fae even angrier.

"You keep her as chattel to feed on?"

Hugh's stomach roiled at the thought.

"Of course not! I've never fed on her, and I never will." He hesitated, then decided to put it all out there. "She's my daughter."

Rykoff went still.

"Your daughter," he said flatly.

"I found her when she was seven days old. She'd been abandoned in a dumpster like the one at the truck stop," he said. "I took her in, and I went through the proper human channels to adopt her."

"You found her? Impossible. Stole her, more likely. No fae would abandon their child."

Hugh wasn't sure how anyone could abandon their child, discarded in the trash. There were two fire stations and a hospital within walking distance from the Ruby Tuesday where he'd found her. She could have been dropped off somewhere safe easily, but she hadn't been. She'd been left by the side of the dumpster like trash. Not a day went by that Hugh didn't thank whatever gods there were that he'd found her.

"I found her," he repeated firmly. "I went back every day for three weeks, hoping to find who'd left her. But there was never any trace."

There wouldn't have been any, not if she'd been left by a fae, he realized. At least none *he* could detect.

"Where."

"Cincinnati."

"And you've left her alone in Cincinnati?"

Hugh tensed. "No. She's at a summer camp with her friends."

"Camp? In the forest?"

"Yes. She's gone every summer for years. She loves it."

Some of the tension bled out of Rykoff's posture, but he still clutched the sock with a death grip. "Of course she does. It is how we recharge. Being in this realm is difficult. The only good part about it are the forests, where the veil between realms is thin."

Ruby always came home from camp energized and happy, and he'd assumed that was just normal kid behavior. But maybe it was more. Maybe the way she darted away from him toward her friends when he dropped her off wasn't about her being an independent spirit. Maybe it was part of her feeling drawn to the forest.

"We may walk among you when it is necessary for us, but the fae do not live in the realm of humans."

How would a fae baby come to be abandoned in the human realm? He doubted there were Planned Parenthoods in the fae world, but if children were that precious, wouldn't adoption be a thing? Why leave a child in the human realm to die?

"I'll answer your questions about my daughter if you answer mine about how to keep her healthy in this realm."

Rykoff huffed. "It is impossible for a fae youngling to be raised outside the realm."

"She's gotten by fine for ten years. But I need to know everything you can tell me about the fae. She's my daughter, Rykoff. Your speech about kids being precious? She is. She's my life. I'd die to protect her. Help me do that."

Hugh held Rykoff's gaze even though he was uncomfortable being so vulnerable. Rykoff had the advantage here. Hugh didn't like it, but it underscored how important it was that he find out more about the fae. Did Ruby have powers now? Was she scared or confused? Hurting? Was she hiding them from him, worried she was some sort of freak?

His decision to hide his true nature from her had seemed wise, but now it seemed cruel. His little girl must think there was something wrong with her. She had no idea she wasn't the only one with a supernatural secret.

Rykoff finally relaxed, and Hugh breathed a sigh of relief and let go of his shirt.

"On one condition," Rykoff said. "I want to verify she is alive and well."

Hugh could do that. They could video chat her in the morning. He'd call the camp and make up an excuse—some emergency that would be bad enough he needed to talk to her face-to-face but not so bad he'd have to pick her up. News about her cousin Clementine, maybe. She didn't have any cousins, of course, but it was their code for the times he couldn't pick her up from school and she needed to go home with someone else.

"Tomorrow," Hugh said with a nod. He checked his rearview mirror for traffic and pulled back out onto the interstate.

"This is the direction you were heading," Rykoff said as Hugh merged. "I asked you to take me to the youngling."

Hugh shot him a tight grin. "I told you I would do anything to keep her safe. That includes not bringing the strange fae I just met to meet her. We'll call her."

"I have a duty to reclaim the youngling and take her to court before harm befalls her in this realm."

Bullshit. "My daughter's welfare is no business of yours, but I assure you she's well cared for and happy."

Rykoff snorted. "How can she be happy when she is trapped among humans and living with a vampire? This realm is stifling. One can barely draw a breath."

Hugh silently reminded himself that his daughter was happy and well-adjusted. She'd never seemed the slightest bit distressed by living in the city.

Though she had a certain glow to her when she came home from camp. Fuck. Had he been asphyxiating her for her entire life?

"Is that—is that a thing?"

"It's a turn of phrase," Rykoff said. "She is not actually unable to breathe."

"Is it really that bad here? Is she being harmed by living in the mortal realm?"

Rykoff frowned. "I meant only that this realm dulls my fae senses. I have none of the freedom that the fae realm provides. Think of it as only being able to see half the colors you normally do, or not being able to taste—" He turned in his seat to face Hugh. "Do you eat? I haven't a clue as to the epicurean habits of the vampire race."

"We eat," Hugh said shortly, annoyed. "Our nourishment comes from chi, but we can eat and drink as humans do."

Rykoff pondered that for a moment and then nodded. "It makes sense, evolutionarily. Your race depends on humans for sustenance, therefore anything that sets you apart from them makes it harder for you to survive."

"Senses, Rykoff," Hugh reminded him. "You were talking about Ru—I mean, my daughter's senses here in the mortal realm."

"They're not as vivid as they would be if she were home. And her access to her powers will be dampened."

Jesus fuck. Powers?

"What powers?"

"She won't develop them until she's older, but she is a fae," he said with a shrug. "We have many latent abilities."

Hugh could tell Rykoff wasn't about to share what those abilities were, so he let it drop. For now.

"You said you're here chasing the rogue. Are you some sort of fae official?"

Rykoff stiffened. "My position at court is none of your business."

That sounded like a no. Which was probably a good thing. It would be harder to convince Rykoff to keep Ruby a secret if he held an official post in the fae court. Hugh needed to make sure he wasn't going to step through a portal the moment he got out of the car and spill the beans.

"A bounty hunter, then?"

Rykoff's already glacial expression cooled even more, so Hugh quit while he was ahead. Whatever Rykoff's mission, it didn't involve him.

"What leads do you have? I have friends in a few jurisdictions who can help if you have enough on him to put a BOLO out."

Just because he couldn't always give the bad guys over to the cops didn't mean he never could. Sometimes he got lucky during his hunt and stumbled into a nest of evidence that could put a criminal away, and he always turned that over when it happened. He'd made quite a few friends in law enforcement over the years, and he had access to an even wider network of resources through his supernatural friends.

"What is a bow low?"

"It's an acronym. It means be on the lookout for. Law enforcement uses it to get a person's description out to a lot of officers on the street so they can look for them."

Rykoff shook his head. "Ambrose is dangerous and wouldn't hesitate to hurt a human if they tried to detain him."

"We could frame it as a missing-person report. They wouldn't try to stop him, but they'd send out an alert if they saw someone who fit his description. Do you know where he's heading?"

He didn't have connections for a statewide call, but if Rykoff could narrow it down to a few cities, Hugh might be able to pull some strings.

Rykoff pursed his lips. "It's private fae business."

Hugh bit back a nasty comment. This wasn't any of his business. If Rykoff was too stubborn to take help, then so be it. Hugh wasn't going to spend his summer vacation hunting down a rogue fae anyway.

He had weeks of gluttony and orgies ahead of him. He'd spend some time with Rykoff, get whatever information out of him he could about powers Ruby might develop and anything else he needed to know, and then they'd go their separate ways.

"I don't suppose you have a fae edition of *What to Expect When You're Expecting*," Hugh muttered.

"I haven't a clue what you're talking about."

Hugh glanced over at Rykoff, who had settled back into the seat and closed his eyes. He wasn't exactly sure what normal looked like for the fae, but this probably wasn't it. Rykoff had bags under his eyes, and his skin still had an unhealthy pallor. It was clear he needed to recharge somehow.

They'd been passing billboards for a campground for miles, and when it showed up again, advertising the exit in a few miles, Hugh made the spontaneous decision that they'd head there. It wasn't like they had a plan. Even before Rykoff had intercepted him, Hugh hadn't had an itinerary for the evening. Hell, if things hadn't gone awry, he'd probably be sleeping off his meal in the car at the truck stop.

Rykoff barely twitched when Hugh took the next exit, which confirmed in his mind that he'd made the right choice. The poor guy was dead to the world, tired enough that he conked out with a virtual stranger at the wheel. Hugh didn't flatter himself thinking it meant Rykoff trusted him. It simply meant the fae was too depleted to stay awake.

He'd said being in nature helped, and this campground was the best Hugh could do at the moment. He followed the signs, inky darkness settling around the car as he left the headlights of the interstate behind them.

Five minutes later he turned onto a gravel drive marked by an unilluminated wooden sign that had seen better days. It erased any hope that the campground would have modern amenities like Wi-Fi. Hell, it didn't even have pavement. His car bumped over foliage and pot holes in what had probably once been a maintained gravel road. They'd have their privacy, at least. It didn't look like Lakeland Hills Campground had hosted visitors for years.

The narrow drive gave way to a clearing, Hugh's headlights illuminating a dilapidated tollbooth-style building. He'd known cabins were a long shot, but the sparseness of the setup was still a surprise. The gravel continued past the booth, with mini driveways set up about ten feet apart. Apparently this had been a drive-up campground.

He pulled into the first campsite and killed the lights. He'd put good money on Rykoff's night vision being even better than his, and his was pretty damn good.

The fae stirred when the engine turned off, blinking hard as he roused himself and took in their new surroundings. Hugh was charmed by how cute and rumpled he looked, and he had to remind himself that Rykoff could probably snap his neck like a twig if he wanted to. This wasn't a guy he'd picked up at a bar. This was a fae, who was a total unknown quantity.

"We needed to stop somewhere for the night, and this seemed as good a place as any," Hugh said when Rykoff frowned at him.

"What is this place?"

"An abandoned campground," Hugh said as he climbed out of the car. He had blankets and a pillow in the back, since he'd planned to sleep in his car at least part of the time anyway. "To be fair, I didn't know it was abandoned when I chose it, but we'll be fine."

They were two apex predators. There was nothing in these woods as scary as them. The worst part was having his hopes of indoor plumbing dashed.

Rykoff stretched as he stood, his shirt riding up to expose sharp hip bones. He looked undernourished, and the urge to feed him overwhelmed Hugh. He rifled through the trunk, looking for supplies. Even though he enjoyed it, and it was part of his routine now, Hugh didn't technically need to eat. And since his vacation budget wouldn't even extend to a shoestring, he hadn't brought unnecessary food. He nearly crowed with delight when he found a box of fruit jerky shoved in a corner. Probably forgotten after a shopping trip. He grabbed that and two bottles of water from his stash and wandered along the dirt path, looking for Rykoff.

He found him nestled against the base of a tree like he was sitting in a plush recliner.

"You must be hungry," he said, shoving the box at him.

Rykoff didn't take it. "I've eaten food in the mortal realm before, and it doesn't agree with me."

Hugh didn't doubt that. Highly processed food made Ruby sick, which was why he spent a considerable amount of his meager salary on organic food from the bougie grocery store in town. The granola bars she'd tried to sneak to camp to sell for quarters cost almost four dollars apiece.

"Try this," he said, nudging the box at Rykoff until he huffed out an annoyed sigh and took it. "No added sugars or preservatives. It's basically fruit and water mashed together and baked."

Rykoff gave it a skeptical look but unwrapped one and took a bite, then another, barely chewing as he finished the first bar. He accepted the bottle of water Hugh held out and took a deep drink from it before wiping his mouth.

"These are acceptable," he said as he unwrapped a second bar. "Thank you."

Hugh shrugged. "My kid has a lot of food intolerances and allergies. I figured you might be the same."

"Our bodies aren't designed to handle food as the humans have evolved it," Rykoff said. "We live closer to nature than modern humans do, and we rely on it for our sustenance. Fruits are good. Vegetables. Nuts. Things freely given to us by the forest in exchange for our protection."

That was a weird way to phrase it. Almost like nature was sentient. Or maybe it was in the fae realm?

"Do the plants really give themselves to you to eat?"

Rykoff snorted. "Like a sacrifice? No. But it is easy to live in tune with nature if you try. Nature is a fickle mistress, but she's also a nurturing one."

That put Hugh's visions of giant man-eating flytraps to bed, then.

"That said, we have many species that no longer exist here. At one time the fae and mortal realms were one, but when mortals began their destructive quest to tame the land, the fae court split us from them."

God, that would be a botanist's dream. Stepping into the fae realm must be like traveling back in time. What if there were—

"There are no dinosaurs," Rykoff said, breaking Hugh out of his reverie. At Hugh's curious look, Rykoff laughed. "You're not the first I've told about the fae realm. Dinosaurs always come up eventually."

Hugh watched as Rykoff gathered leaves, molding them into a bed that ended up looking quite comfortable. Well, as comfortable as sleeping outside on the ground could be.

"I need to rest," Rykoff said, tucking himself into the leaf bed.

"I can stand watch while you sleep."

"Unnecessary," Rykoff answered. "You would benefit from some sleep as well. The rogue isn't anywhere near here, but even if he was, he wouldn't be able to sneak up on us."

He laid a hand at the base of the massive tree he'd built his nest under. His eyes glowed amber briefly. Hugh swore the bark shivered at his touch.

"The forest will let us know if anyone with ill will approaches."

Hugh was too tired to parse that. Apparently Rykoff was forging alliances with trees now, and the forest was sentient enough to stand guard. Maybe he did need to go to bed before he lost the remainder of his sanity.

He'd planned to offer Rykoff his pillow and blanket, but the fae seemed unfairly comfortable in his bed of leaves. He seemed to fall asleep as soon as he closed his eyes, which also annoyed Hugh. He dragged himself back to the car and spent a few minutes adjusting the passenger seat so he could stretch out as much as possible, which unfortunately wasn't nearly enough.

He couldn't see Rykoff from the car, which bothered him more than it should. Logically, he knew the fae could protect himself. Even if the trees "standing watch" thing was bullshit—which it had to be—he'd seen Rykoff fight. After recharging in the woods, he should be back to full strength.

It would be ridiculous to leave the car and sleep on the ground with Rykoff. Hugh had always hated camping, and this barely even qualified as that. No tent, no sleeping bags, no s'mores. Just a nest of leaves that Rykoff seemed to find as comfortable as a feather bed and a tree that had that weird glowy thing going on.

Hugh tossed and turned restlessly for half an hour before a tap on the hood of the car startled him into sitting straight up. Rykoff stood there with an amused smile on his face.

"Your anxiety is keeping me awake," the fae said. "Come. I've made you a bed."

Hugh hoped that meant what he thought it did. Hugh would much rather be in Rykoff's bed than one on his own. He climbed out of the car, stretching his sore muscles as he did. He was confident he wasn't imagining the flash of lust in Rykoff's eyes, and he definitely wasn't imagining the curl of heat in his own stomach. If he and Rykoff were stuck together for the foreseeable future, they could at least have a good time.

Hugh leaned into Rykoff's warmth. His lack of smell was disconcerting, but he was still warm and firm and unmistakably male, even without a scent.

Rykoff's breath stuttered, and Hugh nuzzled against his cheek. The touch was electric, almost dizzying. When Rykoff didn't protest, Hugh leaned in and pressed his lips against his in a brief, teasing kiss.

Or what he'd meant to be teasing. The moment their lips met, he felt Rykoff's aura like a physical touch. It drove his senses wild—like coming out of sensory deprivation. He still couldn't smell him, but he could feel him, which was even better. Rykoff's hand on his shoulder was like a brand. The heat of it nearly had Hugh sweating. He couldn't imagine what it would be like to have Rykoff wrapped around him. Maybe something like stepping into a fire.

He'd like that very, very much.

"What if I'd rather have your bed?"

Rykoff jolted and stepped back. The intoxicating feel of his aura died as soon as the contact ended. Hugh missed it immediately.

"I could certainly trade beds with you. Though they are of the same caliber."

Hugh bit back a laugh as he followed Rykoff into the trees. Ruby was rigidly literal too. Was it a trait all fae shared?

"I meant I'd like to share it with you in it," Hugh said, enjoying the way Rykoff tripped over a tree root in response.

"This is hardly the time to share intimacy," Rykoff said.

Were the fae prudes? Hugh wouldn't have thought so, given how close to nature they seemed to be, but it probably wasn't fair to make assumptions about a race he'd only just learned existed. Rykoff had practically bolted after their kiss after all.

"What better time than this?" Hugh asked. "We need to rest and recharge. Sex helps with that. I'm attracted to you, and I'm pretty sure you're attracted to me. Why not have some fun?"

Rykoff pursed his lips. "I'm well aware of how casually vampires view being intimate with others."

Hugh laughed. "Are you slut-shaming me?"

"I don't know what a slut is, but I am saying you should be ashamed to be thinking of coupling at a time like this."

Sharing intimacy, coupling—Rykoff sounded like a character out of one of the Regency romance novels Hugh's mother loved and he used to sneak as a teenager.

"Suit yourself." Hugh wasn't going to pressure Rykoff into sex. "But you're missing out. Casual sex is fun."

Rykoff huffed and tucked himself into his bed under the large oak tree, which was several feet away from the nest he'd prepared for Hugh. A respectable, puritanical distance. A wave of shame swept over him as he watched Rykoff turn woodenly to face away from him. He'd never meant to offend the fae. Hugh realized too late that he was being disrespectful of

Rykoff's beliefs. Whether they were personal or cultural was irrelevant. He was upsetting the fae, and that was a shitty thing to do.

"Look, I'm sorry," Hugh said as he lowered himself into the pile of leaves. They were shockingly comfortable. Whatever Rykoff had done was nothing short of a miracle. The leaf bed was miles more inviting than the car. He felt even worse for his flippant words now. Rykoff was being kind, and he was being an ass. "You're right. We obviously have different views on sex. I'm not apologizing for mine, but I am sorry for teasing you. I don't know anything about the fae, and I stepped in it by coming on to you. I won't do it again."

Rykoff was silent for a few beats. "What did you step in?"

Right. Idioms were out.

"It means I messed up. And I'm sorry."

"And 'coming on' means an invitation for coupling?"

Hugh choked on his own spit. "Uh, coming can mean something very different. But coming on to someone means showing them you're interested in them."

Rykoff turned back over. Hugh could see his eyes, which seemed to glow on their own without help from the moon.

"I am not disinterested in you," Rykoff said gruffly.

Hugh let that sit, quietly watching as Rykoff rolled onto his back, breaking eye contact with him.

"You'll notice I did not stop you from kissing me, though I should have. The fae don't do casual couplings. That's why I assumed you'd kidnapped the youngling. The fae do not abandon their children. How she came to be here makes no sense. A child is a blessing in our culture. Fae life spans are long, but the ability to bear children is not gifted to everyone."

So Ruby was even more of a miracle than he'd realized. And from the reverent way Rykoff talked about her, Hugh would definitely have to fight him to keep her here in the mortal realm.

He'd deal with that once he learned more about the fae. He needed Rykoff's help, and he wasn't going to jeopardize it by telling him he'd fight him to the death to keep his daughter if need be.

CHAPTER SIX

"IT TASTES of plastic."

Hugh grinned around the Twizzler in his mouth. "You eat a lot of plastic in the fae realm?"

"No." Rykoff rolled down the window and spit out his half-chewed candy. The woman in the car next to them frowned, but her scowl melted into a smile when Hugh waved.

"Road trips are the only time I eat them. It's the great American tradition—junk food and interstates," he said as the light turned green.

"It's as disgusting as most human traditions. Like building these concrete monstrosities."

Hugh loved cities. So many people, so many emotions. It was easier to feed and easier to blend in. Not to mention he was fond of human amenities like twenty-four-hour pizza delivery.

Though Cleveland wasn't one of his favorites. There were plenty of opportunities to feed, but the pall of desperation and urban decay that hung over the city didn't exactly make it a vacation hotspot.

Not that they were there to sightsee. They'd video chatted with Ruby—with Hugh introducing Rykoff as a friend of his from work—so Rykoff could do a welfare check on her, and he'd grudgingly agreed she seemed well-adjusted and the picture of health.

After that, Rykoff had wandered off deeper into the woods to open a portal so he could check in with whoever was helping him keep tabs on the rogue and found he was in Cleveland, of all places. Rykoff had been tight-lipped about what Ambrose might be seeking, so Hugh could only assume it was not good. He needed Rykoff to get Ambrose back to the fae realm so he could wash his hands of them both.

Maybe he and Ruby should move after this. He didn't exactly distrust Rykoff, but he didn't trust him either. Rykoff had such a rigid moral compass. What's to say he wouldn't take Ruby himself, claiming it was for the greater good?

Hugh couldn't take a chance like that. He'd sort this out and then look for a new job. They could move across the country. Buy a house somewhere with lots of forest so Ruby could recharge whenever she wanted.

"You may as well take a nap or something," Hugh suggested. "We've got forty-five minutes until Cleveland."

Rykoff sighed. "I am well rested enough, thank you."

Hugh didn't have to be able to sniff out his aura to know that was a lie. Rykoff had tossed and turned all night, like Hugh had. The sexual tension between them hadn't diminished because Rykoff put the brakes on. He'd become off-limits, but that didn't mean Hugh didn't still want him.

"We could get to know each other," Hugh offered. "You could tell me more about the fae."

"I already know all I need to know about you," Rykoff said, his nose wrinkling when Hugh took another bite of Twizzler.

"But you remain a mystery," Hugh muttered.

Rykoff settled back in his seat. "Perhaps I will take a nap."

"You told me you'd help me with Ruby if I proved she was all right," Hugh reminded him.

"I don't even know where to begin. Fae younglings like Ruby—they may be born to two parents, but they are raised by the greater court. Surrounded by adults who love and care for them. Guide them. Teach them. I don't know how one person could do it. Especially one person who is not fae."

That stung. Not because Rykoff was insinuating that Hugh couldn't raise her alone, but that there was a vibrant community Ruby should be a part of and wasn't. His heart hurt thinking about it.

"That came across harshly," Rykoff said, his tone apologetic. "It was meant as more of a criticism of my ability to communicate what you need to know than any fault of yours."

Hugh swallowed and tried to clear his mind. He had about an hour with Rykoff, and then he'd be dropping him off and going his own way. He doubted they had cell phones in the fae realm. When Hugh left him, he wouldn't see Rykoff again. His link to information about the fae world would be severed. So he needed to set aside his pride and find out as much as possible.

"I want to be the best father possible for her. And that means finding out about what she is and how I can help her as she grows into the powers you were talking about. So hit me with it. Start talking."

Rykoff laughed. "I can't give you a summation of what it means to be fae—not even if I had sixty days instead of sixty minutes."

That was fair, but Hugh needed him to try.

"There are others who live in this realm," Rykoff said before Hugh had gathered his thoughts enough to speak. "Fae who have left the court to live among humans. Some remain in contact with the fae realm, others disappear with intent to never be found. I will connect you with someone who can guide you. I was not being facetious when I told you I cannot be of much service. Fae lines are continued by the eldest. I am not the eldest. I will never have the opportunity to bear a youngling with a mate. I am largely kept in the dark about what raising one entails."

That was heartbreakingly unfair. And it helped Hugh understand Rykoff's reaction to finding Ruby's sock last night. Rykoff clearly wanted a child, but he could never have one. It surprised Hugh he was willing to help at all. It had to be the worst kind of insult to find that a vampire—a creature Rykoff obviously had a huge amount of disdain for—was raising a fae child.

"I appreciate it more than I can say," Hugh said. "And I'm sorry."

Rykoff shrugged. "It is what it is. I may not be able to have younglings, but I can contribute to the realm in other ways."

"Like hunting rogues."

His smile tightened. "This particular rogue, at any rate."

Hugh didn't push for more information, letting the rest of the ride pass in silence as he digested what little he'd learned about the fae world. He'd rather find out more now, but the urgency diminished. He enjoyed hearing Rykoff talk. His odd turns of phrase were endearing. Hugh had only known him for a few hours, but he would miss him when he was gone.

He dropped Rykoff off at a park. Hugh offered to stay and help, but Rykoff rebuffed him gently. Ten minutes after they'd arrived, Hugh was back on the road with the address of a fae who lived in Nebraska and a car full of buzzing silence. It seemed louder than the silence between him and Rykoff had been, but he didn't want to break it by turning on the radio.

It took him almost three hours to make it to Detroit, and he was tempted to stay in for the night and catch up on sleep instead of going out to meet his police contact. But wallowing in his loneliness wouldn't do any good, so Hugh changed into something more appropriate for the club and headed out.

He didn't need to feed, but it wouldn't hurt him to eat again so soon either. His body had become accustomed to the feast-or-famine diet. He liked to think of it as a tank he had to fill. If he fed enough over the summer, he'd be able to survive with small top-offs throughout the year.

Was it as satisfying as draining someone every time he was hungry? No.

But was it enough to sustain him?

Also no. But he could limp along, getting weaker and hungrier, until winter break when he could slip away again for a quick meal. He wasn't sure how the discovery of Ruby's true heritage would affect his feeding schedule. He didn't want to think about it now. He'd punt that problem down the road for later.

Jared was waiting for him at a high-top at the back of the noisy club. The pumping music was overwhelming to Hugh's enhanced hearing— he couldn't imagine how much it must hurt Jared's far more sensitive ears. Hugh grabbed a beer for each of them on his way over.

"How have you been, Hugh? I've been looking forward to this all year!"

Hugh reached out and shook Jared's hand, palming the flash drive Jared slipped him and putting it in his pocket as he sat on the stool.

"Can't complain," he said, picking up his beer to tap against Jared's when the man held it up to toast.

Jared was the captain of a police precinct here in the city. Hugh had met him ten years ago when Jared had been a patrol officer. He'd come upon Hugh stopping a mugging, and when he realized Hugh was a vampire, he'd flashed his amber eyes at him. Being a werewolf on the police force meant Jared lived under the same kind of secrecy Hugh did, and they'd become fast friends bonding over their struggles. Soon after,

Jared started compiling cases for Hugh. Mostly criminals who needed to be taken off the streets but who the police or prosecutors couldn't make a case against for whatever reason.

It also helped that Jared's father was a representative on the Supernatural Council. That was handy for smoothing over messes that bled through from the human world into the supernatural. Not that it happened often.

Hugh was careful to keep a low profile and only feed where he wouldn't be discovered, since he didn't want to put Jared in the position of having to cover for him. He was sure Jared played a part in getting the police reports about the deaths taken care of quickly, but he never asked questions. They had no communication about the list other than the thumb-drive drop. Jared would find out about the deaths at the same time the rest of the world did.

A commotion at the bar drew both their attention, and Hugh didn't miss the way Jared's hand went to his waist automatically. Always the cop.

"We've had a serial rapist on the loose. No solid leads, but women say he starts a fight at a bar, uses the distraction to drug their drinks, and then leads them out back to an alley to rape them."

"Think this could be the guy?"

"Fits the description. Average height, average weight. The women have all said he was nonthreatening, even when he was arguing."

The guy looked like a run-of-the-mill drunk bro arguing with the bartender who was cutting him off. But when Hugh looked harder, he didn't see the haze of drunkenness in his aura. The guy was slurring his speech and weaving around, but his aura was crystal clear. And dark.

Hugh tapped the table and stood. "I've got it. I'll see you around, Jared."

Jared nodded and stayed put as Hugh made his way to the bar. The cloying sick-sweet stench coming off the would-be rapist, who was leaning against the very drunk woman next to him, was not a good sign. It was lust but mixed with something more sinister. There was no question his intent was to harm.

He might not be draining the guy, but he would get a good long drink out of him.

Hugh hunched forward a bit to make himself look less intimidating and shuffled closer, his attention fixed on the bartender like he was walking up to order a drink. His target didn't acknowledge him at all, which was good. He didn't mark Hugh as a threat, though the woman who was trying to pull her arm away from the guy seemed to recognize the malice that glinted in Hugh's eyes was aimed at her attacker, not her. She stopped struggling, her gaze trained on Hugh as he approached.

The man took advantage of her sudden capitulation and pawed at her more aggressively. Hugh separated them easily, grabbing the guy around his neck and tugging him backward into a bear hug.

"Louis, buddy! I haven't seen you in forever."

He leaned in and placed his lips against the shell of the man's ear. "We're going to walk outside and have a little chat. Struggle and I'll hurt you. Go willingly and I promise you'll walk away from this."

The man trembled in his embrace but stayed silent. From the miasma of addiction, violence, and lust leaking out of him, Hugh figured this might be the first good decision the guy had made in a long while.

Hugh nodded to the bartender, who motioned over her shoulder.

"There's a staff door to the rear that's unlocked from the inside. You'll need to walk around to get back in, but uh, it'll give you some privacy for your, um, reunion. Thanks for getting him off the floor."

Hugh wasn't a mind reader, but being able to taste a person's aura was almost as good as being able to see their thoughts. This guy he'd grabbed had a plethora of ill intentions on his mind, and from the depth of the depravity and darkness that streaked through his aura, Hugh wouldn't be surprised if he turned out to be the serial rapist Jared had told him about.

This guy would be fine after Hugh finished with him. Once he dove through the man's baser lusts, he found a well of self-loathing and fear. From the remorse coming off him, he might even be able to turn his life around after Hugh fed off the fount of misogyny and lust that made him prey on women. He'd likely lose his sex drive, but that was nothing less than he deserved.

Hugh forced the man onto the bench of a weathered picnic table in the small staff area. The cement was littered with cigarette butts and the stink of transactional sex. Hugh's mouth watered, a Pavlovian response to the smell.

The man shrank into himself as Hugh closed in on him, the taste of his fear cloying and sweet on Hugh's tongue as he leaned in and took a deep breath. He didn't get to savor feeding like this often. Letting his guard down enough to feed with abandon took a moment, since he was so used to keeping himself in check as he drew small snacks from the humans around him.

He had no reason to keep his eyes from glowing amber, though. It added to the man's fear, which amped up Hugh's hunger even more. Splinters from the rough wood bit into his hand as he braced himself against the bench, using his other arm to wrap around the guy to keep him in place as Hugh nosed along his neck.

He took a deep pull from the man's aura. The chi flowed easily now that Hugh had shifted his focus to feeding. He could feel the hard cement through his shoes and the sting of the splinters in his hand, but those sensations were distant. All that mattered was the flow of energy he was sucking out of his prey. He'd had human friends describe the effect alcohol had on them, and Hugh assumed this was similar. He felt euphoric. Invincible.

The flow of chi slowed, and Hugh concentrated on probing the man's aura to make sure he'd stripped the darkness out of it. He didn't touch the well of depression. Taking that would be a kindness, and Hugh wasn't feeling kind after draining all the man's homicidal rage and lust. This man had hurt women in the past, and if not for Hugh's ability, he'd hurt more in the future. He deserved far worse than he was getting from Hugh.

He let the man go, not bothering to catch him before he fainted. The guy slid off the bench, his shoulder taking the brunt of the fall as he collapsed onto the dirty concrete.

A slow clap to his right startled Hugh. His head snapped up, his rising hackles only somewhat assuaged by the sight of Rykoff leaning against the building. He was standing under a pool of yellow light that made his skin almost glow. He'd have been irresistibly attractive if not for the undisguised revulsion in his expression.

"Killing the locals again?"

Hugh scowled. "One, he's not a local. Guys like that don't prey on women in their own backyard. And two, he's not dead. He'll wake up with a hell of a headache, and he'll never be able to get it up again, but he's very much alive."

Rykoff's lip curled in disgust. "So you're going to feed off him and then leave him to keep hunting women? Figures one monster would want to help another."

Anger coursed through Hugh's veins, and he took a very deliberate breath to calm himself. He'd just fed, and he was still on the adrenaline high. Rykoff, on the other hand, looked to be in about as bad shape as he had been last night. He'd clearly tangled with something and lost.

"What would you do? Kill him? What crime can you prove he committed?"

It ate at Hugh that the criminals he fed on could still roam free. But what could he do? Turn them in to the police with nothing but his word that they were bad people? He had no proof, and what kind of person would he be if he waited until after the man had attacked someone before he'd acted? He'd have proof then, but at what cost?

Rykoff drew a knife from a sheath strapped to his boot. "He deserves to die if he harms people."

Hugh nudged the man's unconscious body with his foot. "He won't be able to harm people anymore. The darkness in him is gone. It's like being neutered. He won't have the reserves of rage he used to fuel his violence, and he'll be impotent as well. For the rest of his life. No rage. No lust. He's like a toothless dog now."

Rykoff gave him a calculating look and resheathed his knife. "I underestimated your kind," he said. "Perhaps there's more to your race than I realized."

"I'm so glad to be your vampire tutor. Lesson one, we don't kill indiscriminately," Hugh said as he stalked toward the alley that led to the street. "And lesson two, we don't appreciate it when people sneak up on us while we're feeding."

"I'd think you'd be on the alert for that sort of thing."

"I am, but for some reason I can't sense or smell you. Or Ruby. Which probably means all fae. Unimportant." He stopped and caged Rykoff against the cool brick. "Why are you here? Why aren't you in Cleveland?"

"I fought with Ambrose and then had to portal out."

Hugh took a long look at him. "He kicked your ass?"

Rykoff's eyes narrowed. "He did not kick my ass."

He was definitely the worse for wear. Hugh leaned in, frustrated by the lack of scent. He couldn't assess how badly Rykoff was injured if he couldn't smell him or see his aura.

"My car is a few blocks down. They're kind of short on forests here in Detroit, but I can at least get you to a park so you can heal. Will that work? How many trees do you need? Are city trees as good as your weird sentient country trees?"

Hugh wasn't prepared for Rykoff to surge forward and kiss him, but he adapted quickly. His blood was already up from his feed, and it didn't take much to have him rock-hard and raring to go. He braced himself against the brick to keep from crushing Rykoff as he deepened the kiss, relieved when instead of shying away, Rykoff wrapped his arms around Hugh's shoulders and ground their hips together.

The press of Rykoff's skin against his was amazing. Hugh had never been so aware of his body. Every point of contact between them was electrified. Nothing could compare to this, not even feeding. Part of him was grateful he couldn't taste Rykoff's aura. It would have been too much stimulation.

He groaned when Rykoff's fingers twined through his hair, a shiver running down his spine hard enough to buckle his knees. Luckily Rykoff caught him, taking his weight easily without breaking the kiss.

Hugh nearly came on the spot when Rykoff's hands left his hair and moved to his belt, deft fingers unbuckling it and sliding inside to wrap around his aching cock. It was the most intense thing he'd ever felt, and his heart was in his throat as he gasped for breath, his pulse hammering in time to Rykoff's strokes.

He whined high and desperate as he tried to return the favor, but he couldn't get Rykoff's fly open one-handed. Each stroke sent a white-hot bolt of pleasure through him, each more unbearable than the last, and Hugh didn't know how much longer he'd make it. He buried his face against the hollow of Rykoff's throat, which vibrated as Rykoff laughed in response.

His orgasm took him by surprise. Not because it happened quickly but because it hadn't happened sooner. The spasms were so violent he doubled over with the force of them, and Rykoff held him as he lowered them both to their knees.

Hugh didn't stay come-drunk for long. He clamped his hands over Rykoff's hip bones, urging him up. He nuzzled his face against Rykoff's growing bulge, gratified that Rykoff made the same mewling noises he'd made himself a few minutes earlier. Hugh made quick work of Rykoff's fly, shoving the fabric aside and letting his lips slide against the velvety hot skin of his erection.

Rykoff's lack of scent was even more troubling now as Hugh swallowed down his length, but Hugh didn't let it deter him from what was probably the most enthusiastic and least-skilled blow job he'd ever given. Rykoff didn't seem to have any complaints, and while Hugh didn't have the scent feedback he was used to, he had Rykoff's fingers squeezing his shoulders in a death grip to egg him on.

Rykoff bucked his hips up, and Hugh tightened his grip on him, holding him in place while he fucked him with his mouth until he sent him over the edge. Rykoff's fingers dug into Hugh's skin painfully, and if Hugh hadn't been completely spent himself, he might have come again from the intensity of it. It wasn't unusual for Hugh to get a zing of power from someone's come, but this was different. His lips and tongue were buzzing with energy, even though, like the rest of him, Rykoff's come was disappointingly devoid of smell or taste.

Hugh pulled back, panting, and sat on his heels. He wasn't ready to give up the electric pulse of contact, so he rested his cheek against Rykoff's bare hip. The white-hot searing pleasure where their skin met from earlier had dulled to a pleasant buzzing sensation that was both comforting and energizing.

Hugh dropped his hands and stumbled back so fast he fell on his ass. Had he been feeding on Rykoff? The buzzing sensation—that's how he felt when he drained someone. He scrambled to his feet and took Rykoff's face in his hands, terrified.

"Are you all right? Did I hurt you?"

Rykoff blinked, his sex-drunk expression replaced by concern.

"No, did I hurt you?"

"I—I think I was trying to feed."

Rykoff laughed. "You can't. Not unless I lower my barriers, and I have to concentrate very hard to do that. Trust me when I tell you I would not have been able to do so."

Relief flooded through Hugh. What he'd just shared with Rykoff had been unlike anything he'd ever experienced. It had horrified him when he thought he might have been taking advantage and feeding on him.

He hastily buttoned his fly and straightened his clothes as best he could.

"Yesterday you said fae don't have sex indiscriminately. What changed?"

Rykoff offered him a small smile. "When we create portals, it's not an exact science. I called it magic, and it is. But it is not our magic. It is the forest's. It's why I need trees to conjure one unless I have a totem, something that draws me to a specific place. But somehow when I called a portal to escape from Ambrose and merely asked it to take me somewhere safe, it took me to you."

Rykoff's eyes glowed amber. "I thought it had been a mistake. But then, even though you were angry with me, you offered to take me somewhere I could heal. So then I realized perhaps the mistake was mine, not the portal's. That is what changed."

Chapter Seven

"THE MAN you fed from tonight," Rykoff said as Hugh drove, "this is what you came here to do? Feed?"

"I was at the club tonight to meet a police contact of mine. He gives me information about criminals who for whatever reason the law can't punish."

"And you punish them."

Hugh grimaced. "Not exactly. What I do isn't painful. If their aura has been completely overtaken with evil, I drain them and they die. Like the guy at the truck stop. But life isn't black and white. Most people are gray. So most of the time I drain out the darkness that leads them to hurt others, and that's it. They don't commit more crimes, and my police contact is happy because that's one less criminal for him to worry about."

"It sounds lonely."

"They probably are, but—"

"I meant you. Feeding on despair and darkness, hiding your true nature."

He hadn't always lived like this. Before Ruby, he'd hung out with vampires. Like-minded ones who didn't kill for sport, but honestly that described most vampires these days. And he'd had other supernatural friends. People who understood what it was like to hide parts of themselves away to fit in with the human world.

It hadn't been worth the risk of exposing Ruby to that world, though. So after he'd adopted her, he'd cut off most contact with his old friends, quit his supernatural job, and become as human as he could. He still got the occasional email or Christmas card, but he wasn't going to vampire orgies or playing poker with selkies.

His priorities had changed.

"It is. But parenthood can be lonely. It's not something the supernatural have a stranglehold on. Raising a tiny person is isolating.

53

But Ruby is my family. She's worth it. And I can take care of my vampire needs while she's away for the summer. It works out."

"And the rest of the year? No hunting? No feeding?"

"Of course I don't hunt," he said defensively. "I have small meals when I have the opportunity. Depression, anxiety. Stuff like that."

"But that's not enough to curb your hunger."

"No. But it tides me over until I can have my monster hall pass over breaks."

"Hall pass?"

Hugh winked. "Permission to break the rules without consequence."

Rykoff's frown deepened instead of becoming the smile Hugh had intended to draw with the joke.

"I'm sorry. It sounds like a terrible choice to face. Your daughter or your health and happiness."

Hugh didn't look at it that way. "She's always my first choice, but it's not as bad as you make it out to be. I don't mind being human most of the year. I have a job I'm good at, and I can help people and feed at the same time. There are things I hate, like the PTA, and the neighborhood association getting on my ass when I don't mow the lawn fast enough for them, but it's all worth it."

The parking-lot gate was chained shut, so he pulled up alongside the park's sidewalk and stopped. "Do you want me to circle around or find some place to park on the street?"

Rykoff opened the door. "I'll be fine. You go back to your hall pass."

"That wasn't what—"

"I know," Rykoff said. "But the best way I can help keep Ruby safe right now is to make sure the rogue doesn't know she exists. That means you can't exist either."

His words hit Hugh like a physical blow. Logically he knew it wasn't a rejection, but it felt like one. He'd never resented the life he'd left behind for Ruby, but he came damn close to it now. He'd just met Rykoff, but they shared a connection that was unlike anything he'd ever experienced. Hugh was terrified about what it might mean, but he was also terrified to lose it. Hugh was damned if he did, damned if he didn't.

Rykoff leaned across the console and kissed him. For a moment Hugh was awash in the scent of evergreens and the slight tang of ozone that signaled a storm, overlaid with a heady spice that he couldn't describe. The scent disappeared the moment Rykoff broke off their kiss, leaving Hugh's head spinning.

"Did you just—"

Rykoff's eyes flashed. "I did. You're a special man, Hugh. And your daughter is an incredible gift. Be well. We will meet again, I give you my word."

He was out of the car before Hugh could react. Rykoff had lowered his barriers to share his aura with Hugh somehow. And it had been incredible. He'd thought their hurried sexcapade in the alley had changed him forever, but that fraction of a moment engulfed in Rykoff's aura would be the memory that haunted him. He'd experienced nothing that compared.

Hugh wanted to chase after him, but his practical side kept him glued to his seat. Rykoff was right. They needed to protect Ruby, and right now that meant making sure there was no link between her and Rykoff that the rogue could follow. Which meant no link with Hugh either.

He forced himself to drive away, but he couldn't help but keep his gaze trained on the rearview mirror, hoping for another glimpse of Rykoff. All he saw was darkness.

What the hell was happening? He wasn't like this. Rykoff had said his life sounded lonely, but it wasn't.

Or at least it hadn't been. He missed Ruby like a phantom limb, but he always did when he was away from her. The gnawing unhappiness inside his chest was new, and he had a sinking suspicion it had to do with the man he was trying hard not to think about right now.

The motel was dead when he pulled up. Hugh wanted to curl up in bed and sleep for days to escape his thoughts, but he knew there was no way he'd quiet his mind enough to do more than toss and turn.

He pulled the thumb drive from Jared out of his pocket instead and rooted around in his backpack for his laptop. Hugh normally enjoyed this part of his vacation hunt, but it was more like a chore now.

55

There were three files on the drive. Each would have information about where the target worked and lived plus any other relevant facts. The first time they'd done this, Jared had given him copies of the police files on the perps, but it wasn't necessary. Hugh needed nothing more than his ability to read their auras. It might not give him the exact details a police report did, but it told him what he needed to know.

He'd planned to spend two weeks here, but he could probably get this done in three or four days. The thought of being so far away from Ruby right now made him uneasy, but he didn't want to leave Jared hanging or short himself the feeds he'd need to sustain himself over the coming year. There was no reason to believe Ruby was in danger. It would be ridiculous to head home now because something *could* happen.

Like it was ridiculous to let Rykoff go after that rogue alone on the off chance his involvement twigged the guy to Ruby's existence. He knew nothing about the man Rykoff was hunting, aside from the fact he'd managed to rough Rykoff up enough to make him turn tail and flee. That meant he was a pretty fierce fighter. And Rykoff didn't seem to have any help here in the mortal realm.

Hugh sat in silence for a few minutes, trying to talk himself out of what he was about to do.

It didn't work.

Hugh grabbed a few days' worth of clothes and shoved them into his book bag, along with some toiletries and his phone charger. He left the laptop and the rest of his things. If last night was any indication, they would be traveling light anyway.

He texted Jared to let him know he was going to help a friend for a few days and locked up the motel room. He didn't know if the rogue was in Detroit or if he'd be on the road, but he'd paid in advance for the room, so there was no reason to check out. He'd need to come back here to finish what he started for Jared anyway.

Hugh couldn't believe he was doing this, but not much of his life had made sense over the last forty-eight hours. Why not risk everything to go help a man he'd just met?

The drive to the park seemed to take forever, but he knew that was his impatience talking. He'd left Rykoff less than an hour ago, but who knew if he'd still be in the park now. The man could open portals to another realm, for Christ's sake.

Hugh parked on a darkened corner and sent up a silent prayer that his car would be safe there while he searched for Rykoff. He didn't know how big the park was, but a lot of it was open spaces, which probably wouldn't work for whatever communing with nature mumbo jumbo the fae had to do to heal himself.

The park was deserted, so he didn't worry about masking his speed as he jogged along the trail that led to a large wooded area. That had to be where Rykoff would have gone. It was maddening, not being able to scent him. The brief glimpse of his true aura he'd given Hugh had been staggering, so maybe it was for the best that he couldn't smell him all the time. But it sure as hell would help right now.

He strained his hearing, trying to catch any noise that was out of the ordinary. Someone was dealing drugs on the edge of the basketball court, and there was a couple having sex concealed inside a copse of trees nearby. But that was it. He could hear the heartbeats of the people who were sleeping on the benches, but as he drew closer to the woods, he picked up on one slow heartbeat that had to be Rykoff. It wasn't an animal, but it was too slow for a human.

Hugh ducked into the tree line anyway, hoping against hope that he'd found him. Luckily there was only one heartbeat, so it was unlikely the rogue was there too. He followed the sound until he could see Rykoff up ahead, his skin glowing faintly as he rested his head against the bark of a massive tree.

Hugh slowed his pace and made plenty of noise so his presence wouldn't startle Rykoff. By the time he drew up to him, Rykoff had leaned away from the tree and was waiting for him, eyes flashing amber.

"We agreed you wouldn't become involved," Rykoff said.

He looked healthy. His skin had regained its color, and all his scrapes and bruises were healed. Being in the park had definitely helped him, even though it wasn't truly a forest. That was good. He needed to be at full strength.

"You decided I wouldn't be involved, and I let you. But after thinking on it, I decided you definitely need my help. This guy seems like he's too strong to take on alone. Why didn't they send anyone to help you?"

Rykoff sighed. "I suspect he is part of the disappearance of a prince of the summer court, and I am honor bound to ensure the prince's safe return and bring the person responsible to justice."

That didn't sound good. Hugh didn't know anything about how fae politics worked, but it sounded like a fairly serious thing to kidnap a prince.

"And no one else believes he kidnapped the prince? That's why you're here alone?"

Rykoff's jaw tightened. "The queen believes the prince left of his own volition and will return when he is ready."

"How long has he been gone?"

Rykoff slumped against the tree, looking more defeated than Hugh had ever seen him. He hadn't even appeared this resigned when Hugh had bested him at the truck stop and he'd been too weak to stand.

"Eleven years."

Wow. As cold cases went, that was a hard trail to follow. "And you think this rogue has something to do with it because…."

"The prince would never leave for this long if he had a choice. We know he is still alive, but we cannot track him. That is highly unusual. And as for why I believe Ambrose has something to do with it—he used to be one of the prince's most trusted advisors. When the prince went missing, Ambrose was the one who came to the mortal realm to find him. He returned with news that the prince was dead, but fae royalty have a way of detecting when a line dies out. The prince is the eldest child. If he was dead, we would know. The light for the Harlow line still burns brightly. It has not died out. So Ambrose must be up to something."

"And you want to be the one to find out what that is?"

"You make it sound vulgar. I take no pleasure in it. I don't seek to curry favor with the queen or win a higher place at court. If the prince is being held captive here, I will free him. If he has chosen to stay, I will respect that. But with Ambrose involved, I think it has to be foul play. He has laid low these last few years, after his fall from grace with the court. But my informants tell me he's gathering strength to take over the throne. He's here to gain some sort of power, and I need to stop him."

This was like a fairy soap opera. Rykoff might say he wasn't in it to prove anything to the queen, but there was definite reverence in his voice when he spoke of her and the prince. There had to be more to the story than Rykoff was sharing.

"And you have no idea what this power play is? Or where he might be?"

Hugh still had contacts from his time working for the Greater North American Supernatural Council. If Rykoff had any solid leads, he could help him run them down. The sooner this rogue was back in the fae realm the better, both because he didn't want Rykoff hurt and because Hugh wanted to salvage his summer vacation and be able to hunt down killers and feed without feeling guilty thinking about Rykoff fighting this guy on his own.

"I know where he will be tomorrow. He has a meeting with sprites in Buffalo."

That definitely wasn't good. The political inner workings of the fae might be unknown to Hugh, but he was well-acquainted with those of the sprites. The ones who operated out of Buffalo were particularly nasty. Likening them to the mob wouldn't be out of place. Sprites dealt in information and ley-line energy, since water was often a conduit for both. And that was even more true of the sprites who operated out of the Great Lakes. Ley lines ran throughout them, and all that power converged in Lake Erie. It was like a cauldron where the energy swirled together before passing through Niagara Falls into Lake Ontario.

There was a reason Lake Erie had one of the highest concentrations of shipwrecks in the world. It was the underwater base of operations for the Great Lakes sprites.

"Then let's get going. It's a long drive to Buffalo."

Rykoff shook his head. "I will portal there. I don't want to bring you into this. Besides, I don't even know where the meeting will take place."

"I'm already in it," Hugh said. "And I know exactly where they will be. The sprites have a base of operations at a coin laundry on the banks of Lake Erie in Buffalo."

Rykoff's look of shock was almost offensive.

"I didn't always work in an insurance call center, okay? Before Ruby I worked in supernatural diplomacy. You'll need to tread carefully with the sprites. They won't appreciate you busting in on their deal, and you do not want them as your enemy."

CHAPTER EIGHT

"OKAY, LET'S run through this again," Hugh said as he pulled away from the gas pump and headed back to the interstate. They'd been driving for three hours and were no closer to having a plan of attack than they'd been when they left the park in Detroit.

"Your man Ambrose is headed to negotiate with the sprites because they have information that will help him overthrow the queen. But we don't know what that is or what he's got that they want in exchange for the information."

Rykoff made an annoyed noise. "I've told you everything I know. You know more about the sprites than I do. What do you think they want from him?"

"They deal in information and power. They're also thick in the underbelly of illegal substance trafficking."

"Drugs?"

"Among other things. They do a fair amount of transporting human drug shipments because it's lucrative, but what the council has its eye on them for is selling black market potions and rare ingredients."

Rykoff stared out the window. "Like the kinds of things you might find in the fae realm."

Hugh opened the bag of Twizzlers he'd picked up inside the gas station, ignoring the exaggerated gagging noise Rykoff made in response.

Hugh was fully aware he had lost control of his life, hence the Twizzlers. If he was captaining a road trip to a third-rate industrial town to thwart a power-hungry fae's meeting with sprite kingpins, he was damn well going to do it while eating Twizzlers and Combos.

"I'd say that's a good guess as to what he's bartering. The sprites don't suffer fools—he has to know that. They only entertain serious petitioners, and the price of their assistance is steep. He must have something valuable if he could get an audience with the Niagara sprites."

"And you think *you* will be able to get a meeting with them?"

"I don't think I can get us a meeting, I have already *gotten* us a meeting."

He'd let most of his contacts slide since leaving the council, so he'd been surprised when his 3:00 a.m. text to an old colleague had been returned within the hour. And not only that, she'd been willing to help him set up a meeting with the sprite elders.

After the dust settled from all this, he was going to make a point of reconnecting with his old friends. It would be nice to have a supernatural network again. Hell, now that there was no reason to hide the supernatural from Ruby, maybe he could work for the council again. From a self-serving point of view, it couldn't hurt to rekindle his connections. He and Ruby might need help in the future.

He'd made it clear when he set up the meeting that he and Rykoff had nothing to trade, but apparently the sprites were willing to talk to them for free. Bizarre, but he wasn't looking a gift horse in the mouth.

"I cannot explain why, but I am even more attracted to you at the moment."

Hugh turned and grinned at him around the Twizzler that was sticking out of his mouth.

"Despite your taste in food," Rykoff added.

"Sounds like a competency kink to me," Hugh teased.

"Please take that thing out of your mouth. I can't bear it," Rykoff said. "And what?"

"A competency kink. Where someone does something well and it's a turn-on. Me working my connections in the supernatural world gets your engines revving."

Rykoff laughed. "I suppose. I enjoy seeing you take charge, even if I must protest your involvement."

"Classic competency kink. Wait till you see me folding laundry or making dinner. It'll blow your mind. I am eminently competent."

As soon as the words left his mouth, Hugh worried he'd gone too far, talking about a possible domestic future. But Rykoff's smile only grew.

"I'd like that. The opportunity to see you and Ruby together would be wonderful."

Hugh had meant more than that, but he kept his mouth shut. It sounded like fae choosing to live in the mortal realm was a rare occurrence. They were nowhere near ready to have a conversation about that. He doubted Rykoff viewed what had happened between them as a one-night stand, since he'd made his views on intimacy and relationships clear. But that didn't mean he was picking out wedding china either.

Did they even have weddings in the fae realm?

Hugh took a breath to center himself. One task at a time. They needed to figure out what Ambrose wanted from the sprites and how to stop him. Then they could talk about Rykoff meeting Ruby and what their future might look like, if they had one at all.

"Has Ambrose committed any crime that your realm can punish him for?"

"Rumors and innuendo only. It is my hope the sprites can give us information about his plans that will verify his intentions so I can convince the queen that he is not to be trusted."

That might prove difficult, but they'd cross that bridge when they got to it. He almost laughed at his own water pun but caught himself. This wasn't the time to introduce Rykoff to dad jokes.

"Okay, enough strategizing. If you were in the fae realm, what would you be doing right now? I'm curious about your life there."

"Nothing this interesting." Rykoff's self-deprecating snort only piqued Hugh's interest.

"No, come on. I've told you what I do. I sit in an office and take phone calls from angry people all day. What do you do? Surely fae have jobs of some sort. Or do you all just live off the land in tree houses or something?"

"We have jobs, Hugh. And homes. We don't live in trees."

"So what do you do for your job, then?"

"I'm a carpenter. I make furniture."

An unexpected bolt of lust hit Hugh square in the chest. He'd joked with Rykoff about a competency kink, but this was his. He found men who created things with their hands fascinating. He snuck a glance at Rykoff's, but they were smooth and unblemished. Nothing like the human carpenters or builders he'd dated. Supernatural healing was useful, but it also meant none of the delicious calluses he loved on humans.

"So you sell furniture in the fae world?"

"And the mortal realm. I have an Etsy shop."

Hugh choked on the bite of Twizzler he'd been swallowing. "You have the internet in the fae realm?"

Rykoff snorted. "Of course not. But I have an iPhone. I portal to the mortal realm every few days to check for new orders and to ship the finished pieces. I had to put the store on hiatus while I'm tracking Ambrose."

That opened up so many questions.

"Do you have electricity in your realm?"

"No need," Rykoff said, holding up his palm. The air above it shimmered before it erupted into flame.

Hugh jerked in surprise, nearly letting the car drift into the other lane. "The fuck!"

"We don't need the amenities humans rely on."

Rykoff closed his palm, extinguishing the licks of fire like they were nothing.

"Can all fae do that?"

"No. Those who don't have a fire affinity rely on candles or have others help them. As I rely on my brethren who have a water affinity to provide water when my well cannot. Those with air affinity conjure cool breezes to soothe us on warm nights. All fae have an earth affinity, naturally."

"Naturally," Hugh repeated, sounding as shell-shocked as he felt. "And all fae have another affinity?"

"We do. The affinity chooses its host in the host's thirteenth year."

Thank Christ. Hugh wasn't the most attentive parent in the world, but he'd be gutted if he'd somehow failed to notice his daughter conjuring fire out of nowhere. It was like the parenting memes all over Facebook—*don't feel bad, the mom from* E.T. *had an alien in her house for days before she noticed.* Except, you know. With fire coming out of his daughter's hands.

"So Ruby would be too young to have one yet?"

Rykoff patted him on the knee. "She is not yet of age. Woefully behind on her education, but not yet ready to open herself to an affinity."

It sounded insane. "Open herself? So the elements are sentient in the fae world?"

"They're sentient here too. But humans haven't opened themselves to listen." He shot Hugh a look when Hugh opened his mouth to ask more questions. "There's a ritual. I do not know what would happen if a fae came of age without it. Perhaps an affinity would choose them anyway. Perhaps not. This is why it's best if you let her come to the fae realm. She needs to know this side of herself."

That was becoming more and more apparent. And it was terrifying. This wasn't like sending her off to summer camp.

"If I let her visit, would she be allowed to come home?"

Rykoff's silence stretched on, and Hugh's heart sank more every moment it did.

"I want to tell you yes, but I do not know. It would be up to the queen. This has never happened before, at least not to my knowledge. I'm not a court scholar, but I'm not uneducated in the histories either. Ruby is special."

Damn right she was.

Hugh pushed the rest of his Twizzlers away, his appetite gone. He couldn't begin to imagine a life without Ruby, but he also didn't want to be the reason she never knew her heritage. Who knew what would happen when she came of age. He certainly didn't know how to help her. And if she had a fire affinity like Rykoff, there could be some very serious consequences to her power being unchecked.

Hugh flinched in surprise when Rykoff twined his fingers through Hugh's where his hand rested in his lap.

"These are not problems that must be solved today. When I return to the court, I will secure a promise from the queen that Ruby may pass between the realms as she wishes."

"You have a lot of confidence in your sway over the queen. I thought you'd tried to convince her Ambrose was dangerous. What if she doesn't listen to you about Ruby either?"

Rykoff squeezed his hand. "Then I refuse to give her details about Ruby, the two of you continue to live in the mortal realm, and we find another way to help her. Perhaps the fae healer I told you about who lives in Nebraska could teach her."

The cold pit of fear that had been growing in his belly eased a bit with Rykoff's use of the word *we*.

"You'll help her? You won't just turn her in or leave us on our own?"

"Even if I have to leave the court myself. I would swear it on my fealty to the queen, but that seems traitorous in this instance, so I will give you my word instead."

Hugh swallowed hard and nodded. He didn't have to know Rykoff well to know that what he'd just promised was huge.

"All right. Thank you."

It didn't seem like enough, but it was all he could say. He didn't start any more small talk the rest of the drive.

CHAPTER NINE

"I THOUGHT we were meeting with the sprite elders, not just one person."

Hugh would have smacked him if it wouldn't have been disrespectful to the sprite leaning against the large tumble dryer a few feet away.

"We are. Sprites share a collective consciousness. Like water, it flows through them, connecting them. So meeting with one is meeting with them all."

"Why are we meeting here out in the open instead of at their court?"

The laundromat the sprites operated from was hardly out in the open. The windows were shuttered, and the place hadn't been a functioning laundromat for years. He wasn't sure how the sprites had come to use it as their terrestrial base of operations, but he bet the large drains that led to the lake were the reason they'd chosen it.

"Their court is underwater," he hissed back. "Now shut up."

The sprite pushed off the dryer and walked toward them. She looked like a middle-aged woman, but Hugh could see she was much older than that from her aura. It rippled and flowed with her energies and those of the rest of the elders. It was beyond intimidating.

She stopped in front of them, and Hugh bowed, pleased when Rykoff followed his lead without prompting.

"Rykoff of Harlow," the sprite said, greeting the fae. "Prince of the summer court. Your presence is an honor to us."

Hugh nearly swallowed his tongue. Rykoff was a prince? What the fuck?

The news utterly rocked Hugh, but this wasn't the time or the place to discuss it. He shook his head when Rykoff opened his mouth.

Rykoff was a fairy prince. Jesus.

The missing prince he was here looking for must be his brother. His hatred for Ambrose and his refusal to give up his search suddenly made a lot more sense.

"The honor is ours," Hugh replied after he'd found his voice again. "Thank you for granting us an audience."

The sprite inclined her head in acknowledgment and turned to Rykoff.

"Speak."

"We come seeking information about the rogue fae Ambrose of Wynne. We believe he seeks to trade with you."

"This is true," the sprite said. "We are not the first he has appealed to in his quest for his prize. No one has been willing to help him."

"And will you?"

Hugh flinched at the brusqueness of Rykoff's question, but the sprite did not seem to take offense.

"We will not. We have the information the traitor seeks, but the cost is too great. Meddling in this affair will start a war not only within the fae courts but also with the supernatural world."

"How do we stop him?"

"We cannot answer that. Our neutrality holds the supernatural world together, and we must not risk it."

Rykoff shifted his weight impatiently, and Hugh put a cautioning hand on his arm. They had to tread carefully here. The sprites were as fickle as the water they served, and the more they learned about Ambrose the worse Hugh's gut felt about it. They couldn't risk angering the sprites.

Rykoff ignored him. "But isn't refusing to help him choosing a side?"

The sprite regarded him coolly but merely shrugged. "The flow of information is never free. And the cost of information is dependent on how valuable it is. Your traitor has nothing to offer us that is worth the risk of placing the sprites in the chaos that the information he seeks would cause."

It surprised Hugh when the sprite shifted her eerie azure gaze to him.

"Hugh Whitby. You are the reason we agreed to this audience. We will not trade with the fae traitor for the information he seeks, but we will trade information to you."

What the everloving fuck. Hugh had nothing of value he could give them. Shit. What did the sprites like? He ransacked his memory, trying to recall what he'd traded to them in the past when he'd been here on official council business. It was usually information for information, but he had no knowledge they would covet.

They were magpies, gathering anything that could have value. He wore no jewelry aside from the celestite pendant Ruby had made from tumbled rocks at camp last year. He never took it off. He'd replaced the flimsy silk thread she'd strung it on with a cheap silver chain. It was the shiniest thing he had.

Hugh reluctantly unfastened the necklace and held it out in his open palm.

"My daughter made me this necklace. It is immeasurably valuable to me."

The sprite took the necklace and slipped it into her pocket.

"The fae traitor killed a Harlow prince in the mortal realm eleven years ago. He sought to overthrow the summer court to install a king of his choosing. He was unsuccessful and thinks the prince somehow lives. He does not. A half-blood fae child of his line, human born, walks the mortal realm. Through her the Harlow court will continue. If the fae traitor learns of her existence, he will seek to kill her to extinguish the line before she can lay claim to her status as heir."

Rykoff made a guttural noise and fell to his knees. Hugh wanted to comfort him, but sheer terror rooted him to the spot.

There couldn't be more than one secret fae child in the mortal realm, could there? If the prince died eleven years ago, he could be Ruby's father. What if leaving her behind that dumpster hadn't been an intentional act of abandonment? What if her parents had been hiding her from Ambrose and had been killed before they could come back for her? Holy shit.

"What we have traded to you is yours to do with what you will."

Rykoff regained his feet and stepped forward. "The identity of the child...."

The sprite inclined her head toward Rykoff. "Words, once spoken aloud, cannot be unsaid. Be sure of the intentions of those around you before you say them."

Hugh swallowed hard. That was as good as confirmation that the child was Ruby. His daughter could start a civil war. And she'd never be safe with Ambrose out there.

"I trust him with my life," Hugh said.

The sprite's lips curved into a sad smile, and she held her hands out, cupping his hand between them. "Then now is the time to trust him with hers."

Before he could respond, he saw a flash of color out of the corner of his eye. Hugh whirled around in time to see a man lunge at Rykoff from the shadows. He carried no scent or visible aura. It had to be Ambrose. Had he portaled in? How much of the sprite's information had he heard?

The sprite had already fled, which confirmed that she'd known he was there. Goddamn sprites and their manipulations.

She'd hedged her bets well, giving both sides the information at the same time. But Hugh had an advantage. He knew where Ruby was.

Her camp was hours from here. But by the time Hugh could drive there, Ambrose likely would have found her himself. Rykoff had portaled to Hugh by thinking of him last night. What if that meant Ambrose could do the same now that he knew Ruby existed? Maybe she'd been safe from him only because he'd been looking for the prince, not the prince's *child*.

He had to get her to the fae realm. And it had to happen now. Ruby had to be presented to the court so she could be acknowledged as the queen's heir, or whatever the sprite had said. She would have to go with no assurance she'd be able to return. Hugh had no idea if he'd ever see her again.

He looked down at his hand, surprised to see the sprite had returned his pendant. That couldn't be accidental, but it wasn't something he could worry about now. He stuffed it into his pocket to keep it safe and took a running leap at Ambrose, knocking him off Rykoff.

Hugh hit the floor with a thump that resonated through his bones, Ambrose's full weight on top of him. Hugh was strong, but Ambrose was stronger. Hugh couldn't get the upper hand. Ambrose broke free of Hugh's hold like it was nothing and sent him flying into the front of a washing machine with one solid kick to the ribs.

Pain flared through his side, making it hard to draw in a breath. Hugh forced himself to get up and go after Ambrose, intercepting him before he reached Rykoff again.

Hugh had never been in a fight like this. It made his tumble with Rykoff at the truck stop look like a child's wrestling match. Ambrose seemed to be able to predict Hugh's moves before he made them—hell, before Hugh even knew what he was going to do himself.

He needed to tell Rykoff where to find Ruby. If he could do that and give Rykoff enough of a break to escape, then he'd have a chance at portaling to Ruby and getting her to safety.

He had to believe that would be enough.

Hugh finally caught Ambrose by surprise with a left hook that sent him crashing through the shuttered front window. Rykoff was by his side in an instant.

"You have no idea what he's capable of," Rykoff said. "You've got to get out of here."

Hugh shook his head. "Go get Ruby. Take her to the fae realm."

He hadn't seen a stand of trees Rykoff could portal from when they'd driven up. It was probably strategic on the sprites' part, to make sure they were safe from ambushes. They didn't do anything without protecting their own interests.

Shit. The necklace. The sprite gave it back to him, which had to mean it was important. He dug it out of his pocket and pressed it into Rykoff's hands.

"Ruby found this stone on the banks of a river that runs through her camp. She said it called to her, like it wanted her to find it. That has to mean something. You've said you can portal with a totem. Please."

Ambrose was back inside already, barreling toward them.

"That's not how totems work, they have to be—"

Hugh shoved Rykoff out of the way, taking the brunt of Ambrose's momentum as he tackled him. His head hit the dirty linoleum, and he saw stars for a moment before he could gather himself enough to struggle back to his feet. Ambrose had Rykoff pinned against a wall, choking him.

Hugh staggered and caught himself on a laundry detergent dispenser on the wall. He wrenched it off, the screech of tearing metal loud enough to make him wince. He closed the distance between them in a few steps and swung the metal dispenser like a bat, catching Ambrose upside the head and sending him sprawling.

"Go," Hugh gasped, his broken ribs making it difficult to draw in a breath deep enough to ease his screaming lungs.

"He'll kill you."

That was probably true. God knew Hugh couldn't keep this up for much longer, but luckily he didn't have to. He just had to stay conscious and fight long enough for Rykoff to get to a portal. Ambrose could probably track him, but hopefully Rykoff would find her quickly and get her out. The camp was in a heavily forested area, so opening a portal to the fae realm wouldn't be a problem.

He just had to get him to the camp.

"I'll be fine. Go. Please."

Rykoff gave him an uncertain look but nodded. "I'll be back for you."

He took off for the door as Ambrose climbed to his feet. Hugh kicked his legs out from under him, somehow taking himself down with Ambrose in a tangle of limbs. He laughed, the absurdity of the situation and the lack of oxygen making him light-headed. Ambrose landed a few solid punches before Hugh could roll away.

It was tempting to lie there and let Ambrose leave, but he had to give Rykoff as much time as he could. So he forced himself up again, hefted the nearest washing machine into the air, and threw it at Ambrose. Water spurted from the broken pipe, drenching him instantly.

The fae dodged it easily, but it gave Hugh an idea as it came to rest in front of the laundromat's door.

He pushed a pair of stacked dryers over, further obstructing the way out. He couldn't win the fight against Ambrose, but he didn't need to. He only needed to keep him here long enough to give Rykoff a head start. Ambrose couldn't portal from inside the laundromat, so Hugh's new goal became making it harder for him to leave.

Ambrose tackled him again, and this time Hugh was certain more ribs broke. His breaths came in tiny pants, shards of agony stabbing his chest. The water made the floor even slipperier, which made it impossible to gain any traction to stand up in his damaged state.

He had no clue how long he and Ambrose had been fighting. Probably only minutes, but it felt much longer than that. All he could do was pray it was enough time for Rykoff to get Ruby to the safety of the fae realm.

Hugh's head lolled as Ambrose pummeled him, and he caught sight of a pipe sticking out of the cement. He ignored the way his body screamed as he rolled, then grabbed it and broke off a foot-long section.

Ambrose kicked him hard, but Hugh brought the pipe down and smashed it against Ambrose's knee, sending him skittering backward into a bank of dryers. Hugh struggled to get up but couldn't, so he lay there, braced for Ambrose's next attack.

The front windows imploded in a rain of glass and wood. Hugh curled in on himself as best he could, protecting his face from the debris. He was barely conscious when hands grabbed his shoulders and dragged him to his feet, and he wanted to cry with frustration when he realized it was Rykoff.

Men clad in leather armor streamed into the laundromat around them. Rykoff must have gone to the fae realm for reinforcements instead of portaling to Ruby. Goddammit.

Hugh could barely keep his head up, but he saw the moment Ambrose dove through the shattered windows and made a break for the lakefront.

All the fight leaving him, Hugh sagged against Rykoff. He'd failed his most important task—protecting Ruby.

Rykoff hefted him up and held him against himself with one arm as he pulled out a piece of wood with a glowing emblem on it.

"Your necklace was not a totem. This is a totem. Just so we're clear."

And then the world went black.

When he opened his eyes again, they weren't in the laundromat anymore.

Hugh had expected the fae realm to be a forest, and it was. But that was like saying a protein bar was a meal. Technically it was true, but it didn't hold a candle to the real thing.

This was unlike any forest he'd ever seen. There were more shades of green than he had names for. Dewdrops shone like diamonds, and the forest floor Rykoff lowered him to was as soft as the beds Rykoff made for them when they camped out.

"Ruby," Hugh gasped between pained breaths. His lungs felt like they were full of broken glass. His entire body hurt, and he was colder than he'd ever thought possible. The irony of freezing to death in the summer court made him want to laugh.

"She's here," Rykoff said, cradling Hugh's head in his lap. "I left her with the guards when I brought reinforcements."

Relief swept through him, making him light-headed. Ruby was safe. Hugh's eyelids seemed to weigh a thousand pounds as he lost his fight to keep them open, but that was okay. Ruby was in the fae realm, and they'd take care of her. He could stop fighting now. His daughter was safe.

CHAPTER TEN

THE FIRST thing Hugh realized as he swam back toward consciousness was he wasn't cold anymore. The last thing he remembered was lying on the floor freezing.

As awareness flooded through him, he sat bolt upright, groaning as his broken ribs protested. He was in a bed, naked from the looks of it. Before he could take in any other details, Rykoff slid under the covers next to him.

"Ruby?"

"Shh," Rykoff said, trailing a finger over Hugh's lips. "Your daughter is fine."

Hugh relaxed a fraction at the reassurance. He hadn't missed the fact that Rykoff still acknowledged him as Ruby's father here in the fae realm. That had to be a good sign, right?

"She's being entertained by her grandmother."

Hugh struggled to sit up farther, pain lancing through his chest. "Her grandmother?"

"The queen sends her regards and her wishes for a speedy recovery. She says to assure you the realm will welcome Ruby as a full member of the summer court, as is her due as the Harlow heir."

Holy shit, they were never going to let him take Ruby home. She was a fairy princess. Jesus Christ. His daughter was fae royalty.

Hugh tried to toss the blanket aside to climb out of bed, but Rykoff easily overpowered him.

"Your daughter is being doted on and given everything she could possibly need. She is safe and well. You, on the other hand, are not. You need to feed, Hugh."

He did. He wouldn't heal until he fed, but he wasn't about to leave his daughter alone in the fae realm to go find someone to eat.

"I'll be fine. I need to see her."

Rykoff wrapped an arm around him and tugged him down until Hugh's cheek pressed against Rykoff's bare chest.

"Feed, Hugh."

"I can't."

"I'm giving you permission. Feed from me. It won't hurt me."

Hugh appreciated the sentiment, but he couldn't feed from someone if he couldn't see or scent their aura. He raised his head to look at Rykoff, who was staring down at him with a fond smile.

Rykoff cupped his jaw with his hand, and a pulse of pure contentment and joy ran through Hugh. He stared at Rykoff, confused. The euphoria hadn't been his own. It differed from reading an aura, or even the emotions he felt from Rykoff when they kissed. This had been purposeful. Directed.

"Feed, Hugh."

He lowered his head, resting his cheek against Rykoff's warm skin again. This time the feeling didn't take him by surprise. He tried to align his own chi so he could feed, but it was like sitting in front of a feast not being able to smell the food. He couldn't engage enough to feed.

Hugh closed his eyes and tried his hardest to focus on the moment and pull energy from Rykoff. Nothing.

"Hold on," Rykoff said. He stroked a hand down Hugh's face again, and then gently helped him sit up.

He leaned in to kiss him, and even though Hugh was far from in the mood, he found his body responding. Suddenly, he was awash in Rykoff's aura. Hugh's body reacted automatically, opening himself up to feed from the enormous well of energy Rykoff was offering.

It was so much more than he could process. He'd had pieces of this before—the glimpse of Rykoff's aura the first time they'd kissed, the taste of him when he'd let down his barriers for a split second as they said goodbye in the park in Detroit. But added together, it was overwhelming. Kissing him with his barriers down had tasted like sunshine. Feeding from him was like standing on the surface of the sun.

Every nerve in Hugh's body tingled, awash in more energy than he'd ever seen before. His circuits felt like they were being overloaded, but he didn't need to struggle to keep up—his body let the energy flow through with ease. To say he was feeding on Rykoff wasn't quite right.

He was a conduit Rykoff was sending energy through. The difference between feeding and being fed. It was absolutely amazing.

Normally healing large injuries took time. The pain would be no more than a dull ache. Bones knitting together, tissues healing. But right now, with Rykoff's energies swirling through him like liquid sunshine in his veins, all of Hugh's injuries were healing at once. It was exquisitely painful, but he was too euphoric to care. He registered the agony, but he was somehow above it. Like it was happening to someone else, and he was merely observing it.

His head spun with the complexity of Rykoff's aura. There was so much. He could explore it for days and not come to the end. Were all fae like this? How did they function with this much life force inside of them?

The influx of energy made Hugh giddy. He couldn't decide if he wanted to laugh or cry. He broke the kiss, not wanting to take too much, even though it seemed like Rykoff had a limitless store.

Rykoff pressed a kiss to his nose and let their foreheads rest against each other. Hugh took a few deep breaths, still dizzy and disoriented.

He was strung out from the chi. Almost come-drunk, but without the sex.

"You look much better. Did you get enough? You only fed for a minute."

A minute? It had seemed like hours.

Hugh sat up, breaking the contact between them. It quieted the buzzing at the back of his head and eased his dizziness a bit. He was still buzzing on a high, but he could think again.

He stretched, marveling at moving without pain or any aching hunger. He'd fed well over the last few days, but it didn't compare with how he felt now.

"Your aura, it—"

"I lowered my barriers entirely this time," Rykoff said with a smile. "I shouldn't have risked as much as I did in the mortal realm. It was a foolish slip of my control. There was too much at stake."

Ruby. Ruby had been at stake. Fear flooded back hard and fast.

"Did you know about her?" Hugh asked hoarsely. "Did you come to reclaim her?"

Rykoff shook his head. "I had no idea she existed, truly. Even after you told me about her, I did not know she was kin. The Harlow line's flame continued to burn after my brother disappeared, which we all assumed meant he lived."

The sound Rykoff had made when the sprite informed them of his brother's death had been one of raw grief, and it would haunt Hugh for the rest of his life. "I'm so sorry about your brother."

Rykoff's lips twisted into a sad smile that didn't reach his eyes. "My eldest brother didn't want the yoke of the court. I would have eased his burden if I could, but that is not the way of the fae. The eldest inherits everything. Land. Power. Everything. And if they die before they produce an heir, the throne falls to whoever can win it."

He shifted around and pulled Hugh back down onto his chest. He went willingly, comforted by the contact, especially now that Rykoff's barriers were back up and he couldn't see his aura any longer. The buzzing in his head didn't return.

"Do you want to be king?"

Rykoff's chest shook with laughter. "I couldn't be even if I wanted the throne. But no. I want to make furniture and be free to move as I please. Like my brother Yugen, I have no patience for politics."

"Do you think he meant to stay in the human realm? When he ran away."

"I don't believe so. But if he met a woman and fell in love—who knows. But believe me when I say I know he would never have left Ruby had it been his choice. Never."

Hugh would probably never know exactly what happened before Ruby ended up behind that dumpster at Ruby Tuesday. But he owed it to her to find out as much about her parents' last minutes as he could.

"Have they found Ambrose yet?"

Rykoff nodded. "He has been exiled and sent to a prison in the winter court."

"Did they question him about your brother's death?"

"That is not our way. There are those among us with special abilities. Those who can read intentions and auras. He is guilty of what the sprites alleged."

"And Ruby? No one is investigating what happened to her? Have we confirmed her mother is dead?"

"She is dead. As for why Ruby came to be abandoned behind a dumpster—we will never know for sure. But iron weakens the fae, and if my brother knew he had but seconds to hide her before Ambrose found them, he'd have used that to his advantage. It dulls our senses. Ambrose never knew she was there."

"And your brother just trusted someone would find her?"

Rykoff stroked his hair. "Someone did. The right person did. My brother trusted his daughter's life to fate, and fate gave her the most glorious gift."

Hugh nuzzled against Rykoff's chest. "A disgusting demon bottom-feeder?"

"Ah, you remember."

"I could hardly forget the first words you spoke to me," Hugh teased. He raised himself up so he could look at Rykoff. "I'll show you just how right you were someday. But right now I want to go see Ruby."

Rykoff grinned. "So you don't deny being a bottom-feeder?"

"In the right circumstances, no."

Joking around was nice. He was still worried sick about Ruby, but he knew she was safe. He'd never take that for granted again. The last twenty-four hours had been the scariest of his life.

"I have some clothes you can borrow," Rykoff offered once they'd gotten out of bed. "My mother has never invited a vampire to court before, so there are bound to be a lot of prying eyes around."

Hugh took a finely spun cotton shirt from him and turned it around in his hands as he tried to figure out how to put it on. Rykoff snorted and took it back, nudging Hugh in his newly healed ribs until he raised his arms so Rykoff could dress him.

"No buttons? Are you sure you're fae and not Amish?"

"I'm not sure what an Amish is," Rykoff said as he laced the ties along the neck and sides of the shirt, "but no, court finery has no buttons. I don't know why. We wear buttons in our noncourtly clothes. I carve them by hand out of felled branches."

Of course he did. God. Why was that sexy? There was that competency kink again.

"I want you to tell me more about that later," Hugh said as he stepped into the pants Rykoff handed him.

The ties at the waist were easy to figure out, even if he was weirded out by the lack of underwear. It felt wrong to be going commando to meet the queen.

"Did Ruby have to change to go to court?"

"You sound like a petulant child," Rykoff said as he dressed himself. "She was in courtly attire last I saw her."

"You've seen her?"

"Yes. The healers sat with you while I had an audience with my mother. Ruby was there. She is every bit as worried about you as you are about her."

He looked down at his bare feet. "What about shoes?"

"We rarely wear them here," Rykoff said with a shrug. "It helps us connect to the earth."

Hugh bit back a retort and followed Rykoff to the door instead. He hadn't focused much on his surroundings, and it surprised him to realize they were in a cozy workshop with half-finished woodworking projects scattered around.

"This is my studio," Rykoff explained as he led Hugh out the door. "I often sleep here when I'm working late on commissions."

"So this isn't where you live?"

Rykoff shook his head. "You were in bad shape, and this cottage is closest to the clearing the totem brought us to. It made sense to keep you here."

"And it also made the rest of the court feel safer, since the vampire wasn't in their midst, I imagine."

"That was also a factor. But now that the queen has heard the entire story, you are welcome at court as an honored guest."

The palace was a short walk from the cottage, and while he was intensely curious about the fae realm, all Hugh could focus on was getting to Ruby. She had to be scared out of her mind. One minute she'd been at camp, and the next minute a stranger had appeared and forced her through a magical portal.

At least she and Rykoff had met over Skype once before he'd kidnapped her. Did they make a guide to helping your child overcome the trauma of being forcibly taken through a portal and discovering they were a member of a mythical race? He'd have to check the library when they got home.

If they got home.

God, he needed to contact the camp. They had to be losing their minds. Surely they'd have filed a missing person's report and put out Amber alerts. This was a mess. That would have to wait until after he spent some time with her. He wasn't leaving the fae realm until he'd held her in his arms and confirmed she was okay.

He heard her before he saw her. She was squealing with laughter, and it made him quicken his steps to get to her. He rounded the corner, and his heart stopped. His daughter was floating twenty feet above the ground.

Rykoff grabbed him before he could run to her.

"Watch," he said, nodding toward the woman who was standing underneath her, her hands up in the air.

"My cousin Leelia. She's an air affinity. This is something we do with our children to keep them entertained. See? Ruby is safe."

Ruby didn't look distressed in any way. In fact, he'd never seen her so happy. He'd made the right choice sending Rykoff to her. She needed to be here. This was part of her life, and it wasn't something he could give her.

"Dad!"

Ruby spotted him and started cartwheeling her arms and legs toward him. The fae on the ground lowered her arms slowly, bringing Ruby down. She took a leap at about six feet off the ground, running as soon as her feet hit the grass.

"Dad!"

He caught her as she leaped at him, burying his face in her hair. She still carried no scent, but thanks to Rykoff he could imagine what she would smell like. Sunshine and warm grass, he would bet.

"You scared the life outta me, kid," he said, hugging her tightly. "I thought you'd learned to fly."

She laughed as he put her down. "Leelia said I might have powers like her! Or maybe I'll be able to make fire!"

How long had he been out? Long enough for Rykoff's cousin to tell her all about affinities, apparently. Great. So much for easing her into things.

"That's awesome, kiddo. You've met a lot of new people today. How are you doing with that?"

"They're related to us! Did you know that?" She squinted at him. "Wait. Are you fae? And you never told me?"

Christ on a cracker.

"Your dad has his own special powers, but he's not fae like us," Rykoff cut in smoothly. "Why don't we go back to your grandmother? I'm sure you have a lot of questions."

Ruby grabbed Hugh's hand, something she hadn't done in public in years. "Come meet Naenae, Dad. She's so cool."

Oh God. Had his daughter nicknamed the queen of the fae after a TikTok dance?

"My mother's name is Queen Naenaid. Or apparently Naenae."

Well, at least it was close to her name. And the fae probably didn't follow pop culture anyway.

He looked at Rykoff, who smirked at him as he swung his hips ever so slightly and raised an arm. Shit.

Hugh turned away before he started laughing. Time to change the subject. "It's pretty neat that you found your grandmother, isn't it, Rube?"

She beamed up at him, and he was struck by how different she looked. It was like she'd grown an inch or two since he'd dropped her off at camp a few days ago, and her hair looked longer. Flowers were woven through it, and she was wearing a loose-fitting linen shift dress, the kind she hated at home. She always complained that her clothes hurt her. Now he wondered if it was the synthetics in the fabric.

How many ways had he been hurting his daughter daily by keeping her in the human realm? Not that he'd known she wasn't human. But now that he did, how could he justify taking her away from her family and a place that was designed to keep her healthy and safe?

"It's so cool here," Ruby said as Rykoff led them into the palace. The guards stationed at the door let them pass with a nod. "Wait till you see Naenae's living room. It has a tree in the middle of it that she can sit in."

She ran ahead, and Rykoff pressed in close.

"The throne room," Rykoff whispered in his ear. "Especially with Ruby being a half-blood, my mother thought it prudent to do the acknowledgment ceremony as quickly as possible."

So she'd already been acknowledged as the heir to the kingdom. A lump formed in Hugh's throat. Any hope he'd been holding on to about taking her home died.

"She'll have a formal presentation ceremony later," Rykoff said, misreading the hitch in Hugh's breath. "You'll be able to come to that. I'm sorry that all this has happened so quickly. We did what we needed to do to keep her safe."

"I'm grateful. I'm just upset I won't get to be a part of her life anymore."

"Don't be absurd," a woman said from behind him. "You are her father. You are the most important person in her life."

Hugh turned, caught off guard by the sudden interruption. It was so difficult to be in a place where literally everyone could sneak up on him because he couldn't scent them.

"Hugh Whitby, may I present her beneficence, Queen Naenaid of the summer court?"

The queen waved her son away impatiently.

"We don't stand on ceremony with family," she said, taking both of Hugh's hands in hers. "Welcome to the summer court. I wish your visit could have been under better circumstances, but I am glad you are here."

Hugh wasn't sure if he should bow or not, but she still held his hands in hers, so he guessed not.

"I'm honored to meet you. Thank you for the kindness you've shown me and my daughter."

"Ruby is a delight," she said. He was struck by how much of his daughter he could see in her smile. "I look forward to getting to know you both."

She gave his hands a squeeze and let go.

"The youngling ran through toward the gardens," she told Rykoff. "Will you fetch her? We have much to discuss."

Rykoff shot Hugh an apologetic look and took off down the same hallway Ruby had skipped through a few minutes earlier. Hugh braced himself. The queen obviously wanted an audience alone with him, and he couldn't imagine that was a good thing.

"Come. We'll go in. It will take him a moment to lure her out. She's quite taken with the lilac labyrinth, which is probably where she will end up. The other younglings will likely pull her in for a game of hide and seek."

She led him into a large room that did indeed have an enormous throne in the middle, crafted out of what looked like a living tree. It was unlike anything Hugh had ever seen, both because of its intricate throne-like shape and because of its smooth multicolor bark.

"Rykoff grew it for me," she said, following his gaze. "It's a rainbow eucalyptus. You must visit when it's in bloom. It's truly a sight then."

"He mentioned that he made furniture, but this wasn't what I was expecting."

She laughed. "He does. This was a special case. I did not handle it well when Yugen left. Rykoff was my rock through a terrible time. He grew this tree from a sapling because this species is my favorite. It took him months to coax its growth and shape it. It makes me happy every time I look at it, as was his intention."

Instead of sitting on her throne she settled on a cushion that rested on the stone floor next to a small pond. Koi swarmed up to the surface, and she skimmed her hand over the water, gently running her fingers over their heads. They scattered after the greeting, and Hugh realized there was a stream that cut through the wall and fed the pond.

"Please, make yourself at home," she said, indicating a cushion identical to hers nearby. He folded himself onto it as gracefully as he could. "I'm sure this has all been a shock to you. It certainly has been for me."

Hugh remembered how relieved he'd been when Rykoff had told him Ruby was fine. The queen had gotten the opposite news about her own child today.

"I'm so sorry for your loss."

She smiled without a trace of sadness. "I lost Yugen a long time ago. I am happy to know that he is at peace. He will live on through Ruby."

"It's all so hard to process."

"I imagine so. Rykoff said you thought Ruby was human. So you've been given a great deal to make sense of in a short period of time." She bowed her head. "I am indebted to you for taking her in and keeping her safe and well loved."

"I did what anyone would have."

She raised her head, her eyes flashing the same amber that Rykoff's did when he was angry. "Do not diminish the sacrifices you have made for your daughter. Ruby couldn't have a better adoptive father. And I have no intention of taking her away from you, though I hope that you will let her spend time in the fae realm."

Hugh was taken aback by her honesty. "You'll seriously let her live with me?"

The queen frowned at him. "She is your youngling. I have no wish to take her from the only parent she has ever known."

God, he couldn't even describe the relief her words brought. He could breathe properly for the first time since realizing she was in danger.

"I assumed she would need to stay here. The sprite said she is heir to the throne. Rykoff said her powers will develop soon."

"That is all true," the queen said. "And it is also true that she has known nothing of the fae realm until now. She is a halfling, and as such she belongs in both worlds. At least until she chooses otherwise."

"You'd let her choose to stay in the mortal realm?"

Pain flashed through the queen's eyes. "If, like Yugen, that was what she wanted, then yes."

"Thank you," Hugh blurted. "Thank you for putting her best interests first."

She smiled. "I could say the same. Now, we have so much to catch up on. Rykoff tells me she was at something called a summer camp? What does that entail? I was unaware the humans allied themselves with the summer and winter courts."

CHAPTER ELEVEN

Six weeks later

"YOU'RE SURE you can't come back next summer?"

Hugh grinned at Jared as he stashed his duffel bag in the trunk and slammed it shut.

"I'm sure you'll see me around, but I can't continue our arrangement. I'll make sure someone does, though, I promise."

A lot had happened since he'd left the fae realm a month and a half ago. Summer was almost over. Ruby would start school soon, and he still had to finish packing for their move.

Jared shook his hand. "I don't know what happened, and I'm sure it's above my pay grade anyway, but I'm glad whatever had you tearing out of here was resolved."

Hugh owed him a huge favor. Jared had retrieved his things from the motel and kept them for him until Hugh could make it back to Detroit.

He'd finished the list for Jared, not because he needed to feed but because he was a man of his word and he'd promised to help Jared out. It hadn't given him any pleasure to feed on criminals, not like it had before.

He and Rykoff had discovered that Hugh could take his fill of Rykoff's energy with no ill effects to the fae. In fact, Rykoff was often even more energized by the exchange than Hugh was. It didn't hurt that feeding sessions usually turned into nights of wild sex. As long as they were together, Hugh would never need to feed on another human again, and it was a huge weight off his shoulders.

Hugh was happier than he could ever remember being. He'd been sad to quit his job, but the Greater North American Supernatural Council had come to him with an offer he couldn't refuse. What he was doing would help so many people. The council had created a position for him— law enforcement liaison. He was helping vampires across the country

86

match up with in-the-know police officers like Jared so they could help take dangerous criminals off the streets. The initiative would save a lot of human lives and also help the vampire community stay fed.

He waved goodbye to Jared and slid into the driver's seat, nearly crushing a bag of Combos that hadn't been there before. Rykoff was sitting in the passenger seat, grinning from ear to ear.

"I brought your road trip snacks."

"Abusing the totem your mother gave you again, I see," Hugh teased.

The queen had granted both Rykoff and Ruby permission to move between the two realms as they wished. Ruby was too young to create a portal, so she'd been given a totem that would open a portal to the queen's throne room. When opened from the fae realm, it would bring her straight to Hugh, using the necklace Hugh wore as a beacon.

Rykoff had been given the same one.

"You're lucky he didn't see you. His father's on the council, you know. He'd have reported your ass faster than you could say portal."

"You forget, he can't scent me," Rykoff reminded him, waggling his eyebrows.

When Ruby and Rykoff had gotten totems as their gift from the queen, Hugh had received something different, though no less precious. The enchantments she'd put on his necklace were more than just a beacon for their totems. They also allowed him the ability to smell them and see their auras.

"Let's get on the road. It's a long drive to Cincinnati, and I want to get there before Ruby's bedtime. You know she's going to come through that portal talking a mile a minute, and she needs time to wind down."

Rykoff settled in his seat and dug out one of the fruit leathers Hugh kept in the glove compartment. "Mother sent the guard to inspect the house in Asheville. She says it's acceptable."

Hugh and Ruby needed to pack the last of their belongings this weekend so the movers could load up the trucks and set off for North Carolina. The council was headquartered there, and they'd offered to rent a house for Hugh and Ruby as part of his salary. It was about fifteen minutes outside the city limits on a sizable wooded lot. It was perfect.

He hadn't told the council she was fae. And he wouldn't. The fae weren't part of the council, and that meant they had no power over Ruby. As far as they knew, Hugh wanted a secluded place because he valued his privacy and wanted some separation between his human daughter and the supernatural world he served.

"Well, if the queen thinks it's acceptable, it must be all right," Hugh joked. "She's not the one living there, you know."

She likely would never even visit. Rykoff said the rulers of the fae courts never left the realm. That meant someday, if she accepted the throne, Ruby would be bound to the realm too, but that was far, far in the future. A hundred years or more, if Rykoff wasn't pulling his leg. It was a relief to know that Ruby's lifespan was longer than his own considerable one. No father wanted to outlive his child.

"No, but her granddaughter is. She wants to make sure it's safe." Rykoff paused and slid a glance over at him. "She said there's a wood shop on the property."

Hugh grinned. That had been the deciding factor when he'd agreed on the house. "A local carpenter owns the property. He moved across the country, but the estate agent said he hoped whoever rented it would be a woodworker."

Rykoff's scent changed subtly, taking on a honeyed note that Hugh had learned was excitement.

"Too bad you don't have any interest in carpentry."

"But I do have an interest in a certain carpenter. I was hoping I might persuade you to spend at least part of your time with us. You said you come to the mortal realm often to ship your pieces. Would it be so bad to have a workshop here?"

"You'd share your home with me?"

Hugh hoped to share a lot more than that with him, to be honest. But he didn't have a clue how fae courtships worked. They'd hardly gone a day without seeing each other. Hell, he'd seen Rykoff a lot more than his own daughter over the last month. Ruby had gone back to spend another week at camp—with the alibi of a medical emergency that had only taken a little of Hugh's persuasion to sell to the counselors—before spending the rest of the summer living in the fae realm.

"I'll share whatever you'll let me with you," he said. Innuendo was often lost on Rykoff, so he'd learned to be blunt. "I know living in the mortal realm isn't ideal for you, but I'll take whatever I can get."

"I'm very fond of both you and Ruby," Rykoff said. "And I find this realm is growing on me."

"So that's a yes?"

"That is a yes."

Hugh let out a victorious whoop, laughing when Rykoff started at the sound.

"You'll love the property," he told him. "The owner left a lot of his tools, and the workshop is pretty far from the main house. Nice and secluded."

"Ruby and I can continue her lessons, then."

He and Leelia had been teaching Ruby about the affinities and helping her kindle her earth abilities. She'd been able to make a bud grow into a flower the last time Hugh had visited, and the look on her face had been sheer joy.

"I told Nae that Ruby could spend every other weekend in the realm during the school year. That should help."

Learning to share her would be difficult, but he wasn't going to be greedy with her time. Not after thinking he'd have to give her up entirely. Besides, how could he deny her the right to spend time with her biological family?

He and Rykoff spent the rest of the drive talking about his new job and Ruby's progress. It was nearly dark by the time he pulled into the driveway, and he resigned himself to a late night of Ruby bouncing off the walls and talking a mile a minute.

"Shall I go get her?" Rykoff asked as Hugh opened the front door.

Most of their things were boxed up already. Hugh had done the majority of the packing before he'd left to go back to Detroit. He only had a few odds and ends left, and Ruby's room. It hadn't felt right to pack that up without her.

The house was blissfully quiet, and he wanted a bit of time to enjoy what was probably his last peaceful moment in the home they'd lived in since Ruby was two months old. He'd learned how to be human in this house. Figured out the ins and outs of caring for a tiny person. He was excited for what was to come, but he'd miss this place.

Hugh stood there with his eyes closed and took a breath, centering himself.

"Yeah. I'll order something for dinner while you're gone."

Rykoff disappeared through a portal a moment later, and Hugh called his favorite Thai place and ordered a mountain of food. Once Rykoff had learned that there were human foods that didn't involve preservatives or meat, he'd taken to eating with gusto. Hugh's own appetite had increased too. A byproduct of having his fill of chi to feed on, probably. His body was no longer in starvation mode, and that meant he could enjoy many things a lot more.

Dragging Ruby away from the fae realm always took longer than it should, so Hugh puttered around packing and cleaning until the food arrived. He'd just gotten it arranged on the blanket he'd laid out as a makeshift table when the portal reopened and Ruby and Rykoff stepped through.

"Hey, Dad!"

She'd grown again. God, she was getting tall. She'd be eleven in a few months. It didn't seem possible. Her getting older was even more terrifying now that he knew she'd be developing mystical powers. He'd been worried enough about navigating things like her first period and dating and peer pressure. Now she might be able to make fire shoot out of her fingertips. They didn't write about that in the books he'd read about puberty.

"Hey, Rubes. How was your week?"

She sat next to him and grabbed a spring roll. "Awesome! I missed having real food."

"The food we eat in the fae realm is real food," Rykoff muttered. Hugh noticed it didn't stop him from popping a spring roll into his mouth, though.

"It's berries and vegetables and really healthy stuff. Sometimes a girl needs cheese."

"Or pad see ew," Hugh said, offering her the carton.

"Yessss," she hissed.

"So what were you working on this week?"

"Healing plants," she said around a bite of food. He glared at her, and she made a face. "Sorry."

The normalcy was comforting. He might be raising the next fae queen, but right now she was just a ten-year-old girl who had to be reminded not to talk with her mouth full.

"Do you think my new school will be like my old one?"

They hadn't talked much about how she felt about the move. Part of him wondered if it was too many changes too quickly for her, but it was the perfect job opportunity for him in a place that was a lot better suited to raising a fae child than his 1200-square-foot house with a postage stamp lawn in the middle of a city.

"What? Why? Are you worried about your classes?"

"I'm just hoping they do the thing we always had to do where we write about our summer vacation. Mine will be epic."

Hugh exchanged a panicked look with Rykoff over her head.

"You can't write about the fae realm!" they yelled in unison, and even though his stomach was in knots over this latest development, part of Hugh was thrilled to have someone else to help him carry the load with Ruby.

Ruby rolled her eyes. "I'm not talking about that. They had a goliath swing at camp this year. I went seven times. Anna threw up on it twice! And we played Gaga ball. Do you think we can get a Gaga pit at the new house? I had Naenae make one at court, and everyone loved it."

"No one loved it," Rykoff whispered in his ear as Ruby kept nattering on. "Literally everyone hated that ridiculous game. But no one was going to argue with the queen or her heir, so the entire fae court played Gaga ball with her."

Hugh hid a laugh behind his hand, pretending to cough. He'd love to see that.

Nothing about his summer had gone to plan, but it was without a doubt the best one he'd ever had. Being with Rykoff was the ultimate hall pass, and he hoped that feeling would never end.

Kismet & Cadavers
by Jenn Moffatt

For the real Thomas, Anders, KJ, and Beshter. Love you so much.

ACKNOWLEDGMENTS

THANK YOU for asking me to be a part of this, Rhys. You're the best sister in the universe.

PROLOGUE

2002

THEIR FOOTSTEPS were muffled by the damp ground beneath the canopy of trees that surrounded their Boy Scout camp—at least, the four boys *hoped* they were. The last thing any of them wanted was for one of the camp counselors or, even worse, a parental chaperone to catch them outside their cabins in the middle of the night. Kevin-James Beshter winced when his sneaker cracked a thin fallen branch, and the other boys hissed at him to be quiet.

"I didn't do it on purpose," he whispered back, taking a moment to smack a mosquito that decided to join the other frequent guests at the Beshter Buffet. Both his arms were covered with bumps and scratches from them. No one else in his cabin got munched on like he did, and he hated it even more than he hated the smell of the froufrou bath oil from the Avon Lady that his mom insisted worked to repel the little bloodsuckers. It didn't, and all of his gear smelled like an old lady rolled in pine sap.

Fingers went over lips while the light of the full moon caught in the whites of their eyes as they glared at him. Kevin-James didn't want to be out in the darkness, but it wasn't as if he could tell his "friends" he had no interest in watching the girls in the next camp dancing naked in the moonlight. For all they knew it was a myth, and he didn't like girls that way. He knew it and had for a couple of years. But he couldn't tell these guys. If they found out, they'd probably beat the crap out of him, cover him in honey, and leave him for a bear to dine on, which was way worse than the mosquitos.

He wasn't the smallest of them, but he was the youngest, just twelve years old. His reddish-brown hair was sun-bleached to the point where he was almost ginger, and he had a permanent sunburn across the bridge of his nose, or his freckles had grown into a solid mass. It was hard to tell after being at camp for almost two weeks. He was miserable, and he wanted to go home.

"The girls' camp is over the hill," Dexter, the oldest at thirteen and three-quarters, said over his shoulder as he continued to lead the hike with the flickering light of his crappy flashlight. "We need to pick up the pace. The good stuff happens at midnight."

Bullshit.

"Are you sure?" one of the others asked. Peter was wearing a *Pinky and the Brain* T-shirt and had almost white hair. Kevin-James thought he was kind of cute, which was a thought he'd be keeping to himself for eternity. No one in the scouts could know about him. They'd kick him out, and he was so close to making Eagle Scout. His grandpa would be disappointed, which was the closest thing to real evil he could think of. Letting his parents down was to be expected, but never Papa.

"My brother told me. He saw them two summers ago," said Mickey. He was the smallest, with the darkest skin. If a bear did come at them in the darkness, it'd miss Mickey in the shadows while Kevin-James *figured he* and the blond kid would die.

"Just shut up and walk," Dexter said, not bothering to whisper this time. He was getting annoyed with the younger boys. "Or we'll miss them."

Kevin-James kept following along, doing his best not to step on anything else and glancing into the trees, watching for lions and tigers and bears—or chainsaw-wielding hook-handed serial killers waiting to chop them into stew meat. *Okay, maybe I should stop watching slasher movies with Dad in the man cave.*

He had paused for a moment, reaching down to tug off one shoe and shake a rock out of it, when he noticed a sound on the breeze. It was almost like a giggle or the chiming of a bell. He opened his mouth to call out to the others, but they were gone, and his heart skipped a beat. It didn't take that long to pull a shoe off!

"Where did you go? Jesus, couldn't wait for me!" He was pissed and sank his teeth into the pillow of his bottom lip to keep from shouting. All that would do was catch the attention of things with two legs and four that they didn't want knowing they were out there.

Instead, he reached into his pocket and pulled out the WWII Army compass that his grandfather had given him and tilted it toward the moon so he could read it. What he saw made him gasp. The needle was spinning crazily in the case. It was pointing in all directions!

"Fuck!" Kevin-James shook the compass and angled it this way and that, but the needle kept moving all over the place. "Come on. Show me how to get back." In truth, he knew a compass really wasn't all that much help if you were lost. It was too dark to see any landmarks, and unless he accidentally walked into the lake, he was screwed until the sun came up.

"Guys?" This time he didn't try to be quiet. His voice cracked as it sounded in the shadows, and the crickets and other night sounds suddenly stopped. All he could hear was the chimes and what might be singing. "Not lost if I can follow the music." He was still scared, but it gave him hope. Even if he wandered into the girls' camp, it was better than being lost in the woods.

Fifteen minutes later—which he knew because he was wearing his watch—he paused and checked the compass again. It was pointed in one direction now, toward the singing, and at the edge of his vision, he thought he could see a blue glow. The closer he got to it, the more he could smell cinnamon and other herbs burning, and he was thankful to finally hear clear voices.

When he made his way carefully between a pair of tall standing stones—like something out of Stonehenge—he could see people dancing around a tall bonfire. They weren't only girls. There were men too, and some of them looked weird. He thought he could see wings like fairies at their shoulders, and some of them looked like satyrs. He knew the names of the creatures because he'd memorized the *Monster Manual* cover to cover the summer before last when he'd started to play D&D.

They weren't human. The fire was blue. He didn't have a spell book or a sword. None of this was supposed to be real. *I am so incredibly fucked!*

"What are you doing here, Boy Scout?" asked a tall, thin teenager wearing only a crown of leaves in his dark hair and a pouch slung around his neck. This guy was high school age or older, and Kevin-

James stared at his nakedness with wide eyes, his mouth hanging open and tongue dry.

"I'm l-l-lost," he stammered, not noticing as his compass fell to the forest floor near their feet.

"No shit, Sherlock." The older boy let out a heavy sigh and pointed a finger at Kevin-James's forehead. "Don't move. I need to get my mom."

Kevin-James felt a charge of electricity like when he ran through the house in socks and then shocked the dog on the nose with the collected static electricity, and try as he might, he couldn't make his feet move or make a sound. All he could do was stare as the naked guy walked toward the… dancing horde? Coven? Creatures? The sounds of their revelry vanished until all he could hear was his breathing and his heartbeat, and it was getting hard to keep his eyes open.

"WE GET at least one a summer," Kat Anders said as she let out a sigh and then smiled at her son. Like the rest of the coven, she was skyclad, wearing only a crown of flowers woven into her long dark hair. "Thomas, next time you do a sleep spell, let him lie down first."

"Sorry, Mom. I panicked a little, and I told him to hold still, not sleep. What happens now?" He moved behind the kid and carefully tilted him against his body until he slid onto the ground. Fortunately he wasn't stiff like a board or stone. If anything, he was a little floppy once Thomas started to move him.

"We send him back to his people after we make him forget that he saw us. Same as we do every time." She stepped closer, brushing the kid's auburn hair away from his forehead. "Poor thing. He's being eaten alive out here. So many bites that he feels like a prickly pear."

"He smells weird. It's familiar but wrong," Thomas said.

Her smile broadened as he took another sniff of the paralyzed Boy Scout, and Thomas could tell she was happy he was trying to make the connections to the mishmash of herbs. "Might be some cedar? It's too chemical. Not enough natural ingredients for me to tell." He bent over the scout and breathed in his scent once more. "Easier to smell the rabbit poop he stepped in, in the woods, and he stinks like hot dogs—yuck. Which could be his dinner or a lack of bathing."

Thomas and his mother's attention was drawn toward the thicker trees when they heard shouting.

"Kevin-James! Kev!"

"Dude, where are you?"

"Come on, man. We're going to be in trouble!"

Both hunkered down on their heels while Kat drew the wards that protected their spell circle to conceal them from the search party. Thomas's magic was new. He'd only started practicing with any sort of confidence since puberty hit. He wasn't weak, but he could be sloppy, which was why Kevin-James was staring at them both with wide-open eyes instead of drooling and snoring. "I'm sorry, Mom."

"Shhh!" she hissed, reaching over to cup the side of his face and press her thumb over his lips to silence him. Thomas could see the strain in her eyes. She had to balance the magic of the coven while borrowing from the wards to keep them hidden. It was like trying to direct a fire hose with your bare hands, and he wished he could do something to help her. He prayed to the goddess that being quiet, and keeping Kevin-James from becoming more alert, would be enough.

He nodded silently and watched as the trio of Boy Scouts came loudly toward them, no longer trying to be cautious in their midnight wandering. Unlike Kevin-James, they didn't seem to notice the singing and dancing, nor the blue flames reaching toward the full moon. They were focused on keeping each other in sight, which made sense since he could only assume that Kevin-James had wandered off by himself or been left behind.

Inches beyond the glamour that was shielding the three of them, Thomas noticed something shiny in the dirt. Darting toward it, he carefully reached through the shimmering magic to grab a brass-cased compass with the initials KJB etched on the back. He tucked it into the pouch he had slung across his body and scooted backward when one of the boys came toward him. He barely made it to safety without getting his hand stepped on.

He met his mother's dark eyes, hoping she understood why he took the chance. If one of them found the evidence that Kevin-James Whatever-the-B-was-for was near, they'd never get rid of them to bring the boy back to the Boy Scout camp. She tilted one hand and gave him a thumbs-up that made him beam at her.

It seemed to take forever for the trio to give up, but neither Thomas nor his mother dared speak out loud or move until the calls for the missing boy faded in the distance. And it couldn't have happened soon enough, since Thomas's original spell was starting to crack. Kevin-James was blinking, and he looked like he was trying to talk.

This time Thomas was calmer, and he did the right spell, sending the kid into a deep sleep while his mother let the glamour she'd been holding twinkle away in the night like a swarm of fireflies. "He's out. I should've let you do it, since you can make him forget us. But he was coming to."

"It's all right. Make him think it was a dream," she said as her shoulders slumped from holding the spell for so long. "I'm worn out. You can do it, sweetie. Just concentrate. It'll be easier. You know his name now. Names are power."

"LET'S GO, Kevin-James," Thomas said as he shook the boy, breaking the spell he'd cast on him. While Kevin-James slumbered, Thomas had raced into the camper he and his mom had driven from San Diego and pulled on jeans, a T-shirt, and a pair of Converse. If Kevin-James remembered anything, it'd help if it wasn't being walked through the woods by a naked guy.

"Who?" The kid blinked at Thomas and pushed his glasses up his nose with a frown.

"I'm a counselor," Thomas told him, and it wasn't a lie. He did help with the younger kids at the coven's camp, which included his pain-in-the-ass younger sister, who'd insisted on tagging along to bring the Boy Scout home. "I'm going to take you back to camp."

"What's that smell, Thomas?" Jules asked as she helped Thomas pull Kevin-James to his feet. "It's icky."

"I don't know," Thomas answered.

"Skin So Soft," Kevin-James muttered. "Keeps the bugs off."

"And it does a stellar job of it too." Thomas looped his arm around the younger boy's shoulders to help guide him through the woods and looked at his sister. "You can come, but be quiet. The more he hears, the harder it'll be for me to make him forget. Okay?"

"Okay." Jules trotted to Thomas's other side to keep out of the Boy Scout's view as much as possible. "But can I say one more thing?"

Thomas let out a heavy sigh, rolled his eyes, and nodded.

"He's cute."

"He is," Thomas agreed. "Keep an eye out for trouble, please. I need to make sure I have the spell right." He was nervous. He'd never cast a spell on a normal human who didn't know it was coming before. This wasn't him practicing the work. This was him doing it, and it was a big responsibility. If he messed up, they might have hordes of Boy Scout parents storming their camp with pitchforks and torches, stringing up the witches to keep them from corrupting their little angels.

Humans were not nice to people who were different or things they didn't understand. That was something every different person on Earth knew.

KEVIN-JAMES WOKE up just outside of the picnic area of the camp. His hair was full of twigs and pine needles. Any exposed skin was welted from bugbites and scratches. His mouth tasted horrible, and he wanted a big bottle of water. And a shower, because he smelled like he'd been rolling in a campfire.

"He's over here!" One of the counselors ran toward him, wearing his official camp T-shirt along with the scarf from his Boy Scout troop tied around his throat. "I found him!"

"Not so loud," he said as he rolled onto his stomach and slowly climbed to his feet. A wave of dizziness hit, and he had to grab the nearest picnic table to keep from face-planting into the turf. "My head hurts."

He sank onto the bench and scrubbed at his face with both hands, not looking up until one of the counselors tilted his face back to get a good look at him in the early morning sunlight. "What were you thinking? Going out in the woods alone at night!"

"I wasn't alone," Kevin-James mumbled. He was going to tell them his cabinmates were with him and how they'd left him behind all alone, but then he caught their eyes from where they were standing behind the adults. None of them looked like they'd gotten any sleep. At least that meant they'd looked for him—right?

"There were witches." He snatched a plastic bottle of water from the camp nurse when she held it out to him and chugged down half of it all at once, which sent him into a choking and coughing fit. *Stupid shit.* "I saw them dancing. Heard them singing."

"That's just a story they tell every summer," the camp leader said with a frown that reached right past his eyes and up to his forehead. "Did he hit his head? Should we take him into town?"

"I don't think I hit my head." Kevin-James ran the fingers of his free hand through his hair and winced when he got them caught in tangled hair and twigs. The back of his head was covered in debris and crap. "I think I fell down a hill?"

They didn't believe him. He knew he'd seen witches and fairies. There was magic. "I can show you where I saw them!" He halfway stood, digging into his pockets for his compass, but it wasn't where he usually kept it. It wasn't in any of his other pockets either. "My compass is gone."

"Mrs. Ramirez, I'm going to call Kevin-James's mother and have her come get him. I'd like you to drive him into town to the doctor. I'll have her meet you there." The leader hunkered onto his heels in front of Kevin-James and patted his knees. "Mrs. Ramirez and your cabin-mates will help you pack. We need to make sure that you're all right."

"But I am okay! Please don't call my mom." But it was obvious he was fighting a losing battle. His mother would drive at supersonic speed to come to his rescue. He'd never get to go to the witches' circle to find evidence to prove what he saw, and he'd never find the compass either. Summer was over for Kevin-James Beshter.

ONE

HIS SNEAKERS slapped on the damp pavement of the Pan-Pacific Exposition section of San Diego's famous Balboa Park. KJ Beshter could still smell the green scent of the trees he'd raced through at dawn as he'd started his run, when fog still shrouded his favorite trails. The sun had just come up over the mountain, casting golden light that shone through the century-old buildings that were the foundation of the historic park. Every step and breath he took cleared his head.

It was easy when the air was still cold with the chill of the desert night, unlike the stifling heat that would choke the life out of him in a few hours. Normally it didn't get hot in June. It was traditionally the grayest month of the year, and it was hard to tell which was more depressing—May Grays or June Gloom. Both seemed to warp reality, when you couldn't tell what time it was with the sky being overcast for weeks at a time. But this year a Santa Ana wind snuck in from the desert. The hot air would rip the clouds and fog away in no time, and then the heat would go up.

"Jesus," he scolded himself as he stopped to stretch his aching calf muscles at the big circular fountain that rested between the Natural History Museum and the Fleet Science Center. Propping one foot on the edge, he leaned over his knee and closed his eyes while his knee popped and the burn in his leg lessened.

"Feel better?" asked another runner. KJ recognized the guy. They seemed to be on the same schedule, but this was the closest thing to a conversation they'd had. He was dressed in running shorts, with compression ankle wraps and a shirt tight enough that KJ could easily see the cool air was toying with his nipples.

"Yeah, stepped wrong about half a mile back, but it's okay now." KJ, on the other hand, was wearing sweats that he'd bought at Target a decade ago and a T-shirt that wasn't much better than a rag. His shoes were the only part of his running gear that were new, and even they were a few years old. "I can't run during the school year, so I have to cram it all into the summer."

"I hear that from a lot of teachers." The well-dressed runner glanced at his smart watch and then gave KJ a nod. "See ya around. I've got a few more miles to go."

WITH A heavy sigh, KJ pulled shut the sliding glass door of his apartment. The air conditioner would start in an hour or less, stripping all the fresh air he'd let in the night before. His reddish-brown hair was still damp from his shower as he made his way to what passed as his kitchen to get a cup of coffee and a bagel before he settled in for a little internet research. The bagel was a cheap national brand, which meant it was barely better than a slice of bread, and probably its only redeeming quality was its capacity as a cream-cheese delivery device.

His coffee, on the other hand, was the good stuff, beans from Kona and ground for each pot. He'd set it brewing the second he'd come home. All showers were better if the steam smelled like the coffee you had dripping away. He drank it black. It had to be quality.

Things were easier in the summer, and he could take the time to eat slowly. No need to pour the coffee into a steel jug to drink throughout the day—it was never enough—or try to find a clean sandwich bag for the bagel. Usually he ended up wrapping it in a paper towel and tucking it in with the leftovers he was bringing for lunch, since teachers didn't have time for a food run. It irked most of the staff that the students got a longer break than they did and could hit the myriad of fast-food and taco shops in the area.

With school out for the summer, he could stop thinking about the repetitive act of spreading historical knowledge to his students. It got harder every year to keep the regular classes interested in the county-issued curriculum. Luckily his AP class allowed him to set his own lessons. He focused on the presidents who had been assassinated, their assassins, and his favorite project, the presidents who had been impeached. As he told his students, you study history to make sure it doesn't repeat itself, which was sadly a lesson few of them learned.

KJ plopped in front of his laptop, making sure his bagel didn't knock over his coffee, and opened his browser. At the corner of his screen, a pop-up announced for the fourth day in a row that it was his friend David's birthday, although it no longer said it was coming soon. He'd pissed around for a week plus, and now he was going to have to go shopping. But it was early yet, barely 8:00 a.m. Plenty of time to work on his YouTube channel.

His email was full of comments from his last video, in which he'd toured Seaport Village, where there were supposed to be ghosts hanging out near the old jail. It'd been a bust, which wasn't unusual. So far he'd failed at proving anything actually went bump in the night, and it bugged the shit out of him. KJ knew it was real. He'd seen witches and fairies cavorting when he was twelve. No one believed him then, and according to his comments, not many people believed him now. That didn't matter, though, because whether they believed in it or not, his audience was starting to bring him in a little money. In fact, it was enough money so far this year that he didn't need a summer job to make ends meet.

"No online shopping for you, you jerk," he told himself as he let out a sigh that set his bangs fluttering and then took a drink of the coffee. It was perfect, and he closed his eyes to focus on its rich, nutty flavor. "You are a horrible friend, but a horrible friend with a cunning plan."

A few of his students had given him gift cards at the end of the school year, and while he'd used the multitudes of Starbucks cards to charge his app and Amazon cards to give him a summer filled with basically free books, he had a few cards left.

"If I can find them!" he reminded himself, since he'd been putting off the search since the birthday alerts started, sure that he knew where the card for Equinox and Occult Shop was hiding. If he couldn't find it, he'd see if they had it on record. It was a family business owned by the parent of one of his favorite students, Star Anders. He'd go buy a birthday card at Target and then shove the gift card inside and give it to David on his way to Pioneer Park.

"Has to be around here somewhere."

It took KJ half an hour to find the gift card tucked in one of his folders from the AP class. Estelle "Star" Anders was brilliant—literally brilliant. She'd skipped three grades and was heading into her junior year of high school at thirteen. Nothing got past her. He loved reading her papers and listening to her theories in class. He was going to miss the hell out of her.

Star also had a hot dad who might be on the right team, but parent night was hardly the right place to cruise for a date. Also, it'd be awkward to date a student's parent. That was a line that shouldn't be crossed.

With his plan for the minimum possible shopping time set, he went back to work on his next video, calling up the plans for Pioneer Park and the rest of the research he'd gathered. Amazon was delivering the equipment he needed sometime that day, but after three notices from UPS in his email, each with a different delivery estimate, he had no idea when they'd be there. He still had two days before the solstice, so that was okay. It wasn't as if he had to rush anything.

But the clunking sound of his AC starting made him get off his ass. He was also finished with his second cup of coffee, and the bagel had been gone at least an hour earlier. After the run he'd had, he was still a little hungry. It was time to go out before it got any hotter. He sent the marked-up map to his tablet, placed it and the Equinox card into his messenger bag, and headed out the door.

TWO

"I DON'T want to go to summer camp, Dad. You didn't make me go last year!" There was a whine in Star's voice that was rubbing one of Thomas's many nerves the wrong way. Normally she didn't make him angry, and he bit the inside of his lip to quash the temptation to whine or shout at her in return. It didn't help that she was throwing her clothes into her suitcase with enough force to nearly knock it off the bed.

"I didn't make you go last year because you were with me in Scotland." He leaned his lanky body against the doorframe, his arms folded across his chest. He could taste the anger and hurt radiating from her, but then she'd never been able to hide her emotions from him even when she tried.

"Something could go wrong." She was thirteen and mostly legs, dark brown hair and eyes like him, with her mother's tawny complexion. "Look what happened with the cat."

"You were seven," he pointed out after glancing at the hairless thing licking his privates in the bay window with one paw stretched high over his head. "And I wasn't here when that happened." He still thought about wringing his sister's neck for not keeping a better eye on Star and the cat.

"That's my point. Dad, you won't be at camp either." She was pouting as she shoved three different pairs of sneakers into her suitcase and then pulled out the pair she'd planned on wearing for the bus ride.

The cat met his eyes after taking one last long lick between his legs and rolling onto his side. Between the dark and light patches on his skin were small x's from where Star had stitched up her pet after bringing his lifeless blood-covered body home. In the right light—or maybe the wrong light—you could see tire-tread marks that ended his normal life running across his stomach.

"Don't use me as your excuse, Princess," the cat said. Its voice was clear as a bell without any silly hint of the melodic meow he'd had before. "You love me."

"I do love you, Nate." She turned around and gathered her undead, sentient, talking cat into her arms and gave him a hug.

"Why don't you tell me the truth, then?" Thomas asked as he mumbled a harmless spell that pulled everything out of her suitcase, folded it properly, and gracefully settled it all back inside. "There, now you can close it. Nation's right. If you've got a reason not to go, I'd like to hear it."

"Isn't it enough that I want to spend time with you?" She tilted her head to the side, giving him puppy-dog eyes that would break his heart if she didn't use them all the time to get her way.

"Sweetie, I love spending summers with you, you know that. It's only two weeks. I went until I was sixteen." He let out a sigh and settled on the window seat the cat had been sprawled on and reached for her hand. "I don't understand. You've never been so…."

"Clingy," the cat offered with a purr, which sounded all wrong coming from him.

"Hey, I do not cling." Star closed her eyes and settled the cat on the cushion next to Thomas. "It's Heather Maxwell. She's been fucking with me since I was little. She'll be there again this year. It's always the same people. I just don't want to deal with her."

Thomas frowned. Talking about sex was easier than talking about how to handle a bully, especially since, as witches, they didn't have a bunch of sexual hang-ups to tread lightly around. But he was also aware of Heather, just as he'd been aware of her father when he was at camp.

"I know I've told you for years not to play their games. I've told you that she's probably jealous of what you can do and how I don't send you there every summer. But it's important for you to spend time around other supernaturals. You know very few witches your age. Hell, you know very few people your age in general. Sometimes I regret letting you skip so many grades. At camp you'll be around our people."

"She's evil, Dad. She's a Heather. They're all evil."

"True. I can't argue with that. Her father was a complete jackass to me when I was your age. Although it might've been worse since your grandmother was one of the high priestesses back then. He accused me of hiding under her skirts because I was afraid of him." Thomas floated the Kleenex box across the room to Star. "If you are backed into a corner, you have my permission to use magic to protect yourself. Will that make it more acceptable?"

"It'd help," she said before blowing her nose and wiping her eyes, which smudged the makeup she'd only started wearing a semester ago. "As long as I don't do it first."

"Which is acceptable to me. I love you with all my heart. You are the most important person in the world to me, but Star," he said, "I need some me time. I haven't had a week alone since the last time you went to camp."

"And you'd like to get laid," the cat pointed out.

"Once again, the cat speaks when he's not spoken to."

"Not my fault you're easy to read, Thomas." Nation looked down at his missing balls. "Unlike me, you've still got yours."

"I was seven, Nate, and you were fixed long before you ran into the street. Not my fault," Star pointed out with a giggle.

"No, it was his," Nation said, glaring at Thomas, his golden eyes glowing unnaturally until he turned away.

"We are not having this discussion again, Nation." It was an old one. A sentient cat was both a blessing and a curse—mostly a curse. "You came from the pound pre-fixed."

"Dad, his name's still Nate, short for Nathaniel," Star reminded him. "Named after my favorite boy on *Gossip Girl*."

"His name is Nation, short for Abomination, hon." He laced their fingers together and then tucked some of her hair behind her ear. "Now, finish packing. I need to open the shop and keep an eye out for your ride. Marjorie's already down there."

THOMAS STOPPED in their kitchen on his way to the shop, sighing when he found the water he'd boiled in the kettle far too cold to make tea. Instead of casting a simple spell to reheat it, he hit the button once more and then puttered in the fridge to grab a cup of yogurt and a few pieces of fruit for breakfast. He also took out the lunch he'd packed for

Star's trip and put it on the tray he'd take downstairs. There was a better chance of her remembering it on her way out the door than her checking the fridge.

With the water boiling away, he placed two mugs on the tray along with two tea bags of Earl Grey, one for him and one for Marjorie. There was never any need to bring her food, because she always picked up some sweet pastry from the bakery on the corner or a breakfast burrito from a drive-thru on her way to work. But she was always thankful for the tea.

Star was still stomping around upstairs, making it far noisier in the shop than normal, or at least Thomas thought it was. It had been two years since he'd manned the counter for the summer season. He was not looking forward to spending three months telling wannabe witches and other practitioners which color candle to burn for good luck and which sacred oils to mix with what herbs to find true love or get rich, but it was the family business. It also made it easier to keep track of untrained gifted who might present a problem in the future, which was his other job for the Mage's Council.

"Star is not pleased that she's being forced to go to camp." He gave a shrug and half a smile to one of his regular customers as she glanced at the crystals swaying above his head. "She's a teenager."

"Already?" Mrs. Wilson gave a glance that said she understood. "Is it cliché for me to say I didn't think I'd been coming here that long?"

"Just a bit, but don't worry about it." He reached overhead to stop a trio of sprites from playing with a sparkling glass Pegasus with a large purple crystal hanging from its hooves. It was a pretty doodad and had absolutely no magical powers at all, much like most of the inventory on display in the shop. It was meant as an impulse buy. Something sparkly to make the buyer happy and nothing more. Over the years there was more and more glitz and less enchantment. They did more sales online than they did in the flesh these days anyway. "Have you seen Marjorie?"

"She went into the back to look for something for me. She said you had new purple candles that you hadn't put on the floor yet." The soccer mom played with the end of her perfect ponytail and did nothing to hide that it was meant to be flirtatious. Thomas was used to the customers flirting with him. Most of them knew it'd do them no good since he didn't like women, but Mrs. Wilson apparently liked a challenge. *One of these days I'm going to ask her why me when she knows I'm not interested.*

"Don't worry about Star. Once she tastes a little freedom in the great outdoors and makes some new friends, she'll hate it when it's time to come home."

"I'm not certain that I like that," he said while pulling the tea bag from his mug. He stirred in a trio of sugar cubes from a dragon-shaped bowl near the cash register. "I'm going to miss my little rebel if she decides to conform to the norm."

"If you don't want me to conform, Dad," said Star, balancing her wheeled suitcase on the steps, a bright fuchsia backpack that clashed with the neon green streaks running through her hair slung over her shoulder, "you wouldn't be sending me to summer camp."

"Do you think you're bringing enough?" he asked, his brows rising over the frame of his glasses. "A few minutes ago it was just the suitcase."

"Seriously, Dad?" She let out a snort and offered Mrs. Wilson a nod when she reached the bottom of the steps. "Have I ever left the house without at least a backpack?"

"Your cat didn't stow away, did he?" *Which wouldn't necessarily be a bad thing.*

"Nate's having second breakfast." Star crossed the shop, holding her hand out for the bag of food Thomas had waiting. She somehow managed to get it to fit in the top of her backpack and then zipped it shut. "I told him to be good while I was gone."

"By his standards or mine?" Thomas stepped around the counter and wrapped his arms around his daughter. "I promise to look out for him, and I'll try to keep him out of trouble. Try not to get into any while you're gone." He kissed her forehead before letting her go.

"I'll do my best, Dad. That's all I can offer you." There was a honk from outside, and a dark van with the camp's logo pulled into the loading zone in front of the shop. "Don't worry about Nate, Dad. Try to have some fun while I'm gone. Bye-bye, Mrs. Wilson!" She rushed for the door, too quick to change her mind, and left with a flurry of bells chiming.

THREE

KJ STILL had the windows down in his old Toyota when he pulled into the parking lot of the Mission Valley Target, figuring he could do a little grocery shopping. It was already busy, and if he had to guess, whoever designed the parking lot was high on some shrooms when they'd decided which direction the traffic went. It barely made sense, and he vowed to the gods that next time he'd go to a different Target. Closer wasn't always better.

He found a space closer to the gardening department than the front doors and rolled up the windows—the hard way. His car didn't have electric windows. The locks popped into place when he hit the alarm button on his keys, though, which meant it wasn't completely primitive.

His muscles were still a bit sore from the morning run as he made his way around the bright-red cement balls that kept you from driving too close. Inside, the air-conditioning sent a chill down his spine, and he tugged at the collar of his Henley to make sure it wasn't clinging to his skin before grabbing a red plastic cart. He'd come for a birthday card, but it wouldn't hurt to grab some stock for his pantry and maybe a gag gift for David.

He was sad it wasn't closer to Halloween, because Target's Halloween stuff was epic. Somehow Fourth of July–themed junk didn't have the same appeal as a plastic rat or dragon skeleton. Might still be something fun in the toy section, but first, some groceries.

Pop-Tarts, cheap bagels, a few frozen pizzas, boxes of macaroni and cheese, and to prove that he was capable of eating healthy if he wanted, a bag of red apples and a bunch of bananas in the top part of the basket. He didn't miss one of the other shoppers commenting that he shopped like a college kid, and he also couldn't say she was wrong. Lastly, he snatched a jar of his favorite vice, pistachios.

"So what are you doing?" David's voice sounded in his ear when he tapped on his Bluetooth to answer his call, shutting down his *Ghostbusters* theme ringtone.

"I'm getting some food for my apartment while crossing my fingers Amazon delivers the cameras and lights today. You?"

While talking, KJ sent his cart up the conveyor to the second floor and stepped onto the much less interesting escalator to meet it there. "Anything you think we might need for the park? Batteries? Bug spray?"

"Not a bad plan, although we shouldn't need batteries with the solar-powered motion detectors. But bug spray might not be a bad idea. People walk their dogs there, so there might be fleas and dog shit."

"I'll hit the sporting goods section for bug spray and get Clorox Wipes for our shoes, just in case. At least I know we don't need sunscreen." KJ gathered his cart and glanced around to figure out where he was going. They didn't have much of a sporting goods area at Target, but they should have OFF! somewhere in the store, and the toys were near the baseballs.

"We're meeting at the grave markers, right?"

"That's the plan. I think we decided on six, which'll give us some good time before the sun goes down."

"Then we wait two nights for the big event." David sounded so excited. KJ wished he could promise something scary for them to film, but promises had no place in their recordings.

"Want to get sushi after? It is your birthday, after all. Unless you've got plans with whoever you're dating this month." Unlike KJ, David had a social life—enough of one that KJ had given up trying to keep track of who he was involved with or the level of involvement. The closest he got to paying attention was making sure he didn't date any of David's hand-me-downs, which wasn't always easy since half of the time David dated men.

"It's my birthday. Rather spend it with sushi to go or delivery and beer at your place than with…."

"Are you pretending not to remember their name?" KJ let out a snort as he snatched a couple of cans of OFF! from a shelf and tossed them into the cart. Then he picked up a small first-aid kit, which was something they always forgot to buy and needed. Once in a while the Eagle Scout remembered to be prepared.

"Is it working?"

"Not really. But great, you and me is the best. I think I can buy beer here. We can order the sushi and have it delivered when we get done at the park."

"That's what best friends are for—hassle-free birthdays. See ya later."

With the call ended, KJ turned the cart into the toy section. Deciding on which pair of Funko Pops! to buy David took the most time. He settled on Iron Man and Captain Marvel from the *Avengers* movies, and there was a 90 percent chance they'd be watching one of those tonight while they ate. Maybe more than one movie since neither had a day job to go to in the morning. He could skip his run.

It took far less time to pick up a proper birthday card. He'd skipped right past the rude ones, the grown-up ones, and decided on one for a five-year-old with dragons breathing fire on a knight on it. Dragons and knights were how they'd met in college, when David joined the dorm-room D&D game KJ ran. They'd bonded over all things geek. David was the only person to ever believe his story about the dancing witches. There was no one KJ loved more.

On his way home with his shopping, KJ drove through his favorite taco shop to get some carne asada fries. They were the ultimate guilty pleasure. French fries covered in marinated beef, cheese, guacamole, and sour cream. He could hear his arteries screaming in pain as he settled the cardboard container on his coffee table. After putting away the few perishables and the beer, he settled down for his lunch with the birthday card, Tony, Carol, and the gift card from Star. He put the Pops! into a Mylar gift bag and pulled the drawstring tight on top. Then he signed the card and shoved the Equinox card inside, tossed the outer cover that Star had signed into the empty bag from the taco shop, and sealed the birthday card. On the outside he scribbled: *Here's a sample of my DNA in case you need it someday.*

It wasn't until he'd finished eating and washing the few dishes in his sink that he noticed the purple card from Star on the kitchen floor.

KJ cocked his head. He thought he'd tied the taco shop bag shut, because while he loved Mexican food, the smell of chili and cilantro could become overpowering. It was part of why he was washing the dishes. He knew he'd gotten green sauce under his nails.

The last rinsed plastic storage bowl got propped on top of the drying rack, and he bent down to pick up the card to toss it back out. But it wasn't only the outer card. It was the $25 gift certificate encased in the envelope as if it'd never been removed.

"What the fuck?" His brows knitted as he looked over the breakfast bar to the coffee table, where the gift was wrapped with its card leaning against it. He knew he'd put it inside. He also knew he'd sealed the card.

"How the hell?" He rubbed his fingers together, noticing a hint of shimmering glitter on them that must've come from the Equinox logo, which was a sparkling crescent moon.

A sharp knock on his door, followed by a loud voice yelling "UPS!" kept him from reopening the birthday card. David would understand. Shit happened. He tucked the card into his back pocket and opened the door to collect four smallish cardboard boxes with big smiles on them. The driver was long gone. They never stayed.

"Okay, fine, I get the hint." Obviously he was supposed to go shopping at Equinox, which was fine. He had to take the boxes down to his car anyway, and he had a few hours to kill before meeting David. Maybe they had something he could give David or send to his mom for her birthday in August.

FOUR

BY THE time Marjorie found the purple candles for Mrs. Wilson, her tea was frigid and darker than the pits of hell. It might've passed as pudding. Thomas ended up pouring it down the drain in the workroom where he mixed oils and incense for the customers as well as created a few genuine potions for the rare practitioner who came in.

Mrs. Wilson bought the candles and the purple unicorn that hung over the counter. Thomas carefully wrapped it in tissue that was imbued with antimagic cantrips just in case it had gathered any mystical energy over the months it'd been hanging over his head.

"Do you want me to make you fresh tea, dear?" he asked Marjorie while she finished unpacking the other new candles that might as well be on display. They were very nice—soy-based waxes were all the rage— and their scents were quite pleasant even when mixed with all the other aromas of the shop.

"No, that's okay. I'm sorry it took me so long. Somehow these ended up under two other boxes in the storage room."

"That was probably my fault," he told her as he reached into one of the cabinets behind the counter and pulled out a ceramic bowl of tiny trinkets, a polishing cloth, and a jar of something that Star called unicorn barf. "I put together some online orders last night, and with Star's camp drama, I got sloppy."

"You, sloppy? Never!" Marjorie shook her head. "I'd believe it more if you said the demon cat from hell did it."

"I am not from hell!" Nation's voice rang from the stairs as he came sauntering down with his tail pointing toward the heavens. "I think."

"No, you're from upstairs, where you are supposed to be basking in a sunbeam and not being seen by customers," Thomas pointed out dryly, casting the undead cat a withering look.

"You don't have any. Besides, if I don't talk, they won't know nothing."

"I don't know what's worse, your stubbornness or abuse of the English language." Thomas hastily moved the trinkets and jar of goop out of Nation's way as he vaulted onto the counter. "You are not from New Jersey."

"Does it really matter?" This time Nation added a hint of a British accent. "I learned to talk watching TV. I can do all kinds of accents." He flopped onto his side, showing his hairless belly to Marjorie, who came over to pet him. "Things would be much easier for you, Thomas, if you let me get away with everything like Star does."

"That will never happen. You may stay to visit with us, but if the shop bell rings, you go upstairs or in back. You're a secret, remember?" As a member of the Mages Council of North America and Star's father, he would be held responsible for the abuse of dark magic that his little girl used to bring her cat back from the dead. Their punishments were nothing to laugh about. He could be stripped of his powers. They could take Star. They'd certainly kill the abomination. Only the last option was acceptable.

TWENTY MINUTES later the shop bell did ring. With the sun behind the man who entered, Thomas couldn't see his face, but there was a slight tingling at the nape of his neck that told him he'd been touched by real magic in the past. It was faint, like the brush of a butterfly's wings or the soft velvet of a baby's ear. He'd finished the trinkets and was now adding a pinch of another magic-blocking powder to the inside of "voodoo" bags to prevent any sorcerous accidents.

"Good afternoon," he said as he set the container of dust under the counter, which was when he noticed Nation was not in hiding. The fucking cat was curled into a naked pancake in a sunbeam in the main window to the shop. *Son of a bitch, or whatever the feline version is!*

"Hi." He was about six feet tall, and Thomas could see a strong reddish cast to his dark hair as he came closer. "We've met before. I'm one of your daughter's teachers."

Thomas stood a trifle straighter and held his hand out when the man was close enough to reach. Once he stepped out of the sun, Thomas recognized both his face and the faint tingle of magic he'd felt before at parents' night at the high school. "Of course, Mr. Beshter. You just missed Star. She went off to summer camp a few hours ago."

Beshter's grip was strong, but not in a bad way. It was strange to see him in regular clothes instead of the suit he'd worn at the school when he'd sung Star's praises. "That's too bad. I'd've loved to say hi."

"I want to thank you," Thomas said as he made his way around the counter. Out of the corner of his eye, he noticed Nation stretching like he didn't have a care in the world, which Thomas knew was a lie. Nation's cares normally equated to raising Thomas's blood pressure.

"No need to do that." Beshter's grin was bright, and Thomas couldn't help but return it. "She was the best in my class."

"I know she's brilliant, but you managed to make her feel normal even though she was so much younger than the other students. That was above and beyond in my book." Thomas leaned against the counter, tapping his fingers against the glass for a moment to make sure Beshter kept his eyes on him instead of Nation's shenanigans.

"It's hard when you're different. I know what that's like."

"If you're talking about being gay," Thomas said, "then yes, I know exactly what that's like. It was different for us back in the dark ages of the 2000s."

Beshter let out a bark of a laugh that spiked the magic in his aura to a point where Thomas could actually see it. He reached into his back pocket and pulled out his gift card. "Do you think you can help me spend this? It's my best friend's birthday tonight, and I flaked on shopping."

"What are you interested in?" *Please say me! Really, Thomas, she's only been gone a few hours! Good goddess, slow down, and he just said he has a friend with a birthday.*

"It's funny. I do a lot of magic research for my YouTube channel, but I've only been to three shops in the area over the past few years." Beshter nodded toward the shelves of books and artwork on the walls. "Books are normal, but your atmosphere's a lot nicer than the last shop I was in, but then they were leaning toward black magic. Doesn't feel like you do any of that here."

"Are you a sensitive, Mr. Beshter?" It seemed like the logical question, and it would explain what Thomas was sensing.

"Please, call me KJ. I'm off duty for the summer, and I'm not Star's teacher anymore." He meandered a bit through the shop, stopping before a display of altar supplies. He picked up a statue of the triple-faced goddess and tilted it upside down to check the price. "My YouTube channel is about the paranormal. I saw something when I was a kid, and I want to prove I wasn't imagining it."

"That's fascinating. I don't think there are a lot of believers in the world anymore, or those who admit it. Sadly Prozac and other chemicals seem to be the standard cure for us crazy magical con men, which is what I've been called more than a few times." It was insulting, and Thomas had been tempted to show some rude normal that magic was very much real.

"We should talk about it sometime." Beshter switched to another goddess statue, one with only one face, and a pair of candleholders that represented the god and the goddess, which he took to the counter.

"As an interview for your channel?" Thomas wondered if he could do that. He'd need to ask the council. "It would be good for business. It's rather slow this summer. Most of our sales are online these days."

"The anonymity of the internet. Great for buying sex toys, magic supplies, and watching porn," Beshter said as he pulled the gift card from his pocket and handed it to Thomas. There was a charge like static electricity when their fingers touched, but beyond that Thomas felt something else—he felt Star.

My girl, what did you do this time?

"Your total is $28.75," Thomas said after running the card through the scanner.

"Great." Beshter dug out some change to pay the difference while Thomas wrapped the items carefully in tissue paper imbued with more of the antimagic dust. "Here you go. Maybe we could catch dinner? I'm busy tonight and on the solstice, but I'm free tomorrow and the night after the solstice."

"Tomorrow night sounds lovely. Let me give you my number, and we can decide where to meet." Thomas pulled out a business card for the shop and wrote his personal number on the back. He handed the card and the shopping bag to Beshter and then walked the man out of the shop.

"Cute," Nation said from the top of one of the bookcases. "Don't screw this up, Thomas. He smells good."

FIVE

WITH A slim plastic box cutter caught in his lips, KJ yanked open the trunk of his old Toyota and frowned when he discovered his trunk light was no longer working. He'd need to make sure they had flashlights on the solstice. He did not want to run about in the park, if something scary did happen, by the light of his phone. He grabbed a smallish Amazon Prime box and started slicing through the black paper tape. Inside he could hear the solar-powered motion sensors he'd ordered by the dozen rattling while he worked to get it open, and said a silent prayer to the powers that be that at least half of them were functional.

You never could tell when you bought anything by the dozen. Hell, half the time a carton of eggs had a broken one hiding in the corner by the time you got it home, and he knew he was more careful than the delivery guy who'd left the boxes on his stoop that afternoon. At least it'd been on the porch and not tossed in the neighbor's yard where their dogs would've had a cardboard-munching party like they'd had last week when he'd ordered new underwear. As pissed as he was at the delivery guy, he couldn't help but smile at the horrified look on his neighbor Diana's face when she'd brought the one and only survivor of the underpants-pocalypse to his front door.

Not that he wasn't grateful for the single pair, since he was currently wearing them under his sweatpants. At least the undies were clean, unlike the rest of his clothing. KJ saw no point in wearing clean clothes to prowl around before sunset to install hidden cameras in the groves around Pioneer Park.

"If this place doesn't give you the creeps," he said into the night-vision-capable camera he'd hooked over the edge of the trunk while he assembled his toys for the hunt, "you've never heard about the hundreds of corpses left behind and paved over when the land was donated to the city and turned into a park. They've even got a little monument made of old gravestones at the entrance that I'll show you along the way. When

122

I was a kid, I refused to play in this park. Pissed my mom off, since it's pretty close to where we lived, but the place made my skin crawl. Hopefully that's a good thing now, and David and I'll be able to show you something that really goes bump in the night."

A real shiver ran down his back as the breeze rustled the leaves overhead and ruffled through his auburn hair, so he reached for his hoodie's hood, tugged it down to his forehead, and then started shoving the motion-detecting cameras into the pouch. He decided to plant the first dozen to test how they worked overnight before he opened the other two boxes. It didn't matter if he caught anything on the trial. He just wanted to make sure they worked.

"Hey, dude," David said as he slipped around an SUV that was too big for the parking space it was sprawled in. "How do they look?"

KJ rested his hip against the edge of the trunk and handed David the one light and camera he'd completely unwrapped. "There's a small scissors on top of the box if the box cutter's not good enough. These things have a lot of tape on them. I probably should've checked when I was home. Hopefully we can get a good test if we unwrap half a dozen."

"We also should've met earlier so they could get more sunlight. I don't think we'll be testing much tonight. But they will get a full charge tomorrow." David began carefully trying to cut the thin tape and paper from another of the cameras. "I'll do this. You sync them to your phone and tablet. If you put them on the roof of the car, we might catch enough light."

"Sundown's not until almost eight. That gives us at least ninety minutes. We can do it."

"We have the technology."

"God, you're more of a geek than I am," KJ said as he placed the cameras on the roof with their little solar panels facing west. "And that's not easy."

"We all have our talents," David answered with the scissors caught between his lips. "These are a bitch!"

WITH THEIR pouches and pockets filled with the cameras and sensors, now synced to KJ's devices, the two men stood in front of the plaque that held the names of almost two thousand people who were still buried under the park. Just the thought of it sent goose bumps up KJ's spine.

"Obviously these people did not see *Poltergeist*," David said while testing the mic on his camera. No phone taping for their channel. Only real equipment could handle what they filmed, or more precisely what they prayed they'd be able to film in the future.

"This place is a hell of a lot older than *Poltergeist*," KJ replied as he pulled back his hood for his opening monologue about the history of the old Catholic cemetery under their feet. He never scrimped on history. How could he? It was the closest he could get to chasing ghosts in real life.

It might not be considered a science, but what was geology? The study of the Earth's history by studying stones. Anthropology, paleontology, the study of bones and how the people and animals who left them lived and died. Hell, even the light from the sun was from eight minutes in the past. As far as KJ was concerned, history was the most concrete science of all. Sure, it was written by the winners, but if you were willing to read between the lines, you could learn the truth.

"The ground for the original Catholic cemetery was broken in the 1870s," he said while looking into the camera, listing off facts he'd memorized from his research while trying to make them interesting. No one watched a history lecture to the end, but they did love a good haunting. Or a nasty serial killer, but KJ wasn't into profiling anyone who might still be alive and scary. The dead were safer, and so far he'd never met a witch who was into human sacrifice, which David said they should find because the ratings would be epic.

"At least eighteen hundred people were buried here, and they still are. It was easier to level the land for picnic areas and tennis courts that way. It's not that rare an occurrence either. There are quite a few parks, housing tracts, and schools built upon the graves of indigenous people and pioneers. These are the only tombstones they kept." He motioned with his hand, and David moved the camera to the line of crumbling relics. KJ crouched before them, dusting his fingers over the names that were mostly unreadable from the passage of time.

"It's sad that you can't make the names out on all of them. They stopped taking care of the cemetery over the decades, and in the 1970s they shoved the tombstones into a ditch and broke ground for the park proper. These are all that's left, but there are still small bits and pieces to be found at the outskirts of the park. Kids used to play over them in the ravines until the eighties. Coincidentally, the movie *Poltergeist* came out in 1982, right before the real construction of the park began."

KJ paused, staying quiet while David walked the row of tombstones, taking pictures of the names and dates on the readable ones and taking other images before it got too dark for them to see. He felt the hair on his arms quiver at one point, when David was shooting the best preserved of them, but he didn't think much of it. He'd already had a weird enough day without looking for the strange and unnatural. He just wanted to set the cameras and go home.

"We should get those in place," David said almost like he was reading KJ's mind, but after being friends for so long, that kind of thing happened. "We don't have much time."

"Yeah, and this is not where you want to spend your birthday." KJ woke up his tablet and showed David the map of where people had felt or "seen" spirits over the years. "These are the cold spots. Not a lot here by the monuments, which isn't a shock. We won't be able to plant anything on the flats because the cameras will either be stepped on or stolen."

"Pretty sure we'll lose more than a few to theft as it is. This is not a safe place after dark." David stowed his camera in its case, slung it across his back, and started walking for the nearest cluster of trees near a cold spot. "Come on. I can boost you into the branches, and you can set the cameras."

KJ twisted the mounting wires around a small branch, aiming the solar panel toward the east to make sure the camera charged as much as it could when the sun came up. The lens was aimed toward the ground, where he thought he saw a glint on the twisted roots of the tree. There wasn't anything there when he dropped down beside David. There never was, but he decided trusting his gut wasn't a bad idea.

"Sun'll be down soon," David said, pointing with his chin toward the darkening clouds and sky. "Time to split up for the rest."

"Yeah." KJ reached into the pouch and counted three cameras waiting to be planted. "I'll hit the side toward the ravine." It was the farthest from the entrance and memorial, and he hoped it might be a good spot to catch something on camera besides a mugger or other paranormal hunters. There were almost always people walking through the haunted sites they visited with homemade PKE meters and other ghost-hunting equipment.

He loped across the grassy area to the tree line and crouched near a dark spot on one of the trees. From across the way he'd thought it might be a hole, but now that he was close, he discovered it was a puddle of black wax. Someone had burned a candle there. It was still warm and kind of soft, which might mean it hadn't been done too long ago, but as hot as it'd been all day, that was hard to judge. Using the camera on his tablet, he captured the evidence of what might've been black magic and then set up one of the cameras from his pouch near the spot.

"Hope you come back," he said to himself. "Might end up being something interesting."

"Who?" a voice whispered, and a cold hand brushed the back of his neck.

"Hello," KJ said, holding as still as a deer in the headlights. His breath steamed as the air around him went cold. "I'm sorry to disturb you." He caught a glimpse of a tattered white lace-trimmed sleeve out of the corner of his eye and slowly twisted on his heels to get a better view of the woman in white. *Please be on the camera. Please be on camera.*

She solidified as he watched her, which was not at all what he expected. Any other time he'd seen a ghost, they'd faded away once they noticed he could see them, though that might've been because David was usually with him with the big camera.

"Darkness," she said, pointing at the wax.

"Yeah, I think so too," he said, agreeing with her while his guts turned to ice. "Something bad is going to happen here."

SIX

"DID YOU just make a date?" Marjorie and Nation asked in unison after KJ left the shop. Thomas couldn't tell who looked more surprised.

"It's not that kind of date." Thomas went back behind the counter to retrieve the gift card KJ just used. "He's one of Star's teachers."

"He *was* one of her teachers," Marjorie pointed out while Nation hopped onto the counter and stuck his face into Thomas's long-empty teacup. "One of her hot teachers. I'd ask him out, but he's on your team, not mine."

Thomas brought the card to his nose, sniffing the edge of it, and then ran it along his tongue. He closed his eyes, tracing the touch of power he detected on the card. His shoulders slumped slightly when he opened his eyes to meet Marjorie's gaze. She was looking at him like he was insane. "She put a spell on it."

"She? Star?" Marjorie came closer and took a look at the card. "Some kind of love spell? Those don't work. You can't make someone love you. You taught me that."

"I'm not sure what spell it was. I'd have to cast something bigger to figure it out, or I could just bloody text her at camp." His sigh was heavy as he dropped the card back into the register. "I tried to teach you both the rules. Apparently you pay more attention than my daughter. First she does *that*."

"I am not a *that*. I am a cat!" And to prove his point, Nation reached out and knocked a jar of polished stones from the counter to scatter on the floor at Marjorie's feet.

"Now she's casting some glamour on gift cards to make her teacher do something or other."

Marjorie bent over, scooped the rocks back into their jar, and placed a nice piece of rose quartz in front of Thomas. "I don't think she meant any harm. She never does. Nate is here because she loves him. If she did a spell to make her pretty teacher—her pretty gay teacher—come to the shop to talk to her pretty gay dad, is that such a bad thing?"

"It's meddling. I can't approve of meddling," he said as he moved to help pick up the last of Nation's mess. "I'd rather not dwell on it. I have a date to prepare for in twenty-four hours, and I'm horribly out of practice."

AFTER BIDDING Marjorie good night, Thomas followed Nation up the steps to his house. It was warm in spots and too cold in others. The building was old, and it didn't have very good air-conditioning, just the spare vents they could afford when it was installed in the shop. He thought about upgrading it every time there was a Santa Ana wind, but he never got around to even doing research on it. As long as it worked downstairs and almost worked upstairs, they'd live. The heat, on the other hand, worked great for what passed as winter in San Diego.

Nation sat like an Egyptian statue near his bowl on the kitchen counter, sleek and stoic, never blinking while he waited for his food. It was the only time the undead cat was quiet, which was another flaw in his resurrection. The old furry version of Nate demanded his food with a yowl you could hear from Peru. But not Nation. For him a good glare was more than enough.

"Of course, Your Worship," Thomas said as he pulled the lid from a can of food that declared it was turkey, tuna, and egg. "This smells like skunk. You'll probably love it."

"I do. It is my favorite."

"Yes, until I buy more than four cans of it and you decide you don't like it anymore." He tapped the edge of the can on the bowl and was thankful none of the stinky goop got on his fingers or his clothes. He wanted a shower, not to feel the need to open a fire hydrant to get the nastiness off.

"Contrary," Nation said around a mouthful, "thy name is cat."

"Thy name is pain in the ass," Thomas told him as he headed toward his bedroom, where he toed off his shoes, fell back onto the queen-size bed, and stared up at the ceiling, which was covered in celestial images from his favorite tarot cards. It was cliché, but he liked it. It didn't hurt that there were protection spells mixed into the paint. No magic but his own unless he allowed it in there, which meant Nation avoided the room like the plague. Last time he'd romped through, the edge of one ear had curled up like an old artichoke leaf, and Star was terrified he'd lost a toe. Thomas agreed to set the wards to allow Nation in, but the cat was still wary of his room, which was just fine with him.

Star, hope the trip was good. Mr. Beshter came to spend his gift card today.

Hey Dad! I managed not to puke on the drive. Thanks for the ginger candy! Mr. B is cool. Wish I'd seen him.

He was sorry he missed you too. Star, there was magic on the card, and I know it was yours.

Just wanted to make sure he didn't lose it. He told us he lost almost $100 from Starbucks last summer.

That makes sense. I will check in with you tomorrow before I go on my date. Goodnight sweetheart. Love you.

DATE!!! You better tell me everything. Love you, Daddy.

It made sense. KJ didn't seem to be the most organized person. In fact, the impression Thomas had been trying to figure out seemed to radiate loss of something—not loss of someone—which made him even more curious about the teacher. The pretty teacher. The teacher that had been touched by the supernatural.

"I should not be thinking like this," he said to the painting of the Sun. "What if he senses something? I mean, I know there are normals who know it's real, and he thinks it is. But I've never been the one to break the Silence." The Silence was the unspoken rule that kept the supernaturals from lording it over the normals and vice versa. There were more normals than supernaturals, and by sheer numbers alone, they'd win any war. The lives lost would be astronomical, and while humanity was becoming more humane, the Council didn't trust them in general. Neither did Thomas.

But there were the rare ones, the normals who were touched by the supernatural and were drawn to it, and he knew in his gut that's what KJ Beshter was. He'd seen or touched something in his past, and Thomas was dead set on finding out what it was before he let himself fantasize about anything else. If this turned out to be matchmaking by

Star, she'd be very disappointed to find out that it would go nowhere very, very fast.

Thomas would be disappointed too. He'd told Star he needed alone time, and Nation hadn't been wrong when he'd chimed in that Thomas needed to get laid—not that he'd have put it so crudely. If KJ hadn't tasted of magic, would he be as cautious? Probably not. A normal normal was fair game. He'd have a good time with him and then say goodbye a few days later.

But if something happened with Beshter, he couldn't bid him a graceful adieu unless it really went south. He was important to Star, even if he wasn't her teacher anymore, and Thomas liked his first and second impressions of the man. He just wished it didn't terrify him that the third time might be the charm. They might click, and then everything would get more complicated.

His thoughts were deep compared to his wandering hands. While thinking of KJ, he'd unbuttoned his shirt, letting the last of the sunlight touch his bared chest, and brushed his fingers along his skin to the patch of hair that barely covered the space between his navel and the waistband of his pants. Slipping his fingers beneath the band, he thumbed the button at the top free and then encouraged the zipper down.

Between wiggling and shimmying, he managed to get his pants and underwear off his rump and halfway down his thighs with one hand while he wrapped his fingers around his cock. A quick glance at the bedroom door told him he hadn't forgotten to shut it, and he let out a sound that was a mix of a sigh and a moan as he began slowly stroking at himself. Thomas tried not to think about Beshter while he tightened his grip, but the teacher's amber-flecked green eyes were locked in his mind.

KJ was also a much better thing to focus on than Nation watching him masturbate. It'd happened before, and it cost him in ahi to keep the cat's mouth shut about it. Everyone did it. But they didn't need to know that he did it!

Thomas bit his bottom lip to keep from making more noise. His groin tightened and his nerves fired. He was almost panting as he breathed, and in his mind's eye it wasn't his own hand on him, it was KJ's. And KJ was very good at what he was doing.

SEVEN

WITH A cold bottle of beer in each hand, David plopped onto the couch while KJ divvied up the sushi DoorDash had just delivered. Using chopsticks with the skills of a ninja, he separated the eel rolls that had stuck together in their little Styrofoam container and placed half on the lid he'd torn free from the box along with half a lump of wasabi and a clump of pickled ginger. He didn't need to ask David if he wanted it all in the lid. They'd had enough sushi nights to never need to ask how to serve the food or what to order.

"How do you eat that?" David's nose wrinkled as KJ moved his Philly rolls into the bottom half he was going to use as his plate. "It's got cream cheese. There is no cream cheese in Japan."

"With my tongue and mad chopsticks skills, dude." To show his point, KJ popped one piece into his mouth and chewed it slowly before putting David's spicy tuna and crunchy rolls into his quasi-plate. "There you go, brother, friend of mine. Eat some and I'll give you your presents."

"Oh, presents! You shouldn't have." David took the lid and balanced it on his knees as he opened his own cheap paper-wrapped chopsticks. He frowned when they broke badly, and KJ shrugged. "Why do yours always come out perfect?"

"Because the chopstick fairy loves me." KJ slid onto the floor in front of the sofa. It was too hot to sit near David, who radiated heat no matter the weather. Good to sit near in winter; not so much in summer. He made a great show of dipping his cream cheese and salmon sushi into his wasabi and hummed yummy noises while he chewed. "It's so good. Have you ever even tried it?"

"Haters gotta hate, KJ." He poked one of his pieces with the chopstick like it was a knife and shoved it in his mouth.

"Barbarian. That's why you can't break them right. You can't even eat with them."

"Whatever." David's next piece went into his mouth using his fingers, and so did all the rest until the lid was as empty as his bottle of beer. "Can I open my presents now, Mom?"

"Yes, dear," KJ said, using his best imitation of David's mom's voice, with her Texas drawl and all. "But first, you help me clean up this mess, and then you can have your presents. There's even pie in the fridge for later."

"Pie instead of cake!" David bent over to gather their trash and kissed the top of KJ's head before he could get up. "Dude, it's times like this that I really wish we were into each other. You'd be the perfect boyfriend."

"I know, and I love you too. But we tried and it was fail." KJ leaned on the coffee table to get to his feet and headed for his bedroom to get the presents from Target. He stopped at the bathroom long enough to wash his hands, and then raked his damp fingers through his hair.

He brought both the gifts from Target and the bag from Equinox. He didn't know whether to give the goddess stuff to David or not. He'd wait to see if he liked it, and if he did, KJ could always go to the shop to buy more. Unless the date went really bad, in which case it was okay, since he'd only paid a few bucks of his own money.

"Here you go," he said, trading the Mylar-wrapped presents for a fresh bottle of beer and a slice of pie. KJ climbed into his usual corner of the old brown leather sofa and balanced his pie on his knee. "If you already have 'em, we can swap them. I kept the receipt. They're supposed to be exclusives, but I know what a toy junkie you are."

"Just because you decided to grow up doesn't mean I have to." David popped the ribbon on the gift bag and pulled the two Pops! free. Both were painted in bright red chrome, which marked them as much as the little Target on the label. "Dude, these are so cool. I don't have any of the Target ones. Tony looks sweet in red. Carol does too." With much more care than he'd used on the ribbon, he took Iron Man out of his box and held him up to the light. "I am Iron Man."

"Do not take me to a dark place, David. I'm not over it yet." One would expect that with KJ's fascination with magic, Doctor Strange would be KJ's Avenger of choice, but it was the genius billionaire playboy philanthropist who got to him. It didn't hurt that RDJ was on the top of his "celebrities I'd like to get naked with" list.

"What's in the other bag?" David reached for the other bag, and KJ let him have it. "You went to Equinox?"

"I had a gift card from one of my students. Her dad owns the place. I bought a few things with it. If you like them, you can have them." KJ had to take a bite of his pie to keep from snatching the bag from his friend. *What the fuck is up with that? Yes, Thomas is beautiful, but you do have a date with him. Chill.*

"I've been meaning to stop there, but it's easier to buy everything in life from Amazon." David had taken the other end of the couch, and he spent a minute or two unwrapping the candleholders and goddess figure. "These are nice. Not really my style. You thinking about setting up an altar?"

"I have a few times over the years, to be honest. I was mostly killing time before meeting you, and by the time Thomas and I talked about Star...."

"Thomas, is it? Not Mr. Whatever?" David leaned forward and set them on the coffee table in a safe place before propping his feet on it to dig into his pie. "You said you had a date tomorrow. Did you make a date with him? Dude, she's your student."

"She *was* my student. I teach junior year history. I don't teach senior. That means it's not against my personal code or whatever rules the school district might have, because God knows they probably do have rules like that. And he's really pretty. Also, he said yes."

David let out a snort. "KJ, hate to tell you, but you're pretty too. People don't turn you down often. You just don't ask enough people out."

"It's too hard to avoid your leftovers, and we don't live in a small town. You never went out with him, right? Thomas Anders?"

"Puppy-dog eyes wouldn't help if I did, you know. Nope, don't think so. I'd be too worried he'd cast some spell on me when we broke up because I'm not a commitment kind of guy. Love and leave 'em."

"You're not that bad. There was that Marine from Pendleton you almost moved in with." He'd been a nice guy, one of the few David had him meet in person, which meant he was serious about him.

"Long distance after he got transferred didn't work. Totally my bad, not him. I'm not good at monogamy—especially when I'm being deprived by thousands of miles and a few oceans. I am a bad boyfriend."

KJ licked his lips after finishing his pie and set the plate on the side table. Then he thought better of that and got up to take both their plates to the sink before either of them got an elbow or a foot covered in apple pie goop. "I have noticed your inability to keep little David in your pants."

"I'm just doing my part for both of us. So do you like him? Thomas?"

"There was something about him that felt familiar. I met him before on a parents' night, and he seemed nice and unapproachable. Now it's different. There was literally a spark when I handed him the card."

"Sounds like mojo to me. Maybe Thomas Anders has the answers, and we can skip spending nights in haunted death traps. Speaking of which, we should check the footage if we've got any."

KJ sat back down, turning toward David with his tablet across his lap while he tapped on the app that should let them see what the cameras were seeing. The images were grainy, which was to be expected. Pretty much any low-price night-vision camera was going to take crappy pictures, but they had to make do with what they could afford. It wasn't as if they could leave David's baby in the woods. They'd be using it on the solstice when they watched for something to happen.

"Usual garbage, although it's not as bad as I thought." He tapped on one of the cameras that had caught some movement and was rewarded with the sight of a raccoon hanging upside down in a trash can, fishing out a crumpled box from Popeyes Chicken. "Trash panda's got good taste. We should go there and get sandwiches when we go to the park."

KJ switched from one camera to the next and let out a disappointed sigh. "Well, that sucks. I didn't say anything earlier, but I saw her, the Lady in White. She was near one of the trees where I planted a camera, and that's not all. There was black wax where a candle had been burned to nothing."

"How could you not tell me about that!" David hit him with one of the small throw pillows. "Why does the good shit never happen when I'm with you?"

"Maybe you're antimagic and I'm quasi-magic?" KJ had no idea why it happened. "I just wish the camera had caught her. But it wasn't

aimed in the right direction, or she doesn't film. I was too excited to tell."
He decided not to tell David about her warning or the cold feeling in his
gut. He'd had them before, and nothing came of it. No reason to freak
his friend out too.

EIGHT

THOMAS DIDN'T feel guilty for his fantasy about the teacher. He reasoned that it wasn't any different than thinking about someone you saw on the street or a celebrity who pushed your buttons. It was perfectly normal. Just because you knew someone's name didn't make imagining them licking your balls a bad thing.

"Twenty-four hours, Thomas," he scolded himself as he cranked up the shower, setting the temperature more than a little colder than was his practice. "You can hold off on dirty thoughts for a day." He took the soap and begin lathering his crotch. "And enough out of you until tomorrow too. Now be good, or I'm shutting off the hot water."

A BIT later than he'd planned, and Thomas was lacing up his high-tops and zipping up his jeans. He tugged a long-sleeved, lightweight pullover on and then looped a stuffed-to-the-brim messenger bag across his body. He popped open the bedroom door, careful not to step on Nation's paws where they were reaching through the crack to get his attention.

"Why do you do that?" he said, looking down at the sprawling furless feline. "You're not a cat anymore."

"I like to stick to the classics, Tom." Nation got up and stretched. His back seemed to arch one bone at a time from his shoulders through his tail, and then he flicked said tail at Thomas. "My brain might not be cat... exactly... but look at me. I need to attempt the cute card."

"Good luck with that." Thomas bent down and scooped Nation into his arms, propping his head over his shoulder. "Do you know where your carrier is?"

"I thought you were my carrier?"

"Not in the car, I'm not. We've got a meeting tonight, and then we're going to do a small patrol." Thomas leaned to one side, balancing his bag and Nation while shoving his keys into the pocket of his faded jeans. "I know you hate it, but if we're in an accident, you'll be safer in it."

"We're both pretty sure I can't die," the cat pointed out as he let the tips of his claws sink into Thomas's shoulders lightly enough to possibly be an accident, which Thomas doubted.

"Probably not, but I don't want to explain to anyone why you're not. Nor do I want you clawing me up in a panic if something were to go wrong. So stop arguing and tell me where it is. The sooner we're out of here, hopefully the gods and goddesses willing, the sooner we can get out of the meeting."

"Fine. Star put it in the pantry, and I promise not to fight going into it if you let me pick the music."

NATION WAS balanced on his shoulder like a proper cat when he entered the Sylvester Pattie Tower, also known as the Witches Tower, in Presidio Park. At the start of the 1800s, the adobe-covered building was old and had originally been a prison for eight lost adventurers who were suspected spies. It was a nearly forgotten part of the city park, with few visitors, but well maintained, and it was a perfect place for the district meetings of the Council of Mages, who had enough members on the city council to keep hold of the location for generations to come.

"Hello," he said with a bow of his head as he took his usual seat at the table after placing Nation on the left armrest. "Sorry if we're a tad late. Got Star off to camp this morning, and I haven't caught up yet."

"Don't worry, Thomas," their leader, Dave Milton, said from the head of the table. He was dressed in casual clothes like Thomas, while the other two were fresh from their day jobs, which required suits. "You're still here before Armando."

"Everyone is always here before Armando," said Lea from her seat. Her familiar, a small masked ferret, was curled around her arm and playing with her bracelet. "How are you and Nate?"

"I'm fine," Nation answered for himself. "He made me ride in the carrier."

"Yes, I'm a horrible person." Thomas decided not to roll his eyes. "Be thankful yours don't talk."

"I am on a daily basis," Dave said, petting the ebony cat at his side. "But then we didn't have to get special dispensation for ours either. Are you going to hand him off to Star when she passes her tests?"

"More than likely," Thomas answered, absentmindedly rubbing his thumb between Nation's ears. "He was hers to begin with, and technically he's not a proper familiar." By a miracle Nation didn't tell him to screw himself, or bite him, but he was fairly certain he heard the words in his head. "I took him to keep him in the family after the accident since she was so young."

"You'll miss me," Nation said with a shrug before jumping from the chair and heading for the door with his head and tail held high. "I'll be on the tower."

Thomas knew he'd miss him, not that he'd admit it. Having a sentient semi-immortal demon slash imp or whatever he was for a familiar had been very helpful, but he hadn't been his cat to begin with, and it was Star's power that brought him back to life. Thomas knew he was a placeholder for the creature and hoped his guidance over the years would keep both of them out of trouble once they were bound together. As much as he bitched—or they bitched at each other—Thomas wasn't looking forward to settling for a normal animal companion.

Once Armando arrived in a fluster of excuses they'd all heard before, the Council got down to business. Dave listed off the hot spots for the coming Solstice, and each member listed the problems they'd handled over the past month. It wasn't a formal meeting by any means. Those were only held when required, when they had to show off, or when the Council had to hold a tribunal over another mage in the county. Then they'd dress the part, cast wards, and do whatever was necessary for the greater good.

"I'll be patrolling Pioneer Park this year," Thomas told them. "There's some very dark energy coming from there this summer. I felt the clouds a few days ago, and a scrying spell said that's where the problem is."

"Better than running all over the city," Lea offered. "I ran myself ragged covering for you last year before they gave me North County."

"Depending on the activities this year," Dave said, "we should probably look into training apprentices for backup. There are millions of people living here now. Five people can't be expected to cover the entire county—not anymore."

THOMAS CLIMBED the exterior steps to the top of the building. It wasn't much of a tower, maybe fifteen feet from the ground, but he hadn't been the one to name the old building. He stepped carefully across the pentagram tiled into the rooftop to where Nation was sitting on the waist-high railing, watching moths drawn to the lights. "Did you get your quarterly warning about me?" the cat asked.

"Of course. It's gotten to be part of the ritual after all these years. I don't even bother to protest anymore that if you were dangerous to us, you'd have done whatever evil you have planned years ago." He moved to lean on his hands next to Nation after he unslung his bag to rest it by his feet. "I mean evil besides being a general pain in the ass."

"Well, I am sort of a cat. I'm also practically powerless in this body, and if I wasn't to be trusted, you wouldn't know my true name."

"Unless you lied about it to begin with." Which Thomas doubted. They'd had a very serious conversation when he'd returned to San Diego to a storm of chaos in the shop and his home caused by his seven-year-old daughter and Nation's return from the dead. The cat had been quite gracious—unlike his current behavior—when he'd sworn to protect Star and given Thomas his true name. Thomas could barely pronounce it, but it still held power over the cat, unlike his common names of Nate and Nation.

"So true." Nation twisted around and rubbed his head on Thomas's elbow, letting out a purr. "Anything interesting going on with the powers that be?"

"They voted to allow us to pick apprentices or deputies to help with the patrols, which would be nice. This isn't the same colony my family came to watch over when the Spaniards were finished with the tribes." That was a part of history mirrored all over California—and the rest of the United States, for that matter—but the best he could think about that was he hoped humanity would learn to treat each other better someday.

"Be nice if you and the family could vacation together, and Star'll be on the roster too." Nation stretched until his front paws were on Thomas's shoulder and met his eyes. "I'll take care of her like I do you."

"I know you will. You love her," he said, scratching the hairless skin between Nation's ears. "Come along, beastie. We need to do a little patrol. I can smell something to the east. Don't know what it is, but I don't like it."

THOMAS WAS winding his way out of Mission Hills, where the streets were lined with old Victorian and Craftsman houses. They were lovely, and he often wondered if he couldn't close up the shop and buy a real house for the family. The online business could be run out of a spare bedroom or basement, since most of the houses were too old to have much in the way of garages, but it'd be hard to let the shop go. It might not be as old as the century-old homes in the area, but it had still been around for decades.

"I feel something," Nation said from inside the carrier. He'd hooked his claws on the bars and had his nose pressed through the grate like a deranged hamster. "Smells bad. Let me out."

"Let me pull over." There weren't many parking places in this part of town either, and it took him a couple of short city blocks to find a bank with a small lot. The driveways had chains across to keep anyone from using the precious parking spaces within, so Thomas parked across the driveway. If anyone said anything, he'd have Nation pretend to be sick.

He popped the latch on the carrier and let the cat out. Nation's eyes were glowing with an internal light. He sat on his haunches in the seat and then jumped onto the dashboard, where he had to crouch, his whiskers twitching as he sniffed. "Head down the big street that goes east."

"Guessing that means El Cajon," Thomas said as he restarted the Lexus and pulled back onto the street. He turned right to a lighted intersection that would head them in the right direction. He reached for the carrier and knocked it onto the floor. "University or Washington. I'll work from one toward the other. Get back on the seat. Tell me when I'm getting close."

Having a cat—sentient or not—give him directions was a challenge Thomas could live without repeating any time soon, but eventually they ended up on El Cajon Blvd, heading east. He kept expecting Nation to tell him to turn north once more, but he didn't. Instead they ended up at a boarded-up video rental store that was close enough to McDonald's to make him want fries.

"At least the parking lot's empty," he said as he pulled in and parked. Now he could feel the touch of darkness that Nation somehow caught on the wind. The hairs on his arms and the back of his neck prickled. He opened the car door, letting Nation out, and reached for his bag. "Any idea what you sensed?"

"Nope, sorry." He might not have known what they were facing, but it didn't slow Nation down. He took off like lightning toward the back side of the store, and Thomas had to rush to keep up.

"Wait," Thomas hissed when they came around the corner. The narrow alley behind the store where deliveries would've been made stank, which wasn't a surprise, but it wasn't the typical stench of wet garbage and piss one normally found. It reeked of death.

"Here." Nation was pawing at a broken rear door that was hanging on one hinge.

"I never would have guessed." Thomas's voice dripped with sarcasm as he pulled a long-bladed dagger from his bag. The blade was etched in runes that had been filled with iron and silver—both were known to cause considerable pain to many supernatural creatures. He wedged one leg through the opening, leaving Nation enough room to move before him. "Smells worse on the inside."

Thomas cast a small spell, making what was left of the ceiling tiles glow with a pale blue light. The store was in ruins, displays shattered, and what videos had been left behind were tangled everywhere. "Gremlins, I think," Nation said.

When half a dozen creatures the size of bull terriers poured out of one of the broken air-conditioning ducts, small batlike wings flapping as they hit the ground running while venom dripped from their snaggletoothed jaws, Nation was proved correct. "Lovely."

NINE

TEXTING WAS easier than a phone call. No one could hear if you got the giggles or if anything else embarrassing happened. It also meant that KJ wouldn't accidentally wake up David, who'd crashed on his couch after they got stupid and decided to finish off an old bottle of Cuervo instead of just drinking the beer he'd bought to celebrate. Texting was also easier when you had a slight—yeah, right—hangover.

Thomas, do you know where you'd like to go for dinner tonight?
That would help, wouldn't it?

KJ had no trouble picturing Thomas in a button-down shirt behind the counter at his shop, looking like a hot librarian, and he prayed that Thomas wasn't picturing him sprawled in an unmade bed wearing nothing but his underwear. *Wait a second, there is nothing wrong with that at all.*

Any food allergies? Vegan-ness? No booze?
Shellfish are not my friends. Not vegetarian nor vegan. Booze is also OK.
How about a brewery? We can get food, good beer?
Wonderful, there's a small pub on Adams that I'm fond of.
Small is good. Far from the colleges is good too. 7:30?
I'll see you there.

"Have you made your date?" David asked from the doorway. His hair was defying gravity on one side and matted on the other, and he was squinting against the sunlight filtering into KJ's bedroom. "Also, I can't find the spare toothbrush that's mine."

"I have made my date. There's a new toothbrush in the second drawer. Take your pick. I found your last one on the floor."

"And because you love me, you tossed it. You are the best, best friend," David said as he turned around to slip into the bathroom. "Dude! These are kids' toothbrushes! You are awesome!"

"Haven't I proven that shopping for you is the same as shopping for a ten-year-old?" KJ grumbled as he rolled out of bed and went to stand in front of his closet. It was better organized than most, which wasn't hard. There were work clothes on the rack, including a special door hanger for his ties, and a small hanging shelf with his jeans. Everything else he wore was in his dresser, which was mostly T-shirts, but he didn't want to wear some anime or TV show shirt to his first date.

"Why am I so boring? Why don't I buy myself some going-out clothes?" He let out a sigh and started moving his mostly pale white, off-white, and gray shirts along the rack. His shirts were nice but nothing exciting. He left that for his ties. Some were very weird since they'd been gifts from his students, but he loved those most of all.

When he finally reached the deep, dark, far corner of the closet, he found a jade green polo shirt. There was no logo on the chest— thank God—so it couldn't be dated. It probably fit. He hoped it'd fit, since he couldn't remember when he got it or if he'd ever worn it. It might've been a gift? After pulling it out along with one of his better pairs of jeans, he stood in front of the standing mirror he had tucked in the corner to see how it looked and decided it'd be fine. And if it wasn't, he had hours to go shopping for something else. *Shopping two days in a row! God help me!*

THOMAS HELD his right arm across the counter while Marjorie wrapped a fresh roll of gauze over the bite he'd gotten from one of the gremlins the night before. The balm he'd had her apply was taking the sting from the wound and drawing out any venom that was still in his system.

"Really, Thomas?" she said with a smirk as she pulled the bandage tight. "Trying to lose your hand to get the summer off?"

"Very funny. Nation and I were caught by surprise. He was too fast to get hurt, and I got most of the poison off myself. I'm just not very good at wrapping up like a mummy on my own," he told her before taking his arm back to text the flexibility of her work.

"And I don't have thumbs," Nation said as he hopped onto the counter. "I got one of its eyes, though. Then it got away while Thomas was bleeding."

"It got away because you were licking the eye gunk from your paws."

"It was disgusting! Do you have any idea how sensitive cat toes are?"

Thomas snorted and started clearing up the medical supplies before dropping sugar cubes into his tea. He took a deep breath, savoring the aroma of the Earl Grey, and narrowed his eyes at Nation. "Bullshit. You were licking it off your toes because you liked how it tasted."

"Do you two mind?" Marjorie said as she looked at her breakfast burrito like it came from a dumpster. "I'm trying to eat here. It's time to open, and you either need to go upstairs or stop talking, mister."

"Fine." Nation jumped off the counter, tail held straight up like a mast, and sauntered up the stairs. "Be glad I can't cough up a hair ball anymore."

"On a daily basis." He let out a sigh, tilted his head back, and rolled his shoulders. Their bickering was what they did, but there were days when he wasn't in the mood. "Running into a nest last night was the last thing I wanted to do, next to going to a Council meeting. I must've been distracted."

"You have a date. That's exciting, and you'll probably be healed enough to go without the bandage by then. I'm only a little witch, but I can taste the power of the balm you whipped up. You're amazing, Thomas, and I'm not just saying that because you pay me. But it helps." She finished off her breakfast and then took their dishes upstairs, leaving Thomas to turn over the Open sign and unlock the doors.

"Between you and the damned cat," he tossed over his shoulder, "I don't miss the snarky teenager at all." Which was a huge lie.

KJ ENDED up parking around the block from the brewery. It wasn't very big, and this part of San Diego was too old to have good parking—you had to head into Mission Valley or newer suburbs to find a proper parking lot—but it was a nice night, and he didn't mind. He looked around for Thomas's car and then realized he didn't know what the man drove. Somehow he doubted it was a minivan wrapped in the Equinox logo with a glittery star at the end of each windshield wiper.

"Hey," he said when he came around the corner and saw Thomas climbing out of the passenger seat of someone's car. "I see we've got perfect timing."

"So it would seem," Thomas answered as he shut the car door, and KJ caught the driver, the woman he'd seen working at Equinox, give a thumbs-up. Thomas was wearing a lightweight dark blue pullover and khakis. KJ thought he looked great and debated telling Thomas that he approved.

"Sorry, she's very excited that I'm out and about."

"That's what friends are for. My friend David was thrilled I was going on an actual date. You'd think we were monks or something." KJ stepped beside Thomas, once again happy they weren't too different in height. No awkwardness there if one thing led to another, which would be a very nice way to end an evening.

"We're lucky Star's not here," Thomas said with a snort. "I wouldn't have had a moment's peace. She texted me about you three times today. You have a fan."

"It's only fair," KJ said as he pulled open the door to the brewery. "I am a pretty big fan of hers too. You've raised one hell of a young woman. There's nothing she can't do if she sets her mind to it."

"You have no idea."

They waited a few moments and then were led to a nice table on the outside terrace and sat down. The waiter handed them a menu of the beers they made on-site and said he'd be back in a few minutes to take their orders. KJ noted that even though the waiter was cute, Thomas didn't check him out as he walked away, which was a very nice sign.

"Any suggestions?" he asked, leaning closer to Thomas and tipping the menu toward him.

"I actually like their pear cider. It's not for everyone. Their golden amber's very nice, though. It may have ruined me for any other beer."

"You're not much of a beer guy, then?"

"Not really, to be honest. But I like the cider. I love the food, and it's a very lovely evening." Thomas offered him a warm smile that made the corners of his eyes crinkle a little bit. "My company's also quite nice."

"Thanks. Pretty sure you just made me blush," KJ said as his face warmed.

"There's no 'pretty sure' about it." Thomas's smile grew brighter, and he offered KJ the food menu. "It's all good. I'm going for the mushroom-smothered swiss burger with fries. Like I told you, I am not a vegetarian."

"That sounds great. I think I'll get that too."

THOMAS TOOK a long sip from the pear cider, enjoying the cold as it worked its way across his tongue, and then let out a blissful sigh, watching KJ while he tasted his beer. Out on the terrace, as the sky darkened, he could see more of the shimmer that he'd caught in the shop. There was definitely something special about Star's teacher, and it wasn't only that he was very cute.

Neither one of them was a skilled practitioner of social graces; that much was obvious. It was hard for Thomas to blend in with normals. He didn't do it outside of the shop often enough. He was simply too busy between being a dad, running the shop, and keeping San Diego safe from the things that went bump in the night.

"So tell me," he asked to break what was turning into an awkward silence between them, "how did a history teacher, with a PhD, for that matter, end up hosting a YouTube channel about the supernatural—especially on the side that thinks it's real?"

"I like to keep people guessing?" KJ said with a small laugh before pushing his glasses back up his nose. "With my education, I do read like someone who would think it was all bullshit, but maybe I am a sensitive like you asked at the shop…. I've always known it was real. When I was a kid, I'd have a dream about someone I hadn't seen for a long time, and then they'd show up. My mom stopped telling me that couldn't be true about the fourth time I got it right." He rubbed his thumb along the condensation on his mug, and Thomas could see he was trying to decide how much he could say without looking crazy.

"I know it's real, KJ," Thomas told him dead seriously, meeting his eyes over the rim of his own mug before taking another sip. "And that's not something I'd tell just anyone, but I feel like you need to hear that from me, which is not how I normally handle this sort of situation."

"You mean first dates?"

"Gods no, I've never... not like this." He set his bottle down when the waiter returned with their burgers balanced along his arm and placed them in front of them. "Good thing you're not a reporter."

"No, but I do have my channel. Not that I'm going to blast you all over it." They lapsed into silence once more as they sank into their meals. Thomas cut his burger in half while KJ fought with the entire thing. He closed his eyes and licked his lips. "Damn, there is nothing like a good bar burger. Thanks for picking this place."

"My pleasure." Thomas wiped his fingers clean and then reached across the table to catch a dab of ketchup from KJ's chin. It was forward, but Thomas was in no mood to play it safe. He only had two weeks to squeeze in some personal time, and if that time was spent with KJ Beshter, that was fine with him. But when KJ seemed to be lost after watching Thomas lick the bit of ketchup off his thumb, Thomas began to worry he'd broken the poor man. Instead of saying he was sorry, which he wasn't, he decided it'd be best to get them talking once more. "Did you notice anything odd at my shop?"

KJ WAS glad when Thomas started talking again, even if it was to ask him a question. He was buzzing, and it wasn't from the beer. He'd drunk half of a mug, and it took a lot more than that to get to him.

It might've been Thomas's company. The man pushed all his typical physical buttons. Tall, broad shoulders, but not overly muscled. He wasn't lanky. He was more a swimmer or martial artist—not like the jogger from the park that morning who needed to look good. The buzz was probably because Thomas believed in the supernatural. He'd been told that before. Hell, David believed, but this was different. Thomas Anders was magical. KJ could taste it!

"I noticed there was an aura on some of the stock. It wasn't always there, and it's hard to tell that time of day. There was so much sun coming in, making the dust motes dance, and who's to say some of them didn't have tiny little wings and faces, right?" He leaned closer toward Thomas to make sure no one overheard him. "I also noticed that the things I bought had a shimmer to them, and so did the gift card, but that went away after you put them in the bag. When I got home, it was still gone. They were inert. Just ceramics from wherever."

"Oh, you are good." Thomas's eyes had widened, as had his smile. "You're definitely a sensitive. No one's taken the time to train you, have they?"

"Who'd do that? My mom sent me to therapy after I insisted I saw witches at Boy Scout camp for all of high school, and when I got to college, I stopped talking about it. I think the only person at the university who believed me, besides Dave, was the librarian. Not because I told him, but because I think he could see the old lady in the history section who hovered between the shelves too." KJ shivered and busied himself with some of the bacon from his burger. "Ghosts, I don't like. They're so lost or angry. I don't see them often, which is a good thing. I'm no Danny Torrance or the kid from *The Sixth Sense*. I've seen the Lady in White in Pioneer Park a couple of times over the years, but I've never managed to record her. Never been able to record any of them. Caught a few dishes flying once in a haunted house in Vegas, but that's about it."

"No one's trained you, and you've managed to believe without driving yourself insane. That is impressive, KJ." Thomas reached for his hand and brushed his fingers over the back of it before giving a supportive squeeze. It wasn't a romantic gesture as far as KJ could tell. Thomas was almost in teacher mode, which was an operating procedure KJ knew well. It'd been a very long time since anyone had shown him that kind of support, and it was the first time ever for the paranormal side of his life.

"Thanks." He smiled and decided not to move his hand away from Thomas's unless the other man moved first. Then he'd scramble and pretend it hadn't happened, but only if he had to. "I like to think I'm grounded. It probably helped that while I believe in the supernatural, I didn't let it become my obsession. It didn't distract me from studying history, and sure, my thesis might've been on the hidden wars between the Church and the witches... but I still got my doctorate. How 'bout you? You're a witch?"

"WHAT I am, and what Star has inherited from me, is complex. How you all see us isn't how we see ourselves. I put together spells. I mix potions, but I also have some abilities of my own." Now that the conversation moved to him, Thomas drew his hand back, once again picking up his mug, although there were barely dregs left. He needed to focus, decide on not only what he could tell KJ but whether he should. It wasn't forbidden to share the truth with trusted friends, and it wasn't unheard of to trust someone on sight.

He'd been drawn to KJ months before when they'd first met. Thomas knew he could be a good friend, if not more, and he hoped it would be far more. It was obvious that Star had spelled the gift card to force them together, which meant she believed in KJ Beshter a great deal. As much as Nation liked to think he was the most important person in her life, Thomas knew that he held that position, just as she did for him.

"My daughter is far more gifted than I am," he said, meeting KJ's gaze. "She spelled that card before she gave it to you, which I'll be talking to her about. She's not supposed to do that, and I'm disappointed she broke the house rules. But I'm not angry that she did it."

"Me neither, I guess. I liked you when I met you at the school. So it's not like that."

"No, no, if she'd broken that rule, we would not be on a date, and I'd be on my way to her camp to have one hell of a serious talk." Forcing emotions on another was considered dark magic even if the result was meant to be a good thing. One did not break the free will of another. Of course, one also didn't bring anyone or anything back from the dead, but since Nation was wearing Nate's skin, Thomas had managed to find a loophole to protect his daughter and her abomination.

"We can consider it lightly massaged kismet." Thomas shrugged and took the time to order them refills. They'd been talking so much he was surprised to find his plate empty. "Do you want to get dessert? I must admit to being an ice cream junkie. Pretty much do anything for a pint of New York Super Chunk Fudge or a trip to Coldstone's."

"Wow, you must really like me," KJ said with a bright laugh. "You told me your weakness. I, too, am a lover of ice cream. Why don't we finish our drinks, pay the bill, and I can drive us to the nearest Coldstone? We can talk more and enjoy the night."

"Excellent plan," Thomas said, tapping their mugs together in a toast to an enjoyable night. "Dinner's on me. Ice cream's on you."

TEN

KJ AIMED the Toyota down the narrow alley that ran behind Equinox, keeping an eye on the slightly leaning wooden fence on one side and the scattered dumpsters on the other. Between the dumpsters there were occasional cars, some nicer than others, or vans with company names painted on their sides.

"We're almost there," Thomas said as he shifted in the passenger seat to get his keys from his pocket without taking off his seat belt. "You can turn left after the next telephone pole and park behind my car."

"Okay," he said with a nod, not needing Thomas's directions at all because he could see a shimmering purple glow coming from just down the alley. It grew brighter as he drove them closer, and it was sparkling when he pulled in behind a sleek black Lexus. KJ shut off his car and then pulled his glasses off to wipe them with the front tail of his shirt. He knew it would help with the light show, but he wasn't sure if he should say something or not.

"Home sweet home," Thomas said, undoing his belt and unfolding from the seat as he got out of the small car. KJ watched him stretch, appreciating the brief glimpse of pale skin he was graced with when Thomas's pullover drew up from his waistband.

This was it. He took a few breaths and put his glasses back on before extracting himself from the driver's seat. He stretched too, although he doubted he was giving Thomas any kind of show with that. His shirt stayed down, and with the car between them, there wasn't much for the other man to see anyway.

"I could tell." He rubbed at the back of his neck and set the alarm on the car after they both closed their doors. "It looks like the Main Street Electrical Parade to me. It's even stronger than what I can see on you, which has been getting brighter all night."

Thomas shrugged as he started up the exterior steps that led to the outside entrance to the apartment. "Once we talked at dinner, I stopped

150

trying to block you. Didn't make much sense for me to waste the energy. You told me the truth, and I shared with you."

"And I appreciate it," KJ said as he took the steps behind Thomas, once again enjoying the view. "I like looking at you."

"Do you?" Thomas left his keys dangling in the lock, turned, and captured KJ's mouth in a kiss.

It wasn't awkward. It was fast, but it wasn't rushed. KJ could taste the chocolate from Thomas's ice cream on his lips. He was down a step from Thomas, and since he couldn't reach anyplace convenient on the man, he gripped the stair railing instead. Between the magic, the sugar rush, and the kiss, he was feeling a bit off-balance. "I like that too."

"Thought you might." Thomas turned his attention back to the door and popped it open, with KJ following closely behind.

The air inside the apartment was warm and smelled of spices. KJ blinked a couple of times to clear his vision, but it didn't help as much as he wanted it to. He had to pause, leaning against the doorframe after Thomas closed the door, and breathe. "Did you guys let a unicorn puke all over the place?"

"No, no unicorns, and the only one who pukes is the cat—not that he does it that often."

"Since he's hairless. I saw him in the window when I came shopping."

"You saw Nation?" Thomas got a look on his face that was not at all encouraging, unlike the other looks he'd been sending KJ's way all night.

He narrowed his eyes at Thomas with his hands tucked into his pockets. "He was in a sunbeam. He's not a ghost cat, is he?"

"Nope, not a ghost." Thomas stepped closer, took KJ's hands in his, and brought them to his lips to brush a kiss across his knuckles. "Is it too much for you? We can go to your place if it is."

"Naw," KJ said, his stomach fluttering with each word and touch Thomas graced him with. "I'll get used to it. I promise not to make up for the cat's lack of puke." *Way to go, KJ, ruin the mood.* "I can focus on you. Ignore the rest. You're what matters." The words were the truth. KJ had no idea how they'd connected so quickly, but he knew it felt right. If it took him years to get used to the unicorn sparkle vomit, he'd live with that. Being near Thomas in the middle of a small apartment kitchen felt like heaven.

"I don't know what it is about you, Thomas, but I need you in ways I can't wrap my brain around."

"We can blame the ice cream," Thomas said before capturing his mouth in a biting kiss. "You taste like cinnamon candy and waffle cones." His fingers hooked in the hem of KJ's shirt and he tugged upward, drawing it over his chest, shoulders, and head without dislodging KJ's glasses. "I want to know what you taste like other places too."

"That's something I'd like to find out too, but on you, not me." He was flustered, but since his hands were over his head, it seemed like the right time to run his fingers through Thomas's thick, wavy hair. "I'm not going anywhere tonight except where you take me, Thomas."

"Where we take each other." Thomas dropped KJ's green shirt on the kitchen table and then hooked one of his belt loops to lead him toward his bedroom. "I want to see what you can teach me."

THOMAS GENTLY tugged KJ toward his bedroom. They passed by the front room with its circular carpet that hid floorboards scratched by years of casting magic circles, as well as the scorch marks from a few errant candles. Nation's glowing eyes shone from the corner of the bay window, and the cat stretched on his side to twice his regular length, but much to Thomas's joy, he didn't get up or speak his opinion about the human in their midst.

"Thank you," Thomas mouthed in Nation's direction as KJ started working to take Thomas's shirt off. Nation shrugged and turned over to watch traffic, and Thomas reached down to help KJ. "Your fingers are cold."

"Are they?" KJ looked at Thomas's top, tossed it onto an old rocking chair, and then started to fumble with his belt. "I know how to warm them up."

"So do I, but not out here. I'd prefer not to entertain the cat on our first adventure."

"I like that you call it that." KJ's cool fingers traced a lazy circle over Thomas's skin, and he shivered. "An adventure."

"I know." Thomas wondered who'd made KJ so defensive. It seemed to be a habit of his to clarify what he meant or if he was joking.

He used his shoulder to push the door to his bedroom open, then stepped back to let KJ walk in. KJ's eyes widened as he took a good long look at the room, slowly walking around the large bed that dominated the space. Thomas noted where he locked his eyes and where he stopped, seeing KJ's untrained magical ability track almost every item or sigil of power in the room.

"Fuck," KJ said in a hushed whisper when his gaze was drawn to the tarot cards painted on the ceiling. "They move!"

"Do they?" That surprised Thomas. "My parents had them painted there before I was born. I've touched them and the wards they carry over the years, but I've never seen them move."

"It's their eyes. She's watching you," he said, pointing at the Empress. "The Knight of Swords is watching me. Should I be nervous?"

"You'll be fine." Thomas hoped. He seldom gave himself the time to enjoy a lover, and he couldn't remember the last time he'd brought one home. Strangers didn't come upstairs at Equinox. He'd had a hard time letting Star bring school friends over in case one of them saw and said too much, but they hadn't had any trouble. He knew how lonely it could be not to have friends welcome in your home. That was how he and his sister were raised.

"Mostly they're to protect the house and block magic that's not mine." He moved behind KJ and kissed one shoulder and then the other while wrapping his arms around his waist. "Which comes in handy when my sister or Star make a mistake."

"Oh, so the unicorn puke is their fault?" KJ relaxed against Thomas's chest, and Thomas breathed in the scent of him.

"Oh yes, very much so. My sister was a hellion growing up, and Star is tap-dancing in her footsteps." Thomas kept his mouth moving over KJ's body, a nip here and there, while he worked open KJ's pants. "I promise you, you're safe with me. No one and nothing will harm you."

"Promises are pretty big, Thomas. Shouldn't you be careful about that kind of thing?" KJ said, then gasped when Thomas pulled him tighter against him. "Magic binds with words too, according to my research."

"It does, but I don't think I'll have anything to regret." He turned KJ around until the backs of his legs were against the side of the bed and moved in front of him, never taking his hands off him. Once Thomas was sure KJ wasn't going to trip or lose his balance, he focused on undoing their jeans. "Let me take care of this. Kick off your shoes, and I'll get the rest. You can lean on me or the bed if you need to."

"Don't worry about me. I've done this before." KJ shifted, lifting one foot and then the other as he toed off his shoes. Thomas had already left his shoes behind someplace on their trip to the bedroom—one in the kitchen, the other in the front room. "But now it's my turn to promise—it'll be amazing, Thomas. Going to blow your mind and other things."

Thomas grinned up at KJ as he sank onto his knees in front of him and pushed his pants to his ankles. He trailed his long fingers over a tattoo spread over KJ's thigh. The ink was vivid but not fresh, showing red roses entwined around a compass. "That's pretty."

"Did it for my grandparents. She loved roses, and he gave me his WWII Army compass when I was a kid." KJ giggled when Thomas dabbed the tattoo with the tip of his tongue. "I lost it. Never told him it was gone because I didn't want to let him down. Used all my allowance that summer to buy a new one so he wouldn't know."

Thomas wasn't really listening to KJ's story. He was too interested in exploring his body with his hands to get the younger man's attention. The talking was great—getting to know each other was important—but Thomas was on his knees and peeling KJ's underwear down his hips and was starting to wonder if biting was required.

Settling on curling his tongue around the tip of KJ's cock, Thomas was pleased when all he heard was a gasp before KJ twined his fingers into Thomas's hair, which he took as the universal sign of approval. Humming to himself, he scooted an inch or so forward—there wasn't much more space between the two of them—and gave in to his curiosity about what KJ tasted like from the base to the end and then wrapped his mouth around him. He took his time, testing what KJ liked and what he didn't, until KJ's fingers tightened in his hair and Thomas could hear him.

"Going to make a mess."

"No, you're not," Thomas said quickly, gripping KJ with both hands on his hips to hold him as still as possible while he took him over the edge. He released his grip on KJ, letting him settle on the edge of the bed while he methodically—and, Thomas hoped, enjoyably—cleaned up any mess he might've missed.

"You okay?" Thomas asked as he got to his feet. He leaned over for a long kiss, sharing KJ's taste as their tongues tangled.

"Uh-huh."

Thomas let out a snort of laughter at KJ's eloquent reply and climbed onto the bed with him, hovering over him on the brightly colored satin quilt, and let out a moan of his own when his cock pressed against KJ's thigh. And a much louder one when KJ curled his fingers around him. "I should reciprocate."

"You could, or I could get a condom and lube out of the nightstand."

"I like that idea a lot. Why don't you do that?"

ELEVEN

KJ LISTENED to Thomas dozing beside him on Thomas's bed, watching the lights of a few cars shift over the ceiling as they went by. He rolled onto his side, brushing his fingers over Thomas's biceps in the dimly lit room, entranced by the sparkling magic trails he was leaving on his skin. The colors shifted from red to gold to blue and green before fading away. "Is that from you or me?"

Thomas's eyes opened a crack, and he watched KJ scribble. "Might be both. Never had that happen before."

"You should've seen your hair when you were on the floor." KJ started giggling and tucked his face against Thomas's chest until it passed. "Thought your hair was going to stick up like Doc Brown's."

"You're lucky I like movies, or I wouldn't get that." Thomas shifted slightly, pulling a thin blanket over them. "Are the cards still moving?"

"No, they stopped when you pushed me onto the bed, which is good, since I was afraid they'd watch us having sex." Not that KJ doubted he'd been watched before. He caught too many sparkles and shimmers from the corners of his eyes on a daily basis to think he was ever completely alone or anyplace was truly private, although other than the now-unmoving sigils on the ceiling, Thomas's room seemed to be devoid of anything alive or spooky. No fairies darted through the air, and there were no eyes reflecting in the shadows. "This is nice. Quieter than my place."

"If we go there next time, I'll bring some supplies, teach you how to seal off your home. I don't mind company out there, but I like my room to be mine and mine alone. Nation's not allowed in here thanks to the wards either."

"He's not normal, is he?" KJ had to ask about the cat. "Star told me he was special, and… yeah, there was a sunbeam on him, but he seemed… well, just weird. I can't describe it. I could see marks on him, but not when I looked for them. Also, why do you call him Nation when his name is Nathaniel?"

156

"I call him Nation because it's short for Abomination." Thomas rolled flat onto his back, pulling KJ along with him so he was sprawled across his chest. Thomas's dark eyes got a faraway look, and his forehead creased. KJ knew from his research that magic users didn't exactly tell the world about their business, and he was flattered he was hearing as much as he was.

It definitely meant Thomas liked him—a ton—which was great since he liked him too.

"I was away for the summer when Star was seven and still going by Estelle. Nathan slipped outside and got hit by a car. She found him in the middle of the alley." KJ could hear the sadness and guilt in Thomas's voice, and he hugged him, kissing his collarbone to hopefully make him feel better.

"He was gone. I don't know all the details. Jules told me she was devastated—horrified that it was her fault because she'd run off without making sure the door was shut. I hated that I was half the world away when she needed me. Her tears woke me up in the middle of the night, and when I called home, they were both crying when they talked to me. I promised to try to get home early, since they needed me." While he told the story, Thomas carded his fingers through KJ's hair, which wasn't making it easy for him to pay attention.

"Let me sit up a little. Actually, let me get us something to drink," he said and then laughed. "Like this is my house. Do you have any beer in the fridge, or a bottle of wine?"

"How about I get up and make us some tea?" Thomas offered. "We've still got a few hours until dawn, and I get by on very little sleep."

"And I'm off until August." KJ slid off the bed and gathered up his clothes.

"Unless you're planning on leaving right after," Thomas said as he pulled open a dresser drawer, "we're close enough to share pajama bottoms." He handed KJ a carefully folded pair in black or dark blue—it was impossible to tell in the dimly lit room. "Bathroom's right there. I'll use Star's and meet you in the sitting room or kitchen."

THOMAS RAN his finger over his teeth with a gob of toothpaste and then ran wet fingers through his hair. Tugging at the drawstring in a pair of red bottoms, he padded barefooted into the kitchen and filled the kettle. He set a tea chest with a variety of herbal and caffeinated teas on the table along with a bright gold package of instant Vietnamese coffee. He didn't drink it often enough to have a coffee maker, but sometimes tea did not give him the energy he needed. He also didn't know if KJ preferred leaf or bean. He pulled a couple of bottles of creamer from the fridge, one vanilla, the other hazelnut, to give KJ another choice.

He was pouring boiling water over an Earl Grey tea bag when KJ came in. His hair was sticking up, and Thomas would've had to be blind to miss the bite he'd left on his shoulder. "Sorry about that."

"This? 'Tis merely a flesh wound," KJ said with a sleepy smile, which grew brighter when he saw the coffee. "Hoping for one on the other shoulder so I can have a matching set, to be honest. Really liked how I got the first one, and thank you for this. I love this stuff." He tore open a coffee packet and dumped it into a mug, wrinkled his nose, and poured a second pouch in before adding water and leaving room for extra cream. "Sweet and strong enough to put hair on your chest—although that has yet to work for me."

While they were talking, Nation jumped onto one of the chairs and peered over the edge of the table. He tilted his head to the side, watching KJ intently, before glancing in Thomas's direction. "Does he know?" the cat asked.

"Jesus fucking Christ!" KJ jumped, nearly upending his coffee, and ended up with his back against the pantry door. "He talks!"

"I hadn't gotten that far in the story, Nation," Thomas said before grabbing a slice of American cheese from the fridge. He peeled off the wrapping and broke the slice into smaller pieces for Nation to have a treat. "I was telling him about Star and Jules finding you."

"Oh, not the good parts yet, then." He sat up, placing his front paws on the table, and chewed on a bit of the cheese. Looking over at KJ, he licked his lips. "Star told me about you, Beshter. She thinks you're amazing. So grab your coffee, get comfy, and Thomas can tell you the rest about me while I eat my treat."

Well, that could have gone better or a lot worse. Thomas decided snacks for the two of them would be a nice addition to their hot drinks and would also give KJ something tangible to hold on to while he shared more of Nation's story. He wouldn't tell him all of it, even if his gut told him KJ was not a short-term affair. They were drawn to each other physically, mentally, and apparently magically, which was a hell of a surprise. At the very least, he felt a need to teach the man how to cast a personal ward to protect himself.

By the time he joined KJ in the front room, Nation was leaning against him on the sofa. Thomas could see a small tremble in KJ's hands, making the surface of his barely tasted coffee ripple. He placed a plate covered in a selection of Girl Scout cookies he'd been hoarding since spring on the coffee table and settled into the other corner of the couch.

"Stop being an asshole, Nation. He's terrified of you," Thomas said as he bit into a Thin Mint.

"Not terrified. Freaked out, I'll give you." The other man shifted and reached for a couple of shortbread cookies and then settled back. Nation made no move to leave his chosen spot at KJ's side, but he did roll onto his back, offering his belly for a rub.

"Whatever you do, KJ, do not touch that. It's a trap."

"I was going to ask. My nana had a cat who would throw herself in your way and offer belly, and if you were stupid enough to fall for it, she'd snicker while you bled on the carpet." He bit into the cookie and then dabbed at the crumbs on his chest with a finger. "If you bite me, you get a coffee bath, which would be a crime, because I really need this right now."

"I do not bite without provocation," Nation informed KJ and then decided to snuggle alongside Thomas instead. "But I know when I'm not wanted."

"Really?" Thomas teased and then petted Nation's side with long strokes. Even after so many years, it felt strange to run his fingers over a hairless creature instead of the fluffball Nate had been. "That never seems to work for me."

"Don't be a dick, Thomas. You don't want Kevin-James judging you."

Kevin-James?

Thomas sat up, any further tales of Nation's life forgotten. He'd been looking at KJ all night, had thought about him most of his free time since he'd walked into the shop, but he'd not once wondered what the KJ stood for. He accepted it as his name, and after seeing the compass tattoo, he felt more than a little foolish.

"You know my name?" KJ wrinkled his nose and set his cup on the coffee table. "I haven't used it on anything but official documents since high school. Do you have magic Google or something?"

"Star knows all about you," Nation told him and then turned his attention to chewing on one of the toes on his back feet.

"Star," Thomas said with a sigh, as he scooped up Nation and set him on the floor, and then twisted in the seat to give KJ his full attention. "I am going to be having a very long talk with my daughter when she gets home. I'm sorry if you didn't mean for anyone to know it." He decided it'd be best not to tell KJ/Kevin-James about the power of true names for now, although there was considerable debate on which was your true name—the one your parents gave you or the one you gave yourself. Either way, he did not want KJ more spooked than he already was.

"You've had a lot to absorb since coming upstairs with me last night."

"THAT'S PUTTING it mildly." KJ felt vulnerable, which was not really a surprise. There was a sentient talking cat with glowing eyes licking between its legs across the room and a genuine warlock sitting on the couch. A pretty, very nice, and great in bed warlock, if he wanted to get technical, but he was overwhelmed. "This is so much bigger than the Lady in White talking to me last night."

"She did?" Thomas's eyebrows rose at that bit of information, but he didn't ask KJ to keep going.

"I find out it's all real. It's not my imagination. You're real. The cat's real. The Lady's real. Apparently Star did some digging to find what KJ stands for, not that I was keeping it a secret, but she still… well, I don't know how I feel about that. I'm just… I feel like I took a sip from a fire hose."

"I am sorry, KJ," Thomas said as he got up and stepped around the coffee table. "If Star was here, I'm sure we'd have all the answers, but not being entirely stupid, I think I know where she got the idea to put this in motion. Please don't leave while I get something from my bedroom.

I promise that if you want to go afterward, I won't stop you. But please give me another twenty minutes or so."

"I can't leave gracefully anyway," KJ said with his arms folded across his chest. "My clothes are in your room with my car keys. You've also been honest with me, so I can wait." To say nothing of how curious he was about whatever Thomas needed to show him. "I'll just drink my coffee and eat more cookies until you get back."

It didn't take Thomas long to return, but he brought KJ's clothes with him, neatly folded, and put them on the seat of the empty rocking chair. "This is not incentive for you to get out of my house. When you see this, you'll see that our story is a lot longer than either of us thought."

KJ nodded and took a couple of breaths to try to calm his nervousness. He hadn't had an anxiety attack in years, but he felt like one was trying to come out. "You don't look like an evil mastermind, even if you do have Mr. Bigglesworth's much smarter cousin."

"Good, you're still making jokes," Thomas said as he settled back in his seat. He held out his hand, showing KJ the compass he'd lost at Boy Scout camp all those years ago. "You are KJB. I've had this since the solstice when I was fifteen. When a lost Scout ended up at our ceremony."

"With your naked dancers and blue bonfire." KJ's fingers were shaking when he took the compass from Thomas's palm. It was warm from being in the warlock's hand, and KJ wrapped his grip around it tightly. "I got lost. I heard the chanting. No one believed me. I couldn't even find the place because they hustled me to the doctor and had my mom come get me. I thought I was crazy!"

"You weren't crazy. You dropped the compass when I tried to make you sleep. For some reason my spells didn't work on you. You weren't supposed to remember any of it. Something about you blocked what I was doing." Thomas looked embarrassed to admit his failure and flustered by the situation, which made KJ feel better. Flustered and embarrassed were two states he was good at, but it was obvious Thomas wasn't a frequent flyer.

"I don't remember very much. The chanting. The dancing. I thought there were creatures. There was a goddess—she had flowers in her hair—and she was nice to the boy—the naked boy—who caught me." He shifted his attention from Thomas to the compass, turning it over and over in his hands. The initials etched on the back were his and his grandfather's. Flashes of blue, purple, and green sparks danced over the bronze shell like they had when he'd touched Thomas earlier. When he popped it open, the needle spun about drunkenly until it came to a stop pointing at the warlock. "This is what it did when I tried to use it to find my way back. It stopped spinning when I saw the fire."

"That was my mother—the naked lady. She was one of the priestesses of our coven. I was the naked boy, and now it's my turn to blush for some reason, which is ridiculous considering we spent a few hours naked in my bed." Thomas reached across the small space between them to place his hand on KJ's wrist. "I didn't mean to steal it from you. I brought it into our camp while I got dressed to bring you back to yours and forgot it in our camper. We were on our way back to San Diego when I discovered it. I'm sorry."

KJ didn't draw away from Thomas's touch. Instead he put his other hand over Thomas's to hold him there. "I know people say stuff happens for a reason. It's looking like you and I were supposed to meet and be friends… or more."

"Of all the gin joints in all the world…." Nation quoted *Casablanca* from his perch in the window seat. "Star figured it all out, because she's the most powerful witch of her generation."

"She brought you back from the dead. Figured out I was the kid her dad met naked in the woods before she was born, and that we'd like each other. That's up there on the amazing scale." He could see the horizon brightening and gave Thomas's hands a squeeze. "I'm not running away, but I should go home. You need to open your shop, and I need to get ready for tonight's filming at Pioneer Park. Maybe finding you and the compass is a good sign and we'll finally get a ghost on camera, right?"

"It's possible. I've been feeling something coming for a week or so. Nation too." Thomas got up, and when KJ didn't step away, they shared a gentle kiss. "Would you mind some company tonight? If your Lady in White's warning is linked to what we've been sensing, you might need some help."

KJ nodded before gathering his clothes. "I wouldn't mind the company at all. David's a good guy, and if this keeps going, you'll have to meet him anyway. Why not meet him doing our favorite thing? Will Nation be coming too?"

"More than likely. But hopefully he'll refrain from talking in front of David. I don't mind if you tell him about me or Star, but Nation's situation is precarious."

"Yeah, not a problem. I'm going to get dressed, come back and give you a better kiss, and then head home. I'll text you later to set up where we can meet tonight."

There were three kisses before KJ climbed into his Toyota: one in the front room, another in the kitchen, and the last on the porch. The compass glowed the entire drive home.

TWELVE

KJ'D SLEPT until past nine and then spent hours going over every piece of information Thomas shared with him the night before. It wasn't as overwhelming as it had been at the time. He'd managed to absorb most of it, or he thought he had. Fortunately the compass had stopped sparkling by the time he woke up. It was sitting in the pouch of his hoodie, where he could rub his thumb over the engravings and play with the latch.

He'd talked to Thomas on the phone for the first time instead of texting, setting up plans to meet at Pioneer Park before sunset. Thomas had called, and it meant a lot to KJ that he'd done that. They were good together, and he didn't want to lose that.

A phone call with Thomas was one thing, but KJ didn't think it would do for David. He had too much to tell his best friend, and he was bouncing on the balls of his feet as he waited for David to answer his door. Five minutes later he let out a sigh and started sorting through his keys for the one that would let him in. The tiny bit of shade didn't keep him from the heat, but before he could shove the key into the lock, he heard David call out his name from behind him.

"You just scared the crap out of me," he said with a laugh. "I didn't know you were out."

David shrugged, coming up the walkway with his backpack slung over one shoulder. He was rumpled, which wasn't uncommon. Unless he was working or on a date, David wasn't a clotheshorse, but he had some dried pine needles caught in his hair to add to his unkempt appearance. "I didn't know you were coming. I went to check on the cameras, replacing the ones that wandered off since we placed them."

"Guess it's great any were still there, but that's probably because they're cheap." KJ followed David inside. The apartment was dark, heavy drapes covering the windows, with barely enough sunlight at the edges to show him the way. It was cluttered and smelled stuffy—and weird—like David hadn't run the garbage disposal last time he used the sink.

"Why are you here?" David asked, sounding less than thrilled KJ was there.

"You wanted to know about the date, didn't you?" KJ wove his way past the coffee table, piles of books, and pillows on the floor to yank one of the curtains open. Then he flopped onto a big pillow while David got settled.

"Well, you're smiling and here, so I'm guessing sex was involved."

"Sex was involved, but that's not the important thing."

David let out a snort and leaned back on the sofa. "Since when?"

"Since magic is fucking real, David. Thomas is a warlock or witch. Not sure if they use the different names by sex, but I'll find out. He's got wards on his house to keep ghosts out and tarot card spells in his bedroom that move. It was insane and so cool, and his daughter's a witch too!"

"Tell me more. Tell me everything," David demanded.

KJ couldn't stop talking if he wanted to. He was too far gone, but he still kept to his promise not to mention Nation.

HOURS LATER, David was running late, and not for the first time, KJ regretted that they rode together on filming nights, since it didn't make sense to take two cars when all their gear was stuffed in the back of his friend's SUV.

"Dude," KJ said when David's voicemail answered, but before he could say anything else, David pulled into the parking lot for the complex.

"Sorry," David said as KJ climbed into the seat and hooked on his seat belt. "I lost track of time going over the coverage from last night after you left. Did you look at it?"

"I couldn't see much. I saw movement, dark shapes, but none of it looked usable." KJ angled himself in the seat so he could pull his tablet out of his backpack. He propped it on the dash and then opened the window a couple of inches to get enough fresh air to keep from getting motion sick while looking at the screen. "The cameras were an experiment. They were shit, but next time we can get better stuff."

"Maybe your boyfriend can tell us where to film next. Use his mojo to guide us to the strange and unnatural."

"Not my boyfriend. Sort of a weird situation, David, and I'm not sure that wouldn't be cheating."

"Cheating? Seriously, KJ? He's a wizard or whatever, and he showed you real magic. You're lucky I know you too well to think you were stoned or drunk last night."

"Thanks for that. I think." KJ scrolled through the cameras, looking for the one he'd planted near the wax, where the Lady had spoken to him. "There's something in this one. I just can't see it well enough to know what it is. This is the spot. My gut's almost always right."

"We'll find out soon enough." David parallel parked in one of the only spots left on the street. He squeezed the steering wheel and turned to look at KJ with probably the most serious look he'd ever had on his face. "This guy's the real deal. Okay. He's the naked guy. This is fate or destiny or kismet or whatever. But if he fucks you over, I'll kill him."

"Aw, that's the nicest thing you've ever said to me."

"It got serious so fast, KJ. That's not normal."

"None of this is normal, but please be nice," KJ said as he slipped from the seat onto the sidewalk and shrugged on his backpack, then picked back up his tablet. "He's waiting for us right over there." *Looking entirely too pretty too.* KJ had to admire the fit of the black on black on black outfit Thomas was wearing.

"Who does he think he is, Dresden?" David said mockingly as he hefted the good camera over his shoulder. "Where's the staff? And that is one fugly cat!"

"I don't think he uses a staff, and Harry Dresden wishes he was that hot. We haven't talked weaponry. It's not like we traded character sheets for a Mage game." Which would make meeting a new person so much easier.

THOMAS LET Nation out of the carrier as soon as they got to the park and casually made his way to the gravestone memorial. He patted his messenger bag one more time to make sure his dagger was where he could get to it quickly and that none of the potions he had tucked in the pockets were leaking.

"It feels wrong here," he told Nation. "Not that it's ever felt right. Too many dead here. Too many ghosts. The place could use a truckload of rock salt and holy water."

"Gotta love the classics," the cat agreed before jumping on top of the tallest headstone to begin washing his face. "Here comes Kevin-James and his friend."

Thomas waved at the two of them and then stroked Nation's back, paying special attention to his rump, which kept the cat from talking and made him purr. The air was cooling off fast, which was a good thing. He wasn't dressed for the first day of summer, unlike David and KJ, who looked like a couple of college students in their hoodies and shorts.

"Thomas Anders, this is David Foster, my best friend aka man who handles the camera."

Thomas held his hand out to shake David's. He expected to feel David being protective of KJ, or even some jealousy from the teacher's best friend, but instead he sensed eagerness and need. It was odd. "And that is Nation."

Nation jumped down and twined between KJ's legs to say hello while completely ignoring David in a very catlike fashion. He let KJ pet him and then sauntered off into the bushes.

"Aren't you worried about him running away?" David asked, which told Thomas that KJ hadn't told his friend about Nation as he'd promised.

"He always finds his way home. He's also very good at sniffing out the paranormal where it does not belong," Thomas said as he reached into his bag and pulled out half a dozen small plastic bottles. "These are travel squeeze bottles filled with holy water from the Mission. They should offer you some protection depending on what's making the hair on the back of my neck stand at attention. You feel it too, don't you, KJ?"

"Yeah, I do. Felt it the night before last when we were here, but it's worse now. If I was alone, I'd be getting back in my car right now." He shivered and handed half of the holy water to David. "David doesn't feel any of it. He's not like me—or you."

"Or the magic-sniffing cat," David said as he tucked the holy water away and adjusted the camera. "Where do you want to start? The black wax/White Lady spot?"

Thomas almost fumbled for the compass, then smiled at KJ, who had it in his hand. "It'll show us where to go. It could do that before it came into my possession. Have it show us the way, KJ."

"This is so weird." KJ's knuckles whitened as he tightened his grip on the compass and then popped it open. Like the night before, there was a cascade of multicolored sparks that would've been dazzling if the sun had gone behind the horizon. "Wow. It's doing its spinning thing. Now we wait to see if it points at you again."

"It likes me," Thomas said with a shrug and a smile. Leaning closer to KJ, he caught the spicy scent of his soap and decided it was far better than Skin So Soft, and it also didn't seem to mess up his spells.

The disc snapped in place, pointing to the tree line near the ravine where KJ said he'd found the black wax. "Not a surprise on either thing," KJ said. "I like you too, and that's where I got the warning. Keep the camera rolling, David."

"Battery and two spares are fully charged, dude. I'm ready for whatever happens."

They weren't and Thomas knew it. He hoped that between him and Nation, they could keep them safe from the darkness creeping in the lengthening shadows.

"DUDE." DAVID stopped suddenly in the middle of the grassy field. There'd been a crackling sound, and his face went white. "I just stepped on something. Oh shit."

It was almost dark. Twilight seemed to last hours until the last few minutes before the sun went beyond the horizon. KJ aimed his flashlight at David's feet. "Is that a hand?"

"That's a hand. I'm standing on a hand!" David stepped cautiously backward, panting as he leaned on KJ to make certain there were no pieces of bone trapped in the sole of his sneakers. "What the hell? Is that real?"

"It's real," Thomas said as he attempted to pick up the shattered hand, but when he touched it, it crumbled to so much dust, drifting in a grayish, glowing cloud onto the grass. "And very, very old, as you'd expect in this place." He got back to his feet, scanning the immediate area for more errant body parts. "There's something over there too, but it's too small to see what it is."

"I know they left the bodies when they made this into a park, but aren't they buried really deep? I mean, they added dirt to level the ground and to make sure nothing came up by accident." KJ's eyes were bright. Unlike David, he wasn't shocked by what they'd found. Thomas didn't know if it was because of KJ's sensitive nature or because he trusted Thomas to look after them. Either choice was better than having both of them scared.

"One would think," Thomas said. He reached into his bag and pulled out his dagger. It was dark enough for them not to draw too much attention, so he wasn't worried about being arrested for carrying a ten-inch-long steel blade honed sharp enough to cut wyvern hide. "I can taste the magic used. The spell was strong, but it's not right."

"When is raising the dead right?" KJ asked with a smirk as they started walking once more.

"It might not be that. A novice might've decided he wanted to make a Hand of Glory and thought this was a good place to go shopping." It wouldn't be the first time that'd happened on Thomas's watch, but usually they went for easier-to-get body parts. It was a hell of a lot easier to grave-rob from a fresh burial or sneak into a morgue or funeral home.

David approached another group of bones, carefully making sure he got it on camera this time. "It's the rest of the arm. Guess they forgot to bring a bag to carry the pieces?"

"Remind me to tell you some stories about this kind of thing next time we see each other. Some of it's really funny." Thomas bumped shoulders with KJ and brushed his knuckles against the back of his hand. "There was this kid who was drenched in Skin So Soft who stumbled into our camp one summer."

"He already knows that story, Thomas. Can't blackmail me with it. Hell, your cat knows the story." KJ crouched at the base of the tree where he'd spoken to the Lady in White. "This a lot more than the other night. And they smashed the camera."

Thomas left KJ and David at the tree and walked deeper into the trees toward the ravine that flanked the park. A familiar shape darted from the darkness, and Nation leaped onto his shoulder. "There's a broken circle near the edge with a pit in the middle of it. Stinks like death," Nation informed him from his perch, keeping his voice low so David didn't hear him. "I don't think they should see it."

"Let me have a look before I try to tell them to go home. Neither one of them is likely to listen. They're too determined to capture their white whale."

Nation jumped down to lead Thomas between the scraggly trees. The third time he was scratched by a branch trying to follow the much smaller cat, he complained, "Would you mind leading me through places where I'll fit?"

"Sorry." It was a short and sweet apology, which made Thomas worry more about the danger they might be facing.

"Where are we going?" KJ asked without bothering to be quiet, coming up behind Thomas. "Wow, it's really dark out here. Is this even still park property?"

Thomas said a silent prayer to the powers that be to protect KJ and David, and then let out a sigh. "Nation wanted to show me something. Can't do that without David hearing him talk."

"We've got a few minutes. Something happened with the camera. The battery flatlined, so he's switching to the backup." KJ ducked under a low-hanging branch and then stopped suddenly. "What is that smell? Nothing dead here should smell like that. It's been over a century!"

"One of the first lessons you need to learn, love, is to stop trying to make magic make sense. I don't suppose you'd go back to help David, would you?" Thomas asked as he stepped through the trees. With a flash, the broken magic circle Nation had warned him about sprang into life. Lines of crimson, gold, and orange traveled over the ground like molten metal filling a groove, reconnecting until the circle was fully formed. "Nation, this circle is not broken."

"It was when I went through it," the cat stated firmly from outside of the now glowing ring. "Twice!"

"Well, it's not now." Thomas pulled on his power and felt a sharp stabbing pain travel up his legs and along his back. His spine grew colder as his body's warmth seemed to be sucked into the soil. He lost his grip on his dagger, and it landed on the soil near his feet, point down. Then he fell to his knees beside KJ. "It's also a trap."

KJ FELT the panic rising, and unlike the last time he was slipping into freak-out mode, he felt he deserved to be there. Of course he was scared! The magic in the circle was real. He could feel heat radiating from the crimson sigils and lines like he was standing near a volcano. Thomas shivered beside him, and when he reached for his hand, it was like ice. But the air was stifling hot around them.

KJ rubbed between Thomas's shoulder blades with his free hand. "Are you going to be okay?"

"I don't know." Thomas's eyes seemed unfocused, and KJ could see the trap was causing him pain. "How about you?"

"I'm okay. Feels weird, though. Like tiny claws, pins and needles all over my skin. Kinda wish I had some of that Skin So Soft. Worked to block you, right?" Without letting go of Thomas, he turned his attention to the path they'd taken. "But we're not alone."

"We've got Nation, unless this hurts him too."

"Not just Nation—we've got David. He's gotta be wondering what happened to us, right?" They hadn't been gone that long, but they were best friends, which meant they worried. Also, after stepping on the skeletal hand, David would be in hyperparanoia mode. "David! David! We need help! Dude, where are you?"

"I'm over here!" David called out to them as he made his way through the trees to the outer edge of the glowing circle. KJ noticed that his toes did not touch the lines at all, which was odd, since he shouldn't be able to see it, and there was a blob of something black that looked like wax on his shoe. David never responded to any of the paranormal effects KJ had shown him over the years. He was as blind to them as his cameras.

"Break the circle. It's right in front of you. Kick some dirt over it, or dig your toes into it."

"I can't do that, KJ." A bright smile spread from one ear to the other as David tucked his hands into his pockets and chuckled. "Because David's not here, man."

"Hitcher," Thomas said from between clenched teeth as he fought his way back to his feet to stand firm with KJ. "He's taken David's body."

"And now I get the choice of yours—both of you." The hitcher leaned against the nearest tree and shrugged. "I've been waiting for someone like you for months, Kevin-James, waiting for someone with at least some magic. You YouTube people, it's like going to a buffet! But your potential drew me here, and then when I found out your friend here was null… perfection. So easy to take his place."

"Where's David?" KJ's heart sank into a thick mire of blackness. Terror that his best friend was dead made his stomach lurch, and he had to bend over to catch his breath before he threw up. "When?"

"David's still in there," Thomas told him before the hitcher could answer. "Locked away while whoever runs the show."

"Spoilsport," the hitcher said snidely. "Yes, David's still here." He tapped the side of his head. "He might survive when I leave, but by then neither of us will give a shit. I wanted you, KJ. So much potential to unlock, but now you've brought me Thomas. He's a council mage, a protector, and there's so much power in him!" He leaned forward, pushing off the tree to return to the rim of the circle. "And what you told me about his daughter today! I want her too. By the time I take her body, I'll be the most powerful of my kind."

"And still trapped here," Thomas said with a snarl of his own. KJ felt him fluster when the hitcher mentioned taking Star's power and body, and he didn't blame him. "Because you can't leave your own body behind or take it with you."

"That's not quite right, Thomas," David said, licking his teeth behind his lips. "The more powerful the body I take, the bigger my circle grows. KJ could get me most of the city. You'll get me the entire county, and Star, if she's as powerful as you brag—well we'll see how far I can go then."

"Huh?" KJ asked while he put all the pieces together. "So he's an undead wizard, kind of a lich? And your body's under the park. You're an old resident of this place, which shouldn't make it too hard to find the real you. Right, Thomas?" While he went on, the volume of his voice increased as KJ tried to make sure Nation would understand him. He and Thomas might be trapped, but the magical cat wasn't. And because of his promise to Thomas, David knew nothing about the cat.

"RIGHT," THOMAS said. He had lost a great deal of his power to the circle, but the draining seemed to stop when KJ held his hand. They might've only gotten to know each other, outside of KJ's job, a few days ago, but he thought their link might be more tangible than that—the compass. It was important to both of them emotionally (as was their affection for Star), but the compass had been in Thomas's possession, among his magical tools, for over twenty years. It was charmed by them both, and with it, they might be able to fight back.

"I pity you. Trapped for at least a century in or around this place. It must have been terrifying when they bulldozed over your grave." He gave KJ's hand a squeeze while glaring at the thing in David's body, and then whispered, "Tell me you didn't lose the compass on your way out here."

"No, it's in my pocket." KJ looked at Thomas briefly before he pulled it out. "See?"

"I won't lie," the hitcher said, "that was frightening until one of the workers literally stumbled on me. I took his body. He was terrified of ghosts, and I used that to take him. Learning to use construction equipment was a challenge, but I learn quickly. It helps that I can absorb the knowledge of my host bodies."

"Which is how you fooled me," KJ said while he slipped the compass between his and Thomas's entwined hands. Thomas held his breath while adjusting his grip to ensure that the antique fit in the space between their palms. "You're good. Making me think you were David all along. Really good. I doubt you'll fool Star, though. She's a fuck of a lot smarter than I am."

Thomas licked his lips and sighed, feeling the gentle, comforting warmth of the compass that was nothing like the hellish heat holding them prisoner. He grinned when he caught a whiff of Skin So Soft in the air fighting the brimstone and cadaverous scent of the magical trap he was caught in. There was the taste of KJ on his tongue, and as he gripped KJ's fingers tighter around the disk of bronze and glass, he felt KJ's untrained power tangle with his own just as their bodies had entwined the night before.

I found it, Nation's voice touched Thomas's mind. *It's his skull. Together, Thomas.*

"I am falling in love with you," he told KJ as he brought their foreheads together. "I also have a plan."

"Yeah, sudden, but I'm okay with it," KJ said in return. "I can feel you. How you feel, and I think I'm falling for you too."

"Do you trust me, Kevin-James Beshter?" Thomas asked with all seriousness, because without KJ's trust and belief in him, he didn't know if he could save them.

"I do. Trusted you when I was twelve. Trust you more now." His hazel eyes locked with Thomas's, and Thomas could see the glossiness of unshed tears in them. "Don't let him hurt Star. No matter what, Thomas. Do not let him hurt her."

"I won't. I promise."

With his power braiding with KJ's through their bond—both old and new—Thomas whispered a single word. It was barely pronounceable, a language seldom spoken in several thousand years, an ancient name locked to a tiny golden token stitched into Nation's broken body by a little girl and powered by her love to bring her cat back to life: Thomas spoke the abomination's true name.

Forks of blue, green, and purple lightning crackled around the magical trap, making it glow like a plasma globe. Each time it touched the crimson sigils and lines, it changed their hue to match Thomas's magic. A crash of thunder shook the ground as the hitcher's spell crumbled, and the creature screamed soundlessly as a single bolt of power bore through the impacted soil to shatter its long-buried skull, sending it to its final death at last.

David's body pitched forward, his head striking a stone as he hit the ground like a broken puppet. Thomas held on to KJ, each of them needing the other to keep from falling down. They were breathing hard, the air smelling of ozone. The only sound Thomas could hear was his own heartbeat.

"Check on David," he told KJ when he finally managed to let go of him. "I need to find Nation."

"Okay." KJ nodded against Thomas's shoulder and then tucked the compass away before rushing to his fallen friend. "I'm going to call 911 too. Is that all right?"

"Definitely. I'll be back soon—I hope."

Thomas made his way along the edge of the ravine, looking for a way into the darkness, following the connection his magic had with Nation. The tie was still strong, which he prayed meant the cat was all right, but he had no idea how it could handle the significant amount of power they'd just shared to kill the hitcher. "Nation?"

"Fuck, Thomas," the cat said weakly from the middle of a patch of ice plant. There were scorch marks blasting from what looked like a collapsed tunnel that blackened all but the juicy fireproof plant. "Think I'm broken."

"I'm sorry, buddy," Thomas said as he carefully gathered the hairless creature into his shirt. "I'll get you home and take care of you."

"Spoil me rotten?" Nation asked as he snuggled against Thomas's chest.

"You'll stink for miles."

"KJ?" David's voice was shaky as he opened his eyes. His forehead was covered in blood, and KJ was sure he had a concussion at the least. "What happened?"

"Yep, it's me. Don't move too much. You hit your head." KJ dug out his phone, breathing a huge sigh of relief when he had enough bars to call for help. He pressed his palm against David's chest to keep him from trying to sit up. "My friend had a bad fall in Pioneer Park. We're on the ravine side, in the trees."

Two Weeks Later

"Dude!" David called from the living room couch, where he'd been squatting since being released from the hospital a week ago. He had the TV remote within reach, as well as a big bottle of Gatorade and some more bottles of water. There was also a mostly empty box of Pop-Tarts and half a cold pizza on the coffee table. "You're going to be late!"

"I am not!" KJ shouted from his bedroom, where he was trying to decide between two new shirts to wear to dinner with Thomas and Star. One shirt was teal and the other was lavender, and he had no idea if he could wear either. All he knew was they were the colors he saw in Thomas's magic and his soul, so he wanted to wear them.

"What I am is a dork!" A dork in love, which was very much okay with him. "I'm also nervous," he said as he came into the living room, trying to get both arms through the sleeves of the teal Henley. "What if Star doesn't like me?"

"What?" David just blinked at him from the sofa, where he was surrounded by piles of books on witchcraft and other reference materials KJ'd borrowed from Thomas. "I'm the one with the head injury who lost three days, right? The girl liked you enough to cast whatever spell she did to set you up to see her dad! Of course she likes you."

"I know. I'm being an idiot." KJ grabbed his keys from the kitchen table, along with the flowers he'd bought for Thomas and Star. He cast David a smile filled with fondness. "Are you sure you'll be okay without me? Thomas will forgive me if I take care of you."

"Thomas will strangle me if you miss this dinner, and it's not like you haven't spent a few nights over there."

"When you were in the hospital."

"Kevin-James, get your ass in that car and go see your boyfriend. Now!" David scooted into a sitting position on the sofa and pointed at the door. "I have a friend coming over who will see to my needs. Do not make me throw one of these heavy magic books at you. Get out!"

"Remind me to remind you that this is my house in the morning!" KJ said as he headed out the door.

"As long as it's in the morning, and don't lock the door. That way I don't have to get up to let Tracy in!"

THE KITCHEN smelled like Italian sausage, garlic, and cheese. Thomas bent before the oven, pulling out the largest glass pan they owned, filled almost to overflowing with lasagna. He carefully placed it on the cooling rack so the cheese could firm up before they cut into it. There were three place settings on the kitchen table, a bottle of wine, and a fresh loaf of garlic bread he'd made with sourdough.

It was almost six thirty. He'd left Equinox closed for the day while he prepared Star's—and KJ's—favorite meal. Thomas wanted it to be perfect. She would be home from summer camp any moment, and KJ would be getting there soon as well.

"She's here!" Nation said, his voice flavored with a very feline yowl as he pressed his paws against the bay window. "Star's home!" His injuries had healed within days of their victory over the hitcher, but Thomas was worried he was in for a talking-to once she found out what had happened to the four of them.

Below them, the shop's bells jingled as she let herself in the front door, and then there was the familiar thunder of her feet on the steps. Thomas was gracious and let Nation greet her first by dancing between her legs until she picked him up, and then the cat got wedged between the two of them as they hugged on top of him. "Hey, can't breathe!"

"So glad you're home," Thomas said before kissing her forehead and the top of her head. The green streaks in her hair were now brilliant blue, and she smelled like sunshine, pine trees, and a hint of coconut from her sunscreen. The bridge of her nose was pinked from the sun, and she looked both wild and grown-up at the same time.

"Would've been here sooner if you'd given me permission. Are you guys okay?" Star stepped away, turning Nation over to look at him from end to end for damage. "You were very brave, baby boy."

"I know," Nation said, preening under her attention as she carried him to the front room while Thomas dragged her luggage into her room.

"He was very brave. Saved us." Thomas reached over and scratched the top of Nation's head. "Go wash up. Dinner will be ready as soon as KJ gets here."

"KJ, huh?" Star teased on her way to the bathroom. "I see it's not Mr. Beshter."

"It isn't for me," Thomas told her just as the back door opened and KJ stepped inside. Both of them smiled brightly as KJ crossed through the kitchen to Thomas. "Might still be for you, missy."

"For you." KJ smiled, and they shared a kiss as he handed Thomas a trio of red roses. "These are for Star," he said, holding up a bunch of daisies. "They're your favorite, right?"

"They are," she said, a twinkle in her dark eyes after seeing them kiss. "Favorite dinner. Favorite flowers. Favorite cat. Favorite dad. Favorite teacher. So, you guys got a big story to tell me. Don't leave anything out."

ELF SHOT
BY TA MOORE

To my mum,
who always encouraged me to have my head in the clouds.
And to the Five,
who told me to stop messing around and get my fingers on a keyboard.

INTRO

IT WAS always—*always*—in the name.

They made no attempt to hide it, and yet, as it always was, their very openness served to deceive. We knew it, of course we did after so many years, but…. But. They gave us back our children. How could we look *that* gift horse in the mouth? Even now I don't see what else we could have done, but we should have known.

Because what they took. They changed.

What they took were children. What they gave back were changelings.

-- The Honorable Andrew Boyd, the American Ambassador-at-Large to the Courts of the Otherworld

CHAPTER ONE

"UGH," FINN groaned. He rested his head against the window and glowered at the town as they drove through. "Just when I thought camp couldn't get any worse, they go and make it redneck. We're going to have classes in marrying our sisters and how to chew tobacco in company."

Raising a fey child was a waiting process. Wait to see if the cellophane thing of thorn bones and rose-petal skin that you're given survives the first harsh winter. Wait for it to grow out of the homely and unwholesome years (fingers crossed it would), and then hope against hope that it would become, at least vaguely, less of an asshole.

Conri glanced at Finn out of the corner of his eye. So far his kid had made it through stage one and… most of stage two. All Conri needed now was for Finn to act like a fourteen-year-old and not a feral marten found in a tree stump.

Goals. Every parent should have them.

"I believe the proper term is 'bakky,'" Conri said dryly. "And you don't have any siblings."

"Yeah, don't remind me. I'm socially stunted because I'm an only child," Finn groused. "And *whose* fault is that, Conri?"

Conri took his eyes off the narrow road long enough to give Finn an exasperated look.

"Well, it's not mine."

"Oh, right," Finn muttered as he tucked his chin down and scowled out at the world through copper-red curls. "Throw it in my face that I'm adopted the minute I don't do what you want. That's A-plus parenting, Conri. My future therapist wants to send you a thank-you card."

To be honest, Conri had thought he needed to downgrade his expectations for Finn. Maybe he should give up on "able to socially pass as a person" and aim for "domesticated marten."

"Don't tell me your real dad wouldn't treat you this way," Conri said.

"Well, he wouldn't."

"No. He'd have turned you into a tree and left you for the first stray princess to take on as a project."

"At least he wouldn't abandon me in the wilderness once a year so he could go and lay some pipe."

Conri grimaced. He'd tried his best to adapt to life in LA, but he was still a priest-fearing Cornish boy at heart. Some things he didn't want to hear out of his fourteen-year-old ward.

"It's the law."

"It *used* to be the law that you threw changelings in a roaring fire," Finn said. "Would you have done that too?"

"Some days," Conri muttered under his breath.

"I heard that."

Of course he did. Conri considered an apology, but they'd been in the car for fourteen hours straight. He was going to give himself a mulligan on that one. The rental GPS came to life all of a sudden and told him to turn left on Naecross Road.

Conri swore to himself as he leaned forward over the wheel to peer at the sun-faded street names on the sides of buildings.

Kendall.

Rowan.

Nail and Cross.

Shit.

He spun the wheel to take the corner tightly and then hit the brakes as he nearly plowed into the thin woman halfway across the pedestrian crossing. The car screeched to a halt inches away from faded jeans, and the woman glared at them with dull, small-town suspicion.

"Sorry," Conri said as he stuck his head out the window. It was hot, the sort of hot that hit you like a slap. "GPS. Do you know where the Kemp Farm is from here?"

"I do."

Conri stared at her for a second, then grinned thinly.

"Not going to tell us, though," he said. "Right?"

She spat on the hood of the car, her candy-pink lips pursed with ripe disgust.

"This is a good, church-going town," she said. "Barry Kemp should be downright ashamed he signed that contract. We don't want you around here. You ain't *welcome*. Ain't that supposed to mean something to you people?"

Finn stuck his head out his side. "No, see, you're thinking vampires," he said in his thickest Cali drawl, maliciously helpful and syrup sweet. "Have to be invited? Don't like garlic? Fey don't like iron and small-minded, smaller-town bit—"

His insult was cut off as Conri grabbed him by the back of his T-shirt and yanked him back into the car. He jabbed his finger on the button to roll the window up before Finn could squirm loose, but it was a bit late. The woman had definitely already heard, her ears gone so red they glowed through her bleached-blond hair. Ah well, Conri had tried. The world couldn't ask more of him.

"Go to the farm and rot there," the woman spat at them. "We're not going to stand for the soulless to be brought amongst us like this. Everyone knows what happens to towns that make the likes of you welcome!"

She slapped the hood of the car and stomped off.

Finn watched her go and then turned to glower at Conri. He didn't say anything, just gestured extravagantly after her with one arm. As if the departing Uggs spoke for themselves. Conri supposed he might have a point, not that he would admit it.

"She could have just been homophobic," Conri said.

"Sure," Finn said with an exaggerated roll of spring-leaf-green eyes as he flopped back into his seat. "One look at you and what jumped out at her was that you were gay. Not the rest of it."

Conri glanced at his reflection in the rearview mirror and snorted his admission that Finn was right. The piebald hair and mismatched eyes *might* pass for human, at a quick glance, but the pricked, tufted ears that poked through his hair were less so. Some changelings used glamours to hide what they were, but he rarely bothered. There were many ways to see through it, and once people did, they assumed that you had something else to hide too.

Besides, he'd already lost one face. The one he wore as a boy was long since forgotten, so he didn't want to let this one slip. It might not be what he started with, but he'd had it the longest.

"So there's a few bigots," he admitted as he checked for pedestrians before he rolled the car forward. "Maybe that's why they brought the camp here this year—so you kids learn to deal with them. It's not like you can depend on always living in LA."

"Yeah, because no one ever calls me Oberon there," Finn said, with the ripe contempt for a parent who didn't understand the microaggressions only a fourteen-year-old could muster.

Conri shrugged.

He'd been one of the last waves of changelings handed back—the fourth? fifth?—and for humanity, the joy of their return had worn off to reveal the suspicion underneath. "Oberon" was a helluva lot better than what he'd been called back then. The West Coast might love the idea of the fey more than the reality—who didn't?—but it treated them well. But as far as Conri could tell, progress was surviving long enough that your kids could be angry about the stuff you'd had to shrug off.

"It's three weeks," he said. "You'll survive."

"You *hope*."

"Yeah, sometimes," Conri said.

He ignored Finn's aggrieved snort and followed the GPS's directions, which brought him back to the first street, three blocks back. The camp staff had turned the scramblers on early—*again*—though nobody was going to have a clue how to get there. Every year. Conri swore they did it to agitate people.

"Da," Finn said abruptly. He poked Conri's arm with a bony finger and then pointed down the street. "There they are."

A convoy of jet-black SUVs with blacked-out windows and no license plates pulled out of a gas station and headed north along Main Street, out of town. The Federal and Otherworld Bureau, or the Templars, if you wanted to be crude. FOBs if you were cocky.

"Tell you what," Conri said as he turned into a diner parking lot. "You want to get lunch first?"

For once Finn didn't have a smart remark. He sighed in relief and nodded as he unsnapped his seat belt.

The FOBs weren't necessarily bad news, but they were news. If you could, it was best to stay out of their way and off everyone's radar. Besides, Conri could always eat.

Well, he supposed as he got out of the car and squinted at the aggressively mom-and-pop frontage, if they'd serve the likes of him here.

THREE DAYS later Conri sprawled naked on the balcony of the nicest hotel in the nearest big city he could find. He still received suspicious squints occasionally, as if they needed to check the human under the elf-gift, but so far no one had caused trouble. It hadn't put off anyone at the clubs either.

He stretched, long and lazy and sated in the sun, and reached for the glass of wine. It wasn't as if he didn't date or fuck around with Finn at home, but there were… constraints. Even before he'd spent all those years in the Otherworld, he'd bristled at any attempt to control him.

That independent streak had never actually done him any favors, he supposed as he took a draft of wine and tilted his head back, but he seemed to be stuck with it.

His phone trilled a sharp, barely audible whine that made Conri's ears twitch. It was Finn's ringtone, the only one in his phone guaranteed to poke through the haze of whatever Conri was doing and grab his attention. A dog whistle, basically.

He scrambled up off the lounger and loped back into the hotel room. His clothes were tossed haphazardly over the furniture, but he finally found his phone shoved into the toe of his trainer.

"What is it?" he barked as he swiped to answer the call. It was *something*. Finn wouldn't have called him otherwise. "What happened?"

Someone sniffed wetly on the other end of the line. For a second, Conri thought someone else had Finn's phone. Finn was fourteen and aggressively aware of his own dignity. He didn't cry in front of—for—Conri.

"Da," Finn said. He exhaled raggedly, and Conri heard fabric slide down a wall until the lanky teen wearing it thumped onto the floor. He sniffed again. "I'm sorry I was a jerk, Da. I was lucky my father gave me to you and… and it's okay you never got me a dog. It would have been weird."

He swallowed hard and wiped his nose on something—his sleeve, from experience.

"Finn, enough," Conri said, his voice flat and impatient. He pinned the phone against his ear with one shoulder as he grabbed a pair of jeans that were more or less clean. "What happened?"

There was a pause, and then Finn admitted in a tight voice. "I don't know. Not exactly. The Templars have closed the camp. I tried to find out why, but they wouldn't tell me. I'm the son of—"

Conri snapped his teeth together, a sharp click that shut Finn up midword. It gave Conri notice that his temper had started to slip too. He licked the back of his teeth smooth again.

"You're fourteen," he said. "You're better off if you don't know some things. Okay?"

"Yeah."

"You think you're safe?"

He listened to Finn's breathing, ragged and frightened in his ear for a long moment. There was no blood relation between them, not even a common ancestor six hundred years back, and one day Finn's real father would come to take him back. Once all the hard work was done. That mattered, and it didn't. Right now, Conri was all Finn had in the world, and he needed to get to him.

"Finnigan," he said. "You're not safe?"

"No. Maybe? I don't know," Finn's voice was quiet now, a muffled whisper as though he'd cupped his hand over his mouth. "They took some of the older kids to talk to them. I haven't seen any of them come back. Da, what if they're going to take us all away?"

Conri buttoned his jeans and grabbed a T-shirt. It tangled around his hands, the simple task of arm and head holes suddenly impossible to surmount. His head felt narrow with the slow thud of anxiety. After they were sent back, there had been a few choke points where it seemed something like this was bound to happen. There had been plans—fragile lines of communication between people divided by courts and gifts and stuff the humans would never understand.

That had passed. Things had gotten better. It had been years since Conri worried about what he'd do if armed soldiers came for Finn.

"They won't," he said and hoped it wasn't a lie. "Did something happen to kick this off?"

"… we snuck out of camp last night," Finn admitted. "We—a bunch of us—were going to go to a party. Da, I didn't know…. The Templars met us at the gate when we got back. It was a bit of fun."

Conri felt like he needed to sit down and put his head between his knees as relief hit him like a brick. He doubted that Finn would appreciate it, under the circumstances, but that was good news. Whatever had happened sounded like it was local, a reaction to some bone-headed kids feeling their oats, not the first step in a nationwide countdown.

He hoped.

"Did anything happen? Anyone get out of hand? Or get their hands caught somewhere they shouldn't be."

"I don't know. I got drunk and passed out. I only woke up when we got back here and they turned the floodlights on us. It could have? The locals have been assholes, so when some of the older kids found out about the party, they decided to crash it. Play Stranger at the Feast. I just tagged along, Da. I didn't do—"

He stopped, and his breath hitched raggedly in his throat. In the background Conri could hear a door handle rattle and the sound of heavy, human boots against linoleum and cheap creaky joists. Finn's hand tightened around his phone so much that his knuckles creaked. Or that could be Conri's own fingers. He loosened his grip as he grabbed what he needed from the suitcase and the car fob from the nightstand and headed for the door.

The rest he could get when he came back.

Finn swallowed hard—a wet click in his throat—and took a shallow breath. "I don't think they want parents to know what's going on. They won't let any of the other kids use the camp phone to call home, and the counselors took our phones and everything when we arrived. But you told me I should keep my burner in case. Da, what if they come for me? Or for the little kids? Should we try and get out?"

"No. Do what you're told," Conri told him. "You haven't done anything wrong, so you don't have anything to hide. Even if you *did* do something wrong, that's the story you stick to."

"That doesn't sound like what a hero would do," Finn said. "Or a lord."

"Yeah, well, you'd be surprised what gets left out once something turns into a story." Conri ducked into the elevator and pretended he didn't see the middle-aged couple's agitated jab at the Close button. "And you aren't either yet, Finn. Now keep your head down and a polite tongue in your head. I'll be there as soon as I can."

"When?"

"Soon," Conri promised grimly. "I'm taking the long way round."

OLD WIVES knew that time passed faster in the Otherworld. Conri was too much of a gentleman to argue with them, but they were only *close*. Time didn't pass at all in the Otherworld. It's why the fey liked mortals. They brought time with them. It stirred the waters.

Sometimes boys joined the fairy ring to dance a reel with a handsome fey, only to wake in the morning well used, with a purse of coin and half a century frittered away. Others the youngest daughter finished their quest and found themselves back home the same night they left, those sixty years squashed back into sixteen-year-old skin.

If someone knew how to read the tides, then they could use the silted-up shallows of the Otherworld as a rat run from somewhere to somewhen.

Conri knew how to do it.

As far as the odometer was concerned, they'd covered the same amount of miles as the trip would take in the real world. More, since the Otherworld's topography hadn't caught up with the human world yet. It was still based on the potholed highways and cracked back roads of the 1950s. Conri's ass ached and his throat was parched despite the bottle of water he'd stolen from the creepy, kudzu-buried gas station he passed a few miles back. It had been too long since he'd lived on Otherworld fare. His body had forgotten how to make do with the thinness of it.

A hitchhiker paused on the side of the road to watch him go by, shabby jeans and a denim jacket under a faded backpack. Ragged blond hair hung still around their face despite the wind that kicked up dust and ragged bits of stick. It didn't bother to try and wave Conri down, it could tell he was meant to be there.

Sometimes Conri could too. Still.

He brushed that thought away like a cobweb and leaned forward to squint out the bug-covered window for the turnoff to Elwood. If he missed it, he'd be stuck on the road for another day maybe. Despite the empty road, there were no U-turns in the Otherworld. Or more accurately, no take-backs. If someone regretted something—a missed turn, a missed opportunity, a murder—they could find a work-around, but it couldn't be undone.

And the GPS was no help. It had spent an hour trying to direct him to the second level of Hell—head straight for Gehenna and turn left at Limbo—before it eroded into static and eerie whispers that made fractured promises and threats. So he wasn't going to depend on it.

The turnoff appeared out of nowhere, disguised by dust and the angle of the road. Conri yanked the wheel and felt the weight of the car as it swerved under him. The front tire slipped off the crumbled tarmac into the dirt with a jolt—and a sudden sense of *something* along the road that waited for people who left it—and then bumped back up again.

He was nearly back. Conri could feel the weight of the mortal world pull at his human bones as he got closer to the boundary. Not far now. He reached over to check the map he'd tossed onto the passenger side and took his eyes off the road for a second.

When he looked back up, the man was already halfway into the road. Conri caught a snapshot of dark hair and torn black clothes—was that a *sword* in his hand?—and the bumper of the car clipped the man and flipped him up into the air. He landed on the hood with a crack that made Conri wince and then grabbed blindly at the top of it. His knuckles showed white through abraded skin as he grabbed at the lip.

"Go," the stranger yelled roughly as he waved his free hand at the road. "Move now."

That's when Conri saw the hounds. They were lean and white, built of mist and bone, with red ears where their bloody-handed masters had ruffled them in approval. The road was new to them, and it gave them pause, paws raised prissily as they poked at the concrete, but only for a second. Then they lunged out into the road after their prey in long, ground-devouring leaps.

"Shit."

Conri hit the gas and plowed through them. The hounds shrieked as they bounced off the metal and rolled into the road, long red grazes on their haunches and shoulders. It wouldn't kill them, but they might remember it.

One managed to grab hold of the rearview mirror. Sharp, yellow teeth punched through the fiberglass like tinfoil and the glass shattered. The hound snarled around the mouthful and glared at Conri out of a mad, yellow eye.

"I'll remember you," that glare said.

Then they hit the border. The hound's long body stretched out like a ribbon in the wind, bone ribs sharp as they tore through mist-made skin. It tried to keep up, but hounds weren't one of the things that could pass through the borders. Not alone.

It unspooled, and the car smashed back into the real world, heat like a slap and the stink of hot concrete and wet, boiled earth thick in the air. Conri hit the brakes hard, and the car fishtailed under him. His passenger lost his grip and was thrown off the car. He hit the road hard and rolled.

Conri sat for a second and panted as he waited to reacclimate. He could have left—he considered it. Some black-clad stranger who was stupid enough to wander into the Otherland wasn't his problem.

Then the man propped himself up on one elbow and wiped blood from his mouth. Dark hair hung in front of his face, and that seemed as far as he could go. Conri tapped his fingers nervously on the wheel and then swore to himself as he scrambled out of the car.

The hounds couldn't cross the border on their own, but plenty of things could bring them over.

CHAPTER TWO

IT WASN'T the first time that Special Agent Dylan Bellamy had been unceremoniously thrown out of faerie, and he doubted it would be the last. The fey might have put their mark on the Accords and bound themselves, but the *place* had made no such promises. It still wanted to have its fun, and it didn't appreciate any mortal interference.

But it was the first time he had gone face-to-face with a Toyota.

Bell swallowed a mouthful of blood, slick and salty in his throat, and appreciated the bright, midmorning sun as it stabbed into his aching eyes. It was always dusk or dawn in the Otherworld, never in-between. Once he was fully reassured he was home, he took a quick inventory of his state. Nothing was broken, and all his extremities were there. But the thicket of tightly woven branches and thorny runners he'd had to fight his way through had taken its toll on his skin before the hounds had their pound of flesh.

He had to get up, but there was nothing about to kill him *right this minute*, and the hot gut sickness of the border twisted his stomach like a rag. A minute, he swore as he pressed his knuckles against his forehead, and then he'd get back to work.

Hounds. Bell wiped his mouth on his sleeve and managed to drag himself onto his knees. What the *fuck* were hounds doing out here, in the most mundane hollow of the States the Agency could find?

"Come on," someone said as they put a lean warm arm around his waist and dragged him to his feet. "I'll get you to town, find somewhere to get you patched up."

Cars, Bell reminded himself scathingly as he stiffened his knees, tended to be driven.

Pride did what the threat of death hadn't, and Bell squashed the sickness and the pain down into the box in his head where it belonged. He'd deal with it later. Or not. He got his feet under him and took his weight off his rescuer's shoulders.

"Thanks for the help," he said, his voice clipped and cold. "But I can take it from here, Mr....."

He limped a step back and paused as he took in the fact that his Good Samaritan wasn't human. Not entirely. Not anymore.

Pointed ears stuck up through his shaggy, roughly cut hair that was blotched with gray and white over the ginger base. His too-bright, mismatched eyes looked starkly inhuman in his broad, handsome, and casually human face.

Cute, huh, a stupid little voice whispered in the back of his head. Bell smothered it impatiently to shut it up. It wasn't wrong, but this wasn't the time.

The changeling, having given Bell the same once-over, looked vaguely stricken.

"Fuck," he said. "You're Iron Door."

Bell glanced down at himself. The muddy Kevlar vest that spelled out his affiliation in stark white letters did kind of give that away. The changeling was also dressed like someone from his decade. Other than the stamp of the elf-gift on his face, he looked like any other guy buying hipster veg at the farmer's market. His jeans were faded by design, not work, and his old green T-shirt had a quote from a Dua Lipa song on it.

Which explained his dismay. One of the rules that repatriated changelings agreed to when they got back was that they didn't go to the Otherworld without oversight from Iron Door.

"Is that a problem?" Bell asked quietly. He reached for his sap on his belt and then remembered he'd dropped it sometime between when the car hit him and he hit the road. That left the gun.

The Changeling glanced up and met his eyes for a second. One of his mismatched eyes was a bright electric blue and the other soulful amber. Neither had any white visible.

"You tell me," he said.

His body language was relaxed, hands loose and shoulders down. It was a deliberately unthreatening stance, assumed to look harmless, but Bell couldn't blame him for that.

"Open the trunk," Bell said.

The Changeling looked... tired... but walked back to the car and leaned in to do as he was told. Bell kept an eye on him as he edged around the car. He'd popped the trunk open, and Bell lifted it up cautiously to check inside.

There was a dirty sock wedged between the back of the seats and half a bag of trail mix spilled over the carpet. It smelled of old clothes and Axe body spray. Not *exactly* how Bell would imagine the changeling smelled—grass, lemons, and clean sweat apparently, so he could thank his brain for that—but not illegal.

"Stand at the side of the road," he said. "Where I can see you."

"Maybe not a great idea to hang out here," the Changeling pointed out as he backed up to the side of the road. He leaned against a tree and crossed his arms, all long legs and patience. It should have looked relaxed, but he looked alert instead. "It's a weak spot."

"I know," Bell said. "Why do you think I headed this way?"

He checked the inside of the car. It was a quick and dirty search—under the seats, in the glove box, behind the shades—instead of the forensic exam he should have ordered. Instinct told Bell that it was clean, though. It didn't… *prickle*… at his ears the way active magic did.

"Why'd you break the rules?" he asked.

The changeling shrugged without pushing himself off the tree. "Shortcut."

"You risked prison to cut a few hours off your trip?" Bell leaned against the side of the car and reached around to press his hand over his bicep where the hound's teeth had dug in. Blood welled between his fingers, and he resisted the urge to take a proper look. It was always easier if you didn't look at it. "Hot date?"

The changeling blinked and then grimaced wryly, as if he'd remembered something. "No, that was actually later on. I should call and let him know I won't make it."

He. Bell tried to pretend he *hadn't* filed that away for later. It didn't work. He could feel it as his interest went from *cute* to *possible*. He clenched his teeth and snorted to himself. His arm had been used for dog chew, and he still had an eye out for a date? With someone who was possibly a criminal, if an unusually easygoing one.

Not to mention the other issues. It wasn't exactly forbidden to fraternize with changelings, but it wasn't encouraged either. Conflict of interest and all that.

None of that would fit with his reputation.

"What was so important?"

"Probably the same thing that took you over the border," the changeling said after a second. He pushed himself off the tree and waited expectantly until a nod from Bell gave him permission to walk back to the car. "My son's at camp. He called me earlier."

Bell scowled in irritation. "He's not supposed to have a phone."

"He's fourteen." Apparently that was enough explanation. "Do you want a ride or not? We're going to the same place, I'd guess, and I've already hit you with my car. How much worse can it get?"

The laugh caught Bell off guard. It felt rusty in his throat, but it had been a while. He glanced down at his arm, blood bright on his fingers, and felt the dull pressure of vertigo throb against his inner ear. It wasn't the worst injury he'd ever had, but something about the loose, crumpled strips of skin turned his stomach. He looked away again.

"Good point. You know where the camp is?" Bell asked as he swallowed the nausea and limped around to the passenger side. The seat was a bit too far forward. It pushed his knees against the dashboard, but he wasn't going to move it with his jacked-up arm.

"I found it last time. Eventually." The changeling climbed into the car and closed the door. He glanced sidelong at Bell from under the tangle of Collie dog hair as he started the engine. "And it's Conri."

"Drive, Mr. Conri," Bell said flatly.

"Just Conri," he said and then hit the gas.

THE SKINNY, red-haired kid shuffled resentfully through the door, all straggly hair and bones that he didn't have quite enough meat for. His long thin face was pinched in sullen lines, and he looked like a troublemaker. Not a ringleader, but the sort of kid who started fires and stole wallets to buy beer.

Then he saw Conri, and all the tension bled out of him. He was still a goblin-looking kid, but a desperately relieved one, all of a sudden.

"Da," he blurted and threw himself across the room into Conri's arms. He buried his face in Conri's broad shoulder and wrapped skinny arms around him. "I don't *know* what happened. I swear."

The head of the camp—Dr. Gwen Cordwainer, who'd been at Langley before she transferred to Iron Door after the Return—cleared her throat.

"That's what everyone is saying, Finn," she said in a smooth, modulated voice that meant it was "on." "But someone must have seen something."

Conri rubbed a big hand over Finn's skinny back and lifted his head to give Cordwainer a long, steady look. It made the hair on the back of Bell's neck raise, and out of the corner of his eye, he saw his SSA shift his weight slightly so he'd have a good shot if something went wrong.

"Someone ain't him," Conri said flatly. "He doesn't know what you want. So move on."

"With all due respect," SSA Felix Donnelly said. "You don't know what's happened yet. So how can you know what we need?"

"People say that," Conri said. "All due respect, I mean, when they don't think you're due any."

"That's not what he meant," Cordwainer interrupted. "Mr. Conri—"

"Just Conri."

It had left Bell off-balance earlier. He was gratified to see it threw Cordwainer, briefly, off script as well.

"Please," she said. "Sit."

Conri cocked his head to the side. "Are you being funny?" he asked.

When Cordwainer realized what she'd said, color flooded her face, hot and dark under her makeup, and she spluttered for a second. She was excellent at what she did, but she rarely dealt with changelings one-on-one. It didn't help that Conri made no apparent effort to make himself look more human.

"I certainly didn't—"

Felix snorted. "Sit or stand, it's your call," he told Conri and then glanced at Cordwainer. "And we have bigger problems than the fact your staff can't outwit teenagers, Doctor. So drop it."

Cordwainer glared at him. Scuttlebutt had it she didn't like Felix. But few people did. He'd got as far as he was because he was *very* good at his job, and he stalled there for the same reason.

"What *is* the problem?" Conri asked. He peeled Finn off him and nudged the boy into one of the chairs while he stayed on his feet. "I know that Finn and some other kids snuck out—"

"It wasn't my idea," Finn objected. Under Conri's quick glare, he slouched down in the seat and fiddled with the ragged hem of his T-shirt. He muttered under his breath, "Well, you made it sound like my idea, and it wasn't."

"We know that," Felix said. "It was Robin Mell's idea, but unfortunately we can't find him to ask him anything. Or… Thistle Graves, Shanko Deeds, and Annie Boot either. So that leaves us you and the others who made it back to camp. Only apparently none of you saw anything."

Finn hunched in on himself, more angle and points than seemed natural under his black clothes. He looked up at Conri pleadingly. "I swear, Da, I don't *remember*. It was a party, that's all, nothing bad happened. I had a couple of drinks of punch, and it made me feel sick, so I went to sleep in the back of the van. Next thing I know we were back here, and the FOBs all had sticks up their asses all of a sudden."

It sounded true, but Bell had missed the first round of interviews. As soon as they reached the camp, Felix had sent him out on recon. The other kids' stories could be just as believable and paint Finn as the bad guy.

Bell glanced at Conri's hand on Finn's shoulder, the scarred knuckles and steady reassurance, and hoped not. Stupid, but it would be nice to see someone's faith turn out to be justified.

"I thought the fey could hold their liquor," Felix said.

Conri snorted. "No, you didn't. Now, is anyone going to tell me what actually happened?"

They didn't have to. Any crimes that touched the Otherworld came under Iron Door's jurisdiction. Eventually they might have to explain themselves, but no one could interfere in the middle of their investigation.

Felix studied Conri and Finn for a moment, his expression set and hard to read.

"The problem is that, right now, you know pretty much everything we do," he said eventually in a hard voice. "Robin Mell and a group of kids from camp snuck out to go to this party. Now four of them are missing, and no one seems to have seen anything out of the ordinary."

"And what don't I know?"

Bell rubbed his bandaged arm as he spoke up. It had been his job to make this bit of information outdated, but he hadn't pulled it off.

"A local girl has gone missing too," he said. "Stolen away to faerie. The first in twenty years, since the Accord was signed."

Finn was too ginger to have much color, but he still managed to lose what he had. He was gray as he looked around the room.

"I didn't know anything about that." He reached up and clutched at Conri's hand. "Da, I *swear* nobody said anything about—"

"It doesn't matter," Conri said grimly. "Whether you all knew or not, if the girl is in the Otherworld by anything other than chance...."

"Then the Accord has been violated," Felix finished. "With everything that entails."

THE GIRL.

Nora Kessel, seventeen years old and inexplicably nondescript. The details made her sound like she had it all going for her—tall, blond, blue-eyed, and slim. In the photos her dad and the school provided, it was obvious she was too tall, too thin, and her eyes weren't blue enough, while her hair was too blond.

She wasn't ugly, but she wasn't pretty either. Instead she was just there in photos, with a challenging expression on her face as if she dared whoever was behind the lens to take a good shot.

Bell didn't know why, but he had the strong feeling he'd like her. He laid the photo back down on the desk.

"Is there any reason to think she was targeted?" he asked.

The fey took who they wanted—a midwife to nurse their newborns, a drunk who'd staggered through a fairy ring, or a lawyer who'd slighted them. They sought out—or had, before the long conflict had finally ground to a brutal, exhausted halt—the exceptional. Beauty, talent, wisdom, or wealth—the fey liked to pluck them up and put them in pride of place.

Conri had probably stumbled into the Otherworld by chance, Bell mused absently. He was handsome enough, but the fey tended to prefer pretty to rugged. They kept their pets human too, in appearance, at least. Alterations as extensive as Conri's suggested that he hadn't been a prize.

"I doubt it," Felix said as he unfastened his bulletproof vest and squirmed out of it. His T-shirt rode up as he did it, revealing the weft of old scar tissue that clotted on his stomach. The official party line was that humanity had won, and the fey had been brought to heel. Most people believed it, but it didn't take long on the front lines to realize it hadn't been nearly that clean... or that clean-cut. "Proficient and hard-working is how people describe her, and nice if you press them."

"Nothing wrong with nice."

"Not to us maybe," Felix said as he propped his hip up on the windowsill, his booted foot dangling off the ground. "But it's not a trait the fey admire. Did you find any trace of the missing kids on the other side?"

Bell gingerly lowered himself into the chair. It had hurt when he hit the road, but as the kick of adrenaline faded, he picked up new aches and pains. They'd fade once the faerie salve soaked through his skin, but until then, he'd ache and smell of aniseed and lunary.

"Nothing. No dropped beads, torn clothes, or bits of hair," he said as he stretched his legs out in front of him. His left knee popped, but that was nothing new. Bell had joined Iron Door a decade after the Accord was signed, so he'd never had to face down elf knights with nothing but bad attitude, a mouthful of blood, and a crowbar. But even without the fey to deal with, the Otherworld had plenty to throw at them. "Do schools not teach kids to pull a Hansel the minute they're grabbed anymore?"

It was a facetious question. Bell was surprised when Felix twisted his mouth and shook his head.

"Irrelevant to a curriculum in dire need of modernization," he quoted dryly as he crossed his arms. "I believe most places replaced it with sex ed, which will come in handy if this does break the Accord."

Bell shifted uncomfortably. He could feel his torn skin as it knit back together under his bandages, and it had the same prickly discomfort/satisfaction as a picked scab.

"Will it come to that?" he asked. "After all this time, all the blood shed to get that thing signed, would we really go back to war over one girl? Who might not even have been taken by the fey."

"It was always over one girl, or one boy," Felix said. "It was about every single child that was taken. So yes, if we don't find Nora, it could mean war. Or worse. There are people—plenty of people—who think we gave too many concessions in the Accord. Who think we were the ones who set the terms. This would give them the opportunity to roll a lot of them back."

The sound of children as they shrieked in laughter and kicked a ball around the yard filtered in through the window. Bell watched them. They weren't human children. That was obvious at a glance—too skinny, too fast, too fey. Still children.

"What about them?" he asked. "The changelings."

Felix ignored the question. They both already knew the answer. Bell could remember the Return. Parents had been elated to get their children back, grown grandchildren had been awkwardly awed to grip their grandmother's unlined hands, and then there were the rest—the ones whose families were long dead, who didn't know how to drive cars or use the internet, who hadn't wanted to come back. People were a lot less elated then.

"We need to find the missing children," Felix told him as he levered himself up out of the window. "Then none of us will have to deal with what-ifs. But it needs to be done quickly. Once people catch wind this has happened, it won't take long before both sides are setting fires."

Of course, the changelings had missing children too. Bell had seen the way Conri gripped his son's shoulder. He supposed the others also had people who loved them. Their situation was less dire—the Otherworld already had its stamp on them—but they still needed to come home.

"What about extra manpower?" Bell asked as he sat forward. They had men here, but just because you were Iron Door didn't mean you were a Templar. The fey could take anyone, or anything they wanted, but humans could only cross at certain times or when they met certain random criteria. The seventh son of a seventh son, the descendants of someone the fey had blessed—or cursed—the caul-born, and anyone who'd died of hanging or drowning. Iron Door aggressively recruited anyone who qualified, but there were still only a handful of them in each state. "The Other Side here is a slough, cut off and left to go fallow. There's only one ford in and out, so it's a killing ground there for anything smart enough."

Felix raised his eyebrows. "You think that's why you ran into the hounds? Because it's good hunting. Or were they on guard?"

"I don't know," Bell said. He scratched his arm and felt the dull bruise of nearly healed pain. "It doesn't really matter. I can fend for myself, but if I have a half-dozen kids in tow, it's not going to be so easy."

"Then stick to one," Felix said flatly. "Once we stop this from escalating, we can go back for the rest."

Bell grimaced and tilted his head back against the seat. "So no backup?"

"Not everyone wants to stop this escalating," Felix pointed out. "They can't stop me getting my own men here, but they can slow it down. I'll cover you when you get back, but I can't cross over."

That had been written into the Accord by the fey themselves, in a neat, scratchy script at the end of the document. Bell figured that was evidence enough that all the stories about Felix were actually only half of the legend. If Felix went across the border, the Accord would go up in flames.

Bell ran his fingers through his hair and found burrs from his last trip worked deep into the unruly waves. He picked them out and stuck them in his pocket to get rid of properly later.

"So, I'm on my own," he said. "Well, why change the habit of a lifetime?"

CHAPTER THREE

HE'D BE informed if anything else changed, Cordwainer had told him as two Iron Door guards politely waited to escort him out of the camp. Until then he was welcome to stay in town, with the unsaid rider that he had to *find* somewhere to stay in town.

Conri had hugged Finn and let them give him the bum's rush. He'd be of more use doing something out here than locked up behind the camp's walls, and—let's be honest—if things did kick off, Finn would be safer under Templar guard.

For now.

It didn't take him long to find some of the local kids who'd been at the party when it was crashed. Elwood might not be a particularly tolerant town, but backwoods teenagers still watched TV and dreamed of going to LA or New York. The more their parents told them to stay away from the kids at the camp, the more intrigued they were about changelings and magic and what it had been like to be stolen away by the fey.

Conri wasn't about to tell them—it might be a shitty story, but it was his. As long as they told him what he needed to know, they could write all the romantic fanfic about him they wanted.

None of them remembered much, and nothing they did remember explained how everything had gotten so dramatically out of hand. They'd all been happy to blame it—whatever *it* ended up being—on the kid who'd hosted the party. Jamie Treva lived in a farm just outside of town, and his parents had gone to New York for their anniversary.

Conri stood at the Treva gate and sniffed the air. Cows and grass and gas—anchored, mortal smells. No hint of anything wild and strange that had leaked through from the Otherworld.

The dog chained up in the yard growled at him, a basso rumble of fear-threat from deep in its chest, as it stared fixedly at Conri. People always thought dogs would like him, but they did not. He supposed it was the dog version of an uncanny valley—too close for comfort.

Its chain was looped around an old apple tree next to the house, the bark buckled and warped around the links, so Conri left it to swear at him as he scrambled over the gate.

When the kids in town had said it was a farm, Conri had vaguely imagined the shabby stone buildings of his childhood. The damp, dusty homes of men who got up at four and went to bed at eight, with rags of curtains that no one bothered to pull. Instead it was a box of glass and black metal, aggressively exposed and uncompromisingly modern.

Conri could see most of the ground floor as he approached, and it didn't look like ground zero for a wild rural party. There were long, bare stretches of floor with not a misplaced cushion or discarded beer bottle in sight.

The dog threw itself at him, half strangled as it strained against its collar and gargled snarls as Conri stepped up onto the porch.

Technically Conri could understand what it was saying. In practice it was a dog, it didn't have a lot to say. Most had the vocabulary of a sheltered four-year-old.

Get off, get off, fuck off, Go fuck away.

A sweary four-year-old.

He pressed the doorbell. It didn't ring, but a small light in the kitchen pulsed politely to attract attention. The dog lost its mind at this further disrespect and stood on its back legs as it snarled an invite to fight it out.

Go away! Don't touch my stuff. Fuck off. I'll tell. I'll tell her when she gets back. People aren't meant to be here! Fuck off. Fuck you.

Conri winced at the noise and gave the dog an annoyed look. It was mostly legs and spots, a hound of the indiscriminate sort you found in places where they breed for soft mouths or a rabid hatred of squirrels instead of registries. It looked more pampered than most, with clipped nails and a shiny coat.

"Where's Jamie?" he asked.

The dog fell over itself in surprise when it understood him. Not in the way it had memorized commands and remembered the savory tang of *biscuit* and *treat*, but as clearly as if Conri had barked at it.

It whuffled unhappily at him. *Bad dog.*

Conri growled at it for the insult, and it lifted its lip at him. Before he could press it more, a sudden explosion of sound made both of them flinch. The crack made Conri's head ring, and he clapped his hands over his ears as he hunched down.

Thunder! The dog wailed as it tangled itself around the tree. *Thunder and she isn't here. Bad dog! Bad dog.*

Not thunder. Gunfire. Conri shook his head to dislodge the noise from his eardrum and jumped off the porch to chase it back to its source. The dog barked furiously after him as he loped away.

The barn was tucked around the back of the house, down a long dirt track so it didn't spoil the view from the kitchen. It looked more like what Conri had expected of a farm—paint peeled down to bare wood and broken windows boarded up with plywood. There were bags of empty bottles and forgotten jackets piled in the trunk of a shiny blue car that had been blocked in by a filthy old yellow pickup.

Conri slowed to a walk, and dust kicked up over his boots as he dug his heels and took in the scene.

The boy in front of the barn—a few years older than Finn but *softer*—was presumably Jamie Treva. He was the one with the shotgun. The yellow pickup had an irregular spray of holes punched into the back panel.

The thick-set, slightly older guy in work jeans and sweat-stained, gas-stop-branded T-shirt didn't look impressed.

"I told you," Jamie said. His voice cracked as he raised it, his vocal cords tight with nerves. His shirt was rumpled, the shoulder torn and buttons lost off the collar, and his eye had started to swell. "Move your damn truck, Ned."

Ned spat in the dirt. "Make me, pixie-fucker."

"I didn't fucking invite them!" Jamie shouted. The barrel of the shotgun wobbled around dangerously as he got more agitated. "Someone told them about the party, and they turned up. That's not my fault. I didn't want them here. I told them to fuck off—"

Ned punched his fist back against the door of the pickup with a dull crack of flesh against metal.

"Did you aim a goddamn shotgun at *them*?" he spat. "Or did you just wake up and find your balls this morning? What the fuck happened to my sister, Jamie. Did you let them take her? Did they promise you a suck of their cocks if you got her here?"

Jamie spluttered a flushed denial, and his finger tightened on the trigger as he lifted the gun.

"Shut up."

"Make me."

Conri sped up into a trot. Dead people only answered questions under specific conditions, and he didn't have any favors to call in there.

"Hey," he said, his hands held up and out and slightly in front of his face. It wasn't much of a disguise, but he didn't need it to work for long. "What's going on here."

Ned was sunbaked rather than sunburned, the sort of hot, under-the-skin pink that never really faded. His sandy hair was cropped brutally short across his skull, and he glared at Conri.

"What business is it of yours?" he snapped as he tried to slap Conri's hands out of the air. "Who the hell are you anyhow?"

"Call me an interested party," Conri said. He waited for Ned to grab at him again and caught him by the thumb. A hard twist squeezed a surprised howl out of Ned and put him on his knees. "If you want to find your sister, there's better ways to go—"

It didn't hurt at first. It never did. Conri felt the impact—a blunt smack to the back of the head that vibrated down to his knees—and smelled his own skin singe against hot metal. He tried to make use of that second between realization and pain, but it didn't last long. All he had time for, as the smell of whiskey and blood rose on the air, was to realize he'd made a mistake as his legs went from under him.

"I didn't need your help," Jamie yelled. "I didn't ask for it, and I didn't ask your goddamn kids to come to my party. Why don't you fuck back off to where you came from."

Blood dripped down Conri's face and splattered over the dirt. He ducked his head and wrapped his arms around it just in time. The heavy metal length of the shotgun smacked against the thick meat of his forearms.

Some people you knew they'd kick you—or pistol whip you—when you were down.

Conri absorbed the blows as he waited for the dizziness to fade. When Jamie swung again, Conri grabbed the shotgun before it could connect. He yanked, Jamie held on, and Conri rammed his shoulder into the boy's soft gut and put him in the dirt.

He grabbed Jamie's shirt and yanked him up long enough to punch him. His knuckles caught Jamie in the jaw, hard enough to clack his teeth together and throw him back down into the dirt. He wasn't unconscious, but Conri figured Jamie hadn't taken a lot of beatings in his life. Winded and with a bitten tongue—Conri assumed from the blood that spluttered from Jamie's lips—the shock would keep him down for a while.

Ned, though, had already scrambled up. Red dirt stained his knees and his face was hot under his all-weather tan. He lunged forward, and Conri rolled away from Jamie and onto his feet.

His mistake. Ned hadn't been going for Conri. He'd been after the shotgun, which Jamie had dropped when Conri laid him out. Ned snatched it away from Conri and backed away, sweat on his face and hands clumsy as he fumbled with the weapon.

"Where's my sister?!" he yelled as he jabbed the gun at Conri. "What did you do to her, you filthy—"

"Nothing," Conri said as he slowly backed away over the grass. "I came to talk to Jamie. Nobody needs to get hurt here… as long as you put that down."

Ned's face twisted, and he flexed his hands about the gun, knuckles white under his skin. "You…. We know the stories, you know. This isn't some big city, maybe, but that doesn't mean that we're stupid. I told Nora to stay away. I *told* her, but she wouldn't listen. We know about the deals, the secrets, the orgies in Iron Door, and the girls that never get seen again. Maybe people in LA will keep their mouths shut about it, but not in Elwood. Not with my sister."

Out of the corner of his eye, Conri saw a flicker of movement on the dirt road down from the house, but he couldn't spare the attention to identify it. With his luck, the dog had gotten loose and wanted to revisit what a *bad dog* he was.

"Look, I don't have anything to do with that," Conri said. "And if I've got a hole in me, I can't help find your sister, can I?"

It was the wrong thing to say. Ned's lips skinned back from his teeth in grim satisfaction. Conri relaxed as the cold acceptance that something awful was about to happen seeped through him.

"So you do know where she is?" Ned said triumphantly. "I knew it. I knew you'd taken her. If you don't tell me right now, I'm gonna—"

He lifted the gun to his shoulder without bothering to finish the sentence. Then he froze and sweat popped on his forehead in a greasy film.

"Mr. Kessell," Special Agent Bellamy said coldly as he put his hand on Ned's shoulder. "Put the gun down. Don't make me repeat myself."

His dark hair was nearly black at the roots where the sun hadn't picked out the dark red streaks, and it framed a lean, hard face. For an inappropriate, giddy moment, Conri wondered what it would take to bring a smile to that stern mouth. None of the ideas seemed wise, but buoyed on a flush of relief, they did look tempting.

Of course, he'd *always* had a thing for dangerous men—it had gotten him into plenty of trouble over the years. But there was a difference between having his head turned by a smart-mouthed thief and making eyes at an *Iron Door* agent. One was a bad idea, and the other was the *last* bad idea you got to have.

Ned's chest heaved under his shabby T-shirt as he stared at Conri, the temptation to finish what he started bald on his face. He'd wanted to do it for a while, Conri figured, in a faceless sort of way. His sister had given him an excuse.

Self-preservation won out. Ned held the shotgun out to the side and let Bell take it off him.

"Yours?" Bell asked as he took it.

Ned glared at the barn, jaw set so hard his teeth must have hurt. So Conri answered for him.

"It's Jamie's," he said. Bell glanced at him, and Conri pointed with his chin to the kid on the ground. "He was going to shoot Ned here for trespassing."

Bell made a disgusted face and shook his head. He stepped back, and Conri caught a quick glimpse of the gun that had been pressed against Ned's kidneys before Bell holstered it under his arm.

"Idiots," Bell said. He broke open the shotgun and unloaded the shell. "You think this is going to find your sister?"

Ned turned around and pointedly spat on the ground in front of Bell. "I think you ain't even looking," he said. "Iron Door is compromised. The iron wall is rusted. My sister is a small price to pay for—"

"I know the spiel," Bell interrupted. "I've heard it before. Go home, Mr. Kessel."

Ned bristled. "You aren't going to keep me quiet," he said. "I ain't *alone*, Agent. Word is already out."

Bell's face hardened.

"Go home," he repeated. "Or I'll put you in jail and you can see what good you are to your sister there."

"Iron Door doesn't have any jurisdiction over *god-fearing* human citizens—"

"Not actually true," Bell said. The shotgun clicked as he closed it again and cocked it back over his shoulder. "But you can argue that to the judge when you make it onto the docket. If you want."

It took a second, but finally Ned folded.

"This isn't over," he muttered darkly as he stalked back to his truck and scrambled up into it. The engine coughed to life, and he reversed jerkily until he could turn the truck around on the churned-up ground. He stuck his arm out through the window and pointed at Jamie, who'd sat up shakily. "If you had *anything* to do with this, Treva, you're going to regret it. Your elf knights won't be around to protect you forever."

He hit the gas and peeled away in a spray of dirt and stones.

Jamie wiped blood off his mouth. "I didn' ask for yer help," he slurred bitterly. "Y'just made it worse."

CONRI TURNED on the kitchen sink tap and stuck his head under it. Pink blood and red streaks of dirt splattered the polished black surface of the sink before they spiraled down the drain.

"I never saw a changeling before Iron Door rented the old farm for your camp thing," Jamie said around the cold cola can he had pressed against his mouth. He didn't sound guilty so much as defensive. "None of us had. And I knew that Ned would make something of it."

"It'll heal," Conri said stoically as he pulled his head out of the stream of water. He ran his hand through his wet hair, the water cold as it trickled down his neck, and winced as his fingers found the split goose-egg knot on the back. Maybe he'd grow in a new white streak once it healed. He turned around to look at the kitchen table, which Jamie currently shared with Agent Bell. "So you've never seen a changeling before? How did you manage to offend Robin Mell and his friends enough they drove all the way out here to ruin your party?"

"Who told you that?" Jamie bristled. "I don't *like* the fey, but that doesn't mean I'm going to kick off at them. I'm not stupid. You don't court the fey, not to make them like or hate you. You avoid 'em. I didn't get into it with them. It was Nora's boyfriend, Keith."

Bell leaned forward intently. His T-shirt pulled tight over his shoulders with the motion, showcasing lean, whipcord muscle layered over his bones. Conri had seen Bell move in the Otherworld—fast enough and mean enough to take on a pack of hounds—so he knew the man wasn't as slightly built as he looked when he was at ease. It was still worth a second look.

"Her brother didn't mention that," Bell said, apparently uninterested in Conri's brief distraction. "According to him she wasn't seeing anyone."

"Well she isn't going to tell *him*," Jamie said with ripe, teenage contempt. He rolled the can up over his jaw, where a blue bruise spread under patchy stubble. "You've met him. Would you tell him anything? He's a psycho. Always has been, even before their parents died. Nora is okay, but.... Ned's a nutjob. And there's the whole thing with the money."

"Money?"

"They don't have any," Jamie said with a mixture of pity and satisfaction. His family obviously did. "Or not enough. That's what I heard at school, anyhow. Ned's always been good with pigs, but not much else."

Conri leaned back against the counter. His hair dripped cold water down his back. A wiser man would have taken the hint.

"So, what happened with her boyfriend?" he asked. "Was he jealous that Robin turned Nora's head?"

Ned snorted. "Are you kidding? Have you seen Nora? I mean, she's okay, but she's hardly the sort of girl a fey chases after. She's just…

Nora. Anyhow, I had nothing to do with it, okay? I only know what happened because someone told me after the points showed up—"

He broke off as he glanced at Conri, who was more "pointed" than most of the fey, and flushed dully. Bell rapped his knuckles on the table to get Jamie's attention back on him.

"You can't save that," he said. "So move on."

Conri grinned. He didn't have fangs—a dentist would have been hard-pressed to find anything wrong in his mouth—but his teeth gave the impression of *sharp*. Jamie swallowed hard, the bob of his Adam's apple audible, and looked away. He pressed the can hard against his cheek and tried again.

"Yeah, well, it was nothing big. The… the fey kids had come down into town from camp, and Keith, y'know, helped them out. With a lift to…."

"To?" Bell said.

Jamie shrugged and looked down at the table. The tops of his ears were dull, resentful pink as he muttered something under his breath. Conri heard him anyhow.

"The shit train?" he said. "What's what?"

"There's a landfill about twenty miles north," he said. "Waste on the way there by rail stops here overnight sometimes. Sometimes longer. It smells like… shit."

"It was a joke," Jamie said, the *o* drawn out in exasperation. "Like, none of us want them in town. It's not *normal*. But he left them there to make a point. He didn't do anything to them."

Conri grimaced and pinched the bridge of his nose between his fingers. In his day, admittedly a looooong time ago, people knew the only fragile thing about a fey was their ego. Even a wound from iron healed quicker and cleaner than a blow to their pride.

"It was a joke!" Jamie repeated indignantly as he looked between Conri and Bell in a futile search for a sympathetic face. "They didn't have to come here to ruin my party over it."

Bell raised his eyebrows. "And kidnap your friend," he reminded him.

"Yeah. I mean, of course," Jamie said. He squirmed in his seat, the legs loud as they scraped on the black-tiled floor, and then frowned. His voice was slow as he said, "Thing is, none of us realized they were here at first? I mean, we did but none of us realized that they *obviously* shouldn't be there? It was like they used magic on us, and that's not allowed, right? So, I mean, nothing after that was our fault."

There was probably some sort of rule that said Bell couldn't lie to the people he was meant to work for. Conri wasn't under any such obligation. The bitter taste in the back of his throat at the idea of this soft, spoiled brat telling Finn he didn't belong? That made the lie slip out smoother.

"That's the law," he said earnestly. "Whatever you did, Iron Door can't do anything about it now. Goddammit."

Bell gave him a dry look over the table but let it stand as Jamie exhaled in relief.

"I figured," he said. "But it's good to know. I missed what started it, but Keith and one of the kids from the camp, the blond one, had gotten into it over something. That's when we all realized that they shouldn't be there, and it got a bit...."

Conri remembered the broken boards in the barn walls and the smashed bottles in a new light.

"Violent," he said.

"Not our fault, though," Jamie said quickly. "They used magic on us, right? We weren't in our right minds. And we were drunk. No one got hurt, not *really* hurt, that I saw. The fey gave as good as they got. Then they got the point and left. My mom is going to kill me when she sees what they did to the barn, and they were laughing as they drove off."

"Not all of them," Bell said. He pulled his phone out and slid it over the table in front of Jamie. "Robin. Thistle. Shanko...."

He flicked through the photos of the missing kids. Conri craned his neck to watch the images, upside down, as they skimmed over the screen. He didn't know any of them. That wasn't a surprise. Even if the families were from LA, Conri didn't hang out with other changelings much. Shanko was a changeling—almost human for now, with acne and dark circles under his eyes—while the others were foundlings a few years down the "not looking like a goblin" from Finn.

Except for Thistle, who seemed to have stuck.

"You might not like them," Bell said. "But they have parents, families who'll miss them. What happened after the others left? What happened to Nora? You already told us you didn't know, so now tell us what you *do* remember. Did she leave with them?"

"No. Maybe," Jamie stumbled over his words. "I wanted everyone to leave, okay? I didn't care where they went. But… Keith went after them. With iron."

CHAPTER FOUR

"KEITH RAWLINS," Bell said into the phone as he walked down the steps off the Treva's porch. Back at the camp, he heard his colleague mutter the name under her breath as she wrote it down. Technically Agent Jayne outranked him, but seniority didn't matter when the case involved the Otherworld. She couldn't cross, so Bell took point on the investigation. "Find out if he made it home last night."

"You think they took him too?" she asked, a sour note in her voice. Jayne didn't like anything that came across the border, not even changelings. It didn't impact her work—and she was a hero like Felix, so it didn't matter if it did—but she enjoyed it when they screwed up. "That won't be something that the government can massage out of existence."

"Find out if he's sleeping off some hard cider at home first," Bell told her. "Then we'll know if we need to worry about him or not."

Behind them, the dog, which had been sacked out in the shade at the side of the house, exploded into a frenzy of snarled barks. The chain it was hooked to rattled noisily as it was yanked tight.

"Hounds?" Jayne asked with a flicker of concern in her voice.

Bell turned around and saw Conri at the bottom of the steps. Slabber dripped from the dog's jowls as it snapped the air in front of his worn T-shirt. He stared it down for a second until the dog gave up, snapped the air one last time, and flopped down on its stomach in the dirt.

"Just dogs," he said dryly. "Don't worry about it. Text me when you know anything. I'll get back when I can."

"Safe travels," she wished him.

The line went dead, and Bell tucked the phone into his jacket and watched as the dog, a low, angry growl rattling between her chest and the dirt, glared up at Conri with doleful, resentful eyes. Bell was surprised. He would have expected dogs would like the man, considering…. He

213

glanced at Conri's mottled hair and mismatched dog eyes and supposed a lot of people made that assumption.

He didn't ask. Conri's relationship with dogs wasn't his business, unlike his relationship to this case.

"What are you doing here?" he asked.

"Same thing as you," Conri said. He left the dog to growl and walked over to Bell. "Trying to find out what happened to Nora and the other kids."

"That's my job."

Conri shrugged and grinned. It was a warm, easy smile that creased his face around it and made him look—despite everything—very human. And smug.

"Mine too," he said as he handed over his wallet. Bell flicked it open and frowned at the skip tracer license tucked in next to his driver's license. "I guess this is where we team up, huh?"

"You watch a lot of TV, huh?" Bell said. He tossed the wallet back, and Conri caught it out of the air. "That's not how the real world works. You're the father of a person of interest in this case—in fact, with everything riding on this, you probably *are* a person of interest—and you're going to stay out of my way."

"Or?" he asked with a hint of a smile.

Bell sighed. Changelings could be frustrating. Whatever physical changes their stay in the Otherworld had made on them were nothing to the ones *under* the skin. Even people who'd returned, more or less, to the world they left, didn't always remember the right ways to react.

Or care about them, which Bell suspected was more Conri's problem. He was out of luck that Bell wasn't fey and didn't need someone to play the fool.

"This isn't a negotiation. I don't need to threaten you, Conri. I've told you what's going to happen, and now you're going to do it. Next time I won't be there to stop you getting shot. Understood?"

There was a pause, and then Conri nodded and glanced away from Bell and across the farm. It should have been satisfying, but Bell felt a brief, selfish twitch of regret. He might not need a partner, but he wouldn't have objected to at least a token protest. It would have given him something to daydream about later.

Not—he gave himself a mental slap on the back of the head—that he was going to have time for that anyhow. He had a job to do, and he'd always been better at that than relationships anyhow. Between what he did and what he *was*? One or the other of those had wrecked all of his relationships—not just romantic—over the years. Most people found it hard enough to know someone they cared about might be put in harm's way every day, never mind that harm would be on the other side of a border they'd never cross and he might never cross back. *Would*, one day, never cross back over.

Walkers didn't die, they disappeared. Everyone understood that was pretty much the same thing.

Conri shouldn't be on Bell's radar to be anything other than a distraction. He might *want* someone to be… something… but not today. Not Conri. That was too complicated even for someone who wasn't anything but a fun night on a motel mattress.

"Stay out of Kessel's way," Bell told him. "Once I find out what happened, things will settle down."

Conri scratched his cheek under his water-blue eye. He looked, for a moment, bone-tired under the easygoing charm. "That depends on what happened, doesn't it?"

He wasn't wrong. Bell grimaced to himself. Most of the time, he didn't have to deal with the aftercare side of the job. He'd always assumed that was how the responsibilities were divided—he crossed into the Otherworld and fought monsters, and agents like Jayne held hands and soothed fevered brows—but maybe he was bad at it.

"Go back to town, stay out of trouble," he repeated the order and turned away.

He headed back toward the Iron Door–issued black SUV parked behind Conri's Toyota. His mind was already occupied with a plan of attack for the search—grid patterns and bleak calculations of how much ground one man could cover—so he got halfway before he felt the prickle on the back of his neck. He looked around and into Conri's face, *right* by his shoulder.

"What the fuck?" he blurted in surprise. No one got that close to him without him being aware of it. *Humans* didn't, never mind a changeling who wore the Otherworld like a tattoo. He'd spent too long alone on the far side of the border, where if you dropped your guard even once, something would feel obliged to take advantage of it. "Where do you think you're going?"

"I said I understood," Conri pointed out. "Not that I agreed."

He detoured around Bell and headed for the passenger side of the car. The back of his T-shirt was damp, plastered to the thick muscles of his back, and blood splattered a dingy pattern against the faded gray fabric.

"I don't need help," Bell said roughly, caught on an uncomfortable fork of reluctant attraction and equally unwelcome concern. His job was to get Nora back, not worry over some cheerful idiot who was probably more resilient than Bell.

Conri stood on the frame of the car, one arm hooked over the door he'd already opened. The wind ruffled his shaggy cropped hair and made him squint one eye shut. It should have made him look more human, blurred the edges of the changes the fey had wrought, but somehow it didn't. Some things were more than skin deep.

"Liar."

"I was grateful for your help earlier," Bell said. "Don't push it and don't forget I can still charge you for illegally going to the Otherworld. You have the same choice as Treva—stay out of my way or wait this out in a cell."

"Okay, I guess it's the cell." Conri dropped down into the passenger seat and made himself comfortable. He waited for Bell to yank the driver's side door open and grinned at him as he slotted the seat belt in place. "So, what's it going to be, Agent? You can spend some of Nora's precious minutes taking me all the way back to town to find a cell I can't get out of. Or you can accept my help."

Bell braced his arms against the roof of the car and scowled at Conri.

"I could drag you out of the car and leave you cuffed to the fence."

Something moved murkily under Conri's charm, a hint of something dark that cut the sunshine and easy smiles. It should have made Bell pull back, warned him off. Instead it made his tongue curl for more—like a shot of whiskey in hot chocolate.

"Either we work together or we work at odds," Conri said flatly. He leaned back in the seat and crossed his arms. "I'm not going to sit this out, and where are you going to find someone else in Elwood who *can* cross into the Otherworld, illegally or not?"

He wasn't, and Iron Door wasn't going to get someone to Elwood in time to be of any use.

"What's the price?" he asked.

Most changelings couldn't cross on their own—the Otherworld wouldn't be much of a trap if you could wander home—but those who could paid a price in blood or time or some esoteric item that the fey who'd given them the gift counted their debts in. Bell wasn't going to run Conri as an asset, even an aggressively willing one, if it would kill or maim him.

Conri looked away from him. "There isn't one," he said. "It's none of your business why."

"There's always a price," Bell said. "Have you already paid it?"

"Twice."

A bitter note to Conri's voice sold that claim. Most Walkers were cocky and arrogant. The ones who joined Iron Door were dangerous to know—in a lot of ways—and the ones who hadn't were out for themselves. The one thing they all had in common was that, when they talked about how they'd gotten their gift? None of them sounded sure they'd come out ahead.

Bell thought about it and then swore under his breath. The odds weren't much better with two people on the hunt, but they *were* better. With the entire, tenuous peace with the fey on his shoulders, Bell would take any advantage he could get.

Even one he maybe couldn't trust.

"Okay, you're so useful," he said. "Prove it. There's only one ford into the Otherworld here. How the hell did a couple of kids get from here to where we met? It's a good eight miles and it's the only ford in and out of the slough. Can you tell me that?"

Conri shed his brief, dour mood like a too-heavy coat as he unleashed a wide, crooked smile.

"I can do better than that," he said. "I can show you."

Bell had already given in. He climbed into the car, slammed the door, and started the engine. Then he bumped the car over the ruts and turned out onto the road.

"Probably," Conri hedged as he braced one black-sneakered foot against the dash and slouched down. "You'll see."

"IT'S A tree," Bell said as he leaned his hips against the side of the SUV and crossed his arms. His head throbbed with frustration and pressure. There wasn't exactly a Golden Hour where you could be *sure* you'd get back who, and what, had crossed over into the Otherworld, but sunrise or sunset was when you had a chance. He should be looking for Nora, and Keith now, since his parents had confirmed the other teenager hadn't made his way home last night, not following Conri's vague directions along backroads.

Conri put his hand on the tree, fingers spread, and then pulled it back. He showed Bell his palm, the skin welted with itchy-looking red hives.

"It's a lock," he said.

Surprise pulled Bell up off the car and forward. He took Conri's hand to check the marks, a prickle of interest sharp and ignored in the back of his throat as he rubbed his thumb over the broad, callused palm. No corresponding tingle on his skin, so he turned to the tree. It took him a minute to find the first one, the head half-buried under scabs of overgrown bark. Once he did, though, the others were easier.

Four old iron nails driven deep into the bark of the tree and left to rust. Bell pulled a knife and dug the bark away from one until he could get a better look at it. Under the rough plaque of rust and dirt, it looked homemade, roughly forged and clumsy. He picked at it with his nails, but there was no give. The wood around the nails was stained red and gray, as if it had bled.

"The tree at Treva's house," he said as he stepped back and wiped his hands. "That chain was older than the dog was."

Conri nodded. "Older than the house probably," he said. "We— me and Finn—passed a rock on the way into town that was covered in horseshoes. I thought it was just another unfriendly town. It's been a… while… since I saw anyone try anything like this."

"They closed off the Otherworld," Bell said. The idea felt… strange. It would close every single case that Iron Door had on the books—past, present, and future—but the idea didn't have the appeal it should. The Otherworld was his enemy, but it had been his enemy his whole life. He couldn't imagine it gone. "I didn't know that was possible."

"It isn't," Conri said. "Usually. Anywhere but a slough and the movement of the Otherworld would have either burst the locks or worn itself a new route. Even here, there's one ford left. They probably tried to lock that off too, but it would only have lasted until the first solstice. Then it would burst like a cyst. That would have been a bad year for Elwood."

Bell walked around the tree. There were four nails on the other side too, lower down and hammered in hard enough to flatten the heads. He ran his thumb over the rough metal and closed his eyes.

It was hard to explain what it felt like to cross into the Otherworld. Bell had tried over the years, but he'd eventually given up. People always thought he kept something back, some trick or gadget that would explain how it worked. He hadn't. The border… felt like a threshold, that feeling you had when you were about to knock on a door you knew would be answered.

This felt like the opposite. The broody emptiness of a house you knew was abandoned and the tight expectation of a knock that echoed. It made his chest tighten and the back of his neck itch.

"Interesting," he said as he opened his eyes. Conri had gotten too close again, his shoulder propped against the tree next to Bell's hand and his long body hipshot and angled. Bell resisted the temptation to be charmed and stepped back. "How does it help us? If the ford is locked—"

"An old lock," Conri said. He slapped the tree. "On old doors. Push it hard enough from either side and it would crack open. Not far, not yet, but enough for a few kids to squeeze through. Especially if their blood was up and emotions running high from the scene at the barn. That would have rattled the slough back to life. For a while."

Bell swore under his breath and walked around the tree to run his eye along the skyline. They'd taken the long way around, on rutted country roads with crumbled edges and faded paint, but as the crow flies…. There it was. Bell could see the peaked roof of the Treva barn from here. It would take him ten minutes to reach it if he cut through the fields, probably less for a scared teenage girl who ran track and had enough cider that she wasn't feeling any pain.

"How did they find it?" he asked over his shoulder.

"Local legends," Conri said. "Kids around here probably dare one another to go to the boarded-up doors of the haunted house they made the Otherworld into. Knock, run away, and tell everyone you saw the fey. The kids from camp… you ever get into so much trouble that you run and only realize where you're going when you hit your own front door?"

… his arm throbbed, a hot, sickly pulse of pain that kept time with the slap of his wet sneakers on the road. There was blood—not all of it his, but some of it—and he could taste his own panic with each breath he took. Fear of what was behind him, fear of what would happen if anyone found out, and a rattling cant of every bad thing anyone had ever said between his ears.

It had been Felix he'd run to, though, not his own family.

"Sort of," Bell said, the words dry on the back of his throat.

"For Robin and the other fey, *this* is home," Conri touched the tree with his fingertips and looked wistful. "And it wants them back. But we're not so lucky. If we want to cross over, we have to do it the old-fashioned way."

He started toward the car, loose-limbed and confident. Bell stepped in front of him, fingers steepled against Conri's chest to stop him in place. The T-shirt was thin, and Bell could feel the warm skin and heavy muscle under it.

"How did *you* find it?"

Conri raised his eyebrows and then shrugged the insult off. "It's downhill," he said. "When people panic, they run downhill, because it feels like the smartest decision, even if it isn't. And unless there's water to distract them, they run toward the moon. It feels safer if you can see. So they came in this direction, and I hoped my theory was right. You can feel the ford now, can't you? If you'd known what to look for, you could have found it too, right?"

Maybe. Now that Bell had touched the ford, he could sort of sense it on the edge of his mind, the unfriendly "no" of something that you weren't expected to open. It felt like the connecting door in a hotel room. The one you rattled tentatively anyhow, just to see.

"Could you open the ford again? he asked.

Conri thought about it. "After this long? I doubt it," he said. "Even if you found all the nails and pulled them out, the iron has leached into the wood. The ford would have to be hacked back open to clear it."

"Let's see," Bell said.

He pulled his hand away from Conri's chest and loped around to the back of the car. He opened the trunk and used his thumb to unlock the heavy black box that took up most of the space. The inside was laid out with obsessive order—guns clipped to the back and ammunition directly below them, knives sheathed in custom-made nanoplastic sheathes to protect the edges, and fairy ointment sealed in lead to keep it potent. Bell lifted the knives and reached under to grab the heavy iron chains. They were meant as restraints, but they'd do.

The links rattled as he hauled them out of the trunk and against the back of the SUV. A few chips dinged the glossy black paintwork.

When Conri saw the iron looped around Bell's wrist, he took a quick, long step back. His easy, loose-boned body language tightened, and he shifted his weight onto his toes.

"What—"

"It's not for you," Bell said. "I never asked to be a Walker, but I am. No one gets to close the door on me."

He draped the weight of the chain over his shoulder and crossed the scrubby grass back to the iron-studded tree. Conri lingered out of reach, obviously not entirely convinced. The trunk wasn't that thick compared to those around it. Nails and stagnant magic weren't good for growing things, apparently. Who knew? He looped the chains around the base of the tree twice and then dragged the heavy length that was left back to the car. It rattled and jingled as it untangled.

"That's… if you cut it open, it won't be like a normal ford," Conri warned. He slunk closer, skittish on his feet as the chains rattled near them. "The slough has probably congealed around it. This will be like lancing a boil and then jumping in."

Bell paused with the chains only half clipped to the tow bar and gave Conri a wry look. "Thanks for the imagery. Get in the car."

Conri didn't do as he was told....

"You can't help with this. It's pure, once-worked iron," Bell said. "So get in, and when I tell you to hit the gas, you hit the gas."

Conri looked like he was going to argue but instead did as he was told and scrambled into the cab. He left the door cracked open as he started the engine and Bell locked the chains in place. His fingers were bruised and his knuckles were bleeding from being pinched between the links by the time he finished.

"Now," he yelled over the engine.

There was a long pause, although he was pretty sure Conri's pointy ears had caught the order, and then a muttered *fuck* before the engine revved and the SUV lurched forward. The chains yanked tight, tore the bark off the tree in strips and splinters, and jolted the SUV to a tire-spinning stop. Dirt and grass spewed out the back as the rear fishtailed and white, acrid smoke spewed out around them.

For a second it looked like the tree was going to win, and then Conri slammed the gas down to the floor. The engine made a raw metal groan as it inched forward, and then the tree tore out of the ground in a shower of dirt and stones and thick, tangled roots. It whiplashed through the air like a mace as the SUV shot forward.

Bell swore and threw himself backward. He hit the ground with a thump, and the branches scraped his hands and face as it was dragged over him. It felt like being beaten, but quickly. Then it was gone.

He rolled over, wiped blood out of his eyes, and shoved himself to his feet. His ribs ached, and a raw scrape ran from the middle of his forearm down to his knuckles. By Iron Door standards, he was whole enough.

Conri spun the wheel and hit the brakes before he drove off the other side of the road. The tree bounced twice and then smashed into the side of the car with a crack that tore metal and scattered chunks of broken glass over the tarmac.

"Fuck," Bell muttered. All that soul-searching about whether it was appropriate to work with Conri—a changeling whose kid might *still* be involved somehow and who was too hot for Bell's own good—and he got the man killed. He picked a splinter out of the back of his hand and loped over to the mangled SUV.

The tree was stuck to the side of the car like a burr, branches jammed through the metal and shoved through the smashed windows. Conri slouched in the driver's seat, his skin paler than usual and his eyes closed. He had, Bell noticed, ridiculously pretty lashes.

"Conri?" He grabbed at the branches and wrenched them back until they broke, and he could scrape them out of the window. Something hot scraped his fingers, and he flinched back. It was one of the nails, hot enough to singe Bell's fingertips from the energy that had torn through it. It had left a long mark on Conri's face, half blister and half cut. Bell grabbed it, ignored the sting in his thumb and forefinger, and wrenched it loose. "Are you okay? Con?"

One eye opened cautiously, bright blue squinted through the thick lashes. After a second, the other followed suit.

"Fuck," he said with feeling. "That was close."

Bell would have very much liked to kiss him. The urge caught him by surprise with the sudden intensity of it. He could actually feel it—the firm pressure of Conri's lips and the taste of him on Bell's tongue. It stung like sour candy as he swallowed the ache and made himself focus.

"It worked," he said. He could feel the ford again, the slightly uncomfortable welcome of a wide-open door and no one else around. "We can follow them."

CHAPTER FIVE

WHOEVER HAD nailed shut the doors to faery had done it a long time ago. Cut off from the mortal world and mortal visitors, the slough had, like a freshly dumped lover, let itself go. The shadows of the mortal world, the cursed highways and eerie ghost towns built from stolen time, hadn't fallen into disrepair, they'd been cannibalized by the slough to sustain itself.

It had fallen back into wet, sucking bogland, lush green hillocks broken up with black mud puddles, and overgrown forest. The landscape was tied together by thickets of dense, knotted briars that stretched for miles. The black, thorny runners were decorated with great white roses the size of a hand that smelled like candied, rotted flesh.

Conri swallowed. His throat felt sticky and his tongue dry. He'd never been here before. Probably. Places changed. Memories failed. He didn't *think* he'd ever been sent here. It didn't matter. He still knew *what* it was.

"I guess we wouldn't have been taking the car anyhow," he said dryly.

Bell snorted as he pulled on a Kevlar vest and tightened the straps. He'd shifted his gun down onto his hip, and, while it was hidden under his T-shirt, Conri had seen him slip a fair-sized, silver-alloy blade into a sheath along the small of his back. In another situation it would be overkill. Here it was lightly armed.

"You didn't know that when you wrecked it." He reached out and touched a gloved finger to one of the hook-thorned briars. It made the flowers tremble, the delicate petals almost flesh-toned under the soft pink glow of dawn light. "The roses hadn't bloomed last time I was here. Time's running fast."

Conri nodded. He could taste it on the air, spun out thin and sharp as cotton candy. It had volume but no substance. Heady. "It hasn't had any time to play with for a long time, so now that it has, it's gorged itself.

It's better than the alternative—at least we have a chance to find her before it's too late."

"But less chance that we take back a Nora that anyone recognizes," Bell said grimly. "Or that she'll want to go back."

Silence hung heavily between them as they both—Conri assumed—thought about their own demons. Not that anyone had come looking for Conri, but if they had, they would have struggled to recognize him after only a few days. Would he have gone back then if he'd had to step back into his old life at the minute he left it?

Probably. His mortal life had been shabby and hand-to-mouth, but life in the Otherworld hadn't exactly changed that. If he had a glamour in his pocket to pass as human—he'd never had any desire to pay for his sins, especially ones imposed on him—he'd have stolen back home and pretended he never left. If his imaginary rescuer got there soon enough, Conri might have even been able to convince himself of it too.

But there were plenty of changelings who would have stayed.

"Are we going to ask what she wants?" he asked.

Bell pushed his sleeves up toward his elbows. The slough had decided to be hot, the air muggy and full of the drone of bugs. Bell's arms were wiry, pale skin pulled tight over whipcord muscles and dusted with freckles and fine, dark hair. A few old scars, faded to white ribbons of skin, dented both arms to different degrees. Conri appreciated the view out of the corner of his eye.

"Probably. If circumstances allow," Bell said. "Ask me if I can care what the answer is."

Conri thought of his life in LA—the narrow box of a house that was full of color and mess, the stack of leftovers in his fridge that ranged from Thai drunken noodles to gyros, and Finn's clothes tossed carelessly around as if "Servants will deal with that" were genetic. He thought of Finn, who wasn't his blood even though Conri had been the first and only one to hold him, and…. Okay, the kid was a pain in the ass, but Conri still loved him.

It wasn't the life he'd planned—Conri was pretty sure he'd never heard of Thailand until the Return—but in a lot of ways, it was better. And it was his.

"That's okay," he said as he headed out along the marshy rise of sandbar that ran through the bog. The mud plucked at his boots, and in the back of his head—where it might have passed as his own if he hadn't been wary—the grass muttered about how warm it was and how nice it would be to lie down and sleep. "I already know the answer."

"Let's just find them," Bell said as he caught up with Conri and slapped a hand on his shoulder. "Worry about it too much now and lying down for a nap will sound like a good idea. And if we don't find them, it won't matter."

Conri gave Bell a hard, sidelong grin. "We'll find them," he said. "This is what I do, and I'm really good at it."

THREE HOURS later—by the not entirely reliable clockwork of Bell's watch—the slough seemed to have put its shoulder to proving Conri wrong. A brittle trail of bent grasses, smears of mud, and the occasional muddy blond hair—garishly mundane in the florid overgrowth that framed it—had led them to a hill white with bog cotton back near where they'd started.

"It doesn't want to give them up," Conri said as he sat down on a rock. His throat was tight with the need to pant, but he resisted. He wanted Bell to see him as a man, not a dog. "You can smell how stagnant it has gotten here down in the hollers, like molasses, and it doesn't want to go back."

"You talk about it like it's alive." Bell dropped into a crouch next to him and took a long drink of water from a bottle. "The fey don't."

"The fey don't like to think about things like that," Conri said. "It's why you don't find many changelings who've seen Mag Mell or Annwn. They don't get to visit. They like to play lords of their own creations, and the last thing they want is to tempt the Otherworld with too much mortality, a hit of time, and wake up with their beautiful cities remade into skyscrapers and tenements. That's why they make places like this, the sloughs and estates and crannogs, near the borders so they can enjoy trysts with mortality without getting it all over the floor at home."

Bell offered him the water, but Conri waved it back. He was thirsty, but he could grab a drink from a stream or pool on the way past. Faerie food had bound him once. It wouldn't bother again. Bell didn't have that option.

But he was sweaty. It stuck his T-shirt to his back and under his arms, sour and sticky. He peeled the band shirt off over his head and draped it over the cotton to air out. It would make him itch later, but he could cope with that. He raked his fingers through his hair and scratched at the nape of his neck. The salt from his sweat stung his palm as it got into the blisters, and he swore and pulled his hand down to scratch at it instead.

"You were here a long time," Bell said. He crouched on the dry dirt, flask dangling between his knees, and watched Conri with dark, hooded eyes. His interest wasn't entirely professional—Conri could tell that as Bell licked his lips—but it wasn't completely unprofessional either. "The hair is always the first thing to change. But eyes and ears are more unusual."

"Not *that* unusual."

"Uncommon," Bell compromised. "But here long enough that you can't bear iron? That's rare. The only ones I know of are the diplomats… who do make it to Mag Mell."

Conri picked a shred of skin off his palm. "I never did," he said. "If I had, I wouldn't have seen the Court of Roses or the Hall of Thorns. I would have been relegated to the Stables of Shit, probably. I was only ever a servant, but I was… useful and resilient. Not much in the Otherworld is both. I made a good dog. Still do."

"You're not a dog," Bell said. Because people did, even the ones who didn't mean it.

Conri leaned back so pale skin pulled tight over lean, heavy muscle. He wasn't built for show or speed, but for endurance. His legs sprawled out carelessly in front of him, jeans pulled low and loose around his lean hips.

"If you really mean that?" he said, the words harsh with challenge as he waited for Bell's eyes to move back to his face. "Come over here and prove it."

It was too late to curb his tongue by the time his brain realized that this *mattered*. There was no reason it should. Bell was nothing to him but the temptation of a good lay and a lot of trouble, but Conri could feel his chest tighten with anticipation as he waited for Bell's reaction.

Apparently, though, he was destined for blue balls—mental and physical—since rather than answer, Bell scrambled to his feet. He shaded his eyes with his hands.

"What's that?" He pointed back toward the ford—marked by an X scarred into the greenery with Iron Door–branded graphite paint— as a long slice of the world went thin. It looked like tissue paper for a second, a painted image laid over something else, and then Ned Kessel's battered yellow pickup with a spray of shotgun pellet holes on the side tore through. The world snapped back into place behind it.

The oversized tires dug ruts into the soft, gray-green banks and splashed black, sticky glaur in thick, clotted patches up the doors and over the windshield. A brief try to clear it off with the wipers smeared the mud more and glued the blades up after three swipes.

"Shit," Conri hissed between his teeth. "He must have followed us."

"Well," Bell drawled sardonically as he absently put one hand on his gun. "Thank God I brought you along for your expertise."

Conri swallowed the growl that stuck in the back of his throat. "How the hell did he get across? We ripped the ford open, but it's *still* a ford. He wasn't a Walker."

Sometimes people pinged as Walkers when they weren't, but Conri had never been wrong about who *wasn't*. Ned Kessel ran too hot—too quick-tempered, too resentful, too everything—to play stepping-stones with reality. Walkers could be dumb as rocks—Conri hadn't gotten to where he was by making good decisions—but they weren't rash. If a Walker did something balls-achingly, breathtakingly unexpected and insane, like ripping the Otherworld open like a picked-at scab, it wasn't because they hadn't thought of the consequences. They'd decided the gain was worth the risk.

Bell fumbled in his pockets and pulled out a pair of binoculars not much bigger than a roll of dollars. He unfolded them and lifted them up to squint through the eyepieces as he followed the truck's uneven, breakneck progress over the terrain.

He muttered, "Fuck," and passed the glasses to Conri.

They were so light they barely weighed anything. Conri remembered when he'd first come to the Otherworld and been amazed by their weightless armor and self-taught swords. Now anyone taken would want to know if it was connected to the cloud or not.

He adjusted the lenses and scanned along the raw tracks cut into the bog until he found the yellow truck. It was Ned Kessel behind the wheel, sunburned skin greasy with sweat and hands locked on the wheel. Next to him....

"Son of a bitch," Conri muttered.

Thistle, raw goblin bones still too close to the top of his skin, hunched in the passenger seat. One arm—too long, too skinny, and with the joint subtly in the wrong place—was stretched up over his head. Blood dripped down from the raw welts the cuffs had scalded into his skin and stained his shirt as he was thrown about.

"That answers your questions about how Ned got here," Bell said. "Another fey child in distress at the Otherworld's door."

Conri handed the little binoculars back to Bell, who folded them and stashed them in his pocket. "And another mortal for the slough to tap," Conri said grimly. "It's getting greedy."

He felt Bell's assessment out of the corner of his eye. "You sure you were just a servant?" he asked. "You sound way too knowledgeable about the inner workings of the Otherworld."

Conri's mouth twitched up at the corner. It wasn't exactly a smile.

"The Otherworld?" he said. "No. But I know a fey lord's hunting preserve when I see it and, well, they are what they eat. This place spent years glutted on death and fear and the hot thrill of the kill. Then it was left to starve. It's like a thirsty drunk—water would do to wet his throat but what he wants is rotgut whiskey."

He jabbed his finger down toward the pickup as he said that. The mire under it had thickened, the broken-edged ruins of an old dirt road shrugged up to the surface under Ned's tires. Bell followed the gesture and grimaced as he saw the road.

"And by rotgut whiskey you mean a violent redneck with a gutful of conspiracy theories and bigotry," Bell said. "On the trail of the kids he thinks kidnapped his sister."

Conri grabbed his T-shirt and pulled it on. It was still damp, and he'd been right about the bog-cotton making him itch.

"A hunt is a hunt," he said through the sweaty folds. "And now it has... two? No three... at the same time."

Bell stared at him for a second and then turned to watch Ned, his face set in grim lines.

"My brother drank," he said. There was no emotion in his voice. Conri, as he picked a burr of flower silk out of his hair, regretted the comparison. "Before he died, he drank a lot. I'll tell you one thing he really hated, that was guaranteed to set him off? If you tried to take his bottle off him."

Conri scratched his ribs and shrugged.

"It won't want us to leave," he admitted. "But it doesn't want the hunt to end either. So it isn't going to help Ned."

Bell glanced down at the proto-road the slough had shaped for the pickup and then gave Conri a skeptical look.

"It's the carrot," Conri said grimly. "If the prey thinks there's no hope, they'll lie down and die. A good hunting preserve is designed to keep them on the move, to dangle the possibility of escape—or rescue—close enough to make them think they have a chance but far enough away to keep them running."

Bell looked bleak. "Then it needs to throw something our way," he said as he started back down the hill. The frustration was raw in his voice. "Because we aren't any closer to finding Nora and the others than when we got here."

He was right. Which.... Conri paused, his sneakers balanced on two rocks, and cocked his head to listen to the rattling growl of the pickup's engine as it cut through the eerie silence that had fallen over the slough.

"We have him," he said thoughtfully. "Tell me, if you were trapped here, would you run toward or away from the sound of a car?"

Bell was smart enough to think about that question instead of making an assumption.

"Toward," he said after a second. "However she got here— however Ned got his hands on Thistle—right now all she knows is *that* is something she hasn't heard for a while. Whether she wants to be rescued or left alone, she'll want to see what's going on. If she's free to."

Well, he'd made a few assumptions once he got started. It wasn't his fault. Humans mostly saw what the fey wanted, saw the fey *how* the fey wanted. Conri hopped off his rocks, altered course slightly, and headed on down the hill.

"Not just Nora," he said. "Robin might be fey, but he hasn't been back here since he was a babe in arms. He might have thought he's ready to come back and be a High Lord of the Otherworld, but a place like this is going to rule him, not the other way around. By now, he's as ready to get back to indoor plumbing and fruit that doesn't have an agenda as the mortal children. Finn would be."

Bell let Conri get almost all the way down the hill before he asked, "Even if Finn knew that he'd broken the Treaty? That he might have caused a war? Would he want to face you then?"

Conri fumbled his next step and planted his foot in a puddle of black mud. He nearly lost his shoe, but the time it took to extract himself let him recover his composure.

"Your mistake is assuming that Finn has any shame," Conri said. He scraped black goop off his shoe onto a knot of grass. "He'd expect me to fix it for him."

"And how would you do that?" Bell asked. He didn't bother to make it sound casual. The suspicion was blunt in his voice. It stung a bit, but Conri appreciated the honesty. "If he *had* been involved."

Conri crouched down and plucked a thin, mangled bit of metal out of the mud he'd scraped from his shoe. It was rusted like it had been there for years—iron reacted to the Otherworld the same way the Otherworld reacted to iron—but it was still recognizably a house key attached to a dented fob in the shape of an N. At one point it had been covered with crystals, but only two or three pink studs were left, sparkle dulled under the mud.

Chance or the slough's machinations, he wondered as he lifted it to his nose for a sniff. It was mostly rust and metal, but it had spent years being handled. The oils from Nora's skin were rubbed deeply into the metal, and even in its current state, he caught a thread of it.

Daffodils and coal.

"I don't know," he said as he straightened up and tossed the fob to Bell…. "I'd probably start by not telling Iron Door my plans."

CHAPTER SIX

CONFESSION, MOCKERY, or both?

Bell slouched back against a twisted thorn tree and chewed on that question as he waited for Conri to get back from scouting nearby for any sign of the missing kids. He'd won the coin toss and left Bell to watch Ned as he made a half-assed camp nearby.

It was nighttime, or what passed for night in the Otherworld. Somehow, although Bell couldn't put his finger on exactly what the difference was, they had indisputably gone from dawn to dusk.

Ned had driven stubbornly into the dim light for a while, until the press of purple, whispering shadows around the dimming headlights got to him and he stopped. Thistle stayed cuffed, this time to the handle of the pickup, while Ned hunched bitterly over the fire as if he could suck the heat from gray sticks as they burned. He fed it handfuls of plucked moss and cursed in baffled, barely stifled rage as he burned his fingers but still stayed chilled.

The Otherworld didn't satisfy. It ran on the energy of want, of the grit in the pearl of someone's perfect, fairy life and the itch of always wanting more.

In the back of his head, the old, sticky trauma tried to squeeze out of the box he kept it in. He pushed it back down impatiently. Everything in the Otherworld brought him back to that—*to blood, dirt that smelled like popcorn under his collar, and the ringing in his ears from his dad's fist*—if he didn't give his brain something else to chew on.

Bell closed his eyes and tried to entice his brain back to the question of Conri's innocence… or lack of it. There was a flicker of filthy interest from his libido, but otherwise nothing took the bait. Bell didn't know Conri, but he wanted to trust him. That was probably a bad sign. Instincts lied in the Otherworld. It showed you exactly what you wanted to see before you got pushed in the hole.

233

How could he trust what his instincts were telling him *now* about Conri, when they'd been so wrong before?

Bell grimaced to himself. There he went again, nails dug into the same old scab.

"You asleep?" Conri asked. He flopped down next to Bell and tried to steal half the tree to lean on, all damp warmth and the faint salt smell of clean sweat. Bell kept his eyes closed as he wondered exactly what Conri would do if he thought he had an Iron Door agent at a disadvantage. After a moment Conri snorted. "I can tell you aren't, Agent Bellamy."

Bell was good at his job. There wasn't any other option when you were a Walker. He didn't often feel like an idiot. It turned out he still didn't like it.

"How?" he asked as he opened his eyes. "Special, heightened changeling senses?"

Conri pulled his knees up and rested his elbows on them. "I used to be a thief. Not a good one, but you learned to tell when people were really asleep. It made it easier."

It shouldn't have been funny, but somehow it was. Bell snorted under his breath and leaned forward to rub his hands over his face. He hadn't been asleep, but it was a temptation.

"Aren't you worried I'll arrest you?" he asked. "Theft is a crime."

"It was a long time ago, remember?" Conri said dryly. "The statute of limitations ran out a few decades back. Anyhow, we have more important things to worry about. Someone has set a trap for Ned about half a mile down the road."

Bell straightened up as a flicker of adrenaline washed his tiredness away. He'd pay for this later—he always did—but a sour hangover tomorrow was better than sleeping in the Otherworld. It wasn't quite as bad as eating or drinking here, but if you let yourself sleep, it was comfort of a sort. That could oblige you.

"Our missing kids?"

Conri shrugged. "Probably," he said. "A trap is usually a bit too sophisticated for a hunting preserve to come up with on its own."

"Usually?"

Conri shrugged.

"Never be sure of anything here," he said. "But if you want someone to drive headlong into a trap—"

"You need beaters," Bell finished for him. He got his feet under him and scrambled gingerly to his feet, one eye on Ned to make sure they didn't attract the man's attention. If he wanted to get Ned in panicked motion, he thought, what would he do? The ground was dense and boggy underfoot, but the thin strings of tall grass were dry and brittle. "Fire?"

Conri tilted his head back to look up at Bell. Despite Bell's dislike for being an idiot, he was apparently determined to be one as he imagined other situations that would angle Conri's head like that and soften the line of his mouth thoughtfully.

"Maybe," he said, the word drawn out over his tongue. "It's not something Robin or the other fey kids would do. It wouldn't be sporting. The hunt has to be fair. There are rules about how to engage with the prey."

It was actually reassuring when Bell's stomach sank in disappointment. This whole thing would be easier if he could find a prejudged slot in his head for Conri. Delusional advocate for the fey was *right there* to be filled and well away from anything that would end with Bell doing anything stupid.

Fun, until the other shoe dropped, but stupid.

"Are there really?" he asked. Even though he had been to the Otherworld enough times to know that was a lie. "Rules of engagement?"

"No," Conri said as he scrambled up, easy and graceless at the same time. "But parents are liars, and it's not exactly easy being fey. Even in LA. It's easier to believe in fair play and honor than assholes and murder."

Maybe for some people. It hadn't been Bell's experience.

"So, what would they do? They don't have weapons or numbers—"

Conri didn't get a chance to answer. The herd burst out of the thick woods at full gallop first, broken branches caught in their horns and trampled under sharp hooves that flashed silver when the light caught them. Hot breaths steamed out of flared red nostrils, and their eyes were wide and rolled enough to show the whites, bright in the dim light.

Aurochs.

That's what people called them. *Unicorn* was too fairy-tale a word once they realized the fey used them like cattle—for meat, milk, and leather. Bell had seen them fat and placid in Otherworld fields when he went to check the living conditions of the farmhands hired to tend them.

Virginity, like death, was a mortal concept. At least it was as far the Otherworld and its beasts were concerned. But death had glutted the market, so virginity brought a higher price if someone was willing to hang on to it for a year's farm work.

These things, though. Bell took a step back, as if that would get him out of the way as the herd charged toward them. They had as much kinship to the horn-docked farm animals he'd seen as boars did to pigs. They were hard, knotted muscle and mange-pocked hides, the silver manes knotted with burrs, and their tails stained with shit and urine.

Not exactly the unicorn of legends, except for the horn. It jutted out from thick, armored foreheads like a spear, white as bone and carved with what old wives claimed were the secrets of the Otherworld. Although they didn't usually mention the blood and filth smeared into the grooves.

"Stay on your feet," Conri yelled as he grabbed Bell's shoulder and dragged him out of the path of the things. "Don't touch the horn—"

They didn't get far before the panicked aurochs rolled over them in a tide of muscle, hide, and hot, sweaty stink. One shouldered between Conri and Bell and shoved them apart. A parting kick from its back feet caught Bell in the stomach and knocked the wind out of him. He grunted and struggled to stay on his feet as the pain twisted around his hip bones.

Still lucky. If not for the Kevlar, it would have opened him up like a knife and knocked his guts out.

"A stampede," Conri yelled, his voice thin over the roar of thirty animals moving as one scared beast. "That'd do it too."

"Again," Bell managed to grind out through clenched teeth as the wet, matted flanks of the beasts battered him. The sheer weight of them made it feel like being beaten, his bones sore and legs aching. "So glad I brought you along."

He slammed his hand against a hard, gray shoulder and managed to keep his feet as another sideswiped him on the way past. There was blood on their flanks, so bright and red it looked like paint. It itched when it got on his hands. A big female lashed out with a hoof the size of a dinner plate as she went past. It caught him on the hip and put him on his back in the dirt as hooves thundered past him. He squirmed like a snake to avoid any of them landing on him, with only partial success.

Bell managed to roll over and scramble onto his knees, gray with filth and bruises. He could taste blood in the back of his throat, and his face throbbed with that distinct *broken* sickly heat that was going to hurt soon. As he tried to get the rest of the way up, something about him caught one of the auroch's attention, and it dropped its head. Mad, blue eyes—blue like Conri's eye was blue, liquid as water—sighted along the spike as it charged at him.

He hesitated, but he'd never admit that to Felix, and then he pulled his gun and fired in one smooth, thoughtless motion. The gun bucked against his hand, and a coin-sized blotch of black appeared on the auroch's chest, right in the middle. It staggered at the impact but didn't go down right away. Blood sprayed from its nose in a fine mist as it snorted, and momentum kept it going forward even as it stumbled over its own hooves.

Head shot would have been quicker, but a unicorn's skull was thick as Kevlar. Bell hesitated again as he considered a second shot, but the unicorn was already dead. The news just hadn't reached it yet.

Two more heavy, juddering strides, and then the unicorn's knees went out from under it, and the limp, sour bulk of it slammed into Bell. The tip of its horn scraped down his throat, and the weight of it bowled him over. He landed flat on his back, legs and hips pinned under the dead thing.

The herd surged over them both. They jumped over their dead herd mate, metal hooves tucked up toward their bellies, and stamped at Bell on the way past. He got his arms up over his head and hunched up to protect his stomach as best he could.

Killed by unicorns, he thought with a flash of black humor. *I guess virginity really doesn't grow back.*

"Fuck," Conri said. There was a rough edge to his voice, as if the fricative *f* wanted to be a snarl. "First time I've wished I was ugly."

The weight on Bell's legs shifted—not a lot, but it was enough to wriggle. Bell opened his eyes and saw Conri with his shoulder braced against the unicorn's side. Blood matted his patchwork hair down into one matte-brown mess, and bruises mottled the side of his face and arms. The heavy muscles in his shoulders bulged as he threw his weight against the unicorn and it shifted enough for Bell to yank his legs free.

"Because you'd have still been a virgin?" Bell asked as he flinched away from the hammer blow of a hoof and scrambled to his knees.

He grinned hard as he grabbed Conri and dragged him over closer to the unicorn's corpse. "Pain in the ass when someone points out the obvious, isn't it?"

They hunched down for shelter as close as they could get against its bulk as the rest of the herd detoured around and over them. The unicorn's hide was rough, coarse as an old dishcloth as Bell pressed against it, and the smell of bloody fruit seeped out of it.

"Because I'd have been dead," Conri said raggedly as he panted for air and made a face at the thick-enough-to-taste stink of it. "And this would be someone else's problem. Are you okay?"

Good question. Bell took inventory. He hurt. His legs itched and tingled as the blood seeped back in, but that was probably a good sign. Less so for his nose, which had started to throb now he had time to think about it. Okay was a stretch, but he was alive.

"It could be worse," he said. "You?"

Conri shrugged. "Never seen a wild unicorn before." He pressed the back of his wrist to his mouth—the lush curve of his lower lip split and bloody. "Never really wanted to either, but still. I guess I can add it to the bucket list just to cross it off."

One of the unicorns misjudged its leap over its dead companion, caught a trailing leg on the dead meat, and went down in front of them. There was a nasty distinct snap as it hit, and it didn't get back up. Its screamed was a piercing sound like a ruined trumpet, and it kicked out violently with three sharp hooves and the spike on its head.

Bell caught a kick on the hip as he scrambled away from it, and Conri bled from a fresh cut on his forearm. It tried to get up and went back down as the other unicorns trampled over it. Bell pulled his knife from the small of his back but hesitated. He did this, and he'd have killed two unicorns, and this one wasn't in defense of his life. They were mean animals, he knew that, but….

"Here," Conri said. He grabbed the knife from Bell and darted forward between the galloping legs to slide the knife in, neat and precise, under the unicorn's jaw. It stopped the god-awful screech and went limp, bloody tongue hanging out of a slack jaw. Conri twisted the knife in a vicious, just-to-be-sure motion and scrambled back to Bell. Sweat cut through the blood on his face, but his hand was steady as he offered the knife back. Bell didn't take it. It wasn't exactly procedure to arm changelings, but if Conri wanted him dead, he could have left him. Conri nodded acknowledgment of the gesture and hung on to the knife. "I've done it before. After a while it doesn't feel quite so much like murdering Tinkerbell."

It had only been minutes, but Bell felt like he'd been in a fight for an hour. He gingerly got onto his knees—and had to choke back a yelp as one of them protested with the hot, wire-yank pain of a dislocated kneecap—and peered over the unicorn's broad back. The herd poured through the trees like a grubby tide, and he saw smaller, paler things weave through the heaving bodies on fast, sure feet.

"You've read *Peter Pan*?" Bell asked absently.

"Finn was not always fifteen and too cool to like things," Conri said. He scrambled over and poked his head up above the unicorn's flanks to follow the direction of Bell's stare. "Son of a bitch."

"Hounds," Bell said, his suspicion confirmed as the end of the stampede grew closer. The slim dogs—long, bony, and sharp—snapped at the unicorn's heels and faces to harry them on. Ribs showed under their thin coats, and they had lost some of the *dog* that the fey liked their beasts to have. Still generally dog-shaped—the *intent* of a dog—but they stretched too long and they were too smooth. The details were gone. "I guess we've found Robin."

"He's from Mag Mell. They don't hunt," Conri said. "The hounds wouldn't answer to him. Not this quick."

"They're answering to someone," Bell said. He reached around to draw his other knife and unhooked the sap from his belt. Guns were no good against hounds. Bullets tore through the air where they had been, and it was hard to fire a second time with no face. "And it's not us."

He flicked his wrist and extended the sap. The click as it locked into place—half felt, half heard—was familiar, but the weight of it was off. His old sap had been dented from use, scarred and scraped from impact. He'd been *used* to it.

Time to break this one in.

The last of the unicorns—the old, lame, and young—hammered down onto the road. Splinters chipped up under their hooves as they hit the stone, and Bell caught the sound of the yellow pickup as it growled to life.

Something eerie undercut the sound of diesel combustion—an unnerving rattle. Ned had driven a long way today, and the more mundane an object, the harder the Otherworld ate at it.

A few of the hounds stuck to the chase, but most of them peeled away to surround Bell and Conri. Bloody ears pricked and white, rubbery jowls wrinkled back from sharp, ragged teeth as they growled. Blood streaked their necks and chests as it dribbled from the thin, thorned collars that wrapped around thick, long necks.

Conri put his back to Bell's and growled at them. It was the surprisingly thin, slightly mad snarl of a herding dog at bay, and it made the hounds shy back, but not for long. A lean bitch, whose collar had hooked into the corner of her mouth to give her a wonky smile, lunged forward to snap at Conri. He kicked her back, but the rest of the pack had already committed.

The last time, Bell had run. More often than the Iron Door Press Office was willing to admit, that was the best option a Walker had. They were usually alone, always out-gunned, and far from home. If they wanted to win, they needed to fight smart, not brave.

Time to see how the hounds fared if he stood his ground.

Bell cracked the sap over narrow skulls and against the joints in long, narrow legs. When the hounds lunged at him, he shoved the sap into their jaws, so their teeth cracked on the iron and silver, while Conri slit throats or slashed at stomachs with the knife.

The thorn collars got in the way. They deflected the knives, so the cuts were shallow instead of deep, and they scratched along muscle instead of opening the jugular. If the hounds got too close, the thorns caught on fabric and skin to foul movement and slow them down.

One of the bigger hounds ignored the knife that slashed its sides and slammed into Conri. It ground its teeth down into his arm, through layers of fat and muscle, as they both fell over backward into the mud. Conri groaned and then choked the noise back as he struggled to keep the hound's teeth from his throat.

He wouldn't succeed for long.

Bell swore to himself and left his knife jammed between the ribs of one of the hounds. He spun on the balls of his feet and swung the sap in a short, brittle arc that caught the hound under the front leg. It shrieked in pain around the mouthful of Conri meat, and Conri dug his fingers into the scruff of his neck and tossed it away.

"I think Robin's better at being fey than you thought," Bell said. He wiped blood off his hands so his grip wouldn't slip. "They aren't going to break."

"Not for you," Conri said as he scrambled back to his feet. "They were bred to hunt men. They wouldn't be much good at it if they feared us. Can you hold them for a minute?

Bell grinned with a flash of bleak amusement. "I thought I already was. You can jump in anytime."

He got a snort for that, but before he could enjoy the moment, two of the hounds charged in. The sap cracked one over the head hard enough to stagger it, and he kicked sideways to slam the heel of his boot into the side of the other hound's throat before he could reach Conri. He lost his knife in the meat of a hound's chest and nearly his Achilles tendon to sharp teeth, but his Iron Door–issued boots were thick enough that the fangs only scraped his skin.

In the middle of all that, he was *still*—very briefly—tempted to look when he saw Conri's jeans get tossed aside out of the corner of his eye. When the ragged T-shirt followed them, he did steal a second to glance over his shoulder.

He got a brief eyeful of Conri's long, lean body, and then it blurred, like a child had scraped their fist over a chalk drawing, and snapped back together into a dog. Bell had seen transformations before, but never such a clean one. It was usually a… wet… process, with the leavings left splattered all over the walls.

This time, one second there was Conri, and the next a dog. So neat that Bell wondered if he'd mis-seen.

Except it was obviously still Conri. The eyes were the same, and the scruffy merle-patterned fur now stretched over a rough-coated collie the size of a Newfoundland. Conri-the-dog shook itself, shed what looked like an entire other dog, and then threw itself forward to slam shoulder-first into a hound.

The long, white almost-dog hit the ground and rolled. When it came back to its feet, it snarled and backed away unhappily. Sharp fangs couldn't dig in through the dense, wiry coat, the collie was nearly as fast and thick with muscle, and a thick, nail-studded leather collar around its throat tore their mouths to shreds when they tried to take it down.

One snuck around to go for the collie's flank, but Bell grabbed it by the scruff of the neck. The thorn collar tore his palm open as he dragged it back and put it down with a short, sharp blow from the butt of his sap to the base of the skull. He shot another, the quarters too close for the hounds to twist out of the way, and got his knife back from one dead hound in time to slash it across another's face.

As the hound staggered backward, one eye and one ear wet with blood as it shook its head, a shrill whistle cut through the trees. The hounds all pricked their ears—the ones that could—and then slowly broke away from the fight to flee into the trees.

The last living hound stood her ground, head dropped and lips curled as she glared at Conri. He shook his head—and maybe his fur wasn't as thick as all that, because he splattered blood—and waited with his paws braced.

Then she snapped at him, the click of her teeth loud as they hit each other and turned tail to follow the rest.

Conri groaned once she was gone and flopped down to roll on the ground as if the dirt would help his bites. Maybe it would. Bell pressed the ball of the sap against his thigh and retracted it as he stepped forward.

"Conri?" he said as he extended his hand. "You still in there?"

The narrow, pointed head that swung toward him didn't have enough room for a human brain, but the spark of Conri was still there in the mismatched eyes. He wagged his tail as Bell stroked his soft ears and wondered how insanely inappropriate that was. Then the dog scrambled back to his feet for a quick scratch before he took off at a trot after the hounds.

Bell wiped his face on his arm—regretted it as it hurt—and supposed that made sense. He didn't know if they could save the Treaty anymore—the kids had obviously been trapped here for more than a scary few days—but maybe he could still save Nora.

It wouldn't change anything. He used to think it would, but no matter how many people he did save, it would never make up for the one he hadn't. Not to him, not to anyone. But it was still worth doing.

CHAPTER SEVEN

IT FELT too good to be back on all fours again. Conri could feel the press of the Otherworld's approval against his bones. *This* was the shape it thought suited him, the skin he should wear, and the thoughts he should think.

There was no malice to it. It was how the Otherworld worked. In the mortal world, people talked about form over function as though it was a bad thing, but here they were the same. Lovers grew more beautiful, bards could—literally—sing like birds, and Conri got turned into a dog because that was how his life always went.

The Otherworld thought he'd make a good dog... and it had been right. Like it or not, no matter what that Kessel hound dog said, Conri was a good dog. It was a shame he'd always wanted more, or he could have been happy.

The stink of the hounds hung on the air like burnt caramel, so strong he could almost reach out and snap off a thread of it. He could taste their blood in his mouth, thick and slippery and undersalted, and the rose-thorn magic that bound them.

Something else too. He ran his tongue over the roof of his mouth and along his teeth as he tried to identify it. Meat and smoke and the crack-slurp of marrow between their jaws.

Loyalty, he realized. It was the smell of loyalty.

That put his ears back. The hounds weren't loyal. They were *hounds*. They were hunger wrapped in mist-skin and given bone teeth because the fey wanted dogs to hunt with. Conri's old master had bred mortal dogs into the line, but that was because he liked their belling howl, not for any doggy attribute.

He'd had Conri for that.

A quick shake of his head dislodged that thought. Collie or man, Conri had never seen any point in worrying about what couldn't be fixed.

244

The hounds had been here a long time, with nothing mortal enough to make killing it worthwhile. Maybe, like the slough itself, they were happy to be back to work.

Cold water splashed Conri's paws and belly as he landed in a thin, brackish stream. He stopped for a second to stick his muzzle in it and slurp up the water. It let Bell catch up with him.

Bell flopped belly down on the bank of the stream and stuck his head into it. Dark hair floated on the water and bubbles trickled up from his nose. Then they stopped. Conri shoved his nose into Bell's ear and snorted to make Bell surface, spluttering water and blood.

"I'm not drinking it," Bell said, after Conri woofed at him. He propped himself up on his elbows and let the water drip off his face. His nose was crooked, his eyebrow split and scabbed, and a dark bruise was rising to the surface along his jawline. The scar the unicorns had given him had already faded to a thin, silver line—actual silver that glittered dully when he turned his head. Conri would have to talk to him about that, when he had words again, anyhow. "I needed to…. How far are they ahead?"

Conri tilted his head to one side and then the other. He was still a person in a dog skin—more or less, less if the Otherworld had its way—but how the hell was he meant to convey distance? Bark once per yard?

"Fair enough," Bell said. He wiped the water off his face and flicked it away. "Far?"

It was a bit undignified, but Conri shook his head.

"Then we want to see what we're getting into before we have to deal with it," Bell said. He pushed himself back and into a sitting position so he could fish the trow ointment out of his belt. "Don't rush in. Stay back and give me a chance to assess that situation."

Conri laid his ears back.

"You nearly got shot sticking your nose where it didn't belong back in the mortal world," Bell said. He cracked the seal on the ointment with his fingernail. It was potent enough that even the smell of it perked Conri up like a good cup of coffee. "I'm not out of line to think you might not wait for me to catch up."

Conri scrambled out of the water and shook himself. He paced back and forth, sniffing the air as Bell rubbed the ointment straight onto his skin. Open wounds first—they didn't heal immediately, but blood dried up—and then a bit for his nose and the knee he'd favored the last half mile.

Once he had the ointment on, Bell took a second to close his eyes. He looked oddly young when he did that, and Conri realized with a start that he actually *was*. After a while in the Otherworld, you stopped trying to work out ages. Old enough for morality was the only standard he really worried about.

Bell, with the set of his jaw softened and the hard impatience he approached everything with faded, was only in his twenties. Mid to late, but still. He was probably younger than Conri had been when he was brought to the Otherworld, before he'd been a Walker.

"Let's go see who we're trying to save," Bell said after a single deep breath that he slowly exhaled. He was still injured, but the ointment dulled the pain enough that Bell was able to scramble easily to his feet. "Then see what the unicorns left of Ned."

Conri bounced on his paws in agreement and took off again. He followed the track of the hounds through the trees, over and under the twisted thorn runners decorated with brown-edged white blooms the size of his head. Up close they looked less like roses and smelled like nothing at all. Spots of blood stained them, bright and indelible.

Cheater's Rose, his old master had called them with disdain. Fey grew them in hunting preserves to make the chase easier. Blood stained them forever, or at least until a frost dropped the petals.

Only mortal blood, though. Even a changeling who'd been in the Otherworld any length of time wouldn't leave much of a mark. So however long had passed for the mortal teenagers, it hadn't been *too* long.

The brittle blood-toffee scent of the hounds thickened, pliable and fresh in the air, and Conri slowed down. He stopped behind a thicket of Cheater's Rose and brambles when he heard the harsh clash of voices. After a minute Bell caught up and crouched down next to him, one arm slung over his shoulder.

"Good… work," he murmured as he listened to the voices bicker, the "boy" caught behind his teeth. Conri huffed down his nose in amusement and wagged his tail, 'cause… well… fuck it. It *did* feel good. He'd enjoyed praise before he was a changeling. "Let's see what's going on and with whom."

He pulled on a pair of gloves and scrambled up the thorny twist of the rose briars, the hooked thorns not sharp enough to pierce through the fabric. Conri paced at the bottom for a second, the dog anxiety in the back of his head like pressure, and then forced himself to leave Bell to it as he slunk under the underbrush until he could see into the clearing.

The hounds sprawled around the clearing in awkward, angular piles of bone and hair. Like greyhounds at rest, they looked like puppets with the strings snapped. In the middle of them, a skinny, darkly tanned youth with bleached white hair crouched next to the big female that led the pack and fussed over her like a pup. Thin, gloved fingers, with "nails" that were thorns broken off the roses and sewn onto the fingers scratched behind her ears and under the crease of her long thin jaw.

Good? Yes. Good me. The hound huffed to herself in satisfaction. Her bony whip of a tail slapped the ground twice and then spasmed weirdly as *dog* instincts tried to kick in and got lost halfway through. *Kill more. Kiss pet. Pet kiss. Good me kill. Food?*

The other hounds lifted their heads at the mention of the food and moaned a weird, wavering noise.

Kill? Food? Food Kill. Yesssss. Good? Me good. You? Good!

A few of them, caught up in the question of who was good, snapped and snarled at one another. The skinny youth jumped in and pulled them apart, backed up by the big female who asserted she was the *good* until the others slunk away from her.

Conri glanced past the hounds and their keeper to….

It had been the Hunting Lodge at one time, but the slough had picked the brick and timber down to a shell of a landmark. In its place was a shabby trailer, the painted sides blistered and warped from time. Prisoners sat hunched around it, filthy sacks of sticks and bones with thorn collars around their throats to chain them to the ground.

Conri had to squint to get his brain to cooperate with numbers. Dogs definitely couldn't count in the Otherworld's view of things. He overrode that.

Four prisoners.

Not enough for all the kids who'd been taken, but graves were easy to miss out here. He glanced up into the tree to judge Bell's next move as Bell apparently forgot everything he said and dropped out of his perch. He landed easily, knees flexed to absorb the impact, and snapped the gun up to point at the hound's master.

"Call them off," he snapped the command in a cold voice. His finger tightened slightly on the trigger. "Now. Or I kill you and see if they have the heart for a fight then."

The hounds growled and whimpered as they milled around and looked to their master for direction.

No. No. Bad! Kill bad?! Kill good? What if good goes like olds? Food?

One of them, bony and young, decided to take the risk. It lunged at Bell, teeth bared behind wrinkled back lips. Conri scrambled under and through a tangle of bush and briar that stripped chunks of hair out of his coat. He scuttled forward, low and fast, and skidded under the hound on his belly. Then he stood up abruptly and knocked the hound off its feet. He was shorter than it—he could have nearly run under it without stooping—but there was more of him.

The hound rolled over on its back, and Conri pinned it down with his teeth at its throat. The thorns ripped at his lips and gums, but he ignored them.

"Stop!" the hound's master said in a low, anxious voice as they raised gloved hands. "Don't hurt them!"

The hounds were driven mad, writhing over and under one another like leggy worms in a storm at the kindness of it. Whatever they'd been before the Otherworld overlaid dog on them hated the weakling sentiment, but at the same time, they wanted to show belly and get scritched by their master.

Fey weren't kind.

Conri loved Finn, and he'd lived with Finn, and it had taken him fourteen years to bully the idea it wasn't compulsory to be spiteful into the boy.

He let the cowed hound slide from under him and sidled forward a few steps to sniff at the hem of the hound master's coat. It was old leather, cured with unicorn piss and too much blood, and it smelled of the thin ozone-and-infusions scent of the fey. In this case smoked salt and the nose-prickle stink of a lightning strike. Under it, though….

"What have you done, Nora?" Bell asked tightly. The gun didn't waver, the muzzle aimed directly at the nondescript if darker-tanned face of the girl they'd come to find. "What were you planning to do?"

For a brittle second, Conri could feel the violence curdle in the air as the slough sucked in an anticipatory, metaphorical breath. This was what it wanted, all the dark, hot emotions that would stir the sluggish Otherworld into life. Conri put himself between them—old habits—and growled a warning at Bell. It made Bell's eyes flicker down to him for an instant, but the gun didn't waver.

Nora stared at Bell with faded blue eyes and a blank expression on her face.

"Who the *fuck* are you?" she asked abruptly, then scowled. "Did you hurt my dogs?"

THE CONVERSATION stuttered along outside the trailer. It had been a while since Nora had anyone to talk to but her hounds, and she frequently stopped only to splutter out a sudden stream of information when Bell prodded her.

Conri sat on the narrow cot with his head in his heads and tried to muster up the will to finish getting dressed in his scavenged gear and go outside. So far it hadn't worked. He buried his fingers deeper into his hair until his knuckles dug into his skull and he half-seriously wished for the old days. Back then, with the threat of his master's whip over his shoulders, he never dallied long, no matter what he felt like.

Cheer up, he thought bitterly to himself, *we could still end up back there*.

He didn't register the silence outside until someone rapped their knuckles against the trailer door.

"You okay?" Bell asked. He probably thought Conri had fallen asleep or something.

"Yeah," Conri said. He didn't lift his head as he worked his hands down to the soft-furred points of his ears and traced them absently. "Give me a minute."

The only person he'd had to answer to for over a decade had been Finn. All he would have done is make a disgusted noise and stomp off. So the creak of the door as it opened to let Bell scramble in surprised him.

"So far it's like Jamie told us," Bell said. All Conri could see of him without looking up was his boots, scarred and stained from the bog. "I figured you'd want to hear the rest of it."

Of course, he did. He had to pull himself together and get up. It was all done and dusted now anyhow. There were no takebacks in the Otherworld.

"Is this…? I wasn't going to shoot her," Bell said suddenly. It didn't sound like he quite believed that any more than Conri did. He might not have decided to shoot Nora, but it had been on the table as they stared at each other. All it would have taken was for one thing to fall differently, and it would have ended differently. "It's just not the first time that I—"

Conri dropped his hands to dangle between his knees. "Not everything is about you, Agent Bellamy."

"Yeah, that's not news," Bell said, a crack of old, bitter humor in his voice. He crouched down, the worn fabric of his trousers pulled tight over his knees and his lean, wiry forearms crossed on top of them. "What is it about?"

It was stupid to care. At this point what did it matter? Conri knew that the same way Bell knew not everything was about him. Painfully.

"It's not every time," Conri said. His voice was low and rough in his throat. "But sometimes when I turn back, not *all* of me turns back."

He hadn't cared about the hair, and he could live with the ears—nearly everyone had pointy ears—but it had been a shock the day he looked in a mirror and didn't see his own eyes. To not even see *human* eyes in your face. He took a breath and was embarrassed to taste the salt and snot of incipient tears in the back of his throat. It was stupid. He couldn't shapeshift in the mortal world. The laws of physics were enforced there, and he'd had time to forget this bleak, helpless fear.

Maybe this time what he saw in the mirror wouldn't be something he could accept as *him*. Or what if, no matter how bizarre it was, he could? That almost seemed worse.

"What about this time?" Bell asked. He probably talked to victims in that low, steady tone, to confused kids and kelpie-nipped horse girls. Or maybe did. "Did you lose something?"

Ah, Conri thought dryly, just when he thought he couldn't feel more stupid.

"I don't know," he admitted. "I'm scared to know."

Bell reached between Conri's braced forearms and pinched his chin between thumb and forefinger so he could lift it up for a look. Conri let his arms drop to his sides and clenched his jaw as he braced himself for disgust. Worse. Pity.

Serious, dark brown eyes searched Conri's face for a second, from his hairline to the tightly set line of his jaw. His grip on Conri's chin shifted as Bell slid his hand up to cup the side of his face.

"Nothing's changed," he said. "You look like you."

A twitch of a bitter smile pulled at Conri's mouth. "Only half dog, then," he said.

Bell snorted and pulled him forward into a kiss.

Surprise froze Conri in place as Bell's mouth pressed against his, soft and still bloody-sweet from the fight. He felt dumb as a virgin who'd realized that *this* was what all the fuss was about with girls… only not girls. It wasn't that he hadn't figured Bell wanted him, he just hadn't expected Bell to make a move.

Either of them to make a move, since it was such a stupid thing to do.

He exhaled into Bell's mouth and kissed him back, hungry and *desperate* in a way he vaguely knew he didn't want to understand right then. It wasn't the sex. Conri didn't have any trouble there. LA had a whole subculture of people who wanted to bang changelings. Something else.

And hadn't he already decided that knowing wouldn't do him any good?

He buried his fingers in Bell's dark hair, loose strands knotted around his fingers, and pulled him in closer. Bell made a low, pleased sound against Conri's mouth and stretched up into the kiss. His free hand was braced against Conri's thigh, warm through the stolen leather, as he bit Conri's lower lip and flirted with his tongue.

Hunger flooded Conri's body, hot as liquid sugar that stung his skin as it coated his bones. It was a heady, mortal rush that cast into sharp relief the empty, shallow pleasure of the Otherworld.

The phantom of a quick tumble on the floor of the trailer hung over them. It would have been easy. All one of them had to do was push the other down, wet kisses and hasty hands and stickiness. It would put the itch to bed once and for all. There'd be a grubby patina over any potential meetings in the future, the memory of dirty floors and messy distraction.

That would head off a lot of problems.

The possibility faded away as the hounds shrieked at one another over a length of unicorn leg outside and Nora yelled at them. None of the fey had quite decided what accent to adopt from America—so her thick, southern vowels were a blunt-weapon reminder that they had other responsibilities.

Bell was the one who pulled back. Dark hair tangled in sweaty curls around his ears, and the hard lines of his face had softened. He looked young and bemused, and Conri felt the old, seductive urge to do what he wanted and screw the consequences. He turned his head to kiss the inside of Bell's wrist and felt the flush of blood under the thin skin.

"So," he said. "This is a thing?"

Bell thought about that for a moment and then smiled wryly with a tight, crooked slant of his severe mouth.

"Yeah," he said. "It is as far as I'm concerned, anyhow."

"Huh," Conri leaned over to press a quick, hard kiss against that dry smile. He rested his forehead against Bell's when he finished, their breath tangled together. "For the record, everything shoulders down is still... you know... as God made me."

Bell spluttered out a surprised laugh and pushed himself to his feet. He scraped his fingers through his hair to untangle the curls. "Good to know," he said.

"Oh, you have no fucking idea," Conri said as he reached over to grab the shirt some fey had left in the wardrobe—either when they fled or because it had gone out of style—and shrugged it on. The fabric pulled over his shoulders. Fey tended to be built along leaner lines. "That I checked."

Bell shook his head and turned to head back to the door. His hand was on the doorknob when Conri cleared his throat.

"Look, thanks," he said awkwardly as he stood up. It was easy to flirt, even roughly, but that touch of honesty felt raw. "It's just... been a while."

Bell stepped outside and turned to look at him, eyebrows raised curiously. "Since someone kissed you?"

No, but it felt like it had been. Conri's assignations before he came back to Elwood had been satisfying, but compared to the tingle of Bell still on his lips, the memory of them was sepia and faded.

"Not exactly," he admitted. "I do okay."

"It has for me," Bell said. "A good while. I'm glad it helped, but I didn't kiss you to get you to pull yourself together. I did it because I've wanted to kiss you since I searched your car."

The deal-with-it-later urge tickled down Conri's spine to clench his ass. "Not before?"

"I don't lust after bad guys," Bell said. "It's sort of a rule. I wanted to be sure you were a good man first. Get dressed. We'll be at the fire."

He jumped down off the steps and walked away to rejoin Nora. Conri absently straightened the shirt over his shoulders and buttoned it up as far as it would go.

He was a good dog. A good man, though? He didn't know if he'd ever been *that*.

CHAPTER EIGHT

THE KISS lingered on Bell's mouth.

He tried to ignore it as Conri dragged a log over to the fire to sit down, even though it felt like it had to be visible, bright pink and lemon sharp. The pale fire cast shadows over Conri's face, picked out the heavy bones of his face and the russet patches in his hair as he leaned in to grab a skewer of unicorn meat.

"… I don't know who they are," Nora said. The almost-pretty girl in the photos had been pared down to raw bones and fierceness. Her hands were scarred and callused, and her face was lean and grave. She ate quickly and untidily with her fingers, every other bite of charred flesh shared with the big pack leader who sprawled at her feet. It licked Nora's fingers clean as she glanced over at the sullen chain-line of prisoners. "They were here when we got here. Like these poor puppies."

She turned her hand absently to scratch under the hound's chin. Its ears went floppy with delight, and it leaned against her with a grunt of satisfaction. The bony whip of a tail thumped the ground.

Bell didn't look at it. He *knew* what the hounds were, down to his bones, while to Nora they were abandoned dogs, dumped in the woods after hunting season like the spotted hounds that couldn't tree back home. It was better the pack believed in Nora and didn't remember Bell's version of them.

"Why are they chained up?" Bell asked.

He rubbed his hands together, his thumbs pressed into the palms as though they could squeeze out the tense ache from his grip on the gun—a reminder of how close he'd come to shooting the girl they'd come to save. He hadn't pulled the trigger, but for a cold, clear second it wasn't Nora he saw, and he'd come close. Part of him hoped that Nora would say something now that would prove that if he *had*, he'd have been justified.

"I don't want to kill them," Nora said. She wiped her fingers on her trousers and scrubbed her hands through her hair in frustration. A frown pinched at her face under the unruly, sun-bleached mop. "I tried to talk to them at first, but they aren't *really* people anymore. They're just... they're just *him*."

Her voice broke a bit, and she shuddered. The hound stuck its long, beaky muzzle under her arm and snorted fretfully into her armpit.

"Robin?" Conri said.

Nora gave him a startled look and then laughed. Sort of. It was a bitter choke of a chuckle that caught in her throat.

"Sorry to disappoint you," she said. "He's not here. Your prince is in another castle."

She scrambled up from the fire and walked over to one of the grubby, hunched figures on their hobble. The hound trailed at her heels with a snarl for the prisoners as one of them spat at her. Nora wiped her cheek on her sleeve and grabbed one of the men by the hair to yank his head up.

"They're Keith," she said, and she had the grace to sound bemused, as though it occurred to her how mad it was when she explained it aloud. "I know it doesn't make sense, but they're all him. *Versions* of him anyhow. Old him, one-eyed him, ugly him, pirate him—all of the worst bits of him."

Not particularly imaginative versions, Bell guessed as he got up to look at the other prisoners and the slightly unique stamps of their faces. But nothing he'd heard about Keith suggested he was a clever boy.

"And the real Keith?" he asked.

One of the prisoners threw himself at Bell, only to strangle on the end of the chain. He fell back onto the ground with a grunt and glared up at Bell with burning, empty eyes. There was maybe the outline of a teenage boy under the grime and scavenger clothes, in the cheekbones and hairlines, but it was well hidden.

"You'll never get him back," he said. The words were garbled in his throat, almost there but not quite. "We'll kill him first. You bitch. Fucking bitch. Whore."

The hound snaked in low and mean to snap at the prisoner's hands and face until he recoiled back into place, mouth shut as he hunched down, cowed before the sharp teeth and pinned-back ears.

"They don't have a lot of words," Nora said, unflappable and quietly cold. "They reuse and recycle what they have, cut and paste it together to try and talk. It's kind of pathetic."

Bell stepped back. The Otherworld was alien, fluid, and strange, but it was usually efficient. The line of half-made, halting clones was more unsettling for how half-assed it was.

"It's wrong anyhow," he said. "We're not here to find Robin. We're here for you, Nora. We're going to take you home."

She gave him the same blank, uncomprehending look as she had when he'd had a gun pointed at her.

"I'm not going," she said. There was a clean, shocking purity to the passion that filled her face. "I'm not going *anywhere* without Robin. I love him."

At least, Bell thought tiredly as he saw the last chance to save the treaty fall apart in his hands, she still had the self-awareness to say "I" not "we."

"NO ONE *stole* me," Nora said irritably as she packed up her camp. "No one forced me to come here. It's not illegal to go to the Otherworld. People queue up to get visas to go and work there. You're here."

"I'm an Iron Door agent," Bell said. He glanced at Conri, who had stepped aside to study the prisoners. The tips of Bell's ears felt hot as he looked at Conri, and his stomach tightened pleasantly, but he kept his voice businesslike. "He's been deputized, and people know we're here. You disappeared in the middle of the night, after a fight at a contentious party. It's not the same situation."

"Fine," Nora said. She held her hand up beside her face and rattled off, "I hereby attest that I want to be here and that I'm here of my own free—"

Bell pulled her hand down and put his hand over her mouth to muffle what she'd been about to say. The theologians hadn't yet agreed on where the Otherworld stood with regard to any gods—some theorized it *was* God—but it would take any oath or prayer for itself.

"You're seventeen," Bell said. "You legally can't make that decision or swear to it by anything."

Nora shoved him away and wiped her mouth on the back of her hand. "I'm not seventeen. I've been here—"

"Not quite a day," Bell said.

That news rocked Nora back on her heels. She gawped at him and then turned away. Her shoulders hunched up to her ears, and Bell realized how skinny she was under the bulky duster.

"I thought it had been over a year," she said. "That it had passed my birthday, at least."

Bell would have been relieved. He *had* been relieved the first time he staggered back to the mortal world and found only a few weeks had passed. Nora sounded as if her world had fallen in.

"Why did you follow Robin through the border?" Conri asked as he stepped away from the clones. "What did he offer you?"

Nora wiped her face on her hands, sniffed hard, and turned to glare at him. The tears made her eyes look more of a watery blue, but her expression was fierce.

"He was grateful," she said, her voice thick with contempt. She raised her chin stubbornly. "He said 'thank you,' he asked me to dance, and I think maybe I got him killed. So I'm not going anywhere, Agent. Not until Robin's safe."

She clenched her hands into fists, and the hounds fell into position behind her. They'd forgotten they were meant to be dogs, the cocked heads and expressive tails dropped like a sheet from the killing machines that had always been underneath.

Bell dropped his hand to his sap out of habit but didn't pull it. If it was a question of getting Nora back to the ford and to safety, he'd bet on himself against the hounds. He might not come out intact, but he could do it. But kidnap was different from rescue. An unwilling passenger would change the odds a lot.

It was Conri who broke the silence.

"My son was at the party too," he said as he stepped forward. The apparent non sequitur made Nora give him a confused look that he ignored. "You might have met him. Finn, red hair and a Cali accent. Still looks a lot like a goblin."

Nora looked annoyed. "Maybe," she said. "A lot of the fey kids at the party had red hair. I didn't talk to him. I didn't talk to anyone but Robin. Good girls don't. They don't talk to fey. They don't eat the fruit. They miss out on a *lot*."

"Well, he was," Conri said. "So now he's in the crosshairs of Iron Door because of you and Robin. The minute the news leaves the county, bounces out of state, the treaty will be torn up… unless we take you back and you tell *everyone* the right story."

Bell stalled for a second on *right* instead of *true*. The implication stuck in his throat, even though he knew Iron Door would take the same approach. It was hardly the corrupt agency that Ned wanted to paint it as, but everyone involved had bled for that treaty.

Literally. If you looked at the original, there were bloody fingerprints smudged on the corners.

It still didn't feel right to put the weight of that on Nora.

"We have time. Why don't you tell us what really happened?" he said as he held his hand out.

She didn't take it. Bell supposed he'd nearly shot her, so he couldn't blame her for that. After a pause, she nodded stiffly, and the hounds relaxed. One of them tried a yawn that went *way* too far back.

"While we walk," she said as she turned to grab the last of her things and stuff them in a backpack. The bag had been pink once and maybe even as stylish as a girl could get with a pig-farm wage. Now it was grubby and stitched, patched with hide and thorns. "I went to a lot of effort to stampede those unicorns. I don't want to waste it."

Conri shrugged at Bell and scattered the greasy bones of their meal with his foot. The heavy leather singed lightly as he stirred the embers.

"Where are we going?" Bell asked.

Nora lifted her hood up to cover her pale hair. "I *told* you," she said as she struck out. "I'm going to rescue Robin and the others. With luck, the stampede will have attracted Keith's attention, and him and Ned can keep each other busy while I get into his camp."

The hounds slunk off into the trees, glimpses of mist through the branches the only evidence they kept pace. Only the big female stuck with Nora, glued to her shadow.

Bell weighed Felix's instructions against the current development in the field. He still didn't need to get Robin and the others back to the mortal realm, but he at least needed to get them to the border if he didn't want to have to fight Nora all the way there.

And she was definitely more resourceful than he expected.

Useful and resilient, the memory of Conri's voice sighed in his head. That described him and Nora, and Bell filed that away for later.

It took a few paces, but finally Nora cleared her throat and started to speak.

"Keith only dated me because it meant he got to hang out with my brother and shoot guns," she said flatly. There was no room for sympathy in her voice. "I don't think he even liked him, which was okay because I don't think I ever much liked him either. But I was the pig-farm girl, and he was a football player, so why not? So I wasn't *surprised* when he started being a dick to some fey kids from the summer camp, but this time he took it too far...."

THE STORY was much the same as the one that Jamie had told him, although sharper edged from someone who'd been there. The prank was meaner, the fey kids less gullible, and Keith didn't leave them there so much as flee with his tail between his legs.

"He left me there, on the ground," Nora said. "I thought I was gonna get a pig nose or something for my trouble. They do that in the stories. And—"

She stumbled over her own tongue as she glanced back over her shoulder at Conri. Color slapped her cheeks, and even though he didn't react, it took her a second to compose her thoughts again.

"Anyhow, all Robin did was help me up. He thanked me for trying to stop Keith and the others, even though they were my friends. He said I was as brave as I was beautiful." Nora paused halfway over a tangled briar and smiled at the memory of that. Her fingers tightened around the wood knot of the rose runner, thorns sharp where they stuck between her knuckles, and she lifted her chin. "I told him he was full of shit, and that made him laugh. They walked me back to town and… you know what was the most magical thing about it? Not that they were fey, but that they didn't come from *here*. Robin grew up in Providence and Shanko was from Brooklyn and… the farthest I've ever gone is over the state line for a pig fair. They left me at the gas station—I wasn't going to let them meet my inbred bigot of a brother—and figured that was it. That was going to be my story. When I was seventy-two and had spent my whole life on the pig farm with my brother and his family, this would be my big brush with fairy-tale romance. The summer I was *almost* a fairy bride. Pathetic, but better than most people's romances around here."

She stopped, shrugged, and jumped down onto the boggy dirt track that faded in and out between the trees. The hound followed her in an easy, long leap that stretched over the thorns.

"Except then he came to the party," Conri said. He boosted himself over the knot of briar and dropped easily down on the other side. "And asked you to dance."

He looked at ease here, Bell noted. In the borrowed fey leathers, amidst the thick white alien roses that hung from trees like kudzu, Conri looked like he was made for this. He had been, from what he'd shared, but it still rubbed Bell the wrong way.

It wasn't suspicion. Bell didn't know if Conri could be trusted in a wider sense, but he obviously loved Finn, and that meant he was on Iron Door's side *this* time. The irritable itch in the back of Bell's head felt more like… jealousy, like the moment you saw your boyfriend laugh at an inside joke with his ex and they didn't include you.

Bell wanted to roll his eyes at his neurotic approach to a one-night stand. A *pending* one-night stand, at that. It was stupid and needy, neither of which he was. But he could still taste the resentment in the back of his throat for the boggy ground underfoot and the smell of salt and roses on the air. Something old and dark and sullen dug its heels into his mind and chewed on old wounds like they were ribeye steak.

The Otherworld didn't get to take anyone else from him.

Bell swallowed the sour-skin taste of that old memory and left it to fester while he focused on his own scramble over the vine.

"That didn't please Keith," he said. His boots hit the ground with a sticky squelch, and he could smell the crushed roses on his clothes. It wanted him to run. He could feel it as his heart rate sped up and sweat broke out.

"It wasn't his business," Nora said sharply. "I'd already told him that, but no, he wasn't thrilled. Robin didn't care. He thought it was funny when the fight kicked off. It *was* funny when I was with him—what were a bunch of hick-town kids when you're the son of a prince? He only left because he got bored of it, and I went with him because I was bored of *all* of it. So why not? Except Keith hung out with my brother, goes to the same hateful forums, and when he found out the summer camp was going to be here—"

"He got iron," Conri said grimly. "How much?"

She shrugged. "What he could afford," she said. The fey didn't care for steel much, but it irritated them. It wouldn't end them. That took cold, pure pig iron, and it was illegal to buy without a license and a valid reason. So people who bought it illegally had to pay over the odds for it. "A crowbar. A couple of shells full of iron ball bearings for his shotgun, but he clipped Thistle with it, and all it did was hurt her. But that's when it stopped being funny. Keith was... he didn't even care about me that much. I don't know why he lost his head over this like he did. Robin told Thistle to go and get help—I guess she did—while we ran for it. Keith was going to kill us, Agent, all of us. I don't know how Robin got us through to here, but it was to save my life, not to steal me away."

"Only problem was," Bell said, "Keith came with you."

Nora nodded. "It didn't seem like a problem at first. This is the Otherworld, after all. It's the fey's playground. Robin thought he had the upper hand—we all did. Even Keith agreed to stay out of our way, but... nothing worked the way we thought it would. We couldn't get back, he couldn't find the way out, and there was nothing to *eat*." Her voice broke at the memory, a raw scratch of trauma she'd had no time to do anything but repress. The hound looked up at her curiously, its head cocked to the side. "It was okay, though. We knew someone would come for us. Ned's a crazy bigot, but he loves me, and the camp would send a Walker to get the fey back. It was okay, we just had to keep it together until someone got here. Except, that's when Keith found...."

She reached out and pushed a tangle of briars out of the way with her heavily sleeved arms, thorns hooked into the rough stitchwork. The dim light picked out the bloodstains on the leather.

"That."

Bell ducked down slightly to peer over her shoulder. The ghosts of the old fey structures were there—a stray doorframe slouched crookedly in a stand of grass and old, broken walls used as climbing frames for the briars. The only building that had survived, or been put back together by the diligent slough, was a splintered, gray old house with a bleak aura.

He glanced around at Conri and raised his eyebrows in a mute question. Of the three of them, Conri was the only one likely to recognize the layout of the buildings. Bell had read about the hunts—the Hunt—and come across enough stray hounds, but whatever the fey hunted these days, it wasn't human prey, so it wasn't Iron Door's business.

Conri crouched down to get a good view. He glanced across the space from corner to corner, and a dour frown creased the open, easy planes of his face. He swallowed, an audible squelch of sound in his throat, and answered reluctantly, "It looks like the Stables."

CHAPTER NINE

IT WASN'T a lie, Conri defended himself to the squirming part of his brain that wanted to kiss Bell again. The words were the truth, and it wasn't his fault if they didn't all share the same bleak, background information.

Or it was, but he wasn't going to do anything about it right now.

"The Others were in the stalls," Nora said. She'd worked her way through a few different terms for the programmed things before she'd settled on that. Until she had someone to talk to, they hadn't really needed a name. She knew who they were. "I was with him. Shanko too, but he left after we found the clearing to let Robin know. He told us to wait, but Keith never listened to anyone. We went down to explore and found... them."

She nodded down at the two half-formed Keith clones who were driving long spikes into the ground at crooked angles. One of them looked old, his hair gray and face melted like candle wax into folds and wrinkles, while the other had black hair instead of dirty blond.

"They weren't him then," Nora said. "They weren't even alive, just bones and leather, but he was obsessed with them. He said they were murdered people, that it was proof that the fey saw us as prey, that they were probably our ancestors. Nobody has even *seen* a fairy circle in Elwood for decades, but everyone insists they have a grandparent or a great-aunt who disappeared and never came back. They probably left town, but... Keith believed the fey took them."

Keith was probably right. Something had motivated the inhabitants of Elwood to seal off the slough and deal with the repercussions afterward. Fields would have gone sour, fertility of the stock and people dropped, and wells lost their sweetness. Yet based on the state of the tree, not one person had snuck out to try and pull a nail out of the trunk.

There were plenty of complaints that Conri could make about his own time in the Otherworld, but it definitely could have been worse. His old master could be cruel at times, but he'd never been wasteful.

263

"You didn't believe him?" he said.

"Of course not," Nora said impatiently. "My brother used to spout this stuff all the time. I know it's rubbish. It's just excuses for why our town sucks so much. Keith wouldn't listen to me, though. He said that Robin and the others had to explain this before he'd come back to camp. I thought… I thought he'd calm down if I left him alone for a while, so I went to tell them what we'd found. Robin was really excited at first and dragged us all right back there. He said this could get us set up like kings, that we wouldn't have to do anything now until rescue got here."

She stopped and unhooked the water bottle from her hip to take a drink. Her eyes were fixed on the far left side of the barn, where the sour, gray grass was churned up and stained with blood.

"It was a trap," Conri said.

Nora laughed harshly. "Wow," she said. "I wish you'd been here to tell us that *before*."

"He does that," Bell said dryly. "You got…. How did you get away?"

Nora crouched down and hugged the hound around her thick, muscular neck. "Betty here got me out," she said. "I'd fed her scraps from my meals when I could—scrapings and bones mostly. She was skittish, near took my hand off a couple of times, but I guess she decided to hang around. When Keith tried to drag me away, she went for him, and I was able to get away. The others were captured, though. I couldn't help them."

She pressed her face to the hound's shoulder and squeezed. Betty. Conri couldn't remember the last time a hound got a true name, just for itself. His master bred his own, a selected bloodline seasoned with occasional mortality, and even they only had heritage names from the dogs they replaced.

Betty stared at him over Nora's shoulder. Her eyes might look brown in the overcast Otherworld, but in the mortal realm they'd be red. They both knew what she was, but if she wanted to pretend to be a dog right now, Conri didn't see any benefit to them in disabusing Nora of the idea.

"Time to change that," he said. "Are you sure Keith will have gone after your brother?"

Nora wiped her face on Betty before she stood up, her nose pink and eyes watery. She pulled her hood back up firmly to throw her face back into shadow.

"He always has his Others on the borders of my territory," she said. The absentminded claim made Conri twitch slightly, an itch over his shoulder, but what was done was done. "They'd have alerted him about the stampede, but they can't really do much more than that. They're limited. Keith would have to go out and take a look himself if he wants to find anything out. He'd want the jeep."

Bell shifted back a step, away from thorns, and absently checked his gun in the holster. His palm wrapped over the butt and his finger rested along the metal of the gun. The controlled danger in the gesture, the deadly elegance of Bell's hands, made the nape of Conri's neck tingle and his mouth go dry.

"You aren't worried about your brother?" Bell asked. "He's here to rescue you. That might not be something Keith wants."

Nora looked down at her feet and shrugged her shoulders with a sullen heft that was painfully familiar.

"You don't get it," she said. "Keith and Ned are cut from the same crazy cloth. Ned's here to take me back, but that's not the same as rescue. Unless I do what they want, say what they want, and grovel for what a filthy whore I've been? Ned would kick me out on the street to starve the minute he worked out I'm not sorry."

She delivered the last fiercely, as if it were a relief to find out it was still true.

"Maybe it won't be that bad, once he hears what really happened," Conri offered awkwardly. Even he—with the dull ache of his skull as a reminder—didn't believe it, but it seemed like the sort of thing someone should offer her. He hadn't had any family—not until Finn—and nothing in the mortal world to be his anchor. If he had, maybe he'd have left with ears he could hide under his hair. "He's your—"

"He's my brother, but…. He can't love me the way I am right now. So I can't worry about him," Nora interrupted him bluntly. "So, me and Ned are going to have to look out for ourselves. I guess we have been for a long time, anyhow, but we didn't want to admit it."

"So?" BELL asked as they worked their way through the dense briars along the edge of the clearing.

Nora had stayed above with the hounds. She might not care what happened to her as long as Robin was safe, but Conri hadn't paid for Finn's private school all this time to see it all burn down with the treaty. When he crawled out of this bloody slough, it would be *with* the one kid who could stop a war.

The hounds would be useful too.

"So?" Conri repeated Bell's question back at him. Thorns pulled at his hair and plucked holes in the thin cotton of his T-shirt as he scrambled through the thicket. His blood dripped on the Cheater's Roses, but the Otherworld had taken that bit of mortality years ago. It didn't leave a mark. "So what?"

Bell had lost less skin on their trek. Kevlar and reinforced leather did more than look hot, apparently. He wasn't beholden to the Otherworld's rules either—he hadn't run out of water or protein bars yet—so it had to work harder to leave its mark on him. It was a good thing. His blood would have betrayed them.

"What didn't you tell us?" Bell asked. He showed his teeth in a humorless smile as Conri glanced sidelong at him. "Someone told you once that your eyes made you hard to read, right? They didn't spend enough time watching your face."

It wasn't the time, but the words slipped out of Conri anyhow. "And you have?"

"I like your mouth," Bell said calmly. He slowed down so he could maneuver through a tight passage between the briars, turned sideways and with his head canted back. "At least now I can pretend it was for the job."

Heat stung Conri's face unexpectedly at the confession. The memory of Bell's elegant hands on his face, that mouth soft against Conri's, did nothing to cool the sting of it. He swallowed and tried to come up with a good cover story through the flush of lust.

Neither of them made much noise, but the sudden absence of it jarred Conri. He plucked a knot of thorns and hair from behind his ear and turned to look at Bell.

"I might have kissed you, but I'm not a damsel in distress. I'm an Iron Door agent, a Walker, and I have no misconceptions about the

Otherworld or faerie lovers," Bell said. "I don't need protection from the truth, so whatever you're hiding, you need to spit it out."

Conri looked away at one of the great, white betraying roses. It smelled like salt and faintly off meat. "What makes you think I'm protecting you?"

"It can't be as bad as what I'm imagining."

"You'd be surprised," Conri said. He grimaced at Bell's glare and gave in. Why should he be the only one with this squashed into his brain. "Or maybe it's not. We don't talk about it."

"We being...."

"Changelings. Stables are... what happens when a Changeling's mortality runs out and the Otherworld has no particular idea what it wants for them," Conri said. He turned his back on Bell and kept walking. After a moment he heard Bell follow suit. "What's left is a shell that an ambitious young fey lordling can upcycle into a semicoherent court, as long as they don't expect too much. Under normal circumstances they're a bit more sophisticated than these guys, but not by much. Places like this? Stables? They were secondhand stores for broken-down changelings, spare part skeleton keys for any job someone needs half-assedly filled."

Bell grunted softly, as if someone had punched him in the gut. "So Keith was right?"

The answer was yes, but Conri struggled to find a different answer.

"He's not wrong," he admitted reluctantly. "But they weren't murdered. They just... did the closest thing to dying you can do here, at least without iron to ease your passage. Most of the courts frown on it, and few of the lords would pass their changelings on like that. My old master never did."

That had been from arrogance rather than kindness. Like a rich man who'd burn his clothes rather than donate them to charity, he didn't want to see any down-at-heels fey with his castoffs. It devalued what he kept.

"They frown on it," Bell said, his lip curled in contempt. "I'm glad they took a stand."

"A frown from the Lord of Mag Mell has more weight *here* than your highest courts have *there*," Conri said. He didn't know why he felt defensive. He'd tried to escape the Otherworld enough times back when he thought he could. "That's probably why the blank stock were left behind here when whatever fey claimed this place abandoned it. Whatever court he belonged to would have punished him for making them."

"Doesn't do them much good," Bell said as he started walking again. He waited for a second and then asked, "Could we save them? If we take them back across the border, back to the mortal world?"

The details wouldn't take the bite of distaste out of Bell's voice when he talked about the Otherworld. Conri flicked a delicate, jewel-colored butterfly off his bare arm, the delicate veins in its wings flushed to pink threads with his blood.

"No," he said. "Sleeping Beauty is a fairy tale. You can't kiss stock back to life. People have tried. They are more or less dead here, and dead when you take them back."

"At least they'd be able to lie down and rest," Bell said.

Conri growled under his breath. He didn't like thinking about this at the best of times, which this wasn't.

"Rescue the people we're sent for *first*," he snapped. "Let your boss worry about burying the dead afterward. That's his job. Mine is to make sure my son doesn't end up collateral damage from two horny teenagers."

The silence was strung tight between them, ready to snap into real anger if either said the wrong thing.

"They're in love," Bell said after a second, his voice ripe with rueful mockery. "Like Romeo and Juliet, only with more hounds and zombies. Remember when you thought love was all you needed?"

Conri thought about it for a second.

"No," he said.

Bell's laugh was a rough, chopped-off snort of amusement. "Yeah, me neither," he said. There was a pause, and when he spoke again, he'd slipped back into Special Agent Bellamy's brisk professionalism. "Okay, you said you had a way in. What is it?"

It was a hunch and one that could be wrong. Conri didn't particularly want to commit to the plan until he knew it was going to work. Not that he had any backup options he could swap it out for on the fly. Still.

"There's one thing that every fey residence has, be it summer palace or hunting lodge," he said as they finally pushed their way out of the overgrown briars and into the shadows behind the weatherworn gray barn. Conri paused to catch his breath and run his eye along the back of the building. His shoulders relaxed when he picked out what he was looking for against the battered wood. They might still fail and start a war or get themselves killed, but at least Conri wouldn't look like an idiot. He gestured grandly at it for Bell. "The servant's entrance."

Bell wiped sweat off his forehead and squinted one eye shut against the thin light. "So your big plan is a back door?" he asked. "I suppose it's better than going in the front."

That wasn't exactly the reaction Conri had anticipated. He cleared his throat and tried not to let his ears droop in disappointment. Or think about whether he wanted Bell's approval because he wanted the man or because dogs lived for a "good boy."

Of course, it could be both.

"It's not a back door," Conri said softly. He could hear the stock—Keith's shabby attempt at conjuring up his own court of mirror images—parroting their lines back and forth to each other from inside the building. "Back doors are locked, guarded, checked to see if the dog wants in. Whoever lives in the building thinks about it, even if it is to complain about who tracked in the mud and mess from outside. The servant's entrance is there so no one who matters has to think about it, so the cleaners and shit-collectors and greasy, scalded cooks can get on with their jobs without spoiling the aesthetic. So that means no locks, no wards, nothing that would make the lords and ladies have to deal with the unpleasantness of it all."

Conri glanced around to make sure none of the stock had ventured out—they weren't quite people, Nora was right about that, but they could be set to guard and raise the alarm—and then loped across the narrow alley of barren dirt to the hatch half-buried in the dead grass. He grabbed the knotted rope handle and tried his best to remember being his master's favorite dog—the gnaw of worry about what his master might want next, the barely buried resentment, and the bitter smugness that, while he was a servant, at least he was more favored than some. It came back *far* too easily for his peace of mind, but when he yanked the rope, the hatch lifted out of the dirt.

"So all the fey have an open door in the back of their castles?" Bell asked as he skidded up to the wall next to Conri. He sounded prickly, as if the hole in security irked him despite how useful it was about to be. "They never thought that an assassin might sneak in through it? Or a thief?"

Conri hooked the rope handle in place to prop the hatch open. "Even if hired to do a job of work, they're mercenaries," he said. "The servant's entrance is only for servants, and the Otherworld knows who that is. It won't let anyone else in and out."

He jumped down into the shallow, low-ceilinged larder. Dusty bottles of wine and moldy legs of ham were still laid out on shelves, next to rows of once-shiny copper pots and pans. Conri could almost see his face in the verdigris-scabbed metal, the memory of a hundred other similar moments overriding this particular one. He let it pass and stuck his head back up out of the hatch to gesture the all clear to Bell.

It took a second—Conri could almost hear the grind of paranoia as Bell wondered if this was a trap after all—but Bell scrambled in after him. He bumped his head on the roof and cursed softly as he bent his knees and hunched over to fit.

"Now all we need to do is find where Keith is keeping Robin and the others," Bell said. He paused as he heard his voice against the narrow walls and adjusted the volume. "Any ideas?"

Conri grimaced. "One," he admitted. "But maybe Keith is less of an evil little shit than I think."

Bell took his sap off his belt and extended it with a sharp flick of his wrist. He held it down and slightly out from his side, the handle of it gripped loosely in his hand.

"Let's assume he's exactly what you think," Bell said. "Where do we go?"

Conri sighed and reached for the door. Before he pulled it open, he leaned over and, when Bell didn't pull away, stole a quick kiss. It was a quick, crooked scrape of his mouth over Bell's, enough for a reminder of sweetness and a mingled breath on both their lips.

"For luck," he said. It was a lie. He wanted to chase away the old bitter taste of servitude from his tongue and replace it with the taste of Bell and the promise of *later*. But it could be for luck too. He wouldn't turn it away if they got some. "And stay behind me unless it comes to a fight. I look like I belong here."

"You don't, though," Bell said, his voice unexpectedly sharp. He cleared his throat and pushed Conri toward the door when Conri looked at him curiously. "You left. Don't let this place make you forget that."

CHAPTER TEN

OF COURSE.

Bell gave in to the bile that stung the back of his throat and pulled his jacket up to cover his mouth and nose. The stink of the slaughterhouse still filtered through it, but at least offal and shit mixed with leather, clean sweat, and yesterday's cologne was better than the stink of offal alone.

He leaned against the back wall of the narrow passage that was a part of the maze constructed inside the walls of the Stables. The surface was unfinished, studded with cheap bronze nails and splinters, and was wide enough for Bell to walk through but too tight for Conri. He had to go sideways or else it scraped his broad shoulders.

"I don't want to ask what this was for, do I?" he said.

Conri glanced at him. *Somehow* a couple of days and a few fantasies had normalized the alien, canine eyes set in his human face. Bell's opinion of them had shifted from odd to striking, from alien to Conri's. People always wondered how humans could fall for the more alien-looking fey, the trow and the redcaps instead of the sidhe and the selkies. But it was amazing what you got used to when you really wanted to kiss someone.

Again, if not right now, under these circumstances....

"You can see what it's for," Conri said. "What you don't want to ask about are the details."

The one saving grace was that the room—probably—hadn't been in active use recently. The hooks buried into the low, tarred rafters were tarnished, the knives were laid out on dusty rolls of leather, and the bloodstains had soaked into the wood and dried into black scabs. The only things in the room that had been dusted off and used recently were the slaughtering pens. All the missing kids were there, filthy and miserable, in torn jeans and stained designer T-shirts. Collars had been padlocked around their necks, the chains strung up to rings buried in the rafters, and their hands were cuffed to the bars with cord that rubbed blisters into their thin, fey skin.

"No," Bell said grimly. "I don't need details. How do we get them out?"

Conri shrugged. "Quickly?" he suggested as he pressed his thumb to a knot in the wood. A hidden panel popped out into the room—the kids flinched at the noise and straightened up in their chains—and he ducked through.

The first thing Robin saw must have been the piebald hair and dog's ears, because he clutched the slats and pressed his face against them as he asked hopefully. "Did my father send you?"

The "No" from Conri was uncharacteristically flat. Bell glanced at him curiously as he squeezed past him into the room. The sight of him made Robin and the others flinch back as far as the narrow pen let them.

"We didn't steal anyone," Robin blurted out. "We just couldn't get back."

"You," the sole changeling of the group said bluntly. Shanko. He looked almost human, except for the shimmer of silver freckles on his nose and cheekbones. "You didn't steal anyone. This had nothing to do with me. I didn't start a fight over some lanky human girl. I was only there to get a drink. That might be illegal, but it ain't Iron Door's problem."

The last of the three, Annie Boot, covered her face with her hands and muttered into her palms, "I wanna go home. I just wanna go home." The picture in her file at camp had shown a pretty, round girl with big brown eyes and big brown curls, probably a commoner compared to Robin's gilt-and-ivory blue-blood genetics. Time in the Otherworld had left her skinny and less human-looking, with a deer's huge, liquid black eyes and the soft brown dapples of a fawn instead of freckles.

Bell had never considered that the Otherworld could make over the fey the same way it did changelings.

"We're going to get you all home," he said as he stepped over a particularly large and scabbed stain on the floorboards. That hadn't exactly been his orders, but he wouldn't leave anyone to this. How long, he thought grimly, would it be until Keith worked himself up to use the knives he had on show? "But first we need to get out of here."

"And we have to find Nora," Robin said. He stretched his hand out between the bars to pluck at Bell's arm on the way past. "She's out in the woods, alone."

Shanko contorted his face into a grim scowl. "She's dead," he said gruffly, as if none of them could see the tears in his ears. "Humans aren't meant to be here. The Otherworld doesn't want us. Without us to keep her safe, and with Keith chasing her? She's dead."

The statement made Annie dissolve into tears. Robin looked stubborn as he shook his head. "We don't know that."

"She's fine," Conri said dryly as he grabbed a thick pair of shears from the table. The blades were thick and notched, for bone, Bell supposed, but they snapped easily enough through the heavy brass chains that sealed the pens. The length of metal links clattered to the ground. "Better than you three are, anyhow."

Robin looked like something you'd see in an old picture book about the fey—tall and blond and pretty in that narrow, fox way the elf knights always were. He grinned like a goofy teenager with his first crush, huge and unselfconscious.

"Ha!" he said. "I told you she'd be okay. Nora's awesome."

Shanko looked relieved too, but quickly dragged up a grumble to hide it. "Sure, and she's kind and pretty and smells like the end of summer and—" His voice cracked, and he clenched his jaw as he pressed his face against the slats. "Are we really going to go home? I want my mom and my dad. I wanna say sorry. I didn't know what it was like here."

"It's not all like this." Bell was a bit surprised to hear those words come out of his mouth. He'd have expected it—admired it—from Conri, but it wasn't exactly his job to make the Otherworld seem like a good tourist destination. But it was part of these kids, part of Conri, and it didn't do any good to hate bits of them. Bell knew that from hard experience. He used his knife to saw through the thorn shackles and peel them off. The dense, woody runners didn't writhe under the blade or in his grip, but they felt like they *might*. "Some of it is beautiful, and some of it is weird. This slough is…."

"Sour," Conri supplied. "It was cut off from the mortal world and barely touched the rest of the Otherworld. It was grown for dark deeds—"

"A hunting preserve," Robin said. "Like Annwn's dark forests."

"Close enough," Conri said. "Right now, though, it wants to survive. Unfortunately, that would mean eating you, slowly, and that isn't going to happen."

It was the cooperative work of a few minutes to free all three of them. The collars were last, the heavy locks picked with a thin-bladed knife and a long needle-pick that made Bell's eye itch to look at it.

"What now?" Robin said. He tried to pull himself up to his full height, but that only made him about the same height as Bell. It was as impressive as he probably meant it to be. "How do we get out of here?"

Bell raised his eyebrows at Conri as he gestured back to the narrow corridor they'd exited. The door had swung shut, camouflaged in along the knotholes and splinters of the wall, but Bell could pick it out if he squinted.

"Go back the way we came?" he suggested.

Conri shook his head and scrubbed his hand through his hair as he thought. "You weren't a problem," he said. "The Otherworld hasn't got enough of a taste of you yet to decide that you're one or the other. You might be a servant or you might not, but since you were with me, it was easiest to lump you in with me and let us through. This group? No, the Otherworld knows what they are and where they belong. It's not the servant's quarters."

Robin tilted his chin arrogantly at the idea. "I'd hope not," he said. "My father's a king in Mag Mell."

"No, he's not," Conri corrected him. "There's one king in Mag Mell, and you aren't of his blood. Don't tell lies, not here. It will come back on you."

"Everyone knows Robin's real dad is royalty," Shanko protested while Annie nodded in agreement. "Look at him."

"Maybe," Conri said with a shrug. "He's definitely wellborn, but he's not a Mag Mell lordling. They have a look."

Color stained Robin's face, a glow of pink under the ivory skin, and he glared at him. "How would the likes of you know anything about the lords of the fey?"

"Right now, it doesn't matter," Bell interrupted. He didn't know why it mattered to Conri to burst Robin's bubble, but it wasn't the time. "All that matters is he's too wellborn to crawl out of here."

Conri looked Robin up and down and then cast his eye over the other two. "He is," he said. "Her kin don't come from the courts, but they're not servants either. The changeling… I doubt it. He doesn't have the attitude for service."

"Hey," Shanko protested but stopped as he tried to decide if he'd been insulted or not. Everyone ignored him.

"Neither do you," Bell pointed out to Conri.

"I learned. He hasn't."

The blunt statement of fact didn't require sympathy. Bell still felt a dull ache in his chest, at least part of it anger, at what lay behind those two words. He didn't imagine it had been easy to teach Conri "his place" in the fey scheme of things.

Like everything else Bell wanted to do right now, that could wait till later.

"That means we stick together," he said. "If we can't use the servants' tunnels, we only have one option."

"What's that?" Annie asked after a glance at her friends, who sullenly stayed quiet. "Do you… do you have, like, a SWAT team on standby or something?"

It would have been unkind to laugh. Bell swallowed the chuckle that tried to escape his throat and tried not to think how reassuring it would be to have enough Walkers available for a SWAT team at short notice.

At any notice.

"I'm a Walker," he said. "We don't need backup, and if we can't take the back door, then we'll let ourselves out the front."

THE KNEE bent the wrong way—sideways and back—as the sap hit it. It popped audibly, and the Other went down. Bell's training wanted to follow through, to knock the opponent out of the fight, but instead he vaulted over the body as it writhed. The clamor of bells filled the house, a discordant peal that one of the Others had raised when Bell hadn't hit him hard enough.

He spun and cracked the weighted end of the sap against a tattooed skull, snapped his elbow back into a fastidiously, surgically redone nose, and side-kicked one of the Others in the stomach—whatever alternate-reality fantasy Keith had conjured him from close enough to normal that nothing stood out to hang a nickname on at first. Bell's heel caught the Other under the rib cage, dug into his diaphragm, and rattled his lungs. The almost-Keith's eyes bulged, bloodshot and red-rimmed as it tried to suck in air around how much it hurt.

Bell dropped it with a quick smack of the sap against its temple and kept moving. He jumped over the sprawled bodies, stamped on hands that attempted to grab at him, and ran through the maze of twisted corridors and oddly angled rooms that blended old-world elegance with whatever frat-boy idea of luxury Keith had come with.

He'd taken point to clear the way. Conri brought up the rear to make sure whatever Bell put down stayed down. Between them, the fey kids, armed with knives and spikes they'd gingerly selected from the slaughterhouse, clung to one another and tried to keep up.

He stepped on an empty bottle of wine. It rolled under his foot and then, as he caught his balance, shattered under his weight. Bell staggered and lost his stride. One of the Others grabbed him by his jacket and swung him around to slam him against the wall. Bell grunted as his head cracked against a thickly carved doorframe and the breath was knocked out of him.

"You won't get him," the Other parroted his lines as he grabbed Bell by the throat and squeezed. The thick fingers cut off Bell's attempts to refill his lungs, and he could feel the tendons in his throat creak and strain. "We'll never let you have him."

Bell squinted as dark spots swam across his vision and slammed the heel of his hand up into the Other's chin. The Other's jaw snapped shut on the tip of his tongue, a spray of blood spit over Bell as the sliver of flesh was severed and either bone or tooth cracked.

The Other tried to hang on to Bell using borrowed jock bulk to pin him against the wall. Then Conri grabbed the Other by the collar and slammed him down onto the ground hard enough to stun. To keep it down, Bell kicked it behind the ear, the impact of steel-reinforced toe against bone way too familiar at this point.

"… sorry," Robin stuttered. The young fey stood frozen, a butcher's blade clutched in one white-knuckled hand and a spray of blood stark red against his cheek. "I was going to... I should have but... they look like real people."

"Not your job," Bell said. He shook the static out of his ears and pushed himself off the wall. Things hurt, some sharp and new and others dull under the faded effects of the trow ointment. In a couple of days, he'd pay for them all. "Move. Let's get you out of here."

Conri chivvied the shaken teens forward, first one step and then another and then a shove to get them to shamble into a run. The Others scrambled out of doors and downstairs to lunge at them with knives or grab at their arms and clothes on the way past. Annie yelped as one of the Others got a handful of her hair and yanked her back off her feet. The knife she'd taken dropped from her fingers, and she grabbed desperately at Shanko and Robin as she was dragged backward. Conri stooped down, grabbed the knife smoothly off the ground, and carved the Other's arm open down to the bone as he came up. Severed tendons loosened the Other's fingers around her knotted curls, and Annie lunged away. She left strands of hair tangled in his fingers as she threw herself into Shanko's arms.

The Other didn't have a chance to do anything before Conri flipped the knife in his hand and drove the blade into his exposed throat. As the Other's eyes widened in shock, it looked real. Then they clouded over as he reeled back, a gout of blood spilling down his throat as the knife slid out.

It was Bell's job to keep people safe. To either bring home the mortals trapped in the Otherworld or make sure the ones who decided to stay did so of their own free will. Some of them had fought him, a few he'd had to hogtie and drag home, but he'd never had to kill a human before. It would feel like a failure, no matter how often Conri claimed they were already as good as dead.

There wasn't time to dwell on it.

"Come on," Bell said as he pushed the fey trio forward. "Keep moving."

Conri kept Annie's knife. He held it like he had a good idea how to use it.

They dashed down corridors, sweaty and—at least in Bell's case—sickly aware they'd lost any sense of direction five turns back. Or maybe not. They skidded around one last corner and nearly crashed into the three Others set to guard the door.

"You won't get him back," one of them, scars raked down one side of his face, said as he stepped forward. A hammer hung from his hand and he bounced it against his thigh as he talked. "We'll die first. All of us. Here. Together."

"We'll die first," the other two said, one slightly slower than the other. "… die first."

Bell didn't break stride. He ducked his shoulder and slammed into the Other's stomach at full speed. It lifted the man off his feet with a grunt of surprise, and he grappled briefly at Bell's back before he remembered the hammer. It was too late for that. Out of the corner of his eye, Bell saw the hammer start to life, the head of it scarred bronze, and he grabbed the Other's arm by the elbow and tossed him. The joint popped with that distinctive snap of fucked tendons—like rubber bands stretched too tight—and the Other crashed awkwardly into the ground.

He writhed there, arm twisted around until his hand was nearly backward, until Conri leaned down to grab a chunk of his hair. He dug his fingers into the matted curls and smacked the Other's head off the flagstones once and then again. The second time, the Other made a sick, wretched noise in his throat and went limp.

Bell spun on the ball of his foot and smashed his sap down against the Other's heavily tattooed forearm as he thrust a spear at Conri's side. The metal caught on the joint of the Other's wrist and snapped it brutally back until the thumb kissed the inked phoenix on his skin and the spear clattered to the ground.

The Other screamed in rage, ignored the pain, and lunged at Bell to grapple with him. He managed to trip them both to the ground, and they scuffled in the filth and blood as they punched and kneed each other. Bell had better technique—after years on the job, he fucking should—but technique didn't count for much in a scrum.

He twisted his head to the side. "Get the door," he yelled at Robin, who'd shoved the other two behind him and then frozen. "Get outside."

The order jarred Robin out of his shock. He scrambled over to the door and fumbled with the heavy, rust-thick bar that sealed it. Shanko hesitated but then went to help while Annie dithered behind them.

Bell grunted as the Other rammed a knee up into his stomach and he tasted bile in the back of his throat. He hammered two hard, knuckly punches into the Other's kidney that made the man groan. The Other tried to pin Bell down with his weight—muscle and a bit of flab—but Bell twisted around and sank his teeth into the side of the man's face. His incisors jarred on the hard ridge of a cheekbone and the chunk of flesh in his mouth tasted like sour wine and sweat.

But dirty tricks were good whatever sort of fight you were in.

The Other howled and reeled back, up onto his knees. Blood dripped down his face from the raw, distinctly bite-shaped wound, raw meat visible where the skin had torn. Bell pulled his knees up until they hit the Other's ass. Then he grabbed his arm and flipped him over. The Other grunted as the landing jarred his grotesquely broken wrist. While the Other writhed around the pain, Bell scooped up his sap, weighted his fist with the handle, and punched it down against the Other's temple. The Other's eyes rolled back at the impact and he went limp, mouth slack and bloody.

Bell braced his fist against the man's chest and pushed himself painfully up onto his feet. He wiped his arm over his mouth and glanced around. The kids were still fighting with the bolts on the door while Conri kept the last Other busy.

Bell took a guilty, indulgent second to watch Conri move.

The changeling fought like a… fencer—Bell refused to give the Otherworld the satisfaction of the other comparison—as he bobbed on the balls of his feet and snaked in with the knife to harry the last Other. From the dirt-locked knots of hair and the razor, he was Keith's version of himself as a homeless serial, and he jerked away from each sharp jab of the knife while Conri twisted bonelessly away from the increasingly desperate slashes of the straight razor.

Conri wasn't exactly graceful. He jinked and twisted at odd angles, but his absolute confidence in his body and what it could do made Bell's mouth dry with lust… even though this wasn't the time.

Conri had the Other under control, so Bell shoved himself to his feet and limped over to help drag the heavy bars out of their dented housings. Sweat itched between his fingers as he wrestled with the lock, the insistent pulse of blood the timekeeper in his ears.

"Watch out!" Annie yelped.

Bell turned and the head of the short axe sliced through the air in front of his nose. If he hadn't moved, it would have been buried in the back of his skull. Chips of wood flew as the tip of the blade buried in the door. The Other grunted as he wrenched it back and swung again in a short, efficient arc that made it clear he knew what he was doing. Bell barely managed to twist out of the way, but Shanko wasn't as lucky. He grabbed at the man and lost part of his hand as the Other easily reversed the arc of the weapon.

What looked like most of a finger dropped to the ground. Shanko was too shocked to even scream. The Other flicked the blood off the blade and swung at Bell again.

Shit.

Bell backpedaled along the wall as he tried to divide his attention between the axe and the rest of the room.

The Other spun the axe in his hand with casual competence. Fairy tales always had beautiful fey weapons—jeweled swords that could talk and spears made of ivory and horn. The reality was sweat-stained, unadorned wood handles and dented, uneven bronze axe-heads crusted with dirt and scabs of dried flesh. Bell adjusted his grip on the sap and wished, again, for the familiar off-kilter weight of his old one. He *knew* where the weak points were on that.

"The whore gets nothing," the Other said. "She was *told*."

Conri had dispatched his opponent. The Other, slumped against the wall and stained with blood, looked as if he was still breathing but he wouldn't get up anytime soon. While Conri yanked the last bolts back and shoved the kids out into the pink-tinged dawn, Bell caught the axe on his sap. The blade scraped along it as it slid dangerously close to his fingers. A heartbeat before he lost a knuckle to the edge, Bell let his arms drop, the sap slid from underneath the axe, and he snapped it back around to tag the meat of the Other's thigh.

The Other staggered, and Conri snaked an arm around his neck from behind. Lean muscle stood out against tanned skin as he choked the Other until blue eyes rolled back, and the axe dropped out of a limp hand.

The heavy weapon landed point-first on the wooden floor and buried itself, trembling slightly from the impact. Its owner was dumped unceremoniously next to it.

"You should have stayed with the kids," Bell snapped as he stepped over the Other. His chest was tight with a strange, heady delight that Conri had come to his aid, even if it wasn't needed. This was work, though. "We're here to rescue them, and I—for the last time—can take care of myself. You should have gone. I would have caught up."

He gave Conri's shoulder a shove to shift him out of the way, and Conri fell back a step.

"Yeah," he said, placid as dark water and just as ominous. "Thing is, they wanna talk to you."

Fuck.

Bell wiped his forehead on his sleeve and limped outside to see what had gone wrong *this time*.

CHAPTER ELEVEN

APPARENTLY THERE were faces you didn't get tired of punching.

Conri rubbed his bruised and bloody knuckles as he watched Keith preen and parade in front of the scarred yellow truck. The paint had come in cracked blisters where unicorn blood had splattered it, and the metal was gouged and ripped like it had been through a war. Something had gone through the windscreen, and they'd had to kick it out.

"… saw through her stupid trap," Keith boasted in a tight, cracking voice. "As soon as I caught up with Ned, we headed *straight* back here. Did you forget we had a *fucking truck now*, Nora?"

He swung around on his heel to scream the last words into Nora's face, and she grimaced and flinched back as far as she could, pinned between two of the Others. Ironically, since every Other was made in Keith's image, the ones he trusted the most were apparently the ones least like him. One was thickly built and cabbage-eared, scars cut through his eyebrows, and the other thin as a whip, with Glasgow Smile scars on both cheeks. He was the one with a knife pressed against Nora's tanned throat.

Her hounds were muzzled with thorns and tied up with rough lengths of rope cobbled together around skinny ankles, under the watchful eye of the rest of the Others. The big pack leader—Betty—snarled and fought her bindings, blood bright on white fur, and was wrenched back by the Other who held her lead. Robin tried to jump in as well, but it was Shanko who dragged him back by the collar.

"I hoped you were so stupid you'd get lost," she snapped back at Keith. "Or you'd go back and leave us alone!"

Keith glowered, but it wasn't him who answered.

"Why would we do that, Nora?" Ned Kessell rasped. "We're only here to save you. Once you're home, you'll see that."

No more ignoring the elephant in the room, then. Or—Conri glanced at what the Otherworld had left of Nora's brother—the pig.

283

Not a placid pig domestic porker, though. This was one of the half-wild pigs that Conri remembered from his childhood—mean, scarred slabs of hard meat, fat on acorns and *maybe* two generations away from wild boars. His shoulders had torn through the sleeves of his T-shirt, the heavy hunch of muscle fuzzed with coarse white bristles, and his eyes were red-rimmed and beady under the heavy overhang of his brow. His jaw thrust forward, and his chin had thickened as it disappeared into the thick folds of his neck. Yellow tusks poked from under his lower lip, and his nose was flattened and wet with snot.

Conri had seen worse. The fey liked extremes. The grotesque stirred their senses just as the beautiful did. It was the mundane they shunned. It wasn't Ned's appearance that made Conri's skin crawl. It was seeing his worst, wet-snouted nightmare made into pink, sweaty flesh and boar-bristled jowls.

In the mortal world, probably ten minutes had passed on the clock, and even by the slough's timekeeping, it had been a few days. Conri had never seen someone so completely, confidently remade by the Otherworld in such a short space of time.

It was what Conri didn't want. The possibility that left him sweaty in the dark, his throat full of his own heartbeat, until Bell came to look at him like he wasn't a monster. And the other thing. The one he tried really hard not to think about.

What if flesh wasn't the only thing the Otherworld could shape to order? What had it left him?

"Let her go," Bell said. He stepped forward, lean and deadly in bruises and bloodstained black clothes. "And we can all go home, Mr. Kessell. That's what we all want, isn't it?"

Keith jumped forward and jabbed a grubby finger at Bell. He was skinny, tanned skin stretched over wiry muscle and bone.

"Fuck you too," he said. "We all want to go home and *what*? What then, Mr. Iron Door Agent *traitor*? You'll bury this? Brush it under the carpet so the filthy sidhe and pixies and trow can keep on fucking us over and fucking us up? Not this time. Not with *this*."

"This *what*?" Bell asked. He put his hand on his gun and then moved it away again as the Others tightened their grip on Nora to make her wince. "What do you think you're going to expose, Keith?"

284

It didn't look like Keith would come up with an answer. He opened his mouth and then closed it again without saying anything as his eyes darted around the clearing.

"This," he spluttered out after a baffled second. He waved both arms wildly at their surroundings as he took a stiff-legged step forward. "All of it. They did all this. They made this, and they killed people. When we bring the… the—"

"Iron Hall," Ned provided the names, his voice thick and glottal in the loose folds of his throat. "Salt and Secrets. The police."

Keith nodded along jerkily until Ned finished and then snatched up the thread of his rant again.

"They'll show the world the truth!" he said triumphantly. Bubbles of spit caked white and stuck in the corners of his mouth. "Everyone will see what soulless, inhuman *things* these people are. Fuck the Treaty. When we had the chance, we should have finished this. Not given them quarter."

Conri laughed. It wasn't intentional—the sound rattled out of his throat—but when Keith turned to glare at him, he ran with it.

"I spent decades in the Otherworld." Conri carefully undersold his length of service. Lies here could come back and bite you, but the truth structured to deceive was usually fine. He took a step forward and then another before he stopped as the Other pressed his knife to Nora's throat. A drop of blood dripped down onto the grimy collar of her leather jerkin. She bit her lower lip. Conri stopped and held his ground as though he hadn't noticed. "Do you know how many times my master sat up late at night to talk over tactics with his allies? Or find weapons to arm their troops? None. To you it was a war, to them it was… inconvenient. Wipe them out? Good luck. You couldn't even *find* all the fey."

"Lock them out, then!" Keith said. "We did… our ancestors, our great-grandparents… they sealed the doors and threw away the keys."

Before Conri could point out the problem with that, Bell took a step forward to catch Keith's attention. It was a slow pincer movement, but so far it seemed to be working. This close to Keith, the Others weren't going to act unless on a specific order from him.

Conri wondered if there was enough left of whoever they'd been to understand what was happening. He squashed that thought quickly as Bell talked.

"That's actually your problem," he said, easy and reasonable. "Your great-grandparents. This place was sealed long before the Treaty was signed. Past sins were forgiven across the board."

Keith shook his head. "Because people didn't know! Because you—"

A big, rough-knuckled hand pushed Keith out of the way as Ned lumbered forward. He hunched down to get into Bell's face.

"They stole my sister," he ground out through thick, angled teeth. "That pretty-boy point came to *my* town and stole *my* little sister, and you're lying if you say *that* hasn't violated the Treaty."

He poked a fat pink finger against Bell's shoulder to make his point. It rocked Bell back on his heels, but he didn't shift position.

"Did they?" Bell asked. "Is that what Nora told you?"

Confusion visibly flickered over Ned's face. "That… that's what happened," he said. "They took her away. I have to save her."

From inside the pickup, Thistle stuck his head out the window, dandelion curls matted down and greasy. He had a black eye and one of his ears was swollen, but otherwise he looked okay.

"I told you," he yelled. "I *told* you. We didn't take her. I don't even like girls. Please, you can't trust—"

Keith stormed over to the car and grabbed Thistle by the face, his long, grimy fingers dug in around the narrow jaw and sharp cheekbones.

"Shut up," he said as he shoved Thistle back into the car. "Or I'll shut you up."

Ned made an angry sound deep in his chest. "I told you, leave him alone," he said. "He did what he was told."

"I did, I did," Thistle jabbered as he retreated back inside the cab of the pickup. His face was pale and frightened, but he kicked out when Keith grabbed at him and kept going. "I did what I was told. I did what *she* told me, remember? She sent me to find you. Why would she do that if we weren't friends?"

"Because she wanted to get rescued," Keith said impatiently. "Obviously. Come on, Ned. You know Nora's a smart girl. She knew you'd come for her."

"Then how come he won't let her tell you that herself?" Bell asked, as he nodded at Nora. One of the Others had let go of Nora's arm to clap his hand over her mouth, the blade of the knife poked into the soft skin under her jaw.

"They've brainwashed her!" Keith said quickly. He stepped between Ned and his sister, his hands up as he tried to push the heavy boar bulk of Ned back. "Stupid bitch believed everything they told her, and—"

"Don't call her that," Ned interrupted him grimly.

Keith swallowed hard and glanced around at the Others. "I... I tried to save her, Ned," he course corrected. "You know that. I told you, remember? I chased after them to rescue her."

Out of the corner of his eye, Conri saw Bell move. Barely. He drew and fired in one quick, confident movement. The Other with his hand around Nora's face stared for a second with the one eye he had left and then went down like a dropped puppet.

Nora gagged and wrenched away from the remaining Other. Her hounds kicked up a fuss at the struggle, their voices thick and garbled as blood scarred their muzzles.

"It's *his* fault," she yelled. "Not Robin's. His. He chased us down. He *shot* at us."

"At them!" Keith screamed at her. "I shot at them!"

"I was with them," Nora said. "You could have killed me, and you didn't care. The only reason we're here is that we were trying to get away—"

The Other managed to get his hand over her mouth and lift her up off her feet. She screamed between his fingers and kicked at his heels. Bell's gun tracked the Other as he backed off, but Nora was in the way.

"You shot at my sister?" Ned rumbled. Anger made his shoulders hunch and his face settle into heavier, piggier lines. He gave Keith a shove that nearly knocked him off his feet. Maybe Nora thought that all Ned wanted her for was domestic help, but at least for a second, he was nothing but an angry big brother. "You could have killed her!"

"Yeah, well," Keith said, suddenly calm and his voice thick with venom. "I didn't, but I wish I had. Then none of this would have happened. If this is anyone's fault, it's *hers*. She was my girlfriend, and she went sniffing after that point like a bitch in heat."

Ned grabbed Keith by the shirt and hauled him up onto his toes. He shook Keith hard enough to rattle his teeth.

"This is your fault," Ned growled furiously. "You caused all this."

The Other made Nora yelp, and Ned snarled as he shoved Keith back.

"You can't get back without me," Ned said. "And I'm here for my sister, not you. If those filthy things hurt her, I'll let you rot here."

Keith made an exasperated noise as he stepped back. "Why? This is what we talked about! We're going to end the tyranny of the Treaty. All that has to happen is she doesn't come back, not right away. We'll be heroes, Ned. Famous. All those changelings and fey will be sent back here."

"It's where they belong," Ned agreed. The words dragged over his tongue, as if it were the force of habit that made him mouth the agreement. "They aren't like us anymore."

Conri barked out a laugh. It sounded more like a dog than him. Maybe that was what the Otherworld had taken this time. He'd have to find out once things were less shitty, maybe binge-watch some old comedies.

"Us?" he said. "Have you looked in a mirror recently, Mr. Kessell?"

The thing was it didn't *feel* different. It seemed like it should, like you could tell your ears had changed or you'd lost some of the colors in the world, but Conri had never been able to tell. Not until he looked in the mirror and his brain saw what his body had already accepted. Luckily— or unluckily—his master had been a vain man, and it had never taken long before Conri caught a glimpse of himself.

But where would Ned find his reflection out here with his broken mirrors and smashed windscreen?

"A mirror?" Ned said. He looked around in bafflement and snorted out a laugh. "What? I got something in my teeth? We're in hell. Who cares what I look like?"

Conri showed his teeth in a humorless grin. "Iron Door will," he said. "If the Treaty's broken."

On the other side of the car, Bell gave Conri a quick scowl and mouthed "be careful" at him as he worked his way into position to take the shot. Conri ignored him. He didn't want Bell to carry killing Keith around with him. Despite the hateful idiocy that spewed out of Keith's mouth, Conri didn't want him dead either.

He wasn't much older than Finn, and it was too easy to imagine Finn in his place. The fey had their bigots too, and it was hard work keeping them and Finn apart.

"You're mad," Ned said with the satisfaction of someone who'd solved a problem. "You spent too much time in the Otherworld, and it made you nuts."

"Prove it," Conri said. "Look in a mirror."

Keith butted in. "Where would we find one here?" he said. "What do you care what he looks like anyhow, dog boy?"

"Why do you care that he doesn't know?"

And maybe Robin was from Mag Mell after all, although he didn't have the ears of their king, because when he raised his hand, the water answered him. Dew stripped off the red-splattered Cheater's Roses, and the Jeep groaned and cracked as the radiator burst and spat out stale, old water. It flowed together and extended up from the ground until it was as tall as Ned, the surface flat and reflective as a millpond.

The two boar men stared at each other for a moment. Then Ned shook his head in rejection. He reached out and slapped his hand through the water to dissolve the truth in a spray of bright droplets. Still under Robin's command, the mirror reformed and stitched Ned's altered image back together.

"It's a lie," Keith said. He stuck his hand into the water and waved it wildly about to try and disrupt the reflection. "They're lying to you, Ned. You know me, don't you? You trust me."

Ned felt his face with both hands, moving his fingers gingerly as he explored the new angles. Then he turned to look at Nora. Her eyes were huge and full of pity over the Other's grimy fingers as she looked at her brother. She couldn't nod, but she didn't need to.

Grief made Ned slump for a second, and Conri *felt* the slough shrug that off for him. It occurred to him that he might have underestimated this place. Rage took its place as Ned looked up and trained red-rimmed eyes on Keith.

"You did this," he rasped as he slapped his hand against his broad chest. "All of this. You stupid little bastard."

He lunged forward. Keith hadn't expected him to move so fast and yowled as Ned laid hands on him. Conri could have told him, but he had other things to do. He lunged toward the Others before they could react to the attack on Keith and barreled with his full weight into Nora and the Other holding her. She whoofed at the impact, and all three of them went down, tangled on the muddy ground as feet stampeded over them.

In the background, Conri could hear gunshots as Bell picked off the Others and a squealing roar he assumed was Ned. He focused on getting Nora loose.

It wasn't a dignified fight. It barely qualified as a scuffle. Conri snapped the Other's fingers so he could pry his hand off Nora's face, bruises red and puffy around her mouth, and she squirmed out of her stolen jacket to get away. The Other cursed her in a strangled voice as Conri held him down by the throat and a knee rammed into his gut. He felt a sharp jolt of pain as the man punched him in the ribs, but he didn't give way.

Conri grabbed the Other by the face, hooked his fingers over his teeth, pressed against his tongue, and broke his jaw with a brittle slaughtered-chicken pop.

A broken neck wouldn't kill everything in the Otherworld, but it would put almost anything out of commission for a while. The Other was no exception.

"I… I didn't want any of this," Nora said plaintively as she watched the twitching dead man who looked like her ex. Tears ran down her face. "I just wanted the best story I'd ever have to not be something that *almost* happened."

Exhausted, Conri clumsily pushed himself to his feet.

"You got your wish," he said grimly. "Trust me, this is what that's like."

The look Nora gave him suggested that was the worst thing she'd heard, despite everything she'd gone through. Before she could say anything, Robin, knife finally bloody, shoved through the melee.

"Nora!" He threw himself into her arms, clumsy as he tried to embrace her and hang on to the knife, and pressed his face against her scruffy, greasy hair like the cropped strands were the scented braids of Titania. "My beautiful girl."

Look at that. It was love, after all.

For now, at least.

He left the lovebirds to it and shoved his way toward the pickup. The Others climbed into the back and onto the cab as they reached through broken windows to drag Thistle out. Those who hadn't, hung off Ned as they tried to carve through the layers of pink flesh and red muscle down to his organs. So far they hadn't nicked anything vital.

"We need to get out of here," Conri yelled to Bell as he dragged the Others off the battered truck while it steamed and clicked to itself. He cracked the door and reached in to grab Thistle's shoulder with a growl to silence him when the panicked fey tried to bite him. "Nora and Robin are clear."

"I've got Annie. Shanko's in the brawl," Bell said. "Get Thistle, get out."

Conri could pick a handcuff lock. It wasn't hard. Since he'd left everything in his discarded clothes when he shifted, he settled for yanking the handle off the door. The molded plastic dangled from the skinny fey's thin wrist as he threw himself out of the car and into Conri's arms.

"I wanna go home," Thistle sobbed as he buried his head in Conri's shoulder. His hair was dense and scratchy as his namesake. "I didn't wanna bring him here, but I was scared."

It hadn't been *easy* to learn to be a dad. Conri's own had been useless the few years he'd been around. But by this point, the motions were second nature—the pat on the back and the words that didn't really matter so much as the tone.

Thistle tightened his grip and snotted into Conri's shoulder. Conri dragged the kid back, and he was heavier than he looked and stronger. *Shit.* He'd rather watch Bell's back, but Thistle wasn't about to let go.

"Okay," he said. "I got you. Come on."

He half carried Thistle away from the truck, neck craned around so he could track Bell until he lost sight of him in the scrum, with only the occasional glimpse of black leather as he cut his way toward the foundering Shanko, his bloody hand wrapped in dirty linen as he struggled. The hounds fought against their captors, bodies twisted like smoke around the thorn tethers. In the middle of it, Ned shrugged the

Others off his back and slapped them aside as he dragged Keith toward the trees. And the slough held its breath.

Shit.

Conri tried to peel Thistle's arms from around his neck, but it was too late. He had to watch as Ned lifted Keith up and threw him into the hungry thorns. The vines tightened, pulled, and the Others stopped midstep, midblow, and the likeness to the dead boy faded from their faces. They hunched over, coarse stubble gray and thick as it poked through their reddened skin.

"Shit," Conri said out loud as he finally managed to set Thistle down. "The king is dead. Long live the king."

CHAPTER TWELVE

RIBS CRACKED like sticks under the pressure. Bell ignored the instinct to recoil and pushed down again. He could feel the grit of broken bone against the heels of his hand as he worked.

Twenty-eight.

Twenty-nine.

Thirty.

His shoulders burned worse than they did after a fight as he stopped compressions. It flared and spread over his back like wings as he hunched over Keith to pinch his nose shut and exhale into his mouth.

Again.

Halfway through the second round of compressions, Keith choked himself back to life. Bell felt the stutter of the kid's assaulted heart against his palm as Keith's eyes fluttered open and he sucked in a breath down a throat greased with trow ointment.

"He wanted to kill us," Nora said. There was a hard note in her voice. Despite her own squeamishness about the Others, she evidently had no qualms about her brother doing her dirty work. "You should have let him die."

She turned and stomped away, her scarred hound limping at her heels. Robin caught up with her and pulled her into a hug, his lips pressed to her temple as he muttered something to her.

"Maybe I should have," Bell said to himself as he looked down at Keith's body, mangled and torn even with trow ointment and desperation holding him together. Both arms and one hip were dislocated, bruises wrapped around the abused joints, and there were punctures where the local hollow thorns had slid into veins and arteries to siphon blood. Keith was breathing, but that didn't mean anything. "He still might. But not here."

He pushed himself up, his battered body aching, and pitched his voice for someone other than him to hear. "Help me get him loaded into the truck."

It wasn't aimed at anyone in particular, but only Conri and Thistle came to help, and that only because the skinny fey was Conri's shadow. They picked up Keith's body—limp in unconsciousness and bending in ways that weren't quite right—and lashed him into the back of the truck.

"What about him?" Thistle asked nervously as he jumped down off the back of the truck and glanced over at Ned. He rubbed his scarred, still-swollen wrist in a fretful gesture. "Is he...?"

He trailed off without finishing the question, pale eyebrows scrunched together unhappily. There were plenty of options. Bell weighed them up.

"He came here under his own steam, of his own free will," he said finally. "Until I'm told otherwise, he's not my problem. Not today."

Thistle frowned as if he didn't like that answer. Bell could understand that. There were plenty of reasons Ned deserved to pay for what he'd done. The problem was the one reason he wouldn't.

"We can't fight him *and* the slough," Conri said bluntly as he jumped down off the truck. "If you want revenge, wait until someone bigger and nastier comes along to oust him."

"And until then," Bell said, "he's here with nothing but how much he hates himself for company."

It wasn't *enough* for Thistle, but it would do.

Ned drove them back to the ford. He reeked of animal—a ripe musk mixed with blood—and he didn't talk much, not until it was Nora's turn to go through.

"My dogs," she said, one hand on Betty's thin head and her voice thick with reluctance. After she'd mentally cut these ties, it stung to pick them back up for a favor. "Will you take care of them? They're good dogs."

Ned nodded his big, heavy head. "Farm's yours now," he said. "Sell the pigs or send 'em through to me. Whatever you want."

"I can come... back. Visit?" Nora offered stiffly.

Ned turned his back on her and stalked away, back to the truck. "Don't."

After a thoughtful second, the hounds gave a distinct shrug and followed their new master, fluid and alien again as they shucked the dog game they'd played. Only Betty stayed, stubbornly pressed against Nora's side as they crossed back to mortality.

"Felix will love that," Bell said tiredly as the whip tail disappeared.

Conri shrugged and bent down to grab Keith's ankles. "His problem," he said. "Not mine."

Or Bell's. It was satisfying to shrug off that one responsibility as Bell bent down to grab Keith under the shoulders. He felt the flutter of breath against his cheek. Still alive. Maybe he'd last long enough for Bell to see what they'd brought back across after all.

They stepped through the ford together and out into a circus of Iron Door agents, paramedics, and panicked parents.

Robin, it turned out, had three changeling siblings and a heavyset human stepfather who alternated between threats of eternal grounding and relieved hugs. Nora looked bewildered as she stood to the side and watched her fey prince be treated like a wayward son.

"Dad!" Finn pushed his way through the crowd and launched himself at Conri. He hugged his father desperately for a second and then pulled back, his hand outstretched and dark in the moonlight. "You're bleeding."

Conri touched his hand and looked at his own bloody fingers. "Huh," he said. "So I am."

Bell caught him as Conri's legs went out from under him.

TWO DAYS of debriefs, paperwork, and interviews with brittle, unhappy parents. Human and changeling—the one thing they'd be willing to admit they had in common was that they didn't trust Iron Door.

Bell didn't blame them, not this week. He tossed his jacket onto the chair and sat down on the edge of the bed. The mattress gave under him and released a faint aroma of old linen and fresh lavender. Iron Door didn't skimp on accommodations, but even the best hotel in Elwood was a bit shopworn.

He leaned forward, elbows braced against his knees, and dug his fingers into his hair. The tension had started to loosen in his shoulders when someone rapped their knuckles against the door. Bell groaned under his breath and lifted his head.

"I don't need towels," he said, his voice gruffer than he meant it to be. "And I don't have any fey stashed under the bed."

"Good to know," Conri said.

Shit.

Bell bolted to his feet, surprised by the sudden buzz of excitement, and yanked the door open before…. Well, before anything. Conri was slouched against the door, back in jeans and a dubiously tasteful band T-shirt. His hair was damp, and he smelled of hotel soap and overtreated tap water.

"It's later," Conri pointed out. "Is it still a thing?"

Back on this side of the ford, all the reasons this was a bad idea were in sharp, unforgiving focus. Professionally. Personally. Whatever they'd wanted in a shabby, Otherworld approximation of a trailer, they couldn't do this.

It was stupid.

They'd regret it later.

Bell supposed he should have brought that up *before* he kissed Conri, but hindsight was always twenty-twenty. He tangled his fingers in the old, washed-thin T-shirt and dragged Conri into the room with him. Conri's laugh slid between their lips as he reached back, groped blindly, and slammed the door shut before they gave any locals—or Felix, who was a floor up and two rooms over—a show.

Later could fend for itself. Bell wanted to pretend he was the sort of man who made bad decisions for one night.

Or part of it.

He pulled Conri down onto the bed. The chintzy spread creased under them as they tangled around each other. Conri's body was long and satisfyingly rangy under Bell's hands—long muscle and warm skin. He ran warm, not quite fever hot but more than room temperature.

Bell entertained a weird, brief fantasy of cold months and warm feet tucked against his, when even if this wasn't a one-time thing, he'd never been stationed anywhere cold enough to care about whose feet were hotter. The Otherworld definitely stretched to Alaska, but the colder it got, the weirder it got. Everyone had their own ideas why.

It was a nice thought now. *Cozy.*

He pulled away from Conri's mouth and shoved the other man back down onto the bed when he tried to chase the kiss.

"I want you to fuck me," he said.

Conri grinned and dropped his head back against the pillows. He grazed his hands down Bell's back, over the long, wiry strips of muscle, until he filled his palms with Bell's ass. He shifted under Bell and raised his knee so Bell's already-halfway-to-hard cock rubbed against the hard-muscled length of Conri's thigh.

"And you say I point out the obvious," Conri mocked lazily.

Bell ducked his head down to grab another kiss and then caught the lush curve of Conri's lower lip between his teeth. The bite made Conri groan low and deep in his chest, and his hands tighten.

"I want to have you on top of me," Bell said. He pushed himself up, settled his weight on Conri's hips, and pulled his jersey up over his head. The air-conditioned cool of the room made him shiver as it hit his skin. "Your cock inside me. People sometimes get the wrong idea about what I want in bed, because of what I do."

Conri moved his hands to brush his fingers over the scars that lined Bell's torso. Some of them predated his job and the trow's healing ointment—an operation when he was a baby, the rib he broke so badly when he… fell off the roof of his house that it had come through the skin. And some of them had been bad enough that even the trow's magic was only able to staple him back together.

Not that many scars, really. Four or five. Not compared to some of the Walkers and not many Bell wanted to talk about. Not right now. He caught Conri's wrists and pinned them down against the pillows behind his head.

"So, do *you* wanna fuck me?" he asked.

Conri flexed his fingers, and Bell felt tendons move over heavy bone under his fingers.

"You think maybe this might be why people get the wrong end of the stick?" he asked. "Not the job?"

Good point, not that Bell planned to admit that.

"That wasn't the question," he said.

Conri braced his foot against the bed, hitched his hips, and rolled them both over onto the mattress. His shoulder hit the edge of the bedside table as he misjudged the space, and the small bedside light wobbled and fell over. It hit the ground with the sharp, explosive crack of a broken bulb. They both ignored it.

It was Bell's turn to be pinned down on the bed, Conri's sweaty weight lazily sprawled over him. Lust cramped low and hard in Bell's balls with a tug that dragged dully from his thighs up into the taut line of his stomach muscles. His cock thickened under his trousers, heavy and tight as it pressed against the zipper.

"I'm easy," Conri said. The corners of his eyes creased as his own joke made him smirk. "In a lot of ways."

Bell snorted and dropped his head back against the pillows. "Funny enough, no one's ever said that about me," he said. "My last boyfriend said I was impossible to satisfy."

"Maybe he was bad in bed." Conri kissed Bell's throat as he made that suggestion, his mouth soft and his teeth sharp as he chewed his way along the long tendon down to Bell's collarbone. Heat seeped through Bell's skin, into his blood, hot with pleasure and impatience. "Or he didn't want to try hard enough. Same thing, really."

"Don't think in bed was what he meant," Bell said. "It was… everything else."

Conri rested his chin on Bell's shoulder and looked up at him. Scruffy hair hung over his face and threw his eyes into shadow, but it was still impossible to mistake him for human. His ears pricked forward through the tangled thatch of curls. "Oh, good. I was going to take it as a challenge."

He waited.

"Oh, well, yeah," Bell said with dry amusement. "You're probably right, now you come to mention it."

He could feel Conri's smile against his skin as the changeling pressed a kiss to his shoulder. "I thought so."

Kiss or bite. It was hard to predict what Conri was going to do next as he thoroughly kissed his way down Bell's chest toward his stomach. He lingered over Bell's nipples, his tongue and teeth equally occupied with the nubs of flesh. Bell groaned as the tight, wire-sharp pleasure that knotted through the nerve-rich flesh slid toward tight, wire-sharp pain.

Both of them tugged on threads of *want* that thrummed all the way down into Bell's cock.

He writhed under Conri and tangled his free hand in the scruff of his hair. It was coarse against his palm and thicker as he worked his fingers down toward the skull.

"I've never slept with another Walker before," Bell said. He wasn't entirely sure of the relevance. The storm of sensation under his skin had thrown his thoughts in the air like a deck of cards, but it was true. Not for lack of trying when he'd been younger, but Felix had shut that down without compromise. "Is it different?"

"No. Yes?" Conri said slowly. He rested his chin on Bell's lower stomach and thought about the question, his warm breath cold as it brushed over spit-wet skin. Bell bit his tongue on the urge to tell him not to bother. "You can tell, but it's not… better? It's just sex. It's not…."

"Like fucking the fey," Bell finished for him.

"Don't know. Never did that," Conri said. He shrugged, and Bell felt a small, wary knot loosen in his gut. Sex with the fey was meant to be… *altering*… and even if it was stupid, Bell didn't want to have Conri weigh his ass against that experience. "Tell you what. It's easier to show you than it is to explain."

Bell knew that was the moment to pull the plug. He was Agent Dylan Bellamy of Iron Door, and he'd sacrificed a *lot* to get there—relationships that mattered to him, lovers he'd left behind when he was sent to new cities, and friends who'd never quite understood that yesterday for them was a month for him. That guy didn't risk his career and reputation for a tumble with a changeling with mismatched eyes.

But apparently he definitely would for Conri.

They shed their clothes quickly, suddenly impatient with buttons and zips and laces, and explored their bodies with eager hands and mouths. Bell ignored the white flag of a gauze dressing taped to Conri's ribs as he mapped the hard lines of muscle in Conri's shoulders and back with his fingers.

It was a practical body. Bell had been honed to swing a sap and take a beating. He was fit, but he was a tool designed for a specific task. Conri wasn't so specialized. The Otherworld's influence? Or his life before? He supposed it didn't matter. That was the joy of a one-night stand.

He wrapped his fingers around Conri's cock. It was thick and hard against his palm as he gripped it. The skin slid under his grip as he stroked the length of it, thin and delicate as wet silk. Conri swore, words thick in his throat, and sprawled back over the bed with a fistful of pillow clenched in one hand. All that long, workmanlike muscle was stretched out tight and lean under his tanned skin.

"If you keep doing that," he said roughly, "you'll need to spend the night if you want me to fuck you."

That idea was... surprisingly appealing. Bell ignored it as he reached over the bed and fumbled at the drawer. He'd bought the lube that morning on the off chance he'd stop being a coward and go knock on Conri's door. If Conri hadn't bitten the bullet for both of them, it would have gone in the garbage.

It was slippery and cool on his fingers as he squeezed it out of the bottle. He smeared it along Conri's cock, from his balls to the flushed, taut head, until it was wet and gleaming and Conri's breath was ragged in his throat.

"My turn," Conri said as he snagged the bottle off Bell.

He pulled Bell down on top of him and kissed him, breathless and intent, as if this were their first kiss, while his cock pressed eagerly against Bell's thigh and his fingers spread Bell's ass wide. Bell wasn't sure which of the three dragged the raw whimper out of his throat. It was sweetly, painfully intimate as he drank in the taste of Conri's mouth and his ass squeezed around Conri's fingers.

"Fuck," Bell groaned finally as he pulled his mouth away. He rested his forehead against Conri's, so close that if he wanted, he could have let the changeling blur and pretend he was human. Could have but didn't. "I want you."

"I know," Conri said. It was probably arrogance, but there was something grateful in the way he said it. He worked his fingers deeper in Bell's ass until his index finger grazed the prostate and Bell nearly lost track of what they were talking about. "It's why I'm here."

It was the sort of statement that invited either offense or complication in equal measure. Bell could take it at face value and told Conri to go fuck *himself*, then, or he listened to the hint underneath and let this turn into a mess.

He went with neither.

"Get on with it, then," Bell ordered. He felt Conri's low, amused laugh rumble between their bodies.

"You *sure* you don't want to be on top?" Conri asked.

Bell took Conri's face in both hands, a hint of stubble rough against his fingers, and kissed him until both of them were breathless.

"Good idea," he said as he braced his hands on Conri's shoulders to push himself up. His ass twitched as Conri slid his fingers out and propped himself on his elbows instead. "If you want something done right, after all, do it yourself."

Usually he'd have insisted on a condom, but so far, only the common cold had proven able to survive the trip to the Otherworld. As many times as both of them had crossed over in the last week, it wasn't worth the bother.

Conri's cock was thick under his fingers, the skin pulled taut around the girth as Bell reached back to hold it in position. Blood pulsed thickly in the base of it, fast and hot, and the head twitched against Bell's hole. He slowly lowered himself down onto it, the dull ache of pressure cut through with preemptive jolts of pleasure that twitched down his thighs and tightened his stomach.

Color flushed over Conri's cheekbones, dull under his tan, and he stroked wet, slippery hands up Bell's thighs. He traced the taut lines of muscle with his thumbs and folded his lower lip between sharp, white teeth as Bell took the length of his cock down to the balls.

Bell paused for a second to admire the view. All that heavy, hard muscle was laid out for him under that smooth tawny skin. There was only one scar, a coin-sized whorl of white, shiny skin under his armpit. It had been a brand once—or ink; some of the fey had marked their changelings in silver or gold—and cutting it out was a statement.

But of what?

"You could ask," Conri said, his voice uneven and ragged with strain. "I'll tell you."

Bell touched the scar and watched Conri twitch. "Do you want to tell me?"

"… no."

Bell folded over awkwardly and brushed a quick tease of a kiss over Conri's mouth. He dodged the hungry attempt to prolong it as he straightened back up.

"Then don't."

He braced both hands on Conri's shoulder as he rode him, the long muscles in Bell's legs trembling as he lifted himself up and then thrust back down. His cock ached with each stroke, tight with the need to be touched, and his balls felt heavy and *thick* with the buildup of pleasure.

Close.

Each thrust that stretched him wide, his ass clenched tightly around Conri's cock, pulled the threads of pleasure tighter. It roiled in his pelvis, a knot of nerves and liquid pleasure that needed *a little more* before it would spill over.

Bell's mouth was dry, and he felt each thrust jolt with sticky, honey pleasure along his spine. It dried his mouth and spread hot, tingling flicks of pleasure over the nape of his neck. Then Conri thrust up to meet him, his hands tight on Bell's thighs and his balls pressed hard against his ass. Bell felt the tangle in his gut tighten until he was about to scream at the sensation… but it held. He swore between clenched teeth, his fingers digging into Conri's shoulders as he scrabbled for the threads of control.

Apparently Conri had other ideas. He slid his hands up to grip Bell's ass and flipped him over in one smooth movement that ended with Bell on his back and Conri between his thighs and still mostly inside him.

"Let me," Conri said. He licked sweat off Bell's throat with a slow, savoring kiss. "Pretend you still trust me. And now's when to pay attention."

As if his mind were about to wander?

Bell hitched his hips up and wrapped his legs around Conri's lean waist, his feet pressed against solidly muscled thighs. He groaned as Conri pushed back into him. Each thrust *barely* skimmed against his prostate with a tease of stark, blind pleasure, and his cock was pressed between his stomach and Conri's. Not quite *enough*, the sandwich of slick skin and pressure, but too much to ignore.

He tangled his fingers in the thick hair at the nape of Conri's neck and pulled him down. The curve of his lips demanded a kiss and then down to the taut line of his throat. The scrape of Bell's teeth down the tanned skin dragged a complimentary, satisfying growl out of Conri. His skin tasted of salt and sweat, his pulse fast against Bell's lips as Conri thrust into him with steady, deep strokes of his cock.

A second bite, teeth dug in hard enough to leave a mark, pitched Conri over the edge. He thrust roughly into Bell, until Bell had to brace his hand against the headboard, and came with a shudder and a groan. His cock pulsed inside Bell, warm and—as Conri pulled out—wet. There was something else too, like a pulse against a membrane under them. The Otherworld border flexed around them, thin and warm as skin, and then faded.

Bell reached for his own cock as Conri pushed himself up off him. He dragged his hand impatiently along the length of it, eager to finish, but Conri moved his hands away.

"I said, let me," he drawled as he crawled down the bed to wrap his mouth around Bell. His tongue was slick and clever as he licked Bell's cock from shaft to head, the pressure of his mouth and lips warm around the shaft.

Bell dropped his head back against the pillows, the hand he had braced against the headboard now tangled in Conri's hair. He didn't think about the fey or being an agent or anything but the spill of hot, sweet pleasure that Conri wrung out of him.

THEY SPRAWLED on the wrinkled, stained comforter, sweaty and sticky and too lazy to untangle themselves. The half-crescent bite scar on Bell's upper arm drew Conri's fingers again. He counted each of the teeth that had jabbed into Bell's bicep.

"Redcap," he guessed.

"Selkie." Bell grinned at Conri's quirked eyebrow. "Some rich asshole had lured her into a marina to try and play seal wife with her. Yelled for us when it didn't work. She didn't want to leave, and it pissed her off when she couldn't seduce me."

People *really* underestimated selkies, in Bell's opinion. They expected cute little harbor seals and then yelled for help when confronted with the toothy, six foot plus of marine-mammal-muscle reality.

"Your drinking scar?" Conri asked.

Bell snorted. He'd never thought about it that way, but he supposed it was. The one that was easy to show off and talking about it didn't make him sweat or have pity muscle the drunk out of people's eyes.

He slid his hand down to the gauze square taped over Conri's ribs. It was rough compared to the silky skin it covered.

"I should have come to you," he said.

"Because I'm the invalid?" Conri asked.

"To see how you were."

"You knew how I was," Conri said with a shrug. "Finn said you went with him to the hospital, yelled at the doctors who didn't want to treat me."

A vet, the doctor had suggested, disdain in his voice. *We don't treat animals.*

"Still," Bell said, because… still. He couldn't quite put his finger on what he should have done or why he owed it. It felt like he did or might. "He okay? Finn?"

"Back at camp," Conri said. *That* made him pull away as he rolled over onto his back, extricated his legs from Bell's, and stretched. "Safe and sound… until he might not be."

There was nothing Bell could do about that, nothing he could say. He might understand Conri's viewpoint, but he knew Iron Door's as well. The reminder of the fault line between them cooled him down, and he sat up, one leg tucked under him.

"This can't be a thing," he said.

"What this?" Conri asked.

"Any of it," Bell said. "Your help. What happened in the Otherworld. What happened here. It's done. Let it go."

Conri folded his arms behind his head and grinned that empty disarming smile he'd greeted Bell with the first time.

"Like I said, I'm easy."

Epilogue

RELIEF THAT his dad hadn't decided to die right in front of him hadn't even lasted until they got back to LA. Faced with the first day of school, even the dregs evaporated.

"So, what. I don't see why I have to learn geography," Finn groused as he threw his bag onto the couch and stalked into the kitchen to raid the fridge. "The minute I hit eighteen, I'm going back to the Otherworld, and I'll never have to find fucking Belgium on a map again. Or, you know what, in the actual world."

"You know the Otherworld's mapped over this world, right?"

"Yeah," Finn said. He took a swig of orange juice from the carton and wiped his mouth. "Now ask me if I care."

Conri weighed the pros and cons to having it out about Belgium, and the cons won.

"Go do your homework," he said. "Try and get a report card that doesn't make me regret learning to read."

Finn rolled his eyes, grabbed a whole bag of ham out of the fridge, and slouched off to his room. From the muted sound of conversation and the clicks that filtered out, he was *not* doing his homework, he was playing *Overwatch*. He'd get around to it before dinner. He usually did.

Sometimes Conri wondered why he wanted to come back. The world wasn't what he remembered—the rules had changed, and he'd never really thought about parenthood. But Finn wasn't a bad kid. Most of the time, Conri actually liked him, which was about as good as people with actual biological kids got.

He grabbed a beer from the fridge and headed back over to the case he'd left spread out on the kitchen table. It gave him a bad feeling. The husband said all the right things about his missing wife, but as far as Conri could tell, she'd hidden her trail herself. So, she was either a really underachieving con artist or something was wrong under her roof.

Either way, she didn't want to be found, and Conri had to decide if his conscience needed that on it.

He had picked up her phone records when a knock on the door made him look up.

"If that's the Thai order already," Finn yelled from his bedroom, "the spring rolls are for me."

"Homework first," Conri yelled back. "Before I turn the router off."

He pushed the chair back from the table and went to grab the takeout before the delivery guy legged it. Plenty of places wouldn't deliver to Little Annwn, and he didn't want to dissuade the ones that did. The tip was already in his hand as he opened the door.

Bell—not in uniform and looking impossibly normal, but hot in jeans and a white T-shirt. He glanced at the ten-dollar bill in Conri's hand and raised dark eyebrows.

"I appreciate the thought," he said. "But I didn't travel all this way for a tip."

Conri stared at him as he wavered between relief and panic. He didn't know what scared him more, that Bell was there for him over some Otherworld thing or that Bell was there for him, unlikely as that seemed.

"What are you here for?" he asked.

Bell glanced around. "Can we do this inside?" he said. "I'm not in uniform, but...."

But it didn't matter. Iron Door was worn into Bell's skin like a stain. Around here, that wasn't going to get him killed, but it wouldn't get him welcomed either.

"Come in," he said as he stepped back and waved Bell in. He closed the door behind him and glanced around in an attempt to not stare at Bell. "You want a beer?"

"Sure."

Beer. Small talk. An ache of interest in Conri's balls as the memory of their sweaty hours in Bell's bed ran on repeat through his head. He tried not to pay too much attention to it, but that left him watching Bell wrap his mouth around the neck of the beer. That wasn't any better.

"So," said as he leaned his hip on the arm of the couch. "Why are you here, again?"

Bell fiddled with the beer. He picked at the edge of the label with his thumbnail and peeled off wet shreds. It was the first time he'd really seen Agent Bellamy look off-balance.

"Couple of reasons," Bell said, and he took a drink of beer. Conri watched it go down with more fascination than it was worth, his eyes glued to Bell's throat. "Working together back in Elwood was more successful than I expected, and something that my boss wanted to trial for a while, apparently. Iron Door has authorized me to approach you and discuss a more... official... association."

"I'd be flattered, but I'm going to guess you couldn't find another changeling who'd give the idea the time of day?"

"It wasn't well received."

"What makes you think I would, without my residency and my son's freedom on the line?"

"You said it yourself," Bell said. "You're useful and resilient."

The beer was cold, and the proposal was interesting, but it wasn't exactly what Conri had—*briefly* and *headily*—imagined when he opened the door. It probably should have been. They both knew where they stood when they left Elwood.

"I'll think about it," he said as he finished the beer. "If it's worth my while, I'll let you know."

He used his legs to push himself up and took a step toward the door.

"I said a couple of reasons," Bell said. "The offer is... a good excuse."

Oh.

Conri turned back. "Oh?"

"Yeah."

They looked at each other. It dragged out long enough that Conri felt his mouth twitch at how ridiculous it was.

"Do I have to guess?"

Bell snorted. He rolled the bottle between his hands, condensation wet on his already damp palms. "If you would, it'd make this a lot easier. I wouldn't have to risk that I got the wrong end of the stick."

"If I had to," Conri drawled as he sauntered over until he was a bit too close to Bell on the chair, "I'd say that we both know it wouldn't work if this were a thing?"

Bell leaned back. His face was unreadable as he looked up at Conri, the bottle braced crookedly against his knee. "Absolutely," he said. "I couldn't trust you. You couldn't trust me. That's not going to last."

The tease took on a bitter note in the back of Conri's throat, because that wasn't wrong.

"Not for long," he admitted as he edged farther into Bell's space. He propped his hip on the arm of the chair, his legs lazily tucked against Bell's. "But maybe that's okay. Trust me, lasting a long time isn't always a good thing. Sometimes shorter is sweeter."

"So, if this were still a thing," Bell suggested slowly, "you might want to… do something that doesn't involve dead unicorns sometime?"

Conri touched Bell's face. The thin scar was distinct as a thread. He leaned down to kiss Bell. It was slow and thorough, as if something might have changed since they parted.

"I'd consider it," he said. "I like good food, and that noise you make when you—"

The smack of Finn's door hitting the wall interrupted them. Conri pulled back from Bell as he recalled his… responsibilities.

"Was it the Thai food?" Finn asked as he dragged his headphones off his messy setter-red hair. A frown creased his face as he saw Bell. "What's *he* doing here?"

It wouldn't last, *and* it wouldn't be easy, but Conri thought it might be worth it.

Wolf At First Sight

by Rhys Ford

To everyone who loves things that go bump in the night...

ACKNOWLEDGMENTS

OH, TO the Five… always. And to Bru, who jumped in on this ride. As well as to Elizabeth, Liz, Naomi, Gin, and everyone else at DSP for letting us go crazy with this.

ONE

"GOD, I hate you."

It was a muttered refrain Levi had heard more than a couple of times since he first brought home his squalling red larva from the hospital, only his son's face visible from the swaddling blankets wrapped around his squirming body. There'd been a few long, drawn-out fights when Declan entered adolescence and was conflicted by the rise of hormones every young boy faced. There was anger and a bit of self-doubt, mostly from grappling with the loss of a mother who'd checked herself out of the hospital and disappeared, practically right after they cleaned the afterbirth off the thin, pale newborn.

Then there was also the first time he shifted into his wolf form—a long-legged, gangly thing with too-big paws, no sense of direction or grace, and an overwhelming appetite for pizza and cheeseburgers.

Levi dealt with Declan's little act of verbal aggression with an arched eyebrow, followed by an ice-cold shot back, "Really?"

At fifteen, his son was gaining on him in height but had years to go before he'd reach Levi's muscle mass... if he ever did. Ashley passed on not only her beauty, blue eyes, and long lashes to their son, but also her compact dancer body—a lithe, sleek contrast to Levi's brawler build. To be fair, Levi also spent many evenings tossing out drunks and staring down tipsy supernaturals with enough strength to tear down a streetlamp even in their human forms, so Levi knew he could bank on just a hard look to push his son's bravado back down a few notches.

The *really* was an extra cherry on top of the Levi-takes-no-shit sundae.

Levi waited, holding his tongue in the tense silence. Declan glanced to the side, making the briefest of eye contact, then dropped his gaze down to the living room floor, where his half-packed duffels sat next to piles of folded summer clothes. If he'd been one to buy into the wolf lore some older packs whispered about, building up their own arrogance and need to feel superior over the next guy, Levi could have said Declan's submissive drop of his head and gaze was lupine in nature, an instinctual reaction to Levi's alpha status. Calling bullshit on that type of thing was exactly why the Keller family was split—one side clinging to the old myths and structure while the ones who had a lick of common sense formed a healthier splinter group.

Levi wasn't alpha so much as he was *Dad*.

The silence simmered, bubbling between them until Declan finally broke.

"Sorry," he muttered, a bit louder than before. "You didn't deserve that crap from me. I just want—"

"You want to stay here and hang out at the pub," Levi finished for his son, picking up one of the duffels. He'd heard enough of Declan's varied arguments over the past few days, his objections ramping up as the date got closer. "And you're not. You know why. It's not up for discussion. You can't spend your entire life only surrounded by your own kin. It doesn't work that way in the human world, and it sure as hell doesn't work that way in ours. Only way you're going to learn about other kinds of people is if you're around them. And don't start telling me St. Con's got lots of people you can learn from. That's not the kind of crowd that needs to be teaching you."

Declan flopped down on the living room couch, a heavy overpadded affair Levi was glad he'd paid through the nose for when the kid was younger. His son was hard on furniture, especially as he was growing into his enormous feet and hands. Puberty was rough, and there'd been times when Declan's body ached from sprouting up an inch or two, seemingly overnight. The soft, comfortable sectional, with its wide cushions, made a great nest for him to curl up in. If he'd been thinking, Levi probably wouldn't have chosen to have it upholstered in bloodred chenille, but he liked the color and didn't realize eventually there'd be two wolves in the house and double the fur all over the place once Declan began to shift.

"Dad—"

"Michelle will be here when you come back," Levi said, cutting through the heart of the bramble growing up around Declan's objections. "You're fifteen, and it might seem like she's the love of your life right now, but the truth is, you're barely a blink in the universe at the moment, kiddo. Yes, she's pretty and she giggles when you tell a joke, but if she's serious about you, she'll wait. It's only two and a half weeks at summer camp. There's people you haven't seen in a year, other kids you like and still talk to. Hell, some of them have even squatted in our house for a weekend or two."

"It's just…." Declan laid his head down to stare up at the ceiling, not even glancing at his father when Levi sat down next to him. "It's not like I don't like the place… or the things we do. Some of it's really cool. It's just that when I go out there, I feel like I'm a freak. At least at home, I feel normal. Like I could almost be normal."

"You *are* normal, Deck." Levi shifted over, hooking his arm around his son's slender shoulders. Pulling his son close, Levi kissed the top of Declan's head, wondering when the hell the little boy who'd fit in his lap only a few years ago was suddenly this handsome young man with a storm of confusion in his blue eyes and troubles in his heart. "*We're* normal. Are we different than the people you go to school with? Yeah, you are. But not just because we're shifters. We're different in experiences and culture. There's people out there with centuries of social burdens holding them down, and they've got to carry all of that crap on their shoulders, wondering if something shitty's going to happen to them because of it or if it's going to stop them from getting ahead.

"You've got other burdens, other troubles, and I'm not saying you've got it easy, but you're not alone. I'm here. Your grandparents and some of the other family members are too," he assured softly, wrapping his other arm around his kid to give Declan a tight hug. "I told you a long time ago, we're making this shit up as we go along, and the only thing I have to guide you with is what I've learned myself and what everyone around me has to say."

"Because you're going to listen to Uncle Gibson?" Declan pulled back a bit to wrinkle his nose at his father. "He writes romance books and lives in a cabin out in the middle of nowhere. What's he going to teach me?"

"Probably that having romance in your life is a damned good thing to have," Levi shot back, unwrapping his arms so he could tweak Declan's nose. "I'm not saying I'm perfect. God knows I've fucked up, and I'm always going to adult up and apologize if I'm wrong, but in this, I know it's the right thing for you. Everyone there's got something to teach you about how to be you, and they're people other than me. Because sometimes you're going to need to hear truths that aren't mine, and maybe you've got something to say to someone else to help them figure things out. Just… go up there, have a good time, and for God's sake, don't blow anything up this year."

"Shit, blow up one toilet—"

"You blew up three toilets, and the year before that, you guys were caught making a still out in the canoe shed, which also exploded." Levi sighed. "Seriously, dude, can you just not set anything on fire or bring down hellfire and brimstone for three weeks? Between you and your cousin Dino, I think our family's replaced most of the buildings up there. Go, have fun, and this time, no makey with the boom-boom. My bank account can either feed you or buy a new roof for a cafeteria. Your choice, kiddo."

JUDGING BY the weight of the duffel in his hand, Levi figured Declan shoveled all of his belongings—and possibly the pub's huge kitchen sink—into the two soft-sided totes. Waiting outside for the camp van to come by to grab his kid was a summer ritual, one he'd participated in at least fourteen times himself. Now, on the other side of the pickup, Levi wondered if his own parents worried about making sure he'd been ready to take on the world once he stepped off the curb.

Talking seemed to push back the anxiety of watching his son take another leap forward, and even though he knew in his gut Declan needed to hear others' stories and maybe discover a bit about himself without his old man looming over him, it was still hard to let go.

"Now, remember what I've told you, Deck?" Scuffing his boots on the gritty sidewalk outside of the building where he lived and worked, Levi peered down the street, then clarified, "Other than the no-exploding-things bit."

"No means no. If someone doesn't listen to me saying no, then…." Declan snarled, shifting his canines into wolf-form to make snick-snick noises with his elongated teeth. "Make them listen with a bit of bitey-bitey?"

316

"You're fifteen now. We don't call it bitey-bitey." He covered his son's mouth, looking around to see if anyone was near. "And don't let Grandma see you do that. She'll tear me a new asshole for teaching you that. Bad enough Pops taught me. She'll start saying you look like a chihuahua. And yeah, no means no, but I was thinking more of the whole... keep it wrapped, or better yet, keep it tucked?"

"Dad, anything I can do there, I can do here, just in a bed that doesn't smell like mold and maybe snakeskin," Declan groaned, rolling his eyes. "I love you, but man, I don't want to have a kid before I'm twenty. Maybe not even before I'm thirty. I want to be old when I have crotch goblins."

"Great, now I'm old," Levi chuckled, mocking Declan's eye roll with one of his own. "And that's going to be your new nickname— Crotch Goblin. That's how I'm going to introduce you to everyone. Hey, have you met Crotch Goblin Declan? I made him myself."

"Swear to God, the main reason I'm sorry I'm an only child is because someone else should share the shame of having you as a dad." Declan dug into his jeans pocket, probably looking for something to bind his long brown hair with. The wind picked up a few strands, carrying a hot kiss on it, the heavy mugginess of summer lingering in the afternoon air. "I'm okay. I haven't bitten anyone in years, and to flip things around, if you do decide to bring someone home, make sure they don't wear the same size shoes I do. Unless you want to replace all my Converse again."

"Have you looked at the boats on your feet?" He snorted. "I could just buy you those inflatable Zodiacs and put them on you. It'll be a lot cheaper."

"Yeah, yeah, so funny." Declan narrowed his eyes and peered around his father, pushing Levi's firm shoulder out of the way. "Van's coming."

"Okay, give me a hug before anyone can see you," Levi murmured, drawing his kid into a smothering embrace. "Can't let them see we love each other."

"You are so fucking weird, Dad," Declan grumbled into Levi's chest, but his arms came up, wrapping around his father's back. "Gonna miss you anyway."

Levi closed his eyes, holding on to the moment as tightly as he did his son. They'd come a long way together, battling the world and pushing back anyone who said Levi could only raise hell and not a kid. It'd been a battle with temptations along the way, sins dark and deep enough to pull him off the path he'd set for himself, but he'd overcome them, focused on being the kind of father he'd had instead of the man he'd become. He and his father, Davis, were too much alike, his mother always said, destined to butt heads because they always had to be right. In some ways, Levi hoped she was right, because if anyone deserved the kind of stand-by-you father Davis was to his kids, it was Declan.

"Man, I love you, kiddo." He squeezed tighter. "I would recognize your foul stench anywhere."

"Okay, Dad… um, the van's almost here." Declan squirmed. "You can let go now."

"No, no. Let me have this moment," Levi sighed, rocking Declan back and forth in as dramatic of a roll as he could. "Seeing my little boy off—"

"Dad, do you want me living with you for the rest of your life?" his son mumbled, unable to pull away from Levi's strong hold. "Because this is how that happens. This is becoming a 'Hot For Teacher Sweet, Sweet Waldo' thing, and dying a virgin wasn't on my life plan. Let go before I have to live under my bed."

"Okay, go get into the van, and good luck with the bears." Levi released Declan, then steadied him with a firm hand, clenching his son's shoulder affectionately. "And well, whatever other shifter is up there this year. Send me an email or something if they ever unchain you from the basket-weaving bench, and no—"

"Biting or exploding stuff." Declan picked up his duffels, his shoulder muscles bulging under his thin T-shirt. "Yeah, I know. Same goes for you."

There was a bit of the same old catch-up small talk with Brandon, the camp's head counselor, as Declan loaded his things and climbed into the van, already mostly full with other teenagers in various stages of funk and sullenness. Stepping back onto the curb, Levi watched the van take off, cruising down the road toward the woodland site nestled in the hills. It would be a long drive ahead, or at least long enough for the kids to get caught up on old friendships. A part of him missed those days.

He'd bought the St. Connal's Pub off of his uncle, moving into the large apartment over the bar with an inquisitive five-year-old boy, both of them ready to take on the world. Or at least that's what he told Declan. The truth was he needed to settle down, and the two-story brick building in an old, established neighborhood was just where he felt they belonged. The St. Con was a piece of Keller history, belonging to the family since the 1930s, and now more than ever, Levi felt the weight of its legacy on his shoulders.

"You know, for a pile of bricks and wood, you're not too bad-looking, old man," he said to the building sitting on the corner, the pub's intersection-facing door open in welcome to anyone passing by. The afternoon shift sounded like it was doing well—a bit of laughter tumbling out onto the street and the delicious scent of beef pies beginning to fight its way through the afternoon air. Cocking his head, Levi turned toward the garage attached to the back of the building and smiled. "Been a while since I've seen you on two feet, cousin. Should have come out and said hey to the kid. About time he met you again."

He caught Ellis's scent as soon as they came out the security door. At first, he didn't quite believe his cousin was lurking about. The last he'd heard from the family was Ellis was no longer curled up inside of his wolf form. But making his way out into the world wasn't something Levi expected Ellis to do, not so soon. Not after… everything he'd gone through.

"Last thing the kid needed," Ellis growled. His voice sounded rough, torn around the edges and lacking the lightness of humor Levi always associated with his older cousin. "Came begging for favors. Didn't want to… muddy things up."

"Okay, I can see that." A reunion would have meant catching up and then Declan again not wanting to leave. Levi nodded, then jerked his head toward the apartment's entrance. "You hungry? I can toss together a dinner. Not on the job tonight."

Ellis studied the wrought iron security gate guarding the place's front steps and stoop as if it were an oracle and he could only ask it one question. His gaze shifted, settling on the mudroom and its chaos beyond the open front door, then a quick glance at the curved stairs beyond that, the warm honey-oak steps leading up into the apartment. Something flickered across Ellis's strong face, turning any softness in his features to stone, and for a moment, Levi wondered if his cousin was even aware he was there.

Like most of the Keller men, they shared a strong genetic stamp. Broad-shouldered and lean-hipped, Ellis had at least twenty pounds of muscle on Levi's honed brawn, and his gaze was just as heavy—an ice-flecked cold sweep of constant movement, catching on any changes in his environment with each turn. When they were kids, Levi and Ellis's younger brother, Gibson, haunted Ellis's heels, barely hiding their hero worship for him and some of the other Keller clan.

Ellis coming home, broken and caught in his wolf form, shattered the clan into pieces. Some suggested putting the eldest of the cousin pack down like a dog infected with rampant distemper, while others spat at the suggestion. The schism happened in ripples, the divide between families and kin growing as angry words and resentment over Ellis's treatment made the rounds. Levi landed on the side of letting Ellis be who he needed to be, refusing the family space at St. Con's to discuss the issue on the pub's neutral grounds. He'd taken a stand against his kin, refusing to fall prey to traditions instead of honoring blood and family. In the end, sides were taken and lines were drawn. He distanced himself from men and women he admired and loved, feeling the loss of their presence in his life keenly during the holidays or during times when he felt alone.

Now the furred wedge himself had shown up at Levi's front door, asking for a favor.

The raspy cough of an ill-timed motorcycle turned both their heads, and Levi's hackles rose despite being hidden deep inside his human form. If Ellis was a hauntingly familiar and welcome scent, the scruffy man in road-rashed leathers and denim cutting around the pub's corner turned the air foul. Ellis's wariness rose, his face closing up once again, a granite hardness shaping his expression into solemn disapproval. Levi didn't blame him one bit. Even if Ellis didn't know Charlie Granger was a low-ranking go-between for the Los Lobos MC and probably would stab his own mother for a can of piss-water beer, Charlie's odor of desperate neediness was strong enough to turn a man's stomach. He tried masking it with bravado and tough words, barely hiding his rage at the world behind violent threats and intimidating stares, but Granger wasn't the first bootlicker he'd dealt with and probably wouldn't be the last.

All part and parcel of being the owner of the St. Con's and a Peacekeeper.

The rattling bike came to rest facing the wrong direction, a tiny aggressive flip-of-the-finger Granger seemed to get a kick out of. Planting his feet down on the asphalt, he made a great show of taking off his aviators and giving Ellis the once-over. Up close, he actually smelled, more sweat and soil with an after-tang of grease and stale booze. A fringe of stringy blond hair poked out from under his black turtle-shell helmet— the barest concession to California's riding laws—and his eyebrows were a crawling mess of coarse hair, battling one another for the bridge of his flat, broad nose. Dirt held a firm grip on the large pores dotting Charlie's fleshy cheeks, and a straggle of hairs dotted his chin in a vague attempt at a goatee.

Curling his lip, Charlie finally spat out, "You should move along, asshole. Keller and I have to talk some business."

"Which asshole?" Ellis cocked his head, looking around. It was good to see Ellis's arrogant smirk form, and Levi chuckled, shaking his head when Charlie's face flushed red. "Which Keller? Looks like at least one asshole and two Kellers."

Before Charlie could bristle up into his best bantam flourish, Levi cut him off. "What do you want, Granger? The meet's not until this weekend, and I've already laid out for both clubs about what's going to happen and when. Is Reilly balking and he couldn't come down here himself to talk to me?"

At the mention of his club's leader, Charlie turned even redder, swallowing hard before speaking. "No, I just figured I was in the area, so I'd come by and make sure Paolo got what he wanted in the deal. Because you know, I'm his right-hand guy, so I'm here to take a look around. It's my business to—"

"So, Reilly didn't send you?" Levi glanced up at the sky briefly, as if pleading with the heavens. "Deal is, none of you come around until Friday night when the meet happens. And even then, there's only going to be three of you on each side. That's the rules, Granger. Always have been. What you guys do until then isn't any of my business, but come seven o'clock Friday night, you'll be under my roof, under my rules. Showing up here only pisses on what's already been agreed on. So if Reilly thinks otherwise, I can call—"

"How about if I punch the asshole next to you in the face, and we can see what *I've* got to think?" Charlie leaned forward, his meaty hand clenched into a tight fist. "Then I'll start in on you."

Levi had to give Charlie points for bravery, or maybe just the depth of his stupidity. He was about to respond when Ellis bent slightly forward and bared his teeth, growing out his canines just like Declan had a little while before. Controlling the shifting of their forms was a sign of strength in their kind, and the delicate, gentle manipulation of growing vicious fangs in a human jaw made Charlie suck in his breath.

Snapping his teeth at the rider, Ellis said quite clearly, "Go ahead. Try it. When I'm done, I'll leave your hands so they can figure out who you were from your fingerprints."

The struggle in Ellis's voice lacquered his threat with a deep menace, his throaty growl more like a fighting wolf than an angry man. Levi braced himself, instincts warning him a member of his family was in danger, but he held himself back and let Charlie sift through his options before stepping in.

"Go away, Granger," Levi finally said, letting Charlie off the hook. "I won't tell Reilly you came by and nearly fucked this all up, and you get to keep your nose. Because Ellis here likes cartilage the best. And spinal cords. Bones are just something to bite through to get to the good stuff."

Ellis gave another wicked-wolf grin and nearly purred at Charlie when he pulled the bike away. They watched the motorcycle jerk and sway up the street, nearly hitting the curb as he took the far corner too tightly.

"Grandpa teach you that? Or your dad?" Levi asked, rocking back on his heels.

"Your dad. Then Grandpa came around all hush-hush, telling me not to tell Grandma." Ellis shrugged. "Haven't yet."

"Who do you think taught Grandpa?" Levi smirked at Ellis's rough laugh. "Sorry about that. Sometimes people with the smallest dicks have to flex them to make sure they're still there."

"Los Lobos? Kind of… stupidly obvious."

"Yeah," Levi replied. "They're not the most imaginative people."

"Who was that asshole? And why?" Ellis grumbled. "You're doing a meet for him and who?"

"Not him. Paolo Reilly from Los Lobos and the Vikings' leader, Tom Wheeler," Levi answered. "Lobos are moving into the Yosemite area, and the Vikings are already there. Reilly says he just wants to homestead, but no one believes him. Wheeler's already gone after a couple of the LL riders and Paolo's retaliated. I guess they figured they'd give St. Con's a shot before they try to wipe each other off the face of the Earth. Meet's on Friday. After that, they're on their own. Now, if you're not hungry and aren't looking for a place to crash, what can I do you for, cousin?"

"Looking for a bike." Ellis shuffled back away from the curb and moved closer to the building. Levi didn't like the shadows in Ellis's warm eyes or the strain in his voice. Freed of his wolf form, his cousin was running from something, maybe even himself. His next words confirmed it. "I need to get far from here. Gibson's… great, but I need to run. For a bit. At least. Hoping you can help, but I don't have—"

"If you're going to say you don't got the money for a bike, I'm going to give you that punch in the face Charlie couldn't pull off. Your coin's no good here, El. You've done enough for me in the past. Least I can do for you now." Levi slapped his broad cousin on the shoulder and pushed him toward the double-wide garage attached to the back of the pub. "Come on and let me show you what I've got, including a Softail Deluxe I just finished bringing back up. Asshole who owned it laid it down in front of an old pickup, so I got it cheap. She ain't pretty, mostly primer, but she runs like she's got a fire under her. And I'm thinking she's just about your size."

TWO

IF THERE was anything Lieutenant Joseph Zanetti knew about, it was coffee and violence.

As a cop for nearly twenty years, he'd downed at least a million cups of coffee, both good and bad, and as for violence, seen more than his share of death, sorrow, and plain stupidity. He'd waded through the remains of bloodbaths, stepped over dead bikers dressed in full club gear and clutching weapons that did them no good in the end. He held on to the images of every child who'd had their light snuffed out way too early and stood over mummified corpses discovered in odd places, murder clearly evident even on their dry, desiccated flesh.

Death he could deal with. Violence could wash over Joe, and he'd barely blink. He'd been in the game too long to expect to see anything new delivered up on a bloody platter for him to be all that surprised about what humans could do to one another and themselves.

But as he steeled himself for yet another sip from the battered paper cup he'd rested on his SUV's middle console, sucking down the sticky film off the top of a cold coffee was perhaps the greatest crime he'd ever have to face.

"If you brought one of those steel tumblers Ma keeps buying for you, you wouldn't be complaining about it, Joe," he scolded himself after scraping his tongue against his front teeth. "And why the hell am I sitting here on my day off?"

He knew the answer, and it lay in the by-chance spotting of a biker sporting a full patch on his back from a motorcycle club he'd thought long gone from the city. The roar of the Harley caught Joe's attention first, rumbling around in the tight Chinatown street, filling the long stretch with its throaty, choppy purr. Thinking nothing other than the bike sounded good, Joe was about to make a right turn when the man sitting back on the bike's long seat wove between the lines of traffic to sit between two small imports to wait for a red light to change. That's when the rider's colors popped out at Joe, its Viking-helmet-wearing bear's head and rocker patches confirming what his brain nearly refused to accept.

Because ten years after being driven out of the city by Joe and the rest of the cops on SFPD's Gang Task Force, the Vikings were possibly coming home to roost.

It'd been years since he'd been on the Task Force but he remembered all of the heavy hitters from when he'd led his team back then. The Vikings weren't a club anyone wanted to mess with, and it'd taken a few years to break their hold on the drug supply lines they'd set up in Chinatown's underground markets. He wanted to verify what he'd seen before he contacted the current GTF's leader, Sgt. John Yang.

"No sense going to Yang with only a whisper of information and a half-verified patch," Joe murmured, taking another sip of his hideously cold coffee. "Quick stakeout. How can that hurt?"

As stakeouts went, this one was unofficial but a hell of a lot more comfortable than any of the others he'd been on. Parked under a shady tree in the parking lot of an evenings-only sushi place across the street from the pub, his SUV was air-conditioned with padded seats and space for a cooler filled with ice and soda. It had been a spontaneous decision, driven more by the niggling suspicion of gang activity than anything else. Or, Joe supposed, he was purposely avoiding heading to his parents' house, where a family gathering awaited him, complete with somebody his mother invited as one of her many matchmaking attempts.

"If it wasn't for her marrying Dad," Joe grumbled, "I would have serious doubts about Ma's taste in men."

He was about to call it a day after an hour when a door on the side of the pub opened up and a lanky teenaged boy ambled out, followed by one of the hottest men Joe'd ever seen. The kid obviously was his or at least related, judging by their similar strong features and dark hair. Their body language was familial, a bit of teasing and murmuring banter Joe couldn't make out even as he rolled down his window. Dad was a few inches shorter than Joe, but his compact muscular body and long legs tickled a desire Joe thought he'd buried a long time ago. He didn't have time for sex, much less relationships, but the sexy, scruffy man in torn blue jeans and an old gray T-shirt stretched tight over his sculpted torso brought a wet need to Joe's dry mouth.

They talked, murmuring in low tones, and the kid turned toward his father and snapped his teeth at him playfully, probably showing off a lack of braces or something, because the boy looked about the age Joe was when his own steel gear came off. The dad's words took on a bit of a warning tone—not quite a scolding but mostly cautious, and the kid grinned up at him, easily falling into their banter again.

The man turned, giving Joe a good look at the tight ass beneath those battered jeans. Then he surprisingly pulled his son into a fierce hug. It was hard to watch, mostly because Joe could count on one hand the times his father ever embraced him. There'd been a few slaps across his shoulder and a thousand hair ruffles but never anything as unadulteratedly affectionate as the slightly grubby father fiercely hugging his son out in the open. The boy's arms came up, returning the embrace, but then something changed between them when the boy struggled a bit and the father's deep laughter rolled over the street, a teasing lilt in his undistinguishable words. The teen pushed at the man's shoulder when they separated, and a sleek white van half-filled with teens and driven by a harried-looking middle-aged man with a full beard and a broad smile pulled up.

"Joey, unlock the door and let your grandma inside. It's hot out here. Do you want me to die of heatstroke?" His grandmother's raspy muted voice shook Joe out of his reverie, and he peered toward the passenger-side window, where her heavily ringed, petite hand rapped at the tinted glass. "Are you deaf, Joey? Can you hear me over that horrible music you listen to?"

"Hold on, Nana." The doors unlocked with a flick of a switch, and Joe leaned over to open the door, then held his hand out for his grandmother to take as she fought with a couple of plastic bags, lifting them up into the cab. "Wait, let me get out and…."

Getting out would mean blowing his surveillance, and a quick glance over at the sidewalk gave him not only a good look at the hot guy but at a second one, stepping up to the curb from the shadowy overhang of what looked like a garage next to the alley behind the pub.

Still, it was his grandmother, and she barely kissed five feet tall on a good day.

"I've got it. Thank God someone thought to put a step thing when they made it. Who are they designing for? The Jolly Green Giant? Take the bags. There's food in there for you." She heaved herself up, a trim eightysomething-year-old woman with a froth of impossibly blond-caramel hair and vivid red lipstick wrapped over and around her thin lips. "I was coming home with some of the girls and I saw your car, and I thought, look, there's Joey and he probably didn't bring himself something to eat. You're going to waste away. You, without a wife. Not that you need a wife, being the gay, but still, you should eat more. There's tacos in there. And some peanut butter and jelly sandwiches. I didn't know what you were hungry for. A couple of apples, but I tucked a banana in there for me. I need the potassium, you know."

She was a slice of the East Coast Italian family Joe and his brothers went to visit during the summer when they were kids, and by the time he was ten, Antonina Zanetti decided Tina, her daughter-in-law and Joe's mother, wasn't doing enough to keep her family alive, well, and happy. Mike, Joe's father, wisely decided to stay out of it and built himself a shed in the backyard, filling it with old cast-off recliners and an enormous television—a proto-mancave before they were a thing. The family braced themselves for outright battles, but Tina and Joe's Nana kept to sniping instead, knowing it was better not to make anyone choose a side. But that didn't mean they couldn't take cheap shots at each other.

"Nana, how did you get here?" Joe sighed, resigned to his grandmother settling into the SUV. "And hold on, let me get you something cold to drink. It's hot as hell out there."

"I walked from home. It's not far. What?" she exclaimed, placing a hand over her pink paisley shirt. "Two miles. Maybe. It'll be time to tuck me into the ground next to your sainted grandfather the day I can't walk two miles to bring my favorite grandson something to eat while he's... working." Peering out the windshield, she gave Joe a sly smile. "Or are you working? You've got something going with the Keller boy? Huh?"

She was a tiny powerhouse of a woman who was the first one he came out to as a shaky-voiced fifteen-year-old kid, afraid God would hate him and the family would toss him out on his ear. Nana was his first warrior, the woman who battled his demons when they overwhelmed him and encouraged him to pursue painting even as he chased after his SFPD star. She'd held his secrets and stood by his mother when he got shot at the age of twenty-five in a drug bust gone wrong, putting aside years of acrimony and backbiting Joe wasn't so sure actually existed, especially when his mom nearly broke down and reached for Nana instead of his dad.

There wasn't a bright color in existence that Nana Zanetti didn't love or wear at some point in her life, and the more something sparkled, the better. She had firm opinions on pasta, family, and beer, with a special hatred for the Los Angeles Dodgers and a deep, abiding love for the Chicago Cubs, despite being from New Jersey. Her showing up at one of his stakeouts shouldn't have surprised him, but her knowing the guy on the curb did. Joe leaned back in his seat, keeping one eye on the two guys across the street from them and the other on the tiny dynamo dressed in blinding pink paisley separates nesting herself in his SUV after shoving a pair of rhinestone-embellished sunglasses on top of her head.

"You know the shorter guy? Keller, you said?" It felt weird grilling his grandmother, but Joe knew she'd shrug it off like water beading on a duck's shoulders. If ducks had shoulders. "How do you know him?"

A motorcycle engine cut through his words, and Joe glanced back to the street and swore when he spotted a greasy-looking guy on a bike pull up to the curb to engage in what sounded like a heated conversation with the men. The rattle of the bike drowned out their words even more so than the ambient street noise had between the guy and his kid, and not for the first time in his life, Joe wished he had superhearing... or a listening device stuck on the outer wall of the pub so he could hear what was being said. It looked like something big or at least heated, especially when the bigger guy on the sidewalk leaned toward the bike rider and said something to make the patched club member flinch.

"Los Lobos," Joe murmured, writing the name down on the notepad he'd left on his console. Sketching the biker's patch as quickly as he could, capturing as much detail as he could, he left off when he was mostly satisfied with it and used his phone to catch a zoomed-in photo, hoping it would hold up. "I need a better phone. Been a long time since I sat doing surveillance. You've seen that guy before, Nana? On the bike? Actually, what the hell would you be doing down here? At a biker bar?"

"It's not a biker bar." She sniffed imperiously. "It's a nice place, and one I've been going to for years. We come here after we're done playing canasta. Levi took the pub from his uncle when that man went to Florida to chase after that blond hussy he fell for. She led him a merry chase, let me tell you. Last I heard, they were living on a houseboat, lying naked in the sun, and getting their bits all browned up. Can't be good for you. There's some things that God meant to be left untanned."

"Levi?" Joe studied the man.

"His parents are hippies. Or were hippies. I think he's got an older brother named Hendrix. He's named after the blue-jean guy. Guess he should have been happy his dad didn't like Dickies." She chortled, snapping off the end of her banana. "Get your nana a water, Joey. It's hot outside. Can't believe you do this for a living. Anyway, Levi's a good boy. Raises his son right.

"The mother skipped out before the kid was even dried off, but Levi's done right by him. Very polite. Helps out around the pub sometimes but not behind the bar. Kitchen work's for him. Buses tables once in a while." Nana didn't skip a beat as she finished peeling the banana and took the opened bottle of water Joe handed her from the cooler. "I try to give him a good tip, and he's always there to help us get Fran into the cab when it's time to go. You know how she gets after a couple of Long Island iced teas. Thinks she's Ethel Merman or Barbra once she gets liquored up. Wouldn't be so bad if she could sing, but the woman sounds more like Biz Markie than Streisand."

From the outside, St. Connal's looked like a typical Irish pub—a bit of polished wood, white paint, and brick walls wrapped around the building with a welcoming, propped-open double door. Signs hung from the outer walls on either side of the front entrance, done up as old-country in swinging placards with a wolf wearing a halo staring out under the pub's name in gold letters above it. The place looked solid, and if the paint on the front door was to be believed, it'd been sitting on that corner, welcoming people into its doors since the early 1930s.

But he'd seen a Vikings club member outside its door only a couple of days ago, and that meant it wasn't a place Nana needed to be.

"How often do you go in there?" he ventured carefully, knowing the older woman was fiercely independent and any move by a family member to curtail her would be met with nearly lethal results. There was talk about his uncle Paul once telling his nana she needed to go into the kitchen where she belonged during the beginning of the ERA movement, and from everything Joe heard about that afternoon, Uncle Paul was lucky he escaped with his life. The old man still flinched whenever someone sharpened a knife near him, and the sound of an oven door apparently made him pass out like a fainting goat. "I mean, once a week? A month? How well do you know this Levi guy?"

"Sometimes twice a week." Her shrug was the same one she gave when discussing world events she had no impact on, as if going to St. Connal's was simply a part of life, like rain and ants. "Sometimes once. Depending on how it goes. If Mass runs late, then we stop by. Especially if Father Greer is doing the sermon. Nothing like a good chocolate stout to wash the taste of someone else's sin from your mouth. Levi's been there for years now. That's the second motorcycle guy I've seen here. I don't think he likes them, but I heard him tell the other one that Friday was good to go."

"This Friday? Or when?" Joe looked up sharply, watching the men carefully, noting the bike's license plate as the guy recoiled again, then drove off. "How many times have you seen bikers there?"

"Just that one time. And, well, that one that just left. The other one was there wanting to do a private party in the back room that night, but Levi told him he couldn't have all the people he wanted." She bit into the banana with relish, chewing carefully between sips of water. "Levi was by the kitchen door, and the bunch of us were at our normal table. The other guy was big, but Levi wasn't going to budge. Couldn't really. The back room fits maybe fifteen people. I know, we did Margie's birthday party back there. Levi let us use it for free, didn't even charge us for bringing our own food in. Some places do that. He's a good boy. Rolled out a small fridge so we could put our cold salads in there beforehand and heated up the hot food in his ovens.

"You know, you could do worse than Levi," Nana murmured, dropping a bombshell into Joe's lap. "He likes both sides of the sheets, if you know what I mean. He's a good-looking guy, and I've met his family. Good people, if a little weird, but really, who isn't. I mean, look at your mother. I mean, I understand her wanting to name your brother Michael, because it's not only your father's name but her father's name, but that at least left my Joseph's name for you. Not that it's weird. Just odd she didn't call him Joseph Michael. Or even Michael Joseph. You do better with the name anyway. You're a spitting image of my Joey. Handsome man. Couldn't hold his liquor, so he lived like a nun on water and juice, but still sainted."

"Nana, everyone you love is sainted," Joe replied softly, kissing his grandmother's temple. "I'm just not so sure Levi Keller is."

"Like I said, you could do worse," she reiterated, wagging a stiff finger under his nose. "And you might not do any better. I'll introduce you, but right now, we need to go to your parents' house and try to choke down some of that slop your mother calls lasagna. I swear, I don't know what your grandma Penny was thinking, teaching her to cook her noodles halfway before putting them in the pan, but the woman—God as I love her—should be shot just for that."

THREE

A PHONE call at eight in the morning normally didn't jerk most men out of bed into a blind panic, but Levi not only owned a pub where odd things happened, but being a father of a teenaged boy, any phone call was a potential cry for help or heralding of disaster. It took him a moment to sit up and find the chirruping device he'd put on a wireless charger when he finally collapsed into bed at three in the morning. Having one bartender call in sick was bad enough, but when the serving staff fell victim to the same flu on a Monday night filled with blue-haired ladies intent on partying hard after a rousing bingo session at the nearby Catholic church, Levi really missed having Declan to pinch-hit.

"Okay, I'm coming," Levi snapped at his phone. "I can't even find my eyes yet. Hold on."

"Mr. Keller? This is Stacy at Forest Break," a chipper woman said before Levi could say hello. "I'm hoping—"

"It's only Tuesday. He's not even been there three whole days and there's already a problem?" Sitting up, Levi rubbed at his face, trying to scrape the sleep out of his eyes. His sheets felt rough, and he pondered why until he realized he'd fallen asleep in his jeans, his T-shirt flung over the boxy nightstand Declan made in woodshop a few years back. "Okay, lay it on me. What did Deck blow up this time and how much is it going to cost me?"

"Actually, Mr. Keller," Stacy burbled. "It's not anything he's done so much as... well, we don't normally allow our campers to reach out to home so early in the excursion, but Declan sounded very distressed, so the senior counselors decided to make an exception. Are you okay with him setting up a video call with you in five minutes?"

"Yeah, five would be great." The sleep wasn't shaking off, but Levi didn't think that mattered. "Just tell me he's okay. And I don't owe you guys my left kidney for something he's done."

"He's fine, sir, and no, so far the camp's how it was before Declan arrived. I'm sure this year will be without incident. He's grown so much." Her perkiness went up, and not for the first time in his life when faced with a red-cheeked, bright-eyed supernatural, he wondered if squirrel shifters were actually a thing. "He just insists on speaking with you, and we thought it best to agree, since he's not normally anxious."

Five minutes gave Levi enough time to hit the bathroom, brush his teeth, make a steaming cup of Vinacafe coffee, then boot up his laptop to wait for Declan's call. He'd just gotten his first sip when Declan rang in.

"Hey, kiddo, what's up?" Levi toasted his son with his mug. "Long night. Just getting up, so if I sound rough, it's 'cause I haven't woken up yet. Talk to me. What's going on?"

"Hey, Dad." The boy had only been gone a couple of days, but the expression on his face was one of a madman caught stuffing a dormouse into a teapot. "I'm... don't laugh, okay? 'Cause I need some help."

"Why would I laugh? What's going on?" There was nothing like the worry of a kid falling into trouble they couldn't get out of, and Levi's guts burbled up as much sour as Stacy chirping was sweet. Leaning forward, he set his coffee cup down and gave his kid every bit of attention he had. "Deck, you know you can tell me anything. What happened? Do you need to come home? Do I need to go up there and rip someone's head off?"

"Hold on." Declan shuddered, his luminous eyes growing unfocused as he stepped back from the screen. Shedding his clothes, Declan sighed. "It's better if I show you."

Declan's shift was still rough around the edges—a lengthy stretch of bones adjusting from rapid growth and changing hormones. Levi's shoulder blades ached in memory of his puberty changes, the rush of blood to places he didn't need it, and the instinctive urges to embrace his wolf form when he saw someone attractive. Nothing said uncontrolled teenager like lust and hunger, and it was hell on shifter adolescence. Trying to be comfortable in two skins was never easy, and having both forms growing at the same time was frequently miserable.

"You having problems shifting?" Levi rubbed at the back of his neck, a problematic spot for him when he'd been Declan's age. He'd grown quickly, too fast for his spine to adjust to, and bringing his head up hurt for an entire summer until the rest of him finally caught up. "Does something hurt? And not like…. Holy fucking shit. Deck, what happened?"

Their family line ran to black wolves, sometimes tipped with sable or cream, but the majority were a rich midnight ebony. There were some outliers and even a cousin who shifted to pure silver, much to the disgust of his father. But their bloodline was an old, fierce warrior stock with muscular wolf forms and strong aggressive stances. Declan pulled the Keller Black, glossy-coated even in his young-pup form, and at times he could slip into the shadows without being seen so he could pounce on his relatives as they went by.

The fluffy jet-black canid with its pom-pom cut and rounded ears looked nothing like his son except for his size. Even his tail had been shaped, trimmed up tight around the base to a pouf at the end, its feathery swoop lying softly against Declan's flank, exactly like their great-aunt Myrtle's Pomeranian looked after coming home from the groomer.

All that was missing was a rhinestone collar and a pair of pink bows tied jauntily in the hair on either side of his ears.

Levi bit at his cheek, tasting blood, but he was able to choke down the laughter boiling up from his belly. Schooling his face into the most serious expression he could muster, Levi nodded, not trusting himself to say anything while Declan shifted back. His son grabbed at his discarded clothes as soon as he had skin, pulling on his jeans in a jumping hop toward the office chair he'd been sitting in.

The time it took Declan to reabsorb his wolf gave Levi a moment to compose himself, but there definitely was a high-pitched squeak to his voice when Levi finally asked, "What the hell happened to you?"

"Naomi happened to me," Declan groaned, burying his face in his hands. "She's cute, and Dad, she smells like strawberry cheesecake—"

"God help you, a young woman that smells like dessert," Levi drawled, assuming his somber face when his son peeked out at him from between his fingers. "Sorry. Go on. Tell me how Naomi Strawberry Cheesecake held you down and took electric clippers to you until you looked like Aunt Myrtle's overgrown hamster?"

"It seemed like… the girls in the next cabin were screaming last night about a possum getting into their place, so I went over to help.

It was just a small baby one, and I shooed it out." Another soft moan escaped Declan, muffled by his hands. "We got to talking—"

"You and Naomi or you and all of the girls?" Levi reached for his coffee again, needing a hit of caffeine to listen to the rest of his son's story. "Because—"

"Just talking. About school and stuff. What it's like being a shifter or Other around humans." Declan dropped his hands and glared at his father in mild offense. "It wasn't anything."

"So tell me how you went from nothing happening to… that," Levi said, cocking his head. "Because the dots aren't connecting for me, kid."

"Naomi and her sister are puma, and they were curious if the shift was the same. We were mostly talking about that kind of stuff. So I kind of showed them."

"You've got to get naked to show them, Deck." Levi sat forward, putting his cup down on the table. "Where the hell were the camp people?"

"This was before lights-out, and I was wearing basketball shorts," he protested. "Wasn't naked. I shifted and then kicked them off. I figured I'd turn back in the bathroom and get dressed again. Nothing—"

"Yeah, yeah. Nothing happened." He rolled his eyes. "I love you, kiddo, but I'm not liking this nothing you're getting up to over there."

"Have you seen me? You think *I* like it?" Declan snorted. "So I shifted, and they were… none of the four girls are wolf so…."

"You were playing big dog on campus."

"Like you haven't?" Declan lifted one eyebrow, something he'd learned from every Keller male he'd ever known. Levi returned the look, rumbling a soft throaty growl at his son. "I swear, I wasn't talking them up like that, Dad. Remember? I've got Michelle."

"Right. Michelle," Levi murmured.

"Naomi's mom's a groomer—"

"Ah, here we go."

"Dad, can you just let me get this out?" Declan sighed heavily. "And be serious. This is some hard-core crap for me. Naomi wondered how I'd look if I were trimmed up a bit, and the next thing I know, I'm standing there while she's clipping away at me with some really freaking sharp scissors. I figured I'd let her because they—the girls—were into it, and that the next time I shifted, I'd just be back to normal. But… did you *see* me? I mean, Dad. I've got a howl coming up in a couple of days. I can't show up looking like this. I mean, shit. Bad enough I'm one of the youngest here. You've got to *do* something."

"Yeah, doesn't work that way, Deck," Levi interrupted his son. "It's like everything else. Scars, haircuts, the common cold. All of that. You've got to wait it out. Nothing I can do about it. Same thing happened to me with bleach, hair dye, and a pair of hot jaguar twins when I was sixteen. Took the whole summer to grow that out. Your grandpa used to try to get me to shift so everyone could see it, 'cause he thought I looked like I'd been dipped in polka-dot tie-dye."

"You're serious? About the waiting, not the tie-dye. I can see Grandpa doing that." Flopping his head down on the desk, Declan mumbled, "What am I going to do?"

"I'd say you should go to the howl, shift, and have fun, but that's up to you," Levi said softly, resting his elbows on his thighs and waiting for his son to look up at him. When he got a peek of Declan's mournful gaze, he continued, "Look, kid, we all do stupid things in our lives. Some we can spin into something awesome when we tell the story later, and some we just have to suck up and buy our friends a drink when they bring it up so we can laugh together. It's up to you on how you're going to deal with this. So you fell for a pretty girl with a pair of scissors.

"I'm more concerned about you being in that cabin with four girls late at night, but that's on me. That's society shit I'm carrying, because we're always told to sexualize relationships. I know it, and it's hard, but I'm trying." He knew he wasn't awake enough to do hard-core parenting, and fighting against his instinct to tear apart the camp counselors wasn't going to do Declan any good. "I trust you when you say it was just talking. If it were me at your age in a cabin with four guys *or* four girls—or a mix—your grandpa would have had to trust me to keep my brain on right, so I've got no room to talk. Still, if you take anything out of this, it's that you can't just drop trou when a pretty girl wants to see how sleekit you are."

"Suppose the guys laugh?" His son sat up, worry souring his handsome features. "Or the girls? Dad... I just thought it would go back to how it was once I shifted."

"Do you want to go to the howl?"

"Yeah." Declan shrugged. "It's always just kind of nice to hang out as... who we are without worrying about that kind of shit."

"So, tell a couple of friends Naomi gave you a haircut and seed the field before you go. Make it a thing," Levi suggested with a grin. "Dude, rock the lemon you were given. Own it. Be fearless. Be cute. I mean, you're freaking adorable, and I might be too old to sport the whole manga-puppy look, but you aren't. Go have fun, kiddo, and don't let anyone else tell you that you're anything but fantastic. Okay?"

"Okay," his son murmured, giving Levi a small smile. "Were you telling me the truth about the spots… well, the colors? Or were you pulling my leg to make me feel better."

"Oh, so much the truth," he laughed, shaking his head. "When you get back, I'll show you the pictures. And be safe and have a good time. But kid, do me a favor, and maybe you should just go back to thinking about blowing things up again. One more pass with those clippers and I'm going to have to explain to your grandmother why she's got a Xoloitzcuintli for a grandson."

"Dude, not cool. Do not tell Grandma I did this." The look of horror on Declan's face was comical—nearly as funny as when he discovered eggs came out of chickens' butts, or so his five-year-old brain thought at the time. "Dad, promise me—"

"Kid, the last thing I'm going to do is tell anyone. Okay, I might have to tell your uncle Kawika, but come on, you know he'll be cool about it." Levi crossed his heart with his finger. "Promise. This is yours to tell if you want to share it. Just remember, cat's already out of the bag. Literally. You've got four girls who already know you're sporting a puffball haircut, and word like that's going to spread like wildfire. Do yourself a favor and own it before someone owns you with it."

"You really think so?" His son shook his head. "I dunno about that, Dad. Did you take a *really* good look at me? I mean, I look like I'm on Fangster hoping to be someone's purse dog."

"Yeah, I think so." Levi leaned back, giving his son a stern look. "Now tell me how the hell you know about Fangster."

"ZANETTI, I know what you're saying, but I don't have the guys to put on that place right now," Yang admitted, stirring a lump of sugar into his pungent black tea. "That's the problem with you all clearing out all of those assholes before me. Brass looks over at my guys and tells me to focus on drugs and trafficking. Biker stuff is way down the list of priorities for the city right now. Bigger fish to sushi, my friend."

Joe sat on the edge of Yang's desk, using the relatively clean corner to park his hip against. Like most inspectors, Yang's workspace was piled high with paper, despite having most communication and reports filed through the department's computer system. There was something about staring at a stack of evidence and making notes that appeased the inquisitive mind, and Yang was no exception.

Of course, Joe also wasn't sure what the top of his own desk looked like most of the time, and suspected the cop across of him had an egg salad sandwich buried under a stack of requisition slips from two years ago.

"Not like I have something solid about anything going down over there," he confessed to Yang. His main informant on the biker presence at the pub was an older Italian woman who used to change his diapers and his random spotting of a single club member a few days ago. "Supposedly something's happening Friday, but I don't know what. Looked back at any activity at the property for the past five years, and it's really clean. Suspiciously clean."

"You think someone's wiping off arrests to cover something?" Yang looked up from his nearly ritualistic squeezing of his tea bag against the back of a spoon and paused in midtwist. "How clean is clean?"

"A couple of drunk-and-disorderlies called in by the pub, but nothing else. Kind of strange for a bar in that area. Most other places average two of those calls a week." He scrolled through the reports he'd pulled up earlier that day. "There's four other bars within a ten-block radius from this place, and they rack up a hell of a lot more police activity than this one does. So either the clientele here is very well behaved or something's going on over there."

"Well, from what you told me, it *is* someplace your granny hangs out," the sergeant shot back, returning to his tea bag. "Did you run the owner?"

"Yeah, one Levi Keller. He's as clean as a whistle on paper too. Pays his taxes. Sends his kid to school. Even the kid's record is sparkling clean. Keller does a small side business of restoring motorcycles and runs food drives through his pub." Joe frowned. "Once again, too clean. Nana says he's a good guy, but then we're talking about a woman who grew up in Jersey. Her idea of a good guy is someone who keeps his feuds to the person he's mad at and doesn't go after the guy's family."

"What'd the captain tell you?"

"That I should keep my eye on it and not bug you for a guy to watch the place, because you're stretched thin as it is. Something about drugs and trafficking." Joe chuckled at Yang's snorting laugh. "I'm probably just being paranoid. So what if one biker comes back to the city? Probably just visiting someone he knew."

"And the other guy? The Los Lobos one? That's an unknown to me. Another MC, huh?" The other cop picked up the printout Joe left on his desk and examined the photo taken of the biker's back patch. "Notice them and the Vikings are from the same locale? Or at least that's what their lower rocker says. Think maybe they're going to join up together?"

"Yeah, I noticed that. Haven't ever heard of Los Lobos either, so that makes me wonder if there's new activity." Pondering the two clubs showing up at the same pub within a few days of each other puzzled Joe. Most gangs had firm alliances, but the Vikings were always aloof, apart from most other groups, and they'd gotten no hits at all on Los Lobos. "It's weird. I don't like weird in our city."

"You *do* know you live in San Francisco, right?" Yang peered at him over the piece of paper. "Pretty sure we invented weird. But yeah, something's up. I just wish I could spare someone. Maybe next week, but not now."

"I'm thinking of swinging by tonight to see if anything's happening there. Friday's only a few days away, and maybe I can keep an eye out in the meantime. If the place is full of Vikings, I'll see if I recognize anyone and get back to you." Joe floated his idea across to Yang. "Told the captain I was thinking about it, and he said it wouldn't be a bad idea but to make sure I had some backup, at least in the area, but I don't think I'll need it."

"Other than your grandmother," Yang teased, handing Joe back the photo. "For backup, I mean."

"Hey, you haven't met the woman," he retorted, gathering up his papers. "I'll take her over the wall with me any day. If they don't pass out from her garlic bread, they die waiting to get a word in edgewise."

FOUR

LEVI SENSED the shift in St. Con's the moment *he* walked through the door.

The air changed, tingling with something bordering on excitement and a little bit of fear. In a pub full of predators and wild cards, something—*someone*—caught their collective interest, and for a brief moment, every person in the place held their breath.

Working the bar on a Wednesday night in normal pubs would be an exercise in finding something to pass the time. St. Con's was a different story. Mass getting out at the nearby Catholic church kicked in an eight o'clock rush, and every second Wednesday brought in a gathering of two lifelong rival hedge-witch families whose elders kept their feud up with rounds of darts and beers. Between the Catholics, the various shifters, a few orcs struggling to pass as human, and two handfuls of witches, Levi and Kawika were kept hopping while the kitchen fought against a wave of food tickets and special requests.

So the lull in the constant hum around him brought Levi's head up from a pair of mojitos, and his heart dropped down to his knees.

He never went for the strong, silent type, and sure as hell not the rough-around-the-edges cop type either, because there was no mistaking this guy for anything other than a bleeds-blue cop. Levi's tastes ran to pretty younger men with vacant smiles and no ambition to be in a relationship.

But then, so did his taste in women.

He wasn't looking for anything other than a good time he could have in between raising his kid and running his pub while riding herd as a Peacekeeper for supernatural squabbles. Levi couldn't remember the last time he had a moment to spare for anything other than a quick flirt, much less a round of hot sex, but the guy walking into his place made him want to kick everyone out, clear off a table, wrestle the lean, tanned cop down onto the flat surface, and dig his teeth into him.

The cop wasn't handsome in a way that Hollywood would draw a frame around. His nose had definitely met something it didn't like much, or maybe that was just the genetics he'd been handed, but Levi doubted it. There was a bit of a scrapper about him—a cunning tilt to his lush mouth and a challenge built into his strong jawline. His dark brown hair grew thick, touched with a bit of silver in places. But other than the crow's-feet around his long-lashed eyes, he wasn't wearing a lot of years on him. Enough to make him interesting, Levi decided as he studied the man, and possibly cynical but with manners, judging by him stepping back to hold the door open for a couple of elderly women tottering out into the cool evening air.

There was muscle on the cop's frame, enough of it to give him shoulders broad enough to hang on to or hold down against a mattress, and his hips were narrow below a taut stomach. He'd dressed down in a loose black leather jacket, a slightly dingy white T-shirt, and faded jeans, but his body language was anything but relaxed. It was a bit too warm for the jacket, but the cop vibe was strong enough, Levi would have laid money down the guy was carrying a concealed weapon. If there was one thing Levi recognized, it was a predator who'd come to hunt, and while he didn't know the cop's prey, he'd come into Levi's place with something in mind.

And it sure as hell wasn't to have a good time with an Irish scrub dog who made his living polishing glasses and slinging drinks behind an old pub bar.

The cop's eyes skimmed over the crowd, picking out the likely threats. Levi watched his attention settle on a few of the larger customers, his burnished-gold eyes gleaming as he probably calculated the threats around him. That warm honey gaze picked out and settled on the obvious physically threatening customers, pausing every few seconds on a pair of broad shoulders or a grumpy countenance. Levi ducked his head to hide a shit-eating grin when the cop's attention skimmed over a table of petite elderly women in full cackle, the monthly gathering of spotted-hyena matriarchs chatting over a plate of fully loaded tater tots and apple cider.

Even from across the pub, Levi smelled human on him, graceful but not with the liquid movements of a shifter. If he packed anything other than a gun and a star, Levi wouldn't know until the guy pulled a rabbit out of his hat. But since his eyes didn't seem to notice the string of protection wards carved into the wood mantle above the liquor bottles, it was a fair guess he wasn't one of them.

"Eh, that one looks like trouble, brother," Kawika rumbled, his Hawaiian Island accent rolling deep through his words. "You go take care of that one. You know me. I can't lie to cops. Too much like lying to my dad. This one's on you."

"You're a fucking elemental mage and, like, seven feet tall. You could squish his head like a grape, and you're scared to talk to him?" Levi groused softly, setting the mojitos on the bar for one of the servers to grab and deliver. "You know, for a Pele-worshipping kahuna, you sure as hell tap out of shit a lot."

"I keep telling you, you don't worship Pele. She's not like that." His friend and fellow Peacekeeper shook his head, sending a ripple through the waves of thick black hair he'd tied back for the evening. "She's more of a 'leave presents on her porch so she don't come by and knock on your door' kind of god. Not someone you invite into your heart, but man, the sex is good, and I can set rocks on fire. I just can't lie to cops."

"Yeah, I don't have that problem," Levi countered. "Let's wait him out, because sooner or later, cops always come up to talk to the bartender."

JOE NEVER got up to the bar. Never spoke to the bartenders, although he knew he should.

He'd meant to. God knew, there were parts of his body aching to stroll up to the long stretch of polished wood and gleaming spigots, but none of that had to do with why he'd come into St. Connal's. "Focus on the job, Zanetti" became a mantra throughout the night, but his attention kept drifting off of the crowd and back to the pretty-faced brawler slinging drinks across the bar.

Choosing a corner table near the door seemed like a good idea at the time, but as one hour passed, then the second, Joe realized it'd probably been a mistake. Most pub layouts kept the door clear of people, and St. Con's, as the server called the place, definitely didn't buck the trend. With his back to the wall, Joe had a good view of the entire place, except for the cordoned-off private area past a pair of closed doors to the left of the bar, but it also gave him a ringside seat for every wicked, sexy grin Levi Keller threw to anyone interested in picking one up.

For some stupid reason, it not only took everything Joe had in him to keep his ass firmly planted on the chair, it took even more to muster up every glimmer of self-control he had to not punch every single person Keller smiled at.

Then Keller met Joe's gaze and winked at him.

"Cocky son of a bitch," he muttered, sipping at his Diet Coke only to catch a piece of lemon pulp on his tongue from the slice caught below the ice chips bobbing about against the glass. "What the hell was that?"

"You need anything else, love?" His server sashayed up to him, a wide-hipped older black woman named Debbie, who'd kept his drink filled all night and swapped out his fries for a salad when they got too cold. "Last call's about a minute off, and the bar will be rushed. Might as well get a refill before we shut down in ten minutes."

"Thanks," Joe murmured, flashing her a smile. "I can pay out the tab now if you want."

"Nah, St. Con's doesn't take money from cops, firemen — sorry firefighters —, or paramedics. Usually you've got to be in uniform, but since it's your first time here, I'll comp it out. And before you say anything, don't tell me you're not a cop or I'm going to lose ten bucks to Sherry in the kitchen. She says you're a lawyer." Debbie glanced behind her, following Joe's attention. "Oh, that's Levi. He owns the place. Want me to ask him to come by? If you need to lodge a complaint or something else with the management…."

"No, I'm okay. It's fine," he protested quickly. "A refill would be good, though, and how'd you know I was a cop?"

"'Cause Toni Zanetti comes in here, and if there's one thing that woman likes to do, it's brag about her grandbabies. I spotted you as soon as you came through the door and recognized you from all the photos she's flashed at me. Easiest ten bucks I've made in my life without me taking off my clothes." She chortled at Joe's flushed cheeks. "She was in here yesterday. Said she went on a stakeout with you."

"She climbed into my car while I was trying to coordinate something with another division, so no, not really a stakeout," Joe lied as smoothly as he could, making a mental note to stem his grandmother's gossip. The sane part of his brain laughed hilariously at him and wandered back up front to drool over Levi's strong arms and body-hugging T-shirt. "Nana's... eccentric."

"That's a word. I'll be right back with your Diet Coke." Debbie nodded down at the mostly eaten salad. "And you either finish that up or pick the mushrooms and olives out of it. No sense wasting the best parts."

"Yes, ma'am," Joe said, saluting her with his fork. "I'll get right on it."

"You're going to be hiding those mushrooms under your lettuce as soon as I turn my back," she scoffed, tapping the table with one long pink fingernail. "Your nana told me all of Tina's kids hate raw mushrooms, and that's the last time you're lying to me, mister. Just eat the olives. I'll be back with your drink."

He let himself get one last peek at Levi Keller, then scanned the pub's customers again. The private room was a concern, mainly because he didn't know if there was a back door. Debbie probably would answer him if he asked, and there wasn't any way Joe could trust she wouldn't bring it up to Keller. There were too many clean spots for a busy pub this size, he thought, looking around carefully. Sure, the mountain serving drinks next to Keller probably could bust a few heads open just by lifting his pinkie finger, but tossing drunks usually meant a couple of cop calls a month. Keller looked like he could hold his own, judging by the powerful flex of his arms as he stretched, but Joe wasn't sure if either man could hold their own against a gang of bikers, especially if they came knocking on the pub's door armed to the teeth and ready to tear apart a rival club.

"Hey, never mind about the soda," Joe called out to Debbie before she rounded back to the bar. "I've got to head out."

"You leaving a tip?" She cocked one eyebrow, first at Joe, then at Levi, who cleared his throat and turned away quickly to find something else to do instead of battling Debbie's glare. "Because this one might give away the farm, but my chickens still have to eat."

"Tip being left, ma'am," he said, shooting her a grin as he laid down a few bills. "I'll be back soon, and when I do, I'm paying."

Once outside, Joe leaned into the slight chill outside of the St. Con's heavy door. The day's stickiness surrendered to a nip in the air, a bit of salt-scented breeze carrying up over the lip of the Bay, and Joe shoved his hands into his jeans pockets, warming them up after a couple of hours of cradling an icy glass. The building's buttery-golden brick walls held a bit of the day's heat, but they probably would be cold by morning. The traffic lights at the corner flashed through their colors, flickering a short-spectrum rainbow on the road where Joe first caught sight of Levi Keller speaking to the biker.

"Okay, let's check out how many back entrances there are to this place. Then it's home for you, Zanetti." Joe glanced up and down the street, looking for any activity, but despite being on the early side, the neighborhood seemed to have rolled up, with the exception of a few lights coming from apartments and lofts. "Might as well cut through the alley. Car's parked on the next street over, anyway."

The pass-through cut through the storefronts right behind the garage attached to the pub. While the entrance was too tight for a vehicle to drive through, farther down the way, it opened up, creating a few parking spaces probably reserved for anyone working or living in the street-facing properties. Pacing off the small garage, Joe reconstructed the pub's layout in his head, figuring the garage was long enough to run the span of the front room.

"Okay, so the main room was about that deep," he murmured softly, examining the pair of heavy doors behind the garage. A pair of small dumpsters sat to the left of the doors, their green painted steel exteriors gleaming in the faint light coming from the streetlight behind Joe. There were a few lights dotting the backs of the other buildings, and when he drew closer to the dumpster, his movement triggered a motion-activated flood nearly strong enough to push the night back a few notches. "The first one is probably the emergency exit I saw at the end of the pub. So that means this one goes... where?

"Kitchen had its own swinging door, and the private room was next to that with its own entrance, but nothing says that room isn't connected to the kitchen," he pondered. "They could potentially slip people in from the back, and with that tighter opening by the garage, no one would even notice. Definitely will need to have someone cover the back door if—"

"Hey, asshole," a man called out, his voice booming down the tight stretch between the street and the two back doors. "Thought I'd come back and settle some business with you. Mostly me kicking your scrawny fucking ass."

Joe turned, but all he saw was a silhouette—a slightly overweight, shorter man cast into deep shadow from the garage's jutting overhang. But he was moving fast, quicker than Joe could react. Reaching for his gun, Joe had enough time to skim his fingers along his service weapon's grip when the dark shape moving toward him began to crackle and shake. His attacker started to twist inside of his clothing, shedding his shirt with a wiggling motion, kicking off his loose jeans before launching up toward Joe.

THE SOUNDS coming from the man's body were horrific—soft shifting bones breaking and twisting beneath convulsing flesh. He'd come close enough to be lit up from the edge of the floodlights, but that didn't make identifying his attacker any easier. The man fell to his hands and knees, but that didn't seem to slow him down. A few jumping hops brought the man closer, his palms and joints striking the hard ground with such impact that Joe swallowed hard, nearly gulping down his tongue in surprise. Some part of his mind thought to stare at the attacker's features, hoping to memorize them so he could identify him later, but that proved to be impossible.

The man's face was gone, folded into an elongated meld of meat and bone before he crossed into the light, his skin peeling and fraying off into long shreds as his body changed in front of Joe's eyes. The gun was forgotten. Transfixed by what was happening in front of him, Joe's brain fought to make sense of what he was seeing, unable to fully accept the jut of shoulder blades pushing up from the man's bowed torso. A creaking rattle was the only warning Joe got as the man's spine ripped clear of his skin, lengthening out from the small of his back. Bits of gray-brown fur rippled, seeming to grow or perhaps push out of the peeks of raw flesh flashing quickly before Joe's eyes. Then, as quickly as it began, it all came to a whispering end.

Leaving one of the largest, fattest, mangiest coyotes Joe'd ever seen standing in front of him.

The beast was huge—much larger than any other he'd come across—but it was definitely a coyote. San Francisco had its share of wildlife, and the long-legged creatures were expert scavengers, often coming down from the wooded areas nearby to help themselves to whatever they could pull out of the garbage at edges of the city. But the pub was way too inland for one, or at least too firmly in the middle of an urban neighborhood for a coyote to dare the streets and dangers simply for an uneaten plate of onion rings, no matter how damned good they looked.

Growling, the creature stepped closer, his head down and teeth bared. But it blinked furiously, staring up at Joe's face. It was enormous, easily the size of a large hound. One paw inched forward, and Joe finally found his gun beneath his jacket to draw it. He stepped closer in the hopes his looming presence would push the coyote back. His SIG Sauer held steady before him, he advanced slowly, easing closer to the kitchen door. Banging on it probably wouldn't bring anyone to answer it. He knew from working at his uncle's restaurant as a kid practically nothing could penetrate a fire door, and his only hope would be to ring the service bell. But he couldn't spare a moment to glance and find it.

After taking a deep breath, Joe said quietly, "Okay, I don't know what the hell is going on here, but—"

The heavy steel kitchen door opened suddenly, slamming Joe in the shoulder. Startled, he stumbled to the side, processing the developing situation as the events began to pile up on top of each other. His trigger finger pressed down, but he stiffened his joints before he accidentally let off a shot. Too off-balance to do anything other than sidestep the swinging door, Joe nearly tumbled into the enormous coyote's path. He caught himself before he plowed into the beast, but as he turned, he caught sight of Levi Keller standing at the open kitchen door, hefting a full garbage bag up, a shocked expression working its way across his handsome features.

"Stay back! Hold the door and get back in!" Joe warned, pulling his gun up to aim at the beast as he tried to back away, giving himself some distance. Keller let the kitchen door slam behind him, shutting off their egress. Dropping the trash bag, Keller seemed to sigh heavily, and resignation took over where shock had momentarily been. "Damn it, Keller. We need to—"

If the coyote had been a long shocking moment, Keller stripping off his shirt and unbuckling his jeans broke Joe's thoughts. The man was mouthwatering, and in the confusion of everything happening around him, Joe couldn't spare any more than a glance at Keller before shifting his attention back to the corpulent coyote.

The crackling noises were back, but this time it was Keller's tightly muscled body shifting, his skin splitting apart and drying in long spirals from his sides. Slack-jawed, Joe couldn't move, or at least he didn't dare to. The change to Keller's form went smoother, or perhaps Joe was too overwhelmed, but the creaking bones soon gave way to rippling flesh and darkening skin. Then a wave of black fur covered the man Joe'd lusted after only minutes before.

The emerging beast was broader, leaner in places, and sleek. Powerful muscles bunched and released as he moved away from the pile of clothes he'd shaken off with a disdainful flick of his back legs. His eyes reflected the light, as dark blue as the Mediterranean but flecked with gold and moonlight. If the coyote was large, the ebony wolf standing where Keller once stood was beyond enormous—a prime dire wolf with sharp teeth and a growl deep enough to send tremors through Joe's teeth. He was both magnificent and terrifying. Then he stepped in between Joe and the coyote, and Joe braced himself for what was coming.

There was no way anyone—any beast—was getting out of the situation without spilling blood, and he hesitated to shoot, uncertain if his bullets would even do any good against the transformed men. Still, his SIG was all he had on him, and he wasn't going to let Keller—wolf or man—die defending him. Lifting his gun, Joe aimed at the coyote's flank.

"I'm going to assume you can understand me," he warned, dropping his voice into a command. "Drop down and… stay in place. I don't want to have to hurt you." Joe wasn't exactly sure what he could threaten a coyote with, but he'd been willing to give it his best go. "These may not be silver, but I'm guessing they'll at least punch a hole in—"

He hadn't even finished his warning when the alleyway exploded in a cascade of stars and the back of his head began to throb. His words caught on his tongue, and Joe blinked, his eyes refusing to focus. The world tilted around him, and with a stumbling protest, he hit the ground. Joe groaned, sure his head had been split open, but his protests died when the black creeping over him rose up suddenly, and he passed out, all the while hoping Keller kicked the coyote's ass.

FIVE

"WHAT THE hell did you hit him with? A brick? He's out like a light," Levi complained loudly as they maneuvered the cop's limp body up the stairs to his apartment's front room. "He's *snoring!*"

"Just my fist," Kawika shot back. "I didn't have anything else. I only came back there to toss out the other bag. Didn't know you were trying to get a date."

The kahuna was easily holding up his end of the cop, hefting the man with a firm grip under his armpits. Levi tried to reason he'd gotten the wiggly end. Having to hold ankles and limp legs up on an incline was never going to be easy, but he was also smart enough to realize Kawika could probably have carried both him and the cop up the narrow stairs under his arms, but the journey wouldn't be a pleasant one.

Mostly because the stairwell was tight, and they'd already banged the unconscious man's head against the rail twice just getting him past the security door.

As stupid as it was, the cop was still as smoking hot passed out as he was when he'd been sitting in the corner of St. Con's, studiously avoiding Levi's occasional glance. There was a lot more power in his long body than Levi first guessed—thick muscles now slack beneath his worn jeans. Those jeans weren't on tight enough, because after a couple of tugs on the man's ankles, they settled down on his hips, leaving a bit of his flat belly and hips exposed.

It was that stretch of golden skin with a peek of pale beneath it that drove Levi nuts. The guy obviously was in good shape. His body was sleek, but the contrast between the tan and light gold got Levi to wondering what type of shorts he wore while swimming and if the light swirl of brown hair trailing down from his belly continued on to dust his thighs as well.

He appeared younger than he looked from across the pub, but that probably could have been due to the fact he was passed out. His relaxed features still held their strong, slightly off-kilter beauty, but the softness of his pout gave the cop a vulnerability Levi didn't think actually existed. He'd seen the fierceness on the guy's face as he stared down a much-too-large coyote, his gun trained on the threat despite the wildness in his eyes. There'd been surprise there, but despite what was obviously a shocking situation, he'd stepped in to protect Levi.

Only to discover Levi wasn't anyone who needed protection.

"Eh, take it easy. No push," Kawika scolded. "I gotta watch for the top of the stairs."

"How the hell can I push *up*?" he groused back, looking up at the huge man, the entire length of the cop slumped between them. "I am just trying not to drop him. Son of a bitch is like a noodle."

"Okay, that's the last step, so watch when you come up." The kahuna frowned, moving slowly backward so Levi could feel his way up. "Where do you want him? And what are you going to do about him?"

"Put him on the couch. Shit, he's heavy." Swinging the cop's legs up onto the long couch, Levi sighed heavily. "I have no damned idea what to do here. Guess I've got to talk to him. Providing he ever wakes up."

"He had a gun. It's down there someplace," Kawika reminded him. "And I have to go back and get it. I kicked it under the dumpster so no one would pick it up."

"I've never had to deal with a discovery before. I mean, shit, Gibson was found out, and he married the guy," Levi said, eyeing the cop. "I don't know if I want to go that far to keep us safe from the mundane."

"Didn't you marry one? Or at least was in deep enough with her to have a kid?" Kawika asked, jerking his head toward the photos of Declan hanging on the wall near the front door. "I mean, unless you got Deck in a cabbage patch or something."

"I never told Ashley," he replied with a shrug. Smiling at Kawika's exasperated hiss, Levi sighed. "I figured I'd have time, and then, well, she booked it. So it was never an issue. *This* is an issue. There's some stuff the old Warder told me when I went through training, but most of it was about military situations or while hunting. Not a cop stumbling through the back alley of a pub. Training stuff's out of date. What do you think?"

"We're Peacekeepers, and we're supposed to keep everyone safe from bad shit. Sometimes mundane humans find out about us, brother, but most of the time, our kind just says you ate spoiled shrimp or something." Kawika took a long hard look at the cop. "I don't think this one's going to believe you. And besides, it was your kitchen that gave him the salad, so if you're slinging rainbow mushrooms back there, he's going to bring the health department and the DEA down on your ass. You've got to make the call. I'm junior here."

"Only 'cause you don't want your own place." The air conditioner in the apartment cranked back on, and Levi shivered. He'd dressed hastily, shoving his feet into his boots after dragging his jeans and shirt on. "Can you see if the coyote's colors are still down there? He might swing back around and grab them while we're doing this. Maybe we'll be lucky and this guy won't be a cop after all."

"Oh no, he's a cop." Kawika held up the wallet he'd just dug out of the man's back pocket. "Gold star. So megacop. ID card says Lieutenant Joseph Zanetti."

"Shit." Levi closed his eyes. "Well, it can't get any worse."

"Oh no, brother, it does." His friend shot him a broad, white, shit-eating smile. "Boy here is Toni Zanetti's grandson."

"No! Maybe they just have the same last name. Just because someone—"

"Yeah, here's a picture of the *strega* and Joey here at maybe his cop graduation? Baby cop. Wearing a uniform, and she's hugging him." Kawika flipped the plastic sleeve over. "*To my Joey. You're my favorite grandson. Don't tell your brothers and cousins I told you that. Love, Nana.* Yeah, totally not related. This must be the cop kid she's always talking about. Never saw a photo, but I know the servers have. Debbie could have known."

"Well, then Debbie should have told us," Levi growled, pacing the room. "Shit. *Shit.* We're going to have to call her. He acted like he didn't know. His face was... he was shocked about the coyote."

"Yeah, he was sputtering when I hit him." Nodding toward the unconscious man on the couch, Kawika sighed. "I'll go get the stuff out of the alley and then see if I can get her on the phone. It's late. She might not answer. And she doesn't know me. Different circles, yeah? You might be stuck with him until morning."

"So you know where she lives?" Levi turned from his pacing, scrambling to think of a way out of dealing with a passed-out cop on his couch and the problems he'd brought to his own door. "Maybe we can dump him on her doorstep and have her deal with it."

"No."

The word was a hard stone skipped across Levi's thoughts, leaving ripples where there was already a choppy surface. Sighing heavily, Levi stared at the cop, wondering what he'd done to deserve a mundane human dropping into his life. It was already bad enough he'd been called upon to broker a peace between the Vikings and Los Lobos, but a cop falling into his lap only complicated things.

"Okay, first I'll deal with Zanetti here," Levi said, wincing at the name. "Of all the cops, he has to be Strega Zanetti's kin. I got a look at that jacket the coyote dropped. Not a good look because, you know, carrying this guy up here wasn't easy, but it looked like Los Lobos colors. If it is, then I've got to get ahold of Paolo and have a good talk with him. That guy came here to mess someone up and didn't seem to give a shit about this being a Sanctuary."

"I'll grab that too," Kawika promised. After emptying the fruit from a heavy koa bowl sitting on the dining table, he hefted it up and said, "In the meantime, if he wakes up, crack him over the head again. If I can't get the Italian witch to come and get her grandkid, we might be able to say he slipped or something and hallucinated the whole thing. Because you, brother, are going to have to deal with him seeing you and that coyote. Just hope that strega doesn't turn you into a newt."

THE LOS Lobos colors weren't a full patch. It was missing its rockers or anything else to mark the member as someone of any distinction. Levi sat on the old purple velvet wing chair he'd dragged up from a consignment shop years ago, resting one bare foot on its matching ottoman, its slightly worn nap speckled in places with strands of long black fur. The cop on the couch was still out like a light, and his unconscious state worried Levi, despite Kawika assuring him the man was all right.

"You don't look all right," Levi told his passed-out guest. "You look like you lost a fight with a wall with the back of your head. Which you kind of did."

They'd agreed Levi would stay up in the apartment with the cop while Kawika closed up the pub and tried to get ahold of Toni Zanetti, but now Levi was having second thoughts about the plan. If Joseph Zanetti woke up, he'd have to scramble to handle the situation, and Levi hadn't quite figured out how to approach it.

"Not like there's an instruction manual," Levi grumbled, scraping at the velvet with his fingers. "That would be leaving information out where someone could find it. Stupidest rule ever. We can totally play it off as a game system. Who the hell is going to believe a Peacekeeper instruction manual was anything but some shit set of rules some kids pulled together so they could go play werewolf someplace in the woods?"

His ringing phone pulled Levi away from worrying about the cop waking up and onto the prayer that Kawika had found the strega to come and get her grandson. His hopes were momentarily dashed when he heard his son whisper his name over the phone line. Then alarm struck.

"What's wrong? It's nearly one thirty. Why are you up?" Levi checked the clock on the wall, frowning at how late it was, but the panic at hearing Deck ramped up. "Kiddo, what's the matter? What's going on?"

"Nothing. I'm okay. I just... needed to talk to you," Declan whispered. "I got one of the counselors to loan me his phone, but—"

"You stole his phone?"

"I didn't steal his phone!" Declan protested, his voice squeaking, then dropping back down. "He told me I could use it, but I didn't want anyone to overhear me. Sheesh, steal *one* thing—"

"It was a tank," Levi shot back. "Okay, a Hummer, but still, it was a SWAT vehicle."

"I went like six feet!" his son grumbled. "And I was ten. Who the hell leaves keys in an armored Hummer for some kid to find?"

"So nothing's wrong? You don't need me to come get you from camp?" Levi leaned forward, dropping his foot from the ottoman. Despite the day's heat, the apartment got chilly at night, and the air conditioner needed to be kicked back, but it could wait. "Not that I don't love you, but why are you calling so late? Shouldn't you be in bed? Isn't there a basket-weaving class at seven in the morning or something? What am I paying that camp for if it's not going to teach you life skills like building a fire with a piece of string and a bit of wood? Never know when *that's* going to come in handy."

"Uncle Gibson said you were mad you couldn't ever get that fire drill thing to work." Declan's laugh was mean and low, much like Gib's was when he taunted Levi about their time at summer camp.

"Yeah, well your uncle Gibson could only do the doggie paddle until he was about eighteen," he shot back, happy to hear Declan's laughter. "Now seriously, kiddo. What's going on? You didn't call me in the middle of the night to tell me you know how to start a fire. I got *that* call when you were in preschool."

"You know the girls with the clippers?"

"Yeah, I'm not that old and feeble I can't remember what happened yesterday, kid." Levi pondered the fridge, wondering if he had a bottle of beer in it or if he could somehow convince Kawika to bring up some from the bar, but then Declan was off and running. "Wait… wait… slow down. How many guys ended up looking like poodles? Where the hell are the camp people while you all are being sheared like sheep?"

Levi caught the cop's eye twitch before he heard the man's breathing shift and then saw his body clench tightly. Wrapping Declan up was going to take a few seconds at the most, and he didn't want to startle Zanetti, not when the man had already taken a beating across the head from Kawika's fist. The guy might have fooled a human, probably even a young shifter like Deck, but Levi knew better. He'd known the moment when Joseph Zanetti roused back to consciousness, and it looked like he was going to have to deal with the strega's grandson by himself.

"Okay, Deck, time to get some sleep. Your old man's got to do a few things. I had to work tonight," Levi said, hedging his words around the pub closing and hoping Declan would assume he had to do some cleanup. "I'll talk to you later." Declan cut in with another rambling, sleep-heavy comment, and Levi murmured, "Yeah, I guess I'm glad you're not the only one sporting a Pomeranian cut. And just so you know,

I'm going to be calling the camp tomorrow to talk to the director. Giving you a heads-up because I'm not too happy—"

Zanetti winced almost imperceptibly but enough for Levi to see the squint of his crow's-feet and the deepening of his laugh lines around his mouth. Declan protested a bit on the other side of the line, without catching a breath, giving argument after argument about why Levi should leave things alone. When Declan finally inhaled, Levi slid back into the conversation.

"I'll leave it off this one time, but I'm going to tell you, anything else and I'm dropping a call in," he warned. "I know shit happens at camp. It wasn't that long ago when I was doing all the stupid things, but now I'm on the other side of the job, and I've got to keep you in one piece so I can get my parenting badge from your grandmother. So do me a favor. Keep your pants on, your fur on your body, and yeah, don't set anything on fire. That's still a given. Get some sleep, kiddo. Love you."

"It's nice you tell your kid you love him," Zanetti said, sitting up, then grabbing the arm of the couch to keep himself steady. The warmth in his honey-gold eyes faded, and they hardened, amber stones iced over with a bit of worry. "Now how about if you tell me what the hell happened to me and what the fuck *you* are?"

HIS HEAD throbbed and the pit of his belly churned with sick, but Joe wasn't going to take his eyes off the lean man sitting in a rather-violent-purple velvet chair on the other side of the shotgun-style living room. Or at least as much as he could see through his squint. Joe was lying on something soft, probably a couch, and a tiny shift of his hands and feet assured him he wasn't tied to anything. Keller appeared to be deep into a phone call with what sounded like his kid, more than likely the slender boy he helped into the white van a few days before. The panic in Keller's voice was oddly reassuring, connecting the man to his family in a way Joe could appreciate. He'd heard that elevated concern more than a few times in his own father's voice, especially during the late-night calls he and his siblings sometimes had to make at various points in his life.

Still, he didn't know where he was, although he could guess he was in Keller's apartment over the pub. But his gun seemed to be gone, and he didn't know how long he'd been out. No one knew he was going to St. Connal's, so it wouldn't be on anyone's radar if….

It hurt to think, and for the life of him, he didn't know who or what hit him. Whatever it was, it'd been solid, and he'd seen stars—literal stars—before a black wave seized him and took him down. The last and only time that'd happened before was when his cousin Mike cracked him across the forehead with a bat and he'd come to in a hospital room filled with praying Italian women and a priest assuring all of them he didn't need last rites.

Although he could have used a priest at the moment. Or maybe a shrink, because not only was his brain rattled from being smacked up against his skull, it was flummoxed by what he'd seen in the alley.

Escaping from where he was being held seemed like a good idea, but judging by the massive painful spot on the back of his head, Joe didn't trust himself not to vomit as soon as he stood up. Sifting through the events before he'd been hit, Keller didn't take long to—Joe couldn't believe he was even contemplating what he'd seen—but it wasn't more than a few seconds for Keller to go from man to… whatever it was he'd become.

A wolf? A dog? And what was that other man? It looked like a coyote, but one made by someone who'd maybe only heard of what one looked like. Maybe there'd been something in his salad after all, or the tuna sandwich he'd picked up for lunch earlier was bad, but then why would he have been struck unconscious unless someone was trying to keep secrets?

Shit, if Keller could turn into a huge black dog, what the hell did the Hawaiian guy behind the bar turn into?

"Going with crazy or food poisoning," Joe muttered to himself, taking another peek at Keller. "There's no way a human being can—"

Then the phone call with Keller's kid took a turn, and Joe was left with absolutely no doubt he'd seen what his brain still refused to accept as reality.

Because Keller was talking to the kid about hoping his fur grew back quickly, and yeah, it was kind of funny to see some other kids' faces when they discovered they couldn't simply shift and go back to a full coat.

He still had the element of surprise, and while Joe didn't know what Keller had planned for him, he was going to have to do *something*. Waiting until it sounded like the man was done talking to his kid, Joe forced himself to sit up, swallowing down the wave of sick threatening to boil up from his belly, and fixed what he hoped was a strong cop-stare at Keller.

"It's nice you tell your kid you love him," Joe choked out, hoping Keller didn't notice how he had to grab the couch arm for support. "Now how about if you tell me what the hell happened to me and what the fuck *you* are?"

Keller didn't even fucking blink. Instead, he smiled at Joe, put his phone down, then leaned forward in his chair. "You probably don't want to move too quickly. I think Kawika whacked you a little bit too hard there. Your pupils are huge. Damned kahuna said you probably didn't have a concussion, but he's also the kind of guy who breaks rocks with his forehead, so what does he know? How are you feeling? Sick? Need to throw up?"

"I'm fine," Joe growled out, spitting his words past gritted teeth. "How about you answer some of my questions?"

"How about if I make you some tea or something first? Then we can talk." Keller stood up, and Joe's eyes followed the man's stretch, nausea flirting at the back of Joe's throat when he moved his head. "Lots of sugar. I hear that helps. Don't go anywhere. I'll be right back. And before you think about heading down those stairs, please think again. Took both of us to get you up here, and you're going to get halfway down and take a gainer. I might be able to pick you up, but more than likely, I'm just going to grab you by an ankle and drag you back to the couch. I'd rather not do that."

Joe spent the time Keller fussed around in the kitchen looking around the place. The man—if he was a man—was right. There was no way Joe'd be able to get down the stairs without pitching himself down their length. His head was too fuzzy, and he wasn't convinced they hadn't done something to him while he was out. Patting his pockets, he found his wallet and phone were missing as well, so there'd be no calling for a cab or for someone to help. Keller's phone was across the room, sitting on an ottoman, but by the time he got across to snag it, Keller probably would catch him before he could make a call.

"Not like there's anyone to call." Frowning only made his head ache more, and Joe sighed. "Who the hell's going to believe this?"

The place looked like a normal home—cleaner than he'd expect with a single dad with a teenaged boy, but it definitely bore the stamp of having two males living in close proximity. A collection of shoes and boots were shoved into cubbyholes next to a mission-style bench near the stairs leading down to the street, and the furniture was oversized and soft. Even the sectional piece Joe'd been left on was comfortable and clean, its upholstery unstained and its cushions plump with filling. The art on the walls ran mostly to what looked like kids' drawings—a collection of ten or so papers framed and arranged on the space above the couch. Dogs seemed to be a theme, but Joe knew better now.

If it was the kid's artwork from when he was younger, he'd captured life with a wolf father in all its glory, including what looked like chasing balloons or butterflies in a garden.

"Here, sip this." Keller moved silently on his bare feet, appearing at Joe's side without a whisper of noise. "And here's some ibuprofen for your head. Tea's hot, so be careful." Putting a water bottle down on the coffee table in front of Joe, he said, "Drink some of that too. You're probably dehydrated. Lots of adrenaline earlier. That stuff can burn through your system like nobody's business."

Damn the man for still being hot, because despite the headache and his dry mouth, Keller was a delectable sight. Taking the hot mug, Joe blew on it, then gratefully sipped at the very sweet tea, feeling relief when the sugared brew began to work to calm the throbbing at the back of his head.

Keller pulled the ottoman over, then sat down near Joe, still slightly out of arm's reach but close enough a good lunge would take care of the distance between them. "You probably have a lot of questions, and I'm—"

"Just first tell me what the hell I saw," Joe said sharply. "What are you? What was that guy who was in the alley? The... other guy... said he had business with me. Business he was going to settle, but I'd never seen him before in my life. So, when you're done explaining what you are, you can tell me what the hell have I walked into."

"What I am?" Keller cocked his head, studying Joe with a steady, thoughtful gaze, as if Joe'd been the one turning into some kind of dog by the pub's kitchen door. "I'm a shifter. A wolf shifter. And well, it looks like you've walked into a pack squabble that's about to turn into a war. Or at least it will if I don't do something about it. Which I will. Right after I do something about *you*."

SIX

THE GARRULOUS female voice bouncing up the stairs not only sounded familiar, it brought shivers to Joe's spine. He couldn't make out what his grandmother was saying, but from her tone, whoever she was speaking to wasn't going to like anything coming out of her mouth over the next few minutes. Perhaps even an hour, because if there was one thing Joe recognized, it was his pissed-off grandmother coming down on someone for injuring one of her family.

"Joey?" Nana's frothy hair appeared at the top of the stairs before she did, a cotton-candy swirl of slightly pink curls bouncing furiously up and down as she stomped into the living room. It was obvious she'd hurried to dress, wearing a long red housecoat over a pair of bright yellow pajamas. But oddly enough, she was a sight for sore eyes. "Are you okay? What happened? This Vick kid said you were hurt."

"Kawika," the large Hawaiian man behind her said as he reached the top of the stairs. He stood there, quietly scanning the room. "Kah-vee-kah. Not Vicky, strega."

"You calling my grandmother a witch?" Joe straightened, his head swimming furiously, but he knew that word wasn't a good one, especially hearing his mother muttering it under her breath about his grandmother since he was a little kid. "Because if you are—shit. I think I'm going to be sick."

"Joey, lean back before you throw up all over Levi's rug," his grandmother ordered. "Ah, here I've been calling you Vick all this time. Why didn't you say anything?"

"Not my way," Kawika replied with a wide, assuring grin. "Didn't want to embarrass you. It happens. Names are hard sometimes."

"I'm glad to welcome you into my house, Strega Zanetti." Keller stood up, moving the ottoman back with a push of his foot. "Why don't you sit down, and I'll get you some coffee. Or maybe you'd like tea? Then we can figure this all out."

"Again, with the——" The green rose back up, and Joe gripped the side of the couch, wondering if he was going to be able to make it through a single sentence without losing his salad. "Jesus, I've got a concussion. Pretty sure about it. What did this guy hit me with?"

"Who hit him? What's with the hitting? What happened?" Nana strode toward the couch and patted at Joe's stomach. "Sit down. Let me look at you. You look like you ran into a truck."

Joe sat.

"Um, I'm going to go down and make sure everything's locked up. I figured I'd let you tell her what happened. I mean, I got into some of it, but not a lot. Mostly about… you and the other guy getting into it." Kawika shot a tight grin at Levi, holding up a brown paper bag. "Let me know if you need me, 'cause if you don't, I'm going to head home."

"Coward," Keller said, amusement lighting up his face. "Go on. It'll be fine. The strega and I will deal with it. Thanks for helping tonight. It could have gone pretty badly if you weren't there."

"Yeah, remember that when I start breaking heads on Friday if those assholes can't keep in line," the bartender rumbled. "Have a good night, and, well, good luck."

Nana plopped down on the couch next to Joe, then grumbled at Keller, who stood in the galley kitchen watching a teakettle work up a boil. "Are there more lights in here, or is stumbling around in the dark one of those training rituals no one talks about?"

"Coffee or tea?" Keller asked again, leaning over the island separating the kitchen from the living room to flick on recessed lighting from a switch on the wall. The flare of white made Joe's eyes water, and he flinched when his grandmother touched his face again. "For tea, I've got—all kinds of shit my mom keeps giving me. You've got every kind of twig, stick, and berry to choose from. Coffee, I've got Vinacafe or… some other kind of Vietnamese coffee. Or I can make a pot."

"The coffee is fine," Nana muttered. "Now let me take a look at him. I didn't spend all that time and energy fixing the cracks in his skull from that stupid baseball bat for the likes of you to take him out in an alleyway."

"Nana, I can go to the emergency room. It's better if they——" Joe shifted uncomfortably as his grandmother's hands grew warm, nearly searing hot on his temples. "Look, I've got to get you out of here. There's things here you don't know about. I need to find my—"

"He's a werewolf. I know. The big guy is a kahuna. Which is kind of like a priest but not really. I don't know much about them. He seems like a nice enough man, even when I got his name wrong." His grandmother ran her fingers over the tender spot at the back of his head. "Stay still. Let me look at you. Then we can talk."

"Here's your coffee, Toni," Keller said, setting a cup down on the heavy wooden table, edging a few magazines aside to make room. "I told him I'm a shifter, but that's as far as I've gotten. He looked at me weird, so I'm guessing he thinks I'm nuts. Or he's nuts. One of the two. Maybe even both."

"What the hell did you put in my food? Because I wasn't hallucinating before I went into your place. I watched you turn into a dog." His grandmother slapped his thigh, and Joe pulled his head back. "What the hell? Nana, I'm a cop. I don't do—"

"Now stop moving so I can make sure all your marbles are lined up. I don't think you're that hurt, but I want to make sure. If you've still got a headache when I'm done, we're going to the ER and they can scan you, but it will be a cold day in hell when I can't fix a tiny thing like this," she tsked. "And don't call them dogs. It's an insult."

Joe shot Keller a look over Nana's shoulder, eyeing the man suspiciously. He looked normal, just like he'd looked every other time Joe'd seen him. But the image of his body sculpting itself into something large and furry wouldn't leave Joe's mind. None of what he'd seen made sense. Werewolves were for movies and books, beasts with insatiable appetites bent on chewing their way through whatever prey they hunted down.

And usually that included humans.

"We consider being called dogs derogatory. It implies we're domesticated and bound to humans in servitude," Keller said, his voice quiet but firm. The shift in his demeanor was obvious. A regal tilt to his head and the feral gleam in his steady gaze was enough for Joe to clear his throat, readying an apology. "But you didn't know. I get that. Just don't do it again."

"Yet you called my grandmother a strega," he pointed out.

"That's because I *am* one, Joey. Sixth generation and proud of it." Nana pulled away, examining his face. The back of his head felt better, but his cheeks were still overly warm from where her hands rested on his skin. "There. All better. Nothing too bad, but your junior from downstairs has to be more careful, Levi. Boy doesn't know his own strength."

"I keep telling him that," Keller drawled, crossing his legs. "But usually it's after him throwing someone through the drywall because they're being assholes, so I don't think he's really listening to me when I say it. Okay, *Joey*, all fixed. Gun, badge, wallet, and all of that is gathered up, and I've got a situation with a couple of rival groups I've got to figure out. Are we talking about this now, or are you going to break it to him that there are things that go bump in the night besides thieves and blind bats? Because it's two in the morning, and I'm dead tired."

"Now would be best," the diminutive woman sitting next to Joe proclaimed. "Because Joey was always one who needed proof. He's like his grandfather that way. My Joseph always needed to see things done before he'd believe it. Took him breaking his wrist to finally understand I could help him get it right. Argued with me the whole time."

"Wait, you think you've cured...." Joe moved his head, realizing the throbbing was gone. The churning in his stomach only murmured, an echo of the sick greenness he'd been feeling since he woke up. Turning his neck slowly, he braced himself for the intense vertigo, but it never hit, only a whisper of a mild uneasiness along his temples when he stared at his grandmother. "Okay, what the hell is going on, Nana? Because I think I've seriously lost my mind. How the hell can you be a witch? You're Catholic."

"Oh boy," Keller sighed, then rubbed at his face. "I'm going to make an actual pot of coffee. This is going to be a *very* long night."

IT TOOK Keller working his body through another transformation for Joe to finally accept what he'd seen. The change itself was both fascinating and horrifying. The creaking and twisting of bone and skin into fur and fang wasn't something he thought he'd ever get used to seeing, but the wolf emerging from Levi Keller's human form was undeniably a gorgeous and powerful animal.

With a startling intelligence gleaming in its burnished golden-green eyes.

If there was anything that gave Joe pause, it was the wolf's changing eye color—a rich spectrum running from gold to emerald with hints of deep sea blue at his dark pupils. Or it could have also been the devilish smirk the wolf seemed to have whenever he glanced Joe's way.

There was nothing to show Keller's change—no wispy skin shreds or discarded teeth. Whatever Keller sloughed off turned to dust in a matter of moments after it hit the floor, leaving behind only the slightest hint of grit, and even that seemed to whisper away.

Keller was massive, easily filling the space of his human form, perhaps even made larger by the wealth of pitch-black fur over his lean, muscular body. He was nothing like the other man Joe saw in the alley, something Joe mentioned when Keller walked out of the hall bathroom after he carefully plucked his discarded clothes up off the floor with a delicate nip of his teeth and changed back into his human form.

"Okay, you're a wolf, then," Joe exhaled, feeling the heat on his breath as he wondered if it was too late to switch from tea to whiskey. "Then what the fuck was that guy in the alley? Because he didn't look like a wolf. More like one of those round, bouncing cartoon animals, or maybe one of those make-your-own plushies someone forgot to ease back on the stuffing when filling it."

"Coyote," Keller answered him. "Not a wolf."

"Only for a little bit. Then it sure as hell did not look like a coyote," he challenged Keller with a tilt of his chin. "For one thing, he was a furry deflated balloon. Secondly, he was a *gigantic* furry deflated balloon. Coyotes are a hell of a lot smaller than whatever he turned into."

"If you're an out-of-shape human, you're going to be an out-of-shape… whatever you are," Nana responded quickly. "It depends on weight distribution. Some shifting metahumans bulk up to strengthen their other form. Muscle, fat, and all of that counts."

"Okay, Nana, the words *metahuman* and *weight distribution* are never things I ever expected to come out of your mouth," Joe said with a sigh. "Jesus, my world is upside down. So he was bigger than a normal coyote because that's just how it works?"

"Thing about us shifters is we don't gain or lose mass. It has to go somewhere. Whatever weight you are as a human being, you're going to be close to that no matter what form you have. It's not magic. It's a genetic mutation of some kind," Keller elaborated. "It's not so much as you can't be overweight as a human, but you have to be fit enough to carry the weight you do. So you've got huge coyotes and scrawny pygmy tigers. It's one of the reasons we try not to expose ourselves to the mundane world. Someone's going to see a two-hundred-pound snow leopard in Lower Mongolia and wonder how the hell did that get there."

"What about birds? Like, is there a two-hundred-pound hummingbird out there getting stoned off its ass on poppies?" he asked, giving his grandmother a dirty look when she giggled. "Hey, I'm behind here in class. I'm still trying to get over the whole strega thing."

"Not birds. Usually predators or hunters—like hyena, wolves, and big cats. People think maybe there were sharks, because of gods like Kamohoali'i, but Kawika thinks they were hunted to extinction. No one alive has ever seen one. Just stories to go on." Keller picked up his coffee cup, frowning at whatever was left inside. "And we don't know why we're this way. Not like we can do open research on ourselves. There aren't tons of any one of us, although canids and smaller cats are more plentiful. That could be because of hunting or just population. There's really no history other than oral. Apparently our kind aren't big on writing things down."

"Something you disagree with," Joe guessed, and Keller nodded.

He needed a minute to think. Actually, he debated asking Keller if he had anything strong to drink but didn't think Nana would even let him have a beer after being knocked senseless. There was too much coming at him, and combined with his suspicions about the Vikings gang resurfacing in the city, Joe didn't know what to tackle first—Keller being a werewolf, his grandmother being some kind of witch, or that there was an entire society of people he never knew existed and the motorcycle club he worked so hard to break up was a part of that secret world.

Footsteps on the stairs made all their heads turn, but Keller got to his feet, his shoulders squaring off with the landing. The fluidity of his rise was startling, and oddly enough, Joe reacted to it, drawn to stand by the force of Keller's authoritative stance. He might not carry a star, but Keller's commanding presence defined his place in the mysterious world Nana appeared to live in. Keller was someone to be reckoned with, a keystone in some puzzle Joe was struggling to fit its pieces together. But one thing was clear—Keller might as well have been wearing a star much like the one Joe carried every day.

"Just me," Kawika called out before reaching the top of the stairs. "Levi, had to double back 'cause Reilly just called—"

"Los Lobos Reilly?" Keller's sharp gaze narrowed, and Joe could have sworn he heard a growl roll through the man's chest. "Why'd he call you?"

"Maybe because you turned your phone off? Or it's set to only answer for the kid? Who knows?" Kawika nodded a hello to Joe and Nana, giving them a quick smile. "He wants to meet with you tomorrow. Says there's been a *misunderstanding*."

"He's trying to cover his own ass. That's what it is." Pursing his mouth, Keller paced a few strides, then shook his head. "Probably worried I'm going to judge against him and not hear both sides out on Friday. Handing the whole territory to the Vikings would mean his club will have to find someplace else to squat, and so far, no one up or down the coast is going to give them room. This was their last chance. So either the guy tonight crawled back to Reilly with his tail literally tucked in and told him he screwed up, or Reilly sent him. Either way, it doesn't look good."

"Better coming up and admitting his guy did something than pretending he didn't know." The kahuna shrugged. "He said he'll call you tomorrow around noon. Didn't ask about the jacket or tell me what he wanted to talk to you about, but that's got to be it. Unless he's going to try to frame the Vikings."

"Yeah, thing is, I smelled and saw coyote." Keller chuckled, tapping his nose. "I'm not some old blind wolf dialing this in, here. That kind of dance doesn't cut it at St. Con's. Let's see what Reilly says and go from there."

"Fair," Kawika agreed in a quiet voice. "Okay, heading home now. This *kanaka* is tired."

"This old lady's tired too," Nana announced, yawning widely. "I'm getting too old for these early-morning emergencies. I need to get some sleep, and Joey here is probably going to keep you up all night asking questions. Kawika, can you give me a ride home so I can go back to bed, if you don't mind."

"No worries, auntie," the huge man assured her. "Whenever you want to go."

"Now is good." She stood up, stretching slowly with a hand at her lower back.

"I can take you home, Nana," Joe murmured.

"No, you stay. I'll be fine. Trust me when I tell you no one in our neighborhood's going to mess with me." She eyed Keller, who'd gotten to his feet as well. "I don't want him driving just yet. I'm going to leave him here with you, because his mouth is going to be going for hours, and I love him—he's my favorite—but if I have to listen to him asking me why like he did when he was three, I'm going to give him a knock on his head that's going to make the one he got earlier look like a love bite."

"He can stay," Keller agreed. "Probably better anyway. He can ask some questions, and then I can get some sleep. The next few days are going to be long ones for me."

"Nana, seriously," Joe protested. "I can take you home."

"No, no. You stay and let Levi here fill you in, because I know you, you're going to stick that nose of yours into this because you can't help it," Nana said, patting his shoulder. "Now, if you're good, Levi here will show you exactly why I come to St. Con's with the girls every week, and it sure as hell isn't for the beer."

SEVEN

"OH GOD. Sweet Jesus in heaven, what are you doing to me?" Joe moaned, his eyes closed in rapturous wonder. "How the hell am I going to ever go back to my life without... fucking hell... damn, you're good."

The low rumbling sounds pouring from Joe's parted lips aroused something silken and dark in Levi's belly, and he smiled, reveling in the pleasure he brought to Joe's mouth. There was nothing more passionate than hearing the erotic groans of satisfaction rising in pitch and the nearly imperceptible widening of a man's pupils when he could no longer take any more of what Levi had to dish out.

"Shit, I've got to slow down or I'm just going to pass out," Joe murmured, reluctantly putting his sucked-clean spoon back into the bowl of ice cream Levi handed him a few moments before. "Seriously, this is better than sex."

"Trust me when I tell you I have better sex than I make ice cream," Levi replied, grinning at the red stain creeping across Joe's face.

It was great teasing a cop, and with his guard down, Joe was simply adorable. The man's infectious laugh and easy smile had been hidden behind his star—an impenetrable shield, focused on his commitment to the law—but the guy behind that exterior possessed a warmth Levi felt down into his belly.

And past that as well.

It'd been too long since he'd spent time with a guy for anything other than a hookup or passing time with a friend, and he was beginning to wonder if the strega's grandson was someone he could maybe fold into his life. They shared the same interests—a love for the Cubs and an intense hatred for dry chicken, as well as, apparently, Joe's love for ice cream.

He could get used to seeing a guy who loved ice cream, especially since his own son was now beginning to refuse to taste some of the more wacky things he churned up in their kitchen.

"What am I eating? Exactly?" Joe dipped his spoon into the melting creamy mound, easing through the swirls cut into the rich vanilla-bean-speckled mixture. "I taste the chocolate, and there's… orange? I mean, it's awesome, but what is it?"

"French vanilla bean base with Grand Marnier caramel swirls and dark chocolate ribbons. The chopped-up roasted mac nuts have to be added after you scoop it out or it gets all gummy," Levi explained, pleased at the rolling deep moan Joe made while sucking another bite off his spoon. "Also, some people have nut allergies, so they can do without the brittle part. I like using crushed-up won ton pi chips too, but I don't have any up here. Either one will give you that sweet, salty crunch afterward. One of my better efforts."

"Thought about putting it in stores?" Joe opened his eyes wide enough to give Levi a longing look. "Because this needs to be in my freezer all the time. 'Course I'll have to jog every day to get it off my stomach, but that'll be worth it. Damn, this is good."

"No stores. This isn't… work," he replied, swirling his spoon into the slurry forming at the edge of his bowl. "It's kind of like my downtime stuff. My mad-scientist time. I build motorcycles back up and make ice cream flavors. The pub and Declan are a lot of work. Don't get me wrong, wouldn't trade the kid or St. Con's for anything, but I need something to lose my head into. And it's kind of cool to have something to show for it after."

"What's it called?" The sound of his spoon hitting ceramic brought a frown to Joe's face, and Levi laughed at his heavy sigh. "Hey, remember most of the time, my life is full of microwave burritos and leftovers I can beg off my mom. The cooking gene flew past me, but I can grill the hell out of a chicken. Homemade ice cream is way out of my league."

"This is number forty-two." Joe's eyebrows rose, and Levi explained. "I number them when I come up with the idea of what goes into them. After I shake out the bugs or add them—don't look at me like that, you haven't tasted the candied apple and caramel ant ice cream yet—I finalize out the recipe and enter it into the ice cream book. Most of them go on sale downstairs. We make a few batches. You can grab a pint of whatever's on the board."

"I thought those were beers," Joe confessed. "Makes more sense now. Couldn't figure out why the hell anyone wanted a mango and *li hing mui* creamy ale. Okay, so now that my headache's gone and I'm sugared up, want to shed some light on… well, shit, everything? Because I don't even know where to start, and I know it's late but—"

"Brain's probably going to be too busy to sleep," Levi said softly. "Here. Give me your bowl and I'll get us some water. So long as I get at least four hours in, I'll be okay. Kawika's probably going to kiss your feet for getting him out of taking a run through the park tomorrow. I'll text and tell him he can sleep in."

"You run every morning?" Joe craned his neck to watch Levi stride to the kitchen, wincing when he turned his head too far. "Damn, I thought it was better, but it still hurts a little bit."

"Yeah, stregas… well, any kind of witch… can't heal everything, but they sort of manipulate the body to motivate healing. From what I understand. Sometimes the old girls your grandmother runs with start talking, and I'm all, well, that's nothing I need to know about. I try to keep out of witch business. Safer that way." Levi handed Joe one of the frosted-over water bottles he'd gotten from his fridge. Then he sat down. "I don't run every morning, but sometimes I can con Kawika to go up with me to one of the bigger parks so I can do a good run. Problem is, that man's built for a long hard sprint. Fast as fuck, but only good for about maybe sixty or seventy yards."

"You don't like running alone?" Joe cracked open the bottle, twisting the cap around as he spoke.

"People tend to panic when they see what looks like a large black dog running through a park. Especially when the dog's almost two hundred pounds and doesn't have a collar." He took a sip, chuckling at Joe's sputter. "And no, I'm not wearing a collar. Running in human form isn't as satisfying, and I burn more energy as a wolf. Works off all the tension I've got building up from raising a teenaged boy with a curious mind and a reckless nature. I live for the day when I don't get a weekly call from the school about something he's gotten into. The pub's easier to run, but like my dad says—you get the kid you were, and I don't think the end of his tail ever got its hair back."

Levi Keller was going to be the death of him. Joe was sure of it. Maybe it was the hit on the head or perhaps the residual alcohol fumes folded into the ice cream, but there was no arguing the pub owner was hitting all of Joe's buttons, including a few he didn't even know he had.

Barefoot and dressed in low-slung old jeans and a ratty T-shirt, the man shouldn't have been sexy, but there was something about his boneless sprawl into the corner of the sectional couch that made Joe grateful for the cooling hit of potent ice cream lingering in his mouth. The stretch of his muscles along his long arms and thighs was bad enough, but the sneak peeks of Levi's lean stomach, with its faint whorl of soft hair below the dip of his belly button, were killing Joe.

His insouciant grace when tilting his head back to drink a sip of water led Joe to naughty places, wondering how the rasp of Levi's tongue against the inside of his thighs would feel in the middle of the night or if that long lean throat would reverberate when he gasped during sex. Shaking his head, Joe cursed his grandmother for leaving him and wondered if he could still find a ride home, not trusting his hands on the steering wheel when he was obviously rattled.

"Gotta admit, you're my first human to deal with finding out about all of us." Levi licked at a drop of water on his lower lip, the liquid trembling until his tongue swept it away. "There's conflicting ways to handle something like being seen, but a lot of them are kind of old-school."

"Like what?" Joe shifted on the couch, stretching out his legs. His head was beginning to hurt again, a softer throb instead of the pounding through-the-bone spikes from before, but it was manageable.

"Well, a lot of older instructions pretty much said kill the human and bury its body, but that was back when torches and pitchforks were all the rage," Levi said with a smile that was probably meant to soothe Joe's nerves but did more to rattle them, especially when a deep dimple appeared alongside the smirk. "I'm leaning toward the option of 'no one would believe you anyway and your grandmother would kick your ass if you said anything.' A hell of a lot easier than starting a whisper campaign that you're nuts. That was a big one too, but once it got out of hand in Salem, I think a lot of us Peacekeepers try to avoid it."

"Nana said that. Peacekeeper." Joe sifted through what he recalled his grandmother said before she left. "I'm going to guess you're some kind of cop."

"Sort of," he murmured in agreement. "No gun, and it's kind of a loose association. Not like we have an academy. Usually it's the owner of a business or area where people like me and Toni can meet to hammer things out. Believe it or not, you don't want a war between shifter families or covens rolling out into the street. Bad shit happens, and there's no way anyone will be able to hide from that. And yeah, we like hiding. Means we don't get cut up and examined. I'm big on that. I like my insides to stay right where they are, and I'll fucking kill anyone who comes for my kid."

The passion in Levi's words ran hot and strong. His eyes were fluid, rolling with gold-and-green fire in their warm hazel depths. Joe held up his hands, offering a tacit surrender. "I believe you. I did my time in a patrol car. I know what people can do to each other, especially when there's no one watching."

"Sorry. I have a few soapboxes." Levi let out a long hiss, a slightly bashful expression on his face. "Let me hit the salient points. We don't have a central government. Anyone can become a Peacekeeper, but you have to apprentice with one and learn the ropes. And I'm both cop and judge. I provide a place for people to talk things out, but I'm also the guy they come to when a decision has to be made about something. Usually that's territory. I'm one of the younger Peacekeepers I know of, but I've got a pretty decent track record. Both sides of the argument have to agree on who they want to hear them out, but it's got to be someone within a few hundred miles of where they are. So, like you can't have someone in New York make a decision in California."

"So the Vikings and Los Lobos wanted you, then?" Joe took a stab in the dark, hoping to punch through the fog surrounding the motorcycle gang's return. "Because I'd gotten the Vikings out of the city. Now they're back, and I'm worried they're going to bring their shit back with them."

"They're only here for Friday's meeting, and I was wondering how long it would take you to circle back around to the bikers." Levi laughed. "The Lobos are edging into the Vikings' territory. Don't know if there's drugs or anything else involved. If there are, they know I'll shut them down if they bring it here, so they'll be on their best behavior. We try to police our own, and they've got a lot of mundanes—humans—running with them, but when it's all said and done, we're just people. Some are lawyers and doctors, others are criminals and thieves. We follow the laws in the places we live in. We're not above it."

"Does that best behavior include that coyote attacking us tonight?" Joe asked. "Because I don't know where he was raised, but that's not good manners where I come from."

"That's what the Los Lobos leader wants to smooth over with me." Levi ran his fingers through his dark hair, pulling it back from his face. "He can't deny it was one of his. We've got the guy's colors, but he might try to say it was someone from the Vikings hoping to get the Lobos kicked out of the talk. That happens, and the Vikings win their argument by default. Thing is, the Vikings don't have any coyote running with them, and any shifters they have are family. None of them are canids."

"What are they?" Joe cocked his head, trying to ignore the rush of something warm moving through him when Levi stretched his arms up over his head and he spied another peek at the man's belly. "Unless you can't tell me."

"Bears. Well, not really bears so much as pandas," Levi replied, dropping his arms back down. "Came over with other Chinese immigrants during the railroad-building days. Most Ursidae are on the larger side, so they're pretty beefy in either form, and the pandas are usually right up there. Most of the Lobos are smaller—a mixture of coyote and whatever else they can get to follow them. A lot more shifters in that club and held together by Reilly, their leader. So, if someone went rogue from his group, then he's got cracks around his seams, not something he needs right now. If he can't show a steady, stabilizing presence, then he's got no business claiming space."

"Okay, the fact that I've spent more than a few years chasing pandas out of San Francisco is blowing my mind. But why do they come to you? I mean, most clubs just fight it out. Whoever is left standing wins the area," Joe pointed out. "It's why we try to shut them down. No one wants that kind of violence in their city. Not to mention everything else they bring with them."

"Groups get established in an area and claim territory. Basically they're saying they are the dominant circle, and anything bad that happens, it's up to them to self-police." Levi crossed his long legs under him. He picked at a split along his right knee, pulling at the white threads. "Los Lobos want the right to police themselves, and the Vikings are saying they shouldn't, because they're not capable of staying under the radar. What happened tonight kind of proves that. But that's only if whoever that was actually *is* a part of Reilly's group.

"We run things by a kind of agreement system," he explained in a soft voice. "Break the agreements and the rest of us turn against you. Our sole focus is to keep our secrets, and that means staying deep under the radar. For the most part, the Vikings have been cleaning themselves up, but there's still issues. One wrong move on their part and that whole torches-and-pitchforks idea gets revisited. Like I said, we police our own."

"So this kind of all rests on you deciding if the Lobos can have their own territory, but that carves out some of the Vikings' area." Joe sat back, fitting the pieces of the puzzle together. "And if they refuse to abide by what you decide, they open themselves up to a major ass-kicking."

"Pretty much." Levi nodded. "It's really not that complicated, and there's enough room up there for both of them, but Los Lobos moving into the Vikings' territory means conflict and not just being on the wrong side of the law. I don't care if someone's growing acres of pot. I don't have to. It's legal now, and it's not my job to make sure everyone pays taxes or has the right permits."

"What if it's heroin or something worse?"

"If they're running heroin and someone has evidence of it, I'd turn it over to the cops because that's also not my job. It's what the police are for. We are bound by the laws of the land, Joe. We pay taxes and vote, or we should. Anything connected to the mundane world is out of my jurisdiction," Levi continued. "But if someone's pushing into an area and making it difficult for another group to be who they are, then I get called in. Los Lobos want the right to decide consequences for the actions of their group, and the Vikings want to make sure the Lobos stay on their side of the river so they can do whatever it is that pandas do in the woods. You've got conflicting shifter cultures here, and ones that don't work well together. I'm here to prevent that from flaring up. That's all."

"Judge and jury, then?" Joe teased. "You are so not a cop, then. We don't get to do that."

"Well, most of the time, my back room is used for birthday parties, and St. Con's a good place to get a beer and a burger." Levi shrugged. "But sometimes, it's where groups gather so they don't end up killing each other later on and I get to listen to them argue their cases. St. Con's is a Sanctuary. Big S. Anyone coming through that door is granted a safe place to be—no weapons, no rivalries. Have a beer, and if you get a little drunk and you don't make an ass out of yourself, we'll pour you into a cab. But don't start shit, no matter if you're carrying fur, fangs, or magic, because I'll shut you down. That's the cop part of it. I don't care what someone's problems are. They just can't make them anyone else's.

"And on that note, I'm going to pour you into my bed and crash out here on the couch." He stood, stretching once again. Joe experienced a moment of ecstasy close to the experience of the number forty-two ice cream hitting his tongue when Levi's ass brushed against his shoulder as the man inched past him. "Let me make sure I've got clean sheets on the mattress and a towel you can use. God knows I've got toothbrushes. Damned kid chews through them like he's still two."

"You love him. Your son, I mean," Joe said softly. It wasn't so much a question as a confirmation of the man Levi seemed to be. "I can hear it in your voice. Harder for me to hear it in my dad's, but sometimes I can."

"Deck's my whole world," Levi murmured, turning to face Joe. "Not to say there isn't room for someone else, but he's the start of it. It's not easy dating when your idea of a good time is to turn into a giant black wolf and chase a Frisbee in the park. Cures the need for me to hunt something, but brings out all the weirdos and freaks if you list that on any online dating app. Not guys I want to bring home and meet my son."

"You really like to chase a Frisbee in the park?" Joe leaned back, suspiciously eyeing Levi. "You're pulling my leg, right?"

"Nope, one of the best things in the world to do. It seriously scratches the hunting itch I get sometimes, and it's better than chasing pigeons," Levi said with a wink. "Because it's a fucking bitch and a half getting those damned feathers out from between my teeth, and they really do taste just like rats."

EIGHT

"KELLER, WE need to meet. You and I have to talk."

Levi didn't recognize the voice on the phone, but it was serious enough to get his attention. Or at least serious enough to wake him up.

Blearily glancing to the right of him, he momentarily wondered what happened to his alarm clock and more importantly, why had his bed shrunk so much? His shoulders hurt a bit, and there was something hard at the small of his back. Digging in behind him, he found one of the crochet-covered throw pillows his mother pawned off on him the last time she was in town and tossed it across the room. The ache eased, but his confusion didn't, not until he recalled a pair of warmed-whiskey eyes and the strong Italian face he'd spent more than a few hours staring at before falling into an unconscious sprawl on his living room sectional.

"Hello?" The man on the phone sounded as confused as Levi'd been moments before. "Keller, are you there?"

"Yeah, give me a second. Who is this?" Yawning as he sat up, Levi blinked at the filmy sunlight coming in through the spaces in the room's drawn curtains. "Better yet. Call back in ten minutes. I just woke up, and I've got to pee."

He hung his phone up before he got a response, then shuffled to the hall bathroom, trying to remember if he'd pulled out some clothes to change into, since Joe Zanetti was probably still asleep in his bed.

Ten minutes was just long enough to get a quick shower in and brush his teeth, but shaving would have to wait. Scrubbing a handful of cold water across his face startled his nerves enough to push Levi into full consciousness, but coffee would go a long way in helping his brain fire up.

His phone began to ring as he filled the kettle for his instant Vietnamese coffee, and Levi let it roll into voicemail, figuring the guy would call back or leave a message.

"'Cause you're not the camp. That's got its own ringtone," Levi told his phone, shaking down the *cafe da* packets, then tearing them open to pour into his tall mug. "And I'm going to need some juice in me before I deal with anyone's shit. Hell, I'm not even awake enough to deal with my own shit right now."

Levi had just settled down onto the couch and had a sip of coffee when his phone chirped at him again. Sighing, he answered the call, not quite willing to have the outside world intrude but resigned to the inevitable. Tucking the phone against his ear, he said, "Yeah. Who is this? And why do we need to talk?"

The growl on the other side of the line was faint, a higher-pitched rumble than a wolf but definitely in the same family. Levi was about to hang up when the man finally spoke. "I don't like being dismissed."

"Call before eight in the morning after I've had a long night and you're lucky I even answered the phone," Levi said softly. "You can either start over with me and speak your piece or I move on and call the Los Lobos group out for violating Sanctuary rules. I do that, and you all are banned from coming in to plead your case. Your call."

"How do you know I'm with Los Lobos?"

"Because who the hell else is going to call me up before the damned sun has burned off the fog and toss attitude my way?" Levi snorted. "Sure as hell isn't going to be the Vikings, and there's no one else being a pain in my ass but you guys. Make up your mind, because the offer's only good for the next ten seconds. I rushed through a hot shower for you. That's all the consideration I'm going to give after one of yours attacked someone at my place. Nine seconds."

"This is Scotty. I'm the Lobos' second." Another sigh, and this time, it sounded strained. "I called to tell you Paolo didn't know Charlie was there last night. I just found out this morning when Charlie came stumbling in."

"Paolo's the leader of your group," Levi reminded him in a voice he often used on Deck when his son was on his fifth excuse for why he did something. "Things aren't supposed to happen without Paolo knowing about them. You're not doing your case for your own territory any good here, Scotty. Charlie left his colors in the alleyway, right in front of the guy he was trying to jump."

"A human, right? A mundane?" Scotty's voice reached for anything to hang a bit of hope on. "Late enough and maybe drunk enough to convince he didn't see what he thought he did."

"Yeah, nope. Let me spell it out for you in small words—wasn't drinking, is an SFPD detective, and is Strega Zanetti's grandson." The sucked-in-hard hiss Scotty made nearly tore Levi's ear off, but the profanity that followed impressed him with the second's creativity. "Tell you what, you go wake Paolo up and tell him whatever story you were going to tell me, and when you guys figure it out, call me back. You've got two hours, and no, the solution doesn't include killing Charlie. Maybe by then, I'll have enough coffee in me and I'll be in a better mood."

Levi ended the call before Scotty could reply and went back to his coffee, nearly curling over the steaming cup in the hopes the fragrance alone would shake off the cobwebs in his mind. An intense sluggishness held on to his limbs, and while he'd love nothing more than to fall back into the couch's almost-too-soft cushions, he still had Joe Zanetti to deal with.

The same Joe Zanetti who was standing at the end of the hallway, wearing nothing but the pair of thin cotton drawstrings Levi found for him only a few hours ago, and with very nice-looking arms crossed over his broad, gorgeous chest.

"You often tell people not to kill their own?" Joe's rasp was thick with sleep, an erotic stroke on Levi's tangled nerves. "Heard you talking. Figured you might need some help dealing with all of this. Then I remembered you're a werewolf. What the hell can I do?"

"Not much difference between you and me, other than we bounce a little better with pain and some of us are a hell of a lot quicker," Levi responded, cocking his head back to drink in the sight of the man standing half-naked in front of him. "Oh yeah, and the turn-into-an-animal thing, but really, not something you can put on your resume. That was one of the Lobos. He wanted to cover up the coyote thing from last night."

"I heard you tell him no." Joe fought back a yawn before finally giving in to it. "And then the two-hour deadline. That enough time for them to think up a different line of bullshit to tell you?"

"It's actually enough time for them to wake up their fearless leader, tell him the bullshit story, and hammer out a solution. Because they owe you for the attack, and they owe me a hell of a lot for violating St. Con's. Technically, I can call for them to be disbanded, but then who else is going to take in Reilly's pack of mutts? It's the one thing he's been good at—giving the loners a place to belong." Levi sucked down a bit more coffee, then nodded to the still-hot kettle. "Packets of the Vietnamese are on the counter if you want, and then maybe I can figure out something we can do for those two hours."

"Yeah?" Joe's gaze grew wary but flared with a heat Levi appreciated. "What's that?"

"Oh, I can think of all kinds of things I'd like to do to you, but two hours definitely isn't enough time." Levi chuckled at Joe's bemused expression. "I've got a lot of frustration and energy I need to burn off, and I'm thinking you're just the guy to help me to do it."

"I CANNOT believe I let you talk me into this." Joe kept his eyes on the street, looking for anyone coming by. "And how many Frisbees do you go through in a year? I think I might go buy some stock in the company."

"Look, it helps me concentrate," Levi said through the cracked-open passenger window. The SUV rocked a bit behind Joe as whatever Levi was doing jostled the car. "Where'd I put my jeans?"

"Did you even bring jeans?" It was surprising how easily he'd fallen into pace with Levi, and standing watch outside of the SUV almost seemed like a natural thing to do, as if Levi were changing out of a wet suit instead of shedding the wolf part of himself. *Almost* natural. "How long does it take you to get dressed? People are beginning to look at me weird."

"That's because you're wearing an SFPD T-shirt. This neighborhood only sees cops when someone calls the police on someone who didn't take their trash cans in an hour after the truck comes by. They're probably wondering if you're on a stakeout." Levi made an *aha* noise, and the SUV rocked again. "Found my pants."

They'd spent a good forty-five minutes at a hard run, then a cooldown with a game of Frisbee that made Joe reevaluate everything he'd ever thought about wolves. He must have been half-asleep when

Levi proposed a jog through the park, and even after Levi came out of the bedroom in full ebony-furred glory, he'd been game. There was something about Levi needing to stretch out the other half of his existence, to peel off the human and shake loose a bit. He asked quietly, giving Joe every out, but he reasoned the only other person he could do a city run with was Kawika, and getting out into the woods was practically impossible with the pub and his son.

So Joe relented and found himself working hard to keep up with Levi's long strides on a winding cement path deep in Presidio on an overcast Thursday morning. It was odd but good. His brain constantly reminded him the large black wolf loping in front of him was a man he'd caught himself lusting after the night before. Still, the run did him a world of good, clearing his head a bit and easing the last of the ache pounding through his skull. By the time they logged in a couple of miles, he'd fallen into a good rhythm, enjoying the companionable run.

At no point did Levi become anything other than a man in his mind, and the curious turn of his thoughts kept Joe company until they stopped for their cooldown and Levi dug a Frisbee out of the backpack he'd handed Joe to wear.

"This isn't going to do anything to dissuade anyone you're a dog, you know," Joe reminded him, hefting the gnawed heavy plastic disc in his hand. "And this thing weighs a ton. If I hit you in the head with it, it's not my fault."

It certainly wasn't play. Tossing a Frisbee to a powerful, nearly two-hundred-pound wolf was vastly different than throwing a tennis ball around the backyard for his mom's scraggly-toothed mutt, Josie. Levi stood at Joe's side, watching the disc arc up before taking off, and then he flew, leaving Joe speechless at the speed and strength in Levi's other form.

While people stopped and watched a bit, no one approached. Levi's manner didn't give off anything other than neutral vibes, but his size made people wary. When a toddler ran up to him screaming, "Doggy," he'd good-naturedly taken the abuse of tiny fingers digging into his fur and pulling on his ears while Joe assured the little girl's wide-eyed mother she wasn't going to be eaten alive. Passing Levi off as a K-9 cop seemed to work, and he was damned certain the man tucked into the wolf was laughing his head off at Joe trying to soothe the hysterical woman's nerves.

Or at least that's what he thought when he saw Levi's sharp white teeth peering out of what looked like a wolfish grin.

"Why aren't we going back to your place so you could do this?" Joe asked over his shoulder, catching a good glimpse of Levi's thighs as he struggled to get his jeans up over his knees. "I mean, do you even sweat when you run like that? Or am I going to be the only one running around sopping wet and reeking to high heaven?"

"Nope, don't sweat, but I bathe every day so I don't end up smelling like roadkill," Levi muttered through the open window. "And I try to keep the whole wolf thing under wraps. The alley was a fluke. Only reason I did it was because Charlie was there to tear someone's head off, and I'm going to guess he thought you were me."

"He looked like a water balloon about to pop." Joe shook his head at the memory. "I know how those kinds of bar fights end. The guy thinks just because he's carrying weight that he's going to win. Then he gets his ass handed to him. There's only so much a heavier advantage can give you. You still need to know how to fight."

"Yeah, but I also didn't know what Charlie was bringing to the table. For all I knew, he's won his share. Couldn't risk it." Levi grunted, shifting his weight into the door. "Couldn't risk you."

Joe wasn't sure if he was meant to hear the soft whisper, and when he turned around, Levi was bent over, tying one of his sneakers. He *liked* the guy. Hell, his grandmother liked Levi, and no one was ever good enough for any of her offspring, including her grandkids. Joe wasn't even sure if Nana liked his mom underneath all of the bluster, but the old woman would stand by her to fight off a storm if she needed to.

He had the feeling Levi was the same way—solid, honest, with a bit of mischief just to keep things interesting.

Nana was right. He could do worse, and he might not ever do any better.

"How long did it take for you to become a Peacekeeper?" Joe turned, catching Levi's eye. "A year? Six months?"

"Two years, and I had to be a junior for a year. My uncle wanted to retire, and he thought I'd be good at it." Levi's shrug tossed off any regard his family might have had for his abilities. "I try to be fair, and I listen. That's pretty much the biggest part of it. Sometimes I've got to do some research about things, like if I don't know how a certain sect works or if there's some innate cultural thing built into a shifter type. Nothing that can't be learned, but people have to trust you to do the right thing. And someone can always go to another Peacekeeper to challenge the decision. The less there is of that, the better."

"Kind of like appealing to a higher court," he mused.

"Sort of, but no one's higher than anyone else. I mean, there's Peacekeepers you respect pretty hard because they've been doing it for years, but there's also some you want to avoid because they show bias. You can also get a Peacekeeper kicked to the curb by calling for a review." Levi made a face. "That means gathering up nine of us, and we listen to reviews of every case that guy—or woman—made over a period of time, especially the cases where bias is claimed. Same thing happens when you become a Peacekeeper. Three seniors review if you're ready, and if you are, then boom, you're off deciding how people should live their lives. And not getting paid for the privilege."

"No pay?" Joe pursed his lips. "So you're doing all of this for free? Why?"

"Because it's the right thing to do and someone's got to do it." He looked up, capturing Joe in the moonlight sheen of his hazel gaze. "We have an obligation to keep ourselves together as a society so we can exist in the mundane world. So we hold ourselves accountable.

"I might disagree with how some sects and shifters handle their own personal business, and hell, my own family splintered because of something a lot of us wouldn't agree to, but if I want to bring my kid up in a world where he has to straddle not only the human laws but also a peace we've all worked for, then I sure as shit better show up when there's trouble." Levi's expression grew fierce, then softened. "Now, as far as you getting a shower, we can head back to my place, and I'll bet as soon as we start driving, Reilly will call. Can't claim you're old enough to wear big-kid pants if you've got to show throat to the Peacekeeper deciding your case. And Reilly wants this bad enough he can taste it. So how about if we grab some tacos on the way home and then see what the Los Lobos gang has to say about their little coyote issue?"

"I THINK this is a bad idea," Kawika asserted, a low groaning sigh accompanying his protest. "Like on the scale of bad ideas, this ranks up there with the fried-pickle-and-sardine sandwich my ex liked to have before dinner. Never ended well, and somehow I was the one who paid for it."

"Told you not to date her," Levi reminded him. "She had crazy eyes. And you should never trust a woman who files her long nails into points. That's some Bathory shit right there. 'Sides, he's a strega's kin. He's got a right to call out his attacker on Sanctuary ground. Might live a mundane life, but he's got witch blood."

"Only because she told him," his friend grumbled. "He doesn't need to be here for this. It's not even the main event. Just a—"

"Los Lobos are sweating on this." Levi began to arrange a few of the private dining room's chairs at a round table set in the middle of the space. "Joe's the one who was jumped. He's got a say in this."

"He bringing his grandmother?" Kawika stopped clearing the floor of excess chairs, pausing in midshuffle. "Because that's not someone we need here."

"She's not," he said, shaking his head. "The less in here the better."

"I think you just let him in because you think he's hot." His friend waddled another table to the side of the room. "And maybe you feel bad because he got whacked on the head."

"Considering you're the one who whacked him, don't know why I'd be the one who felt bad about it," Levi pointed out.

"You know, I'm actually within hearing distance of you." Carting in an ice-filled metal tub, Joe edged past Levi to get farther into the room, then set his load onto a small square table. "Here or somewhere else?"

"There's good. There's soda cans and bottled water in the kitchen if you want to stock it. I was debating chips or something, but this isn't us getting together to watch a game." Levi counted the chairs. "They should have three. Told Reilly he should bring Charlie to show proof of life."

"Would he really kill the guy?" The cop stopped in midstride, a serious storm brewing over his expression. "What the hell kind of rules do you all have?"

"A lot I don't agree with," Levi countered. "But I can only do so much, and I'm biased. I'm coming at things from my canid-centric point of view."

"Don't get him started on leash laws," Kawika muttered to Joe, earning himself a hiss from Levi. "Hey, I love this guy. He took you running. Keep him around so I don't have to. This body wasn't built for marathons."

"Yeah, I told him." Levi leaned his hip against the table. "One of the hardest things about being a Peacekeeper is learning how to juggle everyone's quirks and lines. It's why it takes years before you even hit junior status. Kawika here wants to freeload off of me until he's ready to retire, but most step up into their own space after three or four years."

"Eh, the first round standing in front of those guys was bad," the kahuna protested weakly. "Scary as hell. Could have heard my knees knocking from outside. I've got to get ready for doing that again. Maybe next year. Then I've got to find my own place to mark Sanctuary, and you know how high rent is. What am I going to do? Knock over liquor stores until I can pay rent on some place?"

"Like I said," Levi quipped. "Freeloader."

"Any guys like me become Peacekeepers? I mean, without any animal form or whatever you and Nana can do, because I'm still not too clear about what that is yet." The cop glanced at Kawika, sizing him up, then over to Levi. "I get that they'd be at a disadvantage. How much of it is power versus respect and, well, knowing someone's going to back you up if it comes down to a fight?"

"You thinking of becoming a Peacekeeper?" Levi shot a look over to Kawika, who snorted. "The human part isn't the problem. It's the time and coming up with solutions not colored by a bias. You've got to remember, we don't deal with the law. We're keeping the peace by coming up with compromises."

"Not saying me, but just any human," Joe countered. "And there's not much difference between keeping the law and keeping the peace. Sometimes people do things, and the person wearing that star has to decide if what they're doing is actually criminal intent or desperation. A lot of my time on the job is spent talking to people and trying to understand how they see things. I was just... wondering."

"Wondering is how you end up drunk with a red star tattooed under your arm," Kawika grumbled, pulling back his shirtsleeve to show a five-pointed crimson star inked into the sensitive skin under his arm. "Then you spend years getting stuff shoved into your head, and just when you think there's no more room, they shove in even more. One star I can handle, the second or third? Dunno if there's enough beer in the world to make me go through that again, brother."

"It doesn't hurt," Levi shot back, then caught himself before he rubbed at the same spot under his arm. "Okay, maybe a little, but can we just focus for, like, five minutes and get this done? They should be walking through the door soon, and I want this over and done with before St. Con's has to open for the night."

"I would like to know what this is before it even gets started," a raspy voice, heavy and weary with age, called out from the doorway. "I want to know why the Lobos are meeting with the Peacekeeper the day before our arbitration and why I wasn't told about it."

Stocky and short, the elderly Chinese man shuffled in, using a dragon-headed cane to steady himself while a tall, handsome man wearing a younger version of the elder's face kept up a slow pace behind him. Levi caught Joe stiffening his shoulders, coming up to stand closer to him. Dressed simply in cotton trousers and a button-up shirt, the old man looked as if he'd come in from an early-afternoon stroll, where the younger, taller version behind him looked harried and impatient in a lightweight sports coat, crumpled dress shirt, and slacks. A holster played peek-a-boo with the room when the young man slowly guided his elder in, his hands carefully hovering but not touching the old man. Looking up, the younger man appeared startled when he saw Joe, but the expression melted away into concern when the elderly man muttered something under his breath.

Levi was about to greet the head of the Zhao clan when Joe stepped in front of him, much like he'd done when facing down Charlie in the alley behind the pub.

"What the hell are you doing here, John?" Joe's cop voice surfaced, hard-edged and cutting through the tension the two men brought into the room. "And why the hell are you with the guy who bankrolls the Vikings? Or better yet, why don't you explain to me how you're not a dirty cop and covering for them all this time?"

NINE

THE PUB'S noise level was high, especially for a school night, but Kawika squirreled Joe and Yang away into a back corner, cordoning off the area with a string of velvet ropes and a fierce look at a pair of heavyset construction workers with fistfuls of beer mugs. With his back against the banquette, Joe had a good view of the entire pub, including the closed door to the private room to the side of the long bar. Sounds from the kitchen broke through the bright chatter of the filled tables, metal to the sharp rap of words and periodic bursts of laughter. Not long after the old man and Yang walked in, a slender, goateed man with a firm expression on his sharp features strode into St. Con's, the soft-bodied man named Charlie working hard to keep up with his fierce stride.

The discussion of what was going on came in slaps of polite anger and tightly pressed smiles, words lathered and whipped with secret meanings and coded in ways Joe couldn't parse. A few terse curse words from the guy with the goatee who Joe assumed was Reilly, then Charlie turned on his heel to walk away, leaving the room without saying a word with a distinct impression of a tail tucked between his legs. A few seconds later, Joe found himself being hustled out along with Yang, a soft-voiced Kawika closing the door behind them. They worked in silence for about half an hour, straightening tables and prepping the bar while the kitchen staff walked in to begin their shifts. As soon as Kawika unlocked St. Con's front door, he told them both to have a seat so he could get to work.

"I'm not even sure where to start with you," Joe said, running his index finger over the rim of his glass of Guinness. "I handpicked you to take over the Task Force because I thought you would fight to keep gangs and motorcycle clubs out of the city, and instead, I find you walking in with one of the Vikings' head honchos. Explain to me how that happens, Yang. Because I'm having a hard time understanding."

385

"I would think you would know, considering you were in there with two Peacekeepers," Yang replied, wiping a smear of beer froth from his lower lip with his thumb. "I was about to ask you the same thing. What are you doing here?"

"I don't know how much of this is considered need-to-know, and since nobody told me not to talk about it, I'm going to lay all my cards on the table, and I can tell you, I don't have too many of them." Joe spent a few minutes telling Yang what happened and how he'd woken up to an entirely different world with a lump on the back of his head and his grandmother turning out to be a witch. He left out the part about ice cream and Frisbees but explained about the Los Lobos leader wanting to come in to discuss things with Levi. "The Los Lobos name doesn't make sense, not with the whole Viking nickname and Chinese panda shifters, that wasn't as important as me trying to get over feeling betrayed, because it seems like instead of putting the task group into good hands, it sounds like I handed it over to the enemy."

"My Clan is not the enemy," Yang protested softly. "Grandpa Zhou has been trying to get that part of the family out of the drug trade for decades. We used to run opium back in the day, and every time a new high cropped up, they expanded into it. My great-great-uncle Yang Xiying started a benevolent society about sixty years ago, and some guy thought it was funny to call him Viking because he couldn't pronounce my uncle's name. He took the nickname and turned it into the group's name.

"Uncle wanted nothing to do with being Chinese. He got into the whole outlaw culture and pulled in some of his relatives—*my* relatives— and that's how the gang got started," he continued. "I became a cop because I saw how it was tearing my family apart and there was nothing I would be able to do inside of the Clan. Everything my uncle did violated human law, and that's where I needed to take him down. And we did, but now Grandpa Zhou and the others are stuck with the motorcycle club's legacy and reputation. Trying to clean up decades of criminal activity and familial shame is bad enough, but now we've got Los Lobos moving in, and everyone with half a brain is afraid it's going to be Yang Xiying all over again."

"But when I came to you about that guy on the motorcycle, you told me you didn't know anything about the Lobos," Joe pointed out. It was difficult to scratch away the suspicion edging in around his opinion of Yang. He thought he knew the guy, trusted Yang to have his back if ever they went through a door, guns drawn and vests on. They were brothers in blue, but now the connection between them was murky. "And I questioned you about Levi. Wondered if he was getting favors from someone in the department, and you told me no. How many lies have you told me lately, Yang?"

"I knew about Los Lobos being in the city because Reilly was supposed to meet up with Tom Wheeler, who is technically in charge of the remaining Vikings left over from my uncle's days. But when we found out Los Lobos was meeting with Levi the day before the official talks, Grandfather decided to step in. Wheeler's a good guy. He's an old biker they respect, and he's been clean and sober ever since everyone moved up north." Yang spread his hands apart, extending a gentle supplication toward Joe. "The old gang is dying off, but they still command some respect, and we thought Los Lobos would prefer to talk to them about territory. It's complicated. That group up there is stitched together with some pretty thin threads, and everyone tries to work hard to make things peaceful. I'm sorry I lied to you, but I couldn't risk the cops coming down on them before they hammered things out. I knew the Vikings weren't coming back into the city, and the Los Lobos gang isn't either. Everyone attached to this will be gone by Monday, so I figured I would just try to minimize things and there wouldn't be any harm."

"And the thing with Levi?" Joe pressed, leaning forward when Kawika hustled by, hefting a keg into the kitchen in a graceful shifting dance learned from hours of getting past oblivious customers. He didn't want the large Hawaiian man to hear him, wary of probing into Levi's life and having his questions get back to the pub owner. They had something between them, something Joe wanted to explore, but he had to settle things with Yang if ever he was going to trust the man again. "All of that a lie? Is there someone in the department covering anything shitty that goes down here?"

"I don't know." Yang exhaled sharply, keeping an eye on the crowd as people moved around the tables. "Peacekeepers are a different breed. They're outside of their Clan politics. They have to be neutral. Everything I know about Levi Keller is tied into him owning this place and it being a

Sanctuary. I've never really dealt with him. I've haven't needed to. He's got a reputation for being fair and not someone to fuck with in a fight. But you can say that about most Peacekeepers.

"Look, they have their own structure and network. If there's one in the department pulling strings for them, that's outside of any group's influence. You don't mess with Peacekeepers, and you sure as hell don't try shit at where they mark their areas. It's a good way to get your ass handed to you." Yang nodded his chin toward Kawika, who'd taken his place back behind the bar. But Joe noticed the large man glancing their way every once in a while. "From what I know, that one's the gentlest we've got here in the city."

"Kawika's the one who nearly cracked my head open with his fist," Joe snorted.

"Like I said, the gentlest one," Yang shot back with a smirk. "I'm not a major player in my Clan's stuff. I'm a cop, Zanetti, plain and simple. If one of us breaks the law, I run them in. I'm just here because my grandfather needed a ride and was worried Los Lobos was trying to pressure Keller into something. I just wish I knew what was going on behind that damned door. If the Lobos are kicked out of the area, they'll be moving on to someplace else, and that worries me. I don't want them coming down here any more than you would. They're still loose cannons. I don't know what they'd be bringing with them, but it could be trouble."

The private room's door opened and Yang fell silent, craning his neck to watch his grandfather, Levi, and the Los Lobos gang leader walk out. The old man came first, shoulders back and chin held high, his cane thumping on the floor to support his weight. Reilly followed, deferentially a few steps behind, but his eyes were everywhere except for the old man in front of him. Kawika made eye contact with the Los Lobos gang leader, then jerked his head toward the door. Bending his head down, the slender shifter said something to Yang's grandfather, and they shared a smile between them about whatever he whispered. After a handshake with Levi, Reilly eased his way through the crowd, then slipped from the pub, disappearing into the fading sunlight of the early evening.

Yang stood up as his grandfather approached, unhooking the velvet ropes so the old man could sit down, but Zhou refused with a shake of his head.

"We have to go and speak to Wheeler. We have two hours before the Peacekeeper's decision is posted. I would rather everyone hear it from me first," the elderly man said. Turning, he held his hand out to Levi, his expression sobering when Levi took it. "I can only hope I'm not making a mistake. Can I count on your help if it goes poorly?"

"You can count on my help even if it goes well." Levi chuckled. "I'm glad you all came to an agreement. Let's see how this looks in six months. It will take work on both ends, but I have faith. Let me know how you're doing."

Levi stayed on his feet until Yang and his grandfather left the pub. The door had barely swung shut behind them when he slid into the banquette next to Joe. Sliding his hand around Joe's beer when their shoulders touched, he sighed and brought the bottle up to his mouth for a long draught.

"I really needed this. The beer and, well, finding you here outside when I came out," Levi said, inhaling sharply. "And now that this is all over, I kind of need something else. Like good food, great booze, and someone hot to share it with. So how about it, Zanetti? Feel like going on a date?"

"SO WHAT happened?" Joe plucked a piece of tofu out of the bowl sitting between them, the tip of his chopstick digging into the soft white cube. He dipped it back down again into the shoyu-and-green-onion pool, drenching the piece before biting into it. "Or is that something you can't talk about?"

They'd had a spirited but amusing debate on what to eat and where to eat it. Eventually, they both decided they were dead tired, or at least too tired to go out hunting for food. Levi's apartment was cool and inviting, and after a quick call to a delivery service, they started their date with an assortment of appetizers scattered about on a TV tray between them while they sat on the couch cradling bowls of ramen heaped high with *char siu* and soft-boiled eggs and speckled with hot-chili-and-black-garlic oil.

Barefoot and dressed in a pair of soft sweatpants and an old T-shirt, Levi knew he wasn't exactly putting his best face forward on his first date with Joe, but he liked the comfort they knitted between them. He'd taken a quick shower, then came out to find Joe unpacking their food onto the coffee table. Levi drew close and discovered he liked the smell of his own soap on Joe's skin, the slight citrus fragrance clinging to the man from the shower he'd taken after their run. It'd been nice to let Joe take care of him, ordering Levi to sit on the couch while he poured out noodles and creamy *tonkatsu* broth into low bowls. Amused at Joe's exacting placement of each topping, Levi murmured a thank-you when the cop handed him the ramen bowl, following his words with a hot, slow kiss.

He wondered briefly if he'd read it wrong, because the man said nothing for a long moment, staring at Levi with his dark, honey-tipped eyes. His expression was hard to read, his gaze searching Levi's face for something he must've found, because he followed Levi's kiss with one of his own, murmuring between their pressed-together lips for Levi to hold that thought until after dinner.

Levi's body still tingled from that kiss, and it was difficult for him to figure out what Joe was talking about until he remembered the meeting he'd had only a couple of hours before.

"Zhou's agreed to take in the Los Lobos as a part of his group. It's not exactly what Reilly wanted, but it gives him a lot of independence in his own area with the backing of a stronger contingent. What he's doing is a good thing, but it was a hard sell." Levi pinched a few salted bean sprouts from the TV tray and munched through them quickly. "The Lobos are pretty much an island of misfits, shifters, and witches who broke from their own groups or have been tossed out. He's giving them their second or third, maybe even their sixth chance, so it's a huge gamble for Zhou and the Vikings to take them in. Hopefully it'll work out. If not, then they'll have to move on, and it will be harder for Los Lobos to find someplace that'll let them stay."

"Yang and I pretty much went over how I felt, because seeing him walk in—as a cop who lied to me—it was hard," Joe confessed. "I understand how it's important to keep things a secret. Hell, apparently my grandmother has been lying to me my whole life. I still need to get back with her about that."

"Don't be too hard on her. I can't imagine it's easy explaining to someone that the world they know has pieces and parts that they've never seen. There are people out there who can change their bodies into animals or manipulate the energies around them to influence how someone heals or call up a wind." Levi studied Joe through his lashes, watching as the man's attention drifted toward the kitchen windows, his gaze unfocused and poignant. "I'm not going to lie to you and tell you I know how it feels, but I can tell you I know exactly why what we do, what we are, should never become open knowledge.

"My son is my *world*." Levi heard his emotions shatter his voice, a heavy steel hammer on fragile glass. "I never want to see my son cut open, his still-alive body spread apart and his skin pinned down, held fast by hemostats and sharp spikes while a group of assholes who call themselves scientists poke and prod at him to see what makes him shift. I would like to think that it wouldn't happen, when you and I both know that's already been done to people just because they have a different god or skin color or language. For all we know, it's already happening and we just haven't found out about it. That's how scattered all of us are. That's what worries me the most, that there's somebody out there who is already willing and able to tear apart my son, my mother, or even Yang, just because they don't understand us."

He was tired. Levi could feel the stress of the week and the pressure of bringing two volatile groups to compromise building on top of his buried fears. Joe edged the TV tray out, turning it so it was out of their way, then took both of their bowls and set them down on the table. Edging closer to Levi, he clasped their hands together and stroked the back of Levi's hand with his thumb. The touch was enough to soothe Levi's jangled nerves, easing away the tightness in his chest. It was nice to share his worries with someone who seemed to get it. Other people, even his parents, assured him time and time again that their world was safe, that no one would ever subjugate them in the ways Levi's imagination seemed to spin out.

There was just too much evidence of mankind being cruel to itself, and Levi wasn't willing to risk his son's life on maybes. Declan was too precious, and Joe's steadiness was a welcome comfort.

"That's the real reason why you're a Peacekeeper," Joe murmured, nodding his head. "*That* I can understand. I wouldn't want that for you. I wouldn't want that for any of you."

"Besides, your grandmother is a terror, and the less you know about what she does, the better off you are," Levi teased. "Toni Zanetti is a powerful strega, not just because she can influence humors and flesh, but because she has a huge network of people who are not only willing to lend her their powers, but also have some relatives who are willing to break a few kneecaps. Let's just say I was surprised to find out her grandson was a cop."

"Well, I also have an uncle who has an Italian restaurant where people who break kneecaps go to eat." Joe laughed. "How about if we talk less about my grandmother and more about you? And I don't mean the furry side of you, but the guy who runs a pub and seems to have a teenage son with a nose for trouble."

"A nose?" He snorted, unable to count the amount of times he'd gotten calls from the school about what his son had gotten into. "That boy has an entire body for trouble. I'd wonder where he got it from, but my parents cursed me to have a kid just like me, so I guess shifters can do magic after all."

Joe drew another circle with his thumb, searing hot with promise and as spicy as the chili oil lingering on Levi's tongue. "I can't wait to meet him. Or at least, I hope you keep me around long enough to meet him."

There were sayings about crossroads in life or how a single pebble—one single decision—tossed into a river could change its direction. Levi never believed that until Joe's thumb made another circuit along the back of his hand, brushing over Levi's knuckles with gentle strokes. He'd kept every single one of his lovers at a distance, his relationships casual enough to end by not returning a phone call. What Joe was asking was a hell of a lot more than Levi had given, maybe even more than he'd given the mother of his child. Joseph Zanetti wasn't someone to toy with. An older man with a solid career and a strong sense of family—a far cry from the butterflies Levi chased for a good time. He tasted good, better than Levi deserved, and best of all, he *listened.*

Joe wasn't asking for forever, but he was tossing a stone onto that path, placing it carefully down so Levi could take a step.

"I think Deck will like you, and not just because you can throw a Frisbee." He teased a smile out of Joe's sensual mouth. "I like you too. Do you think you're done with your ramen, because I would really like dessert. And I'm not talking about ice cream, Joey."

TEN

As a cop who'd started in a patrol car cruising some of the meanest streets in San Francisco, Joe had more than a few scary moments under his belt. He'd been shot at, stabbed in the ribs, and tackled during his career, usually coming out of the incidents thankful for his Kevlar vest even when a bullet found his flesh. Yet, in all of his years wearing one of SFPD's stars, nothing seemed to have prepared him for the twist of nerves in his gut and down his spine as he reached for the waistband on Levi's sweats. Joe's fingers trembled slightly when he was finally able to slip down the tiny plastic fastener from its snug place against Levi's belly to the end of the drawstrings holding Levi's pants up. Tugging at the loosened pants, he dragged the fabric down around Levi's hips, then gripped the lean, powerful body he'd wanted since the moment he'd seen Levi from across the street.

Joe knew they were rushing things. Or at least it would seem that way to anyone looking in from the outside, but Levi fit into him in ways Joe had never experienced before. It was easy—scarily easy—to laugh and share with a man he'd only laid eyes on a few days before.

The skin of Levi's belly warmed the back of Joe's fingers, the silken dark strands below his belly button tickling Joe's knuckles. Still fully dressed and sitting on Levi's king-size bed, Joe pulled Levi closer, bringing him forward until Levi straddled Joe's thighs. Tugging Levi's shirt up, Joe gently placed his lips on Levi's stomach and closed his eyes while he inhaled the man's sweet, musky scent. There was nothing more erotic than brushing his mouth over the soft skin of a man's most vulnerable parts—the stretch of an oblique or the nearly baby-fine texture of a man's bare-naked hip. Levi tasted as good as he smelled, and when Joe skimmed the tip of his tongue across Levi's belly over to his hip, Levi's hands came up to cradle Joe's head, pressing him in closer.

There was no mistaking Levi's arousal, his need for Joe straining his sweats' crotch, the soft fabric imprisoning his thickening cock. The long fingers scraping through Joe's hair moved in slow, erotic lines, nails lightly scratching in places with enough friction to make Joe hum in pleasure.

"I hate to bring this up right now, but," Joe whispered, luxuriating in the feel of Levi's hands on him, "do we need condoms? I mean, I don't know what... hell, I'm not even sure how to talk about it without sounding like an asshole." He lifted his chin and stared into Levi's hooded eyes. "I don't even know what I'm asking. I know we're different physically, but—"

"I've had my rabies and distemper shot," Levi murmured, then shot Joe a smirk broad and wicked enough for Joe to realize he was teasing. "I've always used condoms, because shit, we're told we can't get this or that, but really, who knows? I know we can test clean of stuff, but babe, I haven't dated anyone serious enough to go bare in forever and a day. It's not that I don't want to, but, so I've got a kid to think about, and it's something we can do later, once... you know I'm safe. That a deal breaker for you?"

"Do you *have* any?" Joe chuckled. "Because I do not. So I was also kind of asking... begging... that you had some stashed away, because I don't think I can walk away from you right now. Even if it's just to go down to the drug store and come right back."

"Yeah, no walking needed." Levi jerked his head toward the side of the bed. "Nightstand. Got everything we need."

The brief glimpses he'd gotten of Levi's trim, muscle-packed body didn't prepare Joe for the beauty of the man beneath the clothes. The first time he saw Levi mostly naked, he'd been sitting with his grandmother in the apartment's living room, watching Levi peel off not only his jeans but the human skin he lived in, revealing the wolf beneath. The strangeness of that lingered, mostly in the back of Joe's thoughts, in a ball of wonder he didn't dare poke at. He was falling for the man pressed against him, their mouths finding stretches of skin to nibble at and kiss, their fingers stroking at wet spots made slick from tongues and then the salty-bitter moisture of their arousal spreading over velvety heads.

Joe's jeans were shed with some difficulty, his rigid cock refusing to get out of the way, and Levi's laugh at their struggles was nearly as erotic as the kiss that followed. The snap of a lubricant bottle opening and the feel of warming oil on his fingers tightened something in Joe's chest. He needed this, needed the laughter and the intimacy with a man who faced down the same demons and angels he did every day when he walked the city's streets wearing a star and a gun. Levi seemed to understand everything Joe needed—from his deep love of family to the drive to keep those around him safe and happy.

The man could also make a mean ice cream, not something Joe would ever dismiss lightly.

Levi worried Joe's lower lip, a tinge of pain hovering at the edge of the pleasure of Levi's mouth on his. His skin, warmed by Levi's roaming hands, grew sensitive to the touch, even the whorl of Levi's thumbs over his nipples knitting a tightness into Joe's belly. The unshaved scruff along Levi's strong jaw left a nearly imperceptible stinging trail along Joe's shoulder, the faint burn an Icarus-warning echo of flying too close to the sun, or in this case, a wolf shifter with the moon caught in his eyes and carrying a now complicated world on his shoulders.

His oil-slicked fingers skated over the curve of Levi's powerful back, tracing down his spine before sliding around the rounded curves of his ass. Joe caught Levi's gasp and traded a bemused chuckle for the sharp exhale when Joe dipped the tip of a finger against the soft curl of Levi's entrance. Capturing Levi's mouth with a deep kiss, he kept them pinned together, exploring Levi cautiously, easing his way past the clenched ring of muscle to the hidden heat beyond.

Levi lay sprawled on the bed, knees up and ankles resting on Joe's hips, his fingers digging into Joe's shoulders. The need in his eyes darkened Levi's gaze, wrapping silken fingers around Joe's desire. There was so much he longed to do with Levi, longed to do *to* Levi, and plenty he wanted done to him, but for now, they were falling into a comfortable rhythm, exploring each other's skin while testing the limits of their control. Bending in closer, Joe nuzzled at Levi's neck, kissing and nipping at his throat, then his collarbone as he began to work his way in.

Stretching across Levi and trapping the heat of the man's body against his skin brought Joe to the edge. He needed to take his time, even as his desire bit into his control, shredding the thin hold he had on himself into tiny pieces. Levi writhed beneath him, throwing his head back with a long hissing growl. And Joe rubbed and pushed, accompanying each tiny intrusion with a kiss or lick to Levi's exposed throat or firm muscle.

"Jesus!" Levi choked out, dropping his head to Joe's shoulder as Joe stretched him with a pull of his finger. "Shit, it's been a long time. Just… go slow. Or fast. Don't know if I can take slow."

"Slow's definitely how I like things," he whispered into Levi's ear, shivering at the feel of the cool sheath Levi rolled down his shaft. "Let me take care of you this time. I'll go as gently as you need."

They found a pace, one they could roll their hips into nearly as soon as Joe slid the head of his cock into Levi's heat. A few strokes in and he was seated deep, curled over Levi's taut torso, his lover's shins resting on his trembling thighs while Joe held still to let Levi adjust to the stretching of his body around Joe's cock.

The roll of Levi's hips into him proved to be too much for Joe. With each downstroke, Levi tightened around him, twisting heat and velvet around Joe's shaft, stroking at his head and length, with Joe alternately diving hard into Levi's grip or prolonging their joining as much as he could.

Levi's hands found Joe's shoulders, fingers digging in until Joe was sure he'd have bruises when they were done. But it didn't seem to matter, not when he was riding Levi's passion, delving deep into the warmth and sensual pleasures he found there. Their mouths grew hot, kisses enflamed with more than desire. He'd found someone he understood, and Joe crested on the edge of an awareness of how life could be.

It wasn't simply sex. They were too steady and mindful for casual intimacies anymore. Something was folding their lives together, hammering at the threads of steel and grit in their souls until they were stronger with each other than apart. Levi whispered into Joe's ear, heavy sweet somethings about liking this, loving them, feeling Joe, and finding satisfaction and contentment in the slap of their damp skin and the laughter hidden in the passionate kisses they shared.

"Not letting you go," Levi murmured, his words strained from meeting Joe's long strokes with hard thrusts. "Shit, this is crazy. We're—"

"Yeah, crazy but…." Joe gasped, reaching for the explosion rising up from his belly and balls, a tingle of fire and stars promising to consume him in a body-shaking orgasm. "Here we are. Too much alike, in two different worlds."

There was so much more he wanted to say, to talk about, even as Joe knew he would lose his words in the storm brewing over them. The first lick of lightning hit him without warning, building up along the length of his cock, then stretching outward in a crackling thread when Levi's teeth sank into his collarbone. It was a punch of sensation, enough to break him, and the pinprick of too-tight-skin feeling rippled over him.

Joe came in waves, the hot smear of his seed pushing far into the grasp of Levi's body, caught against the thin membrane covering his shaft. He continued to rise and fall, bringing as much of himself into Levi's depths, his right hand stroking at Levi's hard cock, rubbing his thumb through the gush of hot silken fluid of his lover's release. The scent of their spill and damp flesh mingled, erotic musk layered with the citrus notes of the soap they'd both used.

Joe's orgasm gripped him, tearing apart his hold on his thoughts. Everything in him at that point was instinct, the need to bring Levi to completion, to hear his name on Levi's lips, and to steal that bit of breath away from Levi's mouth so he could hold it in forever. He was falling hard. Falling fast. Joe knew there was nothing he could do to stop it, and in the end, as his passion gripped him as tightly as Levi held Joe against his sweat-damp chest, Joe knew he never wanted to be let go.

They lay against each other, Joe shifting to roll over onto his side, but he held Levi close, sliding free of his body but not his embrace. Reluctantly, after a few minutes, Levi murmured about being too sticky, and they fumbled about with baby wipes from the nightstand and a near miss of the trash can with the now-discarded condom. Sensitive to the touch, Joe's cock still responded when Levi swiped the damp paper square over its tender head. Joe's stomach clenched and trembled with each careful caress.

"How about if you hold that thought until the morning? As much as I'd like to do a round two—and there's going to be a round two—we've both had long freaking days," Levi whispered, kissing the tip of Joe's cock, then making a face. "Okay, bad idea. Seemed like a good one in my head, but that chemical taste ruined it. I'm going to have to get better-tasting wipes."

"Or we could just use a washcloth," Joe suggested, chuckling at Levi's exaggerated distaste. "Come here. Sleep sounds good, but the morning sounds even better. We've got, what? Three condoms left? One more for me and two for you. Then after that, we'll have to go to the store."

"Or we can have them delivered," Levi teased, then smirked. "Or better yet, we can ask your grandmother to go get us some, and when she gets here, you can ask her why she never told you about stregas or shifters or anything else that makes the world go a little bit crazy during the night."

"Why are we talking about my grandmother?" Joe caught his breath, exhaling hard. "Not who I want in bed with us right now."

"Just weird, and that's where my head went," Levi said, shrugging as best he could while tangled up against Joe. "Maybe it's a Peacekeeper thing. I've got a piece of a puzzle that's not fitting into the whole, so I've got to poke at it. I mean, she's a Strega. Big S. And she doesn't talk about it to her kids or the favorite grandson. It's her legacy. Hell, it's *your* legacy. You could be off turning people into frogs someplace instead of lying here with me—"

"Lying here with you is a hell of a lot nicer than any frog transformations I'd probably screw up. You'd end up with three-headed tadpoles, and some tree hugger would want to shut down SF because the pigeons suddenly speak Italian. 'Sides, it's not really that complex. She promised my dad she wouldn't pull any of the grandkids into it. He's not a believer, or so she told me. Or maybe he is and he's scared of it," Joe confessed softly. "I think he knows something's up but doesn't want to really look at it, and I sure as hell ain't asking him. My dad's very much an evidence-in-hand kind of person. I guess she thought I was too. And if I hadn't seen the bikers coming around St. Con's, I probably never would have ever known. And how shitty would that be, because then I'd never have met you."

"It's kind of funny you came sniffing around because you found out some of the Vikings were in town." Making himself comfortable against Joe's side, Levi squirmed down into the pillows and yawned. "Especially since it was your grandmother who suggested Zhou and the Vikings use me as their Peacekeeper for their arbitration. So in a lot of ways, I've got Toni to thank for landing you on my doorstep… and my bed."

"Yeah, my grandmother definitely likes to stir the pot," he admitted, sleep tugging at him. It was cool enough for a thin sheet and Levi against him to keep him warm enough to fall off, but Joe was reluctant to go under, enjoying having Levi with him while the night embraced the city streets. "Remind me tomorrow to thank her, and then after that, she and I are going to have some very long talks about secrets. Because something tells me, there's a hell of a lot more that I don't know, and she's the best place for me to start."

"Probably," Levi agreed, his words slurred with sleep. "And you might want to start off with the five red stars she's got tattooed under her arm. Because your grandmother's not just a strega, she's also on the region's Peacekeeper council. So technically, right now? I'm sleeping with my boss's grandson."

TWO WEEKS after he'd first led Joe into his bed, Levi was stretched out over the mattress on his back, naked and staring up at the ceiling as the sun stretched its intrusive fingers across his bedroom. Joe lay next to him, silver-shot hair wild from Levi's fingers and probably still slightly damp from the 4:00 a.m. shower they'd taken after Joe came home from a long night's work. The summer had turned muggy, bringing in a damp heat to lave over the daylight hours, but the evenings were a welcome relief. Even better, since Joe came around to help close the pub if he finished work early or if an investigation stream went into the wee hours. Levi spent the time waiting in the apartment, closing out the books for the night, and keeping some food hot for when Joe came in.

When.

Not if but *when*.

Levi felt the air shift as Joe slowly woke up. One thing he'd found out about Zanetti was the man did not wake up instantly like most people in Levi's family. He shook sleep off in stages, unpeeling layers of slumber from his consciousness until his eyes were finally clear and bright and he was able to take on the world again. Murmuring, Joe's breathing deepened, and a familiar crackle of awareness ran over Levi's skin, much like the surge of energy he felt before he shifted. His world fit around him, pieces he didn't know were missing falling into place simply by the presence of a strega-blooded Italian cop with a nose for trouble and justice.

"Hey," Joe mumbled, scrubbing at his eyes. "God, my mouth tastes like I sucked on fish butts while I slept."

"Nice," Levi drawled. "Forget kissing me until you brush your teeth."

"Babe, I'm not even sure I'd talk to myself before I brush my teeth," Joe replied, sliding out of bed and giving Levi a good look at his tight ass as he padded toward the bathroom. "And man, I've got to piss. Be right back. Don't get dressed. I've got plans for you. Unless you need to go."

"I've already been to the bathroom. Had plans to get up, but the bed reached out and grabbed me." Levi sat up, resting his weight on his elbows and grinning at the sight of Joe standing in the bathroom door, framed by the wood-trimmed opening in the dark blue wall. "I tried fighting it, but it was too strong, so I finally gave up and decided to wait until you could rescue me."

"Yeah, sorry about that," Joe shot back, stepping into the bathroom far enough for his words to echo against the tiles. "I was the one who set the trap. Because you know, plans."

"Plans better include waffles, because dinner was a hot dog last night at nine," Levi shouted toward the bathroom as the door closed. "Shit, I don't even know if I have waffles."

His cell phone jangled for his attention from its perch on the night table. Stretching over the bed, Levi grabbed it from the charging pad, only to drag the sheets across his waist when he saw the number on the screen. Fighting a grimace and hoping he had enough money in his bank account, he answered tentatively, "Hello?"

"Dad? Did I wake you up? You sound like you're still in bed," Declan chortled across the line. "Didn't we talk about you going to bed at a decent time? You're getting old, dude. Man needs his sleep."

"I'm not only going to pull the door off your room, but I'm going to roll your bed into the alleyway and rent it out to racoons." He glanced at the clock. "It's not even ten. Close but not yet. And not that I don't want to hear from you, but you've got two days left in camp, and how the hell did you get a hold of a phone?"

"Borrowed it from Brad. He said I could call you, because so far, I've done no property damage—even accidentally—and he figured you were just waiting to be handed a bill once they dropped me off." Declan cleared his throat. "Can you switch to vid? I want to show you something cool."

A quick glance toward the bathroom door assured Levi it was closed, mostly because he and Joe hadn't quite hammered out how to talk to Declan about their relationship. All he could hope for was Declan's fairly steady personality to maintain its course. He'd never had something serious with anyone while raising Deck, and the uncertainty of how his son would react was a heavier weight than the red stars tattooed under his arm.

"Sure, kiddo. Let me just hit the button," Levi replied, turning his phone so Declan wouldn't give him shit about not filming horizontally. "There, before you bitch about it."

The kid looked good. Less like a kid, actually, and Levi sat staring at his son's face while Declan excitedly babbled about how camp was going and what they'd done over the past few weeks. His voice deepened, then pitched back up in rolls, quickly losing the baby squeak of a cub when he laughed, and Levi's heart twisted a bit, knowing he'd miss the little boy he used to be able to lift up into the air. A bit of scruff speckled Deck's chin—more of a ghost of color than anything else, but it was there. There was a confidence about the kid—the young man— he'd sent off in a van to be with others like him, to find a place among supernaturals who needed to live peacefully in a mundane world.

"Okay, so let me show you what I called about. Hold on. I'm going to move the phone. Make sure to tell me if you can't see me." Declan set the device into something, shifting it so Levi could see the wood-paneled office he was calling from. "I need to change. Don't go anywhere."

"Couldn't have grown out much. It's only been a couple of weeks and…." Levi stared at the screen while his son shook off the fine powder of his skin, his fur glistening under the office's pale fluorescent lights. "What the hell have you done to yourself, kiddo?"

The Pomeranian cut was the same, turning Declan's wolfish shape into a cute tumble of foxy features. It had definitely grown out a bit—at least two inches—but instead of the familiar Keller Black, his fur was a riot of colors near his skin. From what Levi could see, the colors were mostly hexagons, a short patchwork rainbow tipped with long black strands spreading over Deck's back, shoulders, and flanks. His face and muzzle seemed mostly untouched except for a curious dot of pink at the tip of his right ear.

"Are we...?" Levi struggled to find a word to fill in the echoing void eating through his thoughts.

For the life of him, no parenting book ever written could have prepared him for what he was seeing, and he knew a phone call to his mother for help would only be met with riotous laughter to the point of gasping breathing and tears. Stepping carefully around a teenaged boy's ego was a delicate thing, but a shifter in a hormonal flux made things even worse, and Levi was fairly certain his response to Declan's coat of many colors would be a fixed point in his kid's life.

"Are we happy about this?" he asked cautiously, angling his head to get a better look at Declan's coat. "I mean, that's some saturation. It looks... good. The colors blend well together. I mean, it doesn't look like someone melted a box of crayons on you. It looks like the color placements were done well so they don't clash. Help me out here, kid. What happened?"

Declan was tugging his jeans on when Joe came out of the bathroom, singing a bad rendition of some song Levi didn't recognize. Levi barely had time to react to Joe's striding into the bedroom wearing a pair of sweats, a smile, and a towel over his head to rub off any excess water. A groan slithered out of Levi's mouth when Declan visibly perked up and grinned at him.

"Who's that?" Deck leaned forward as if he could see around the phone's edge. "Tell me that's Strega Zanetti's grandson. Please? Because I have a hundred bucks riding on you guys hooking up before I turn sixteen."

Joe froze in place, eyes wide and filled with a little panic. Mouthing at Levi, he said he would leave, motioning to the door, but Levi sighed, shaking his head while waving him over. "Might as well say hi. Because apparently my kid's bet on me. And I was going to ask who the hell set it all up, but I only have one person that comes to mind."

"Shit, who else do you know meddles as much?" Declan snorted. "Toni's been trying to get that guy into the pub for, like, a year now. I figured it was just a matter of time. So long as you're playing it safe and he treats you right—because that's what you tell me—I don't care. But see, here's the thing, Dad. If he hurts you, then I'm going to have to call in reinforcements to break his legs, and the last thing I want to do is start a war between the shifters and the strega. Now, you're not going to guess who I met at the camp exchange. Kawika's niece, Ka'ena, is here, and man, she's got some juice. Can't wait for you to meet her. Well, you might already have, but Dad, I think I'm in love."

"That's cool, kiddo," Levi murmured, looking up to meet Joe's amused gaze. "I think I am too."

"Only fair," Joe whispered, leaning over to kiss the top of Levi's head while Declan continued to talk about the sloe-eyed girl who'd given him rainbow fur. "Since I've pretty much known since our first kiss. And we seriously have to talk to my nana. Because, babe, you might be the greatest gift she's given me, but man—"

Levi tilted his face up, kissing Joe's throat, and said, "She's a pain in the ass."

JENN MOFFATT is a proud nerd. Raised on *Star Trek*, *Dark Shadows*, *The Wild Wild West*, and *James Bond*, she learned not to be afraid of things that go bump in the night and to have hope for the future of humanity. She grew up wanting to be a member of the Addams Family or part of the crew of the USS *Enterprise*—and she still does.

She's been soaked to the skin for Chinese New Year and walked in the fog in Frisco. Went to high school in Sin City, and no, she didn't live in a casino. Lived on the slope of an active volcano, and used to snorkel between classes in college on the Big Island. Now she lives in San Diego where she gets to see the ocean and wildflowers in the desert on the same day.

Jenn was born disabled, which gives her a deep understanding of what it's like to be different, but she's never let it hold her back. It just means she gets pretty good parking.

Find Jenn:

Twitter: @thatvulcanbitch
Facebook: www.facebook.com/thatvulcanb1tch
Instagram: @thatvulcanbitch
Website: jennmoffattwrites.com

BRU BAKER got her first taste of life as a writer at the tender age of four, when she started publishing a weekly newspaper for her family. What they called nosiness she called a nose for news, and no one was surprised when she ended up with degrees in journalism and political science and started a career in journalism.

Bru spent more than a decade writing for newspapers before making the jump to fiction. Whether it's creating her own characters or getting caught up in someone else's, there's no denying that Bru is happiest when she's engrossed in a story. She and her husband have two children, which means a lot of her books get written from the sidelines of various sports practices.

Website: www.bru-baker.com
Blog: www.bru-baker.blogspot.com
Twitter: @bru_baker
Facebook: www.facebook.com/bru.baker79
Goodreads: www.goodreads.com/author/show/6608093.Bru_Baker
Email: bru@bru-baker.com

TA MOORE is a Northern Irish writer of romantic suspense, urban fantasy, and contemporary romance novels. A childhood in a rural seaside town fostered a suspicious nature, a love of mystery, and a streak of black humour a mile wide. As her grandmother always said, "She'd laugh at a bad thing, that one," mind you, that was the pot calling the kettle black. TA studied history, Irish mythology, and English at University, mostly because she has always loved a good story. She has worked as a journalist, a finance manager, and in the arts sectors before she finally gave in to a lifelong desire to write.

Coffee, Doc Marten boots, and good friends are the essential things in life. Spiders, mayo, and heels are to be avoided.

Website: www.nevertobetold.co.uk
Facebook: www.facebook.com/TA.Moores
Twitter: @tammy_moore

RHYS FORD is an award-winning author with several long-running LGBT+ mystery, thriller, paranormal, and urban fantasy series and is a two-time LAMBDA finalist with her Murder and Mayhem novels. She is also a 2017 Gold and Silver Medal winner in the Florida Authors and Publishers President's Book Awards for her novels *Ink and Shadows* and *Hanging the Stars*. She is published by Dreamspinner Press and DSP Publications.

She shares the house with Harley, a gray tuxedo with a flower on her face, Badger, a disgruntled alley cat who isn't sure living inside is a step up the social ladder, as well as a ginger cairn terrorist named Gus. Rhys is also enslaved to the upkeep of a 1979 Pontiac Firebird and enjoys murdering make-believe people.

Rhys can be found at the following locations:

Blog: www.rhysford.com
Facebook: www.facebook.com/rhys.ford.author
Twitter: @Rhys_Ford

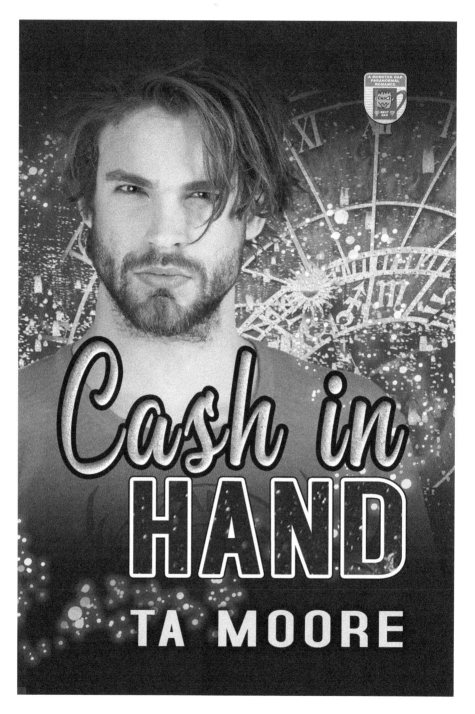

The last monster died a hundred years ago. At least, that's what the monsters want you to think.

Half-monster Cash just wants to keep his head down and raise his daughter, Ellie, to be an upstanding member of monstrous society. Even if she'd rather spend the summer with her human friends than learn the art of man traps at Camp Dark Hollow.

So the last person Cash wants to see is her uncle Arkady Abascal, who's also Cash's ex-boyfriend.

Arkady has more than Ellie's summer plans on his mind. He's there to enlist Cash to find out who's been selling monster secrets. Cash hasn't gotten any better at telling Arkady no, but it's not just his weakness for Arkady that makes him agree. The Prodigium thinks an Abascal exposed them to humans, and now the whole family is at risk—including Ellie.

Recruited to help Arkady identify the culprit—or frame a scapegoat—Cash finds the machinations of monstrous power easier to navigate than his feelings for Arkady. At least, at first. But when things get bloody, he wishes romantic disasters were all he had to worry about….

www.dreamspinnerpress.com

CPSIA information can be obtained
at www.ICGtesting.com
Printed in the USA
LVHW080306151020
668875LV00016B/660